Mischief at Mingela

The Army Cadets

C.R. Cummings

Also By
CHRISTOPHER CUMMINGS

Mischief at Mingela

The Army Cadets

C.R. Cummings

DoctorZed
Publishing
www.doctorzed.com

Published 2019 by DoctorZed Publishing

DoctorZed Publishing books may be ordered through booksellers or by contacting:

DoctorZed Publishing
10 Vista Ave
Skye, South Australia 5072
www.doctorzed.com

ISBN: 978-0-6485361-1-6 (hc)
ISBN: 978-0-6485361-2-3 (sc)
ISBN: 978-0-6485726-9-5 (ebk)

National Library of Australia Cataloguing-in-Publication entry

> Author: Cummings, C. R., author.
>
> Title: Mischief at Mingela/ Christopher Cummings.
>
> ISBN: 9780648536116(hardcover)
>
> Series: Cummings, C. R. The army cadets.
>
> Target Audience: For young adults.
>
> Subjects: Adventure stories, Australian.
>
> Military cadets--Queensland--Fiction.

Cover image © Nick Freund | Dreamstime.com
Cover design © Scott Zarcinas

Printed in Australia, UK & USA

DoctorZed Publishing rev. date: 14/06/2019

Dedication

**The Officers of Cadets and Cadets
of 130 Army Cadet Unit (Heatley)**

This book, while a work of fiction, is dedicated to all the
Officers of Cadets of 130ACU (Heatley) and 140ACU
(William Ross State High School) who have attended bivouacs
at Mingela in May and who shared in the trials, tribulations
and dramas of helping young people prepare for life as good
citizens. By your hard work, common sense and dedication
you have made 130ACU a cadet unit to be proud of. By being
good role models and by showing compassion and sympathy
to young people under stress you have helped many. Your
wisdom and moral courage has assisted the OC in delivering
what he hopes was justice in particular cases and in ensuring
activities were well and safely run.

Also a special thanks to
**the Wheatley and Schneider families
of 'Maidavale' Station, Mingela**
for the use of their property for cadet
exercises over many years.

Thank you.

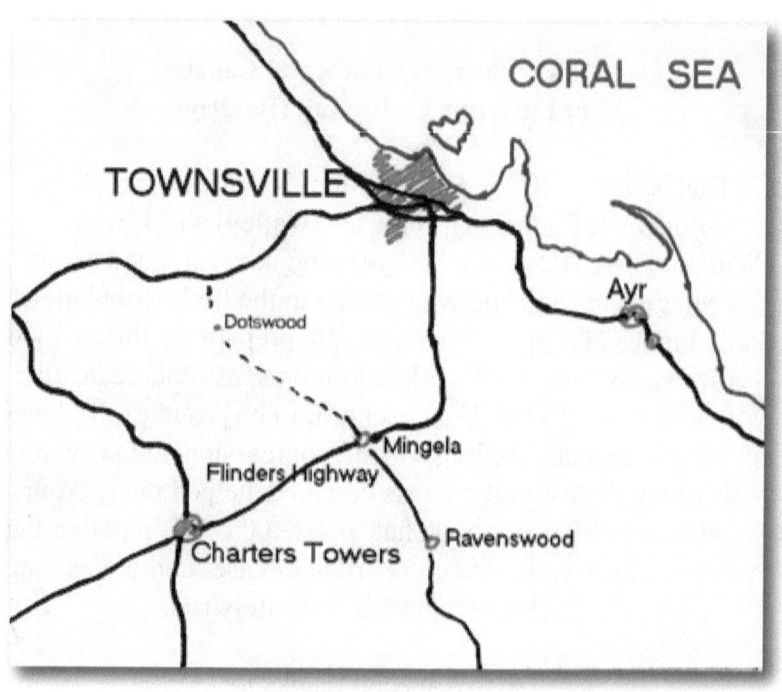

Map 1: Location

Chapter 1

1830 hrs, Friday afternoon
Heatley Secondary College
Townsville, North Queensland

Army Cadet Sergeant Ryan Lepson, sixteen years' old, and the platoon sergeant of Number 4 Platoon of the Heatley Cadet Unit stood on the grass footpath outside the school and supervised the loading of his platoon's gear into the luggage bins of a coach. 4 Platoon was the Senior platoon of the company and was nineteen strong. The platoon was made up of older cadets in Years 10 and 11 who had joined as 'First Years', or of 'Second Years' who were in Year 9.

It was one of these Year 9 'Second Years' who was occupying most of Sgt Lepson's attention at that moment: Cadet Chloe Cummings.

Bloody Chloe! Sgt Lepson thought, looking, but pretending not to, at how her large breasts caused the front of her camouflage shirt to bulge out. He saw that she had only tied her long golden hair in a ponytail instead of a regulation bun. *I must speak to her about that hair,* he told himself, knowing that he was half afraid to do so and that he was totally torn up about how he felt about her. *I wish she wasn't in my platoon. She is a real slut—and real trouble!* he thought.

Chloe's friend Jane, a shapely brunette and also a Year 9 'Second Year', bent to push her pack into the cargo space. As she did Chloe bent over in front of her and wriggled her behind as she attempted to shove her basic webbing into the cargo bin. Jane pushed at Chloe's buttocks.

"Chloe! You don't have to stick your bum in my face!" she cried.

Chloe turned and gave Jane an impish grin. "What's wrong? You've never complained before. Anyway, it's a very nice bum. You should be grateful."

Sgt Lepson shook his head and found his emotions in turmoil. It was a very nice bum, even in the shapeless army camouflage uniform, and he was gripped by fierce desire, a desire which made him burn with shame and frustrated anger. Half of him was revolted by her behaviour and the ugly rumours about her immoral goings-on but the other half was the victim of sheer lust, fuelling an intense desire to have sex with her, to possess her.

"Hurry up and get on the bus you two!" he snapped, annoyed to find that his mouth had gone dry with desire and that his hands were twitching with urgent yearning.

Sgt Lepson had never had sex and had been brought up by his very strict religious father to believe that it was something that should only happen between married couples, and in private.

In fact, Sgt Lepson thought that all females were inferior to males and he believed they should not be allowed in the Army Cadets. To his mind their place was the traditional bed and kitchen.

Adding to his frustration and anguish was the knowledge that Chloe and her friend were the objects of countless stories and rumours about nudity and sex. What made Sgt Lepson's emotions all the more intense was having seen Chloe naked on three occasions. The first had been at the school swimming carnival the previous year. As a dare Chloe had swum a race nude without any of the teachers realizing until she had climbed out at the other end. Even though Chloe had only been a thirteen-year-old Year 8 her appearance had sparked the fires of lust and fantasy in him as she looked more like she was sixteen or seventeen. Now she was a year older and even more shapely.

The second time had been on a bivouac in March the previous year when she had come on the morning check parade wearing only her boots and hat. That had only been a glimpse from 25 metres away and in the half light of dawn, but the third time had been in broad daylight and close up. During a weekend exercise with the Navy Cadets up near Innisfail Chloe and Jane had been kidnapped by some smugglers. They had escaped but were nude. Chloe had come running along the beach to where Sgt Lepson and others, including the OC, Major Wickham, had been standing. She was being chased by one of the smugglers who had then turned and run back to a boat.

The images of Chloe jumping up and down on the beach, her breasts bouncing up and down and of her, to his eyes, perfect golden body, caused Sgt Lepson to experience a rush of desire that caused his penis to begin stiffening up. Not being able to drive such images out of his thoughts or to be able to keep control of his body caused him a spurt of resentment, despising himself as a weakling and her as a cheap slut.

And she is a slut, he thought angrily as he watched her give her name to the officer marking the bus roll before she climbed aboard.

There were numerous stories of her going to parties and letting boys do things to her, even though it was against the law because she was years under age. She was rumoured to do things for money and to romp around naked most of the time. She had even been known to take her top or all of her clothes off at school.

I don't know why she hasn't been expelled, Sgt Lepson thought, his frustration fuelling a strong desire to put her in her place. *She should have been chucked out of the cadets,* he mused. Then another thought added more fuel to his feelings. *I hope she doesn't muck up on this bivouac. If she does and I get a bad report, I may not get selected for promotion to Warrant Officer or Cadet Under-Officer. I will keep a sharp eye on her, and her tart of a mate.*

Memories of taunts about Chloe and Jane by the other platoon sergeants and concern about the reputation of 4 Platoon and of the cadet unit added to Sgt Lepson's strong feelings.

I will try to catch them out and get them chucked out of cadets, or at least moved out of my platoon, he resolved.

*****

As Jane, also fourteen and Chloe's best friend of several years, slid into the seat beside Chloe she shook her head with worry. "Chloe, don't you get up to any mischief this camp," she said.

Chloe turned to look at her, her sparkling blue eyes glinting with impish high spirits.

"What do you call mischief Janie Babe?" she replied.

"You know what I mean," Jane answered. "We are both on report at school and on our second warning at cadets. Any more trouble and we will be chucked out."

"If we get caught," Chloe replied with a grin.

"Please Chloe. I am enjoying cadets and it is important to me to be one. Remember that we did not get selected for the Promotion Course last December because of misbehaviour last year."

"Maybe just a little bit of fun," Chloe suggested.

"Nothing serious please," Jane replied. She settled herself comfortably and then looked up to meet Sgt Lepson's eyes. He seemed to leer back and she cringed inside.

What a creep! she thought, hastily looking away.

To her annoyance Sgt Lepson seated himself across the aisle from her, next to her section commander, Corporal Hankin.

Another creep! she told herself, *and an incompetent one.*

Jane turned to talk to Chloe while the Company Sergeant Major did a headcount to double check the numbers on each bus. There were two coaches and Jane guessed at about ninety cadets attending as the unit had four rifle platoons, each with about twenty in it, plus the headquarters of about ten.

When Jane looked at her friend again she saw that Chloe was staring out the window and looking distinctly down.

Not her usual bubbly self, she thought.

She knew that Chloe had been through a very rough patch in her life over the previous couple of months and hoped it had not damaged her spirit. The worst thing had been a real bitch fight with another girl at school over a boy who had then used Chloe, boasted to his mates, and then dumped her.

Jane knew that Chloe had been hurt, both physically and emotionally.

I hope Chloe isn't too depressed by it all, Jane mused, noting the dark rings under Chloe's eyes and the fact that her friend's face looked almost haggard, spoiling her usual striking beauty.

For a few moments Jane worried about Chloe contemplating suicide or of doing silly things because she was dejected. Then she shook her head. A number of people had suggested that Chloe give up Cadets and take things easy, but she had emphatically refused. She had also said that sitting around brooding and feeling sorry for herself would be worse than getting on with life. So she had done that, putting on a brave face to the world.

And a world full of people who don't like her and would love to see her hurt, Jane thought, being well aware that most girls were scared of Chloe and very jealous of her looks and sexuality.

And there is one of the girls who hates her, Jane mused, noting one of the only three other girls in their platoon, Cadet Kim Keeler.

Kim had seated herself in front of them after a single, sneering glance. Several times over the last few months Jane had heard whispers that Kim wanted both of them out of cadets. The dislike had been sparked by jealousy, Kim blaming Chloe for taking her boyfriend off her. In fact the boy, Cpl Bailey from 3 Platoon, had been the one to chase Chloe. Chloe had not encouraged him at all and did not like him. It had taken weeks of hints and finally blunt rejections before Bailey had given up trying.

*****

What Jane did not realise was the depth or resentment and hatred that had festered in Kim Keeler's mind over the preceding few weeks. Kim blamed all of her problems on them, but principally on Chloe.

The sneaky slut! I'll teach her! she had thought. Slowly a plan had formed which offered what felt like suitable revenge. *I'll get the sneaky bitch chucked out of Cadets, and her stuck-up troll of a mate.*

For she disliked Jane almost as much, Jane having many of the attributes she herself felt she lacked: better looks, a better figure, better school results and an ability to make friends and to meet boys that caused the envy to churn in Kim's stomach every time she saw it.

Her plan, she thought, was brilliant, if risky. *I will play on their reputations and they won't be able to prove it wasn't them,* she had decided.

So she had made preparations, including enlisting the unwilling aid of her friend Chantelle Sandilands. Kim was sure that Chantelle did not believe she would go through with it but that just steeled her determination.

She will see that I really mean it later tonight, or maybe tomorrow night if it doesn't suit.

Now, as she sat in the coach next to Chantelle, Kim ran over her plan in her mind. *It is a good one,* she decided. Through her mind ran the elements that combined to make her sure it would work. Having done several bivouacs with cadets she felt certain that she could harness the routines and procedures of the cadet unit to unwittingly help her.

That bitch Chloe will regret she ever stole my man!

*****

Happily unaware of this Jane watched as the CSM, Cadet Warrant Officer Class 2 Glenn, a strict Year 12 youth, came along for a second count. This time he was satisfied and reported to the Officer of Cadets, Lt Jenny Peters. Lt Peters, an attractive blonde officer in her twenties, seated herself near the front and told the driver he could start. Jane gave a wry smile.

There is another of our enemies, she thought. Lt Peters was usually very strict and had been the source of several disciplinary incidents. *She wants us out as well,* she told herself.

The coach set off and Jane settled back to chat and relax. The drive to Mingela would take about an hour once they were free of Townsville's suburbs. The drive was no novelty to her as she and Chloe had frequently been along the Flinders Highway to Charters Towers. They had also attended a weekend bivouac at Mingela as 'First Years' so she knew roughly what to expect.

As the coach passed through the suburb of Stuart and out into the dry savannah country beyond Chloe stopped staring moodily out the window as darkness set in and said, "I hate this road. It is so boring!"

"Well, we did travel up and down it last weekend," Jane commented. The previous weekend she and Chloe had gone to the inland town of Charters Towers for the annual Country Music Festival. Jane had gone merely as a friend and spectator .but Chloe had entered several of the singing competitions. However, her hopes of winning a prize had been dashed and she had come away with hurt feelings and no awards. They had both played up and flirted with several youths. The young men had been stockmen off a cattle station and their love making had been rough and tough. But when they had discovered the girl's true ages during the competition they had looked aghast and then quickly vanished.

Jane smiled at that but also felt guilty. She had a steady boyfriend, Martin, a Year 12 student at William Ross State High School. Martin was a Navy Cadet Chief Petty Officer and a kind and gentle person but sometimes Jane just needed more.

At least Chloe and I can comfort each other with a bit of a cuddle and a massage at cadets without much danger of being caught, she thought.

Girls were expected to share tents or shelters, 'Hoochies or hutchies' in the army slang. It was against the unit's rules for boys and girls to share, although on field exercises they often slept side by side.

Pressing herself against Chloe Jane murmured, "Cheer up Chlo. I will give you a good cuddle when we are in bed."

"Thanks Janie, but oooh! I need more than just a hug," Chloe replied.

"Well don't you tempt any of these boys and get us into trouble," Jane cautioned.

"Corporal Callan could make me happy, I think," Chloe replied. "Or even Davo or Grey."

"Please Chloe, not at Cadets," Jane whispered.

Chloe shrugged. "I don't care if I get chucked out."

"If you go I go too," Jane said, anxiety for both her friend and her future gripping her.

"You don't have to," Chloe replied. "We would still be best friends."

Jane struggled to find the right answer. She knew that being in Cadets was now extremely important to her, that it was the primary focus of her life and hopes. "It wouldn't be the same without you," she said. "Besides, you like being a cadet, and you are good at it."

Chloe bit her lip and looked thoughtful. "OK. I'll behave," she answered. She then glanced across at where Sgt Lepson and Cpl Hankin sat and whispered, "I don't want that hypocritical prick Lepson catching me out."

"He'd like to get into your pants," Jane whispered back.

"All the boys want to do that," Chloe said with a smile.

"Yeah, but Lepson is one of those turds who frown and criticize but who secretly lust to do it with you," Jane replied.

Chloe nodded. "He is, but he has Buckley's of getting any satisfaction out of me, either way."

"Good!"

*****

Half an hour ahead of the coaches was the Officer Commanding the company, the OC, Major Wickham. He was driving his private car and his thoughts were also on possible problems in the unit.

Our numbers are badly down, he thought. The unit's 'Authorized Establishment' was one hundred and twenty cadets and eight officers but he had only seventy-six cadets and six adult staff attending the weekend. He was particularly concerned that Number 1 Platoon, which did its 'Home Training' at Heatley, had only twelve cadets including its commander and corporals.

They are hardly strong enough to be a separate platoon for tomorrow night's exercise, he mused.

After considering whether to amalgamate 1 Platoon with 2 for the exercise he decided not to. *3 Platoon is strong enough with seventeen and 4 Platoon is doing well this year with nineteen. Things should go well, as long as we don't have any trouble.*

The thought of what sort of trouble might occur shifted Major Wickham's thoughts to personalities and that got him worrying about Chloe and Jane.

I hope that bloody Chloe isn't going to generate more problems this weekend, he thought.

Memories of some of Chloe's escapades made him sigh and shake his head. He was a teacher at their school and taught both girls in History and Geography so had a wider perspective on them than the other OOCs. The memories also caused him some uncomfortable thoughts as he found the images of naked young females forming in his mind. That caused him to angrily shake his head.

They are just kids and they shouldn't carry on like that, he told himself, uncomfortably aware that Chloe had to power to cause him strong erotic fantasies. He was ashamed to admit to having a secret regard for her.

She and Jane are both on their second formal warning, he thought. *If they muck up on this weekend, I will have to discharge them, regardless of how I feel.*

Thinking about what might then happen to the two girls made him feel sad and he wondered what he could do to help keep them on the straight and narrow.

These thoughts carried him on for many kilometres. Darkness set in as he passed the roadhouse at Calcium and after that he was driving through dark bush with only an occasional light to be seen in the distance. There was plenty of traffic, including large 'road trains' and that made the driving unpleasant and sometimes dangerous.

A few minutes later he crossed the concrete bridge at Reid River and sped on south along long straights until he rounded the end of a range of hills near 'Cardington' Station. Once across Oakey Creek he had twenty minutes of fairly boring driving on the two 10-kilometre straights which led Southwest across the flat country of the Haughton River valley. Apart from a couple of lonely cattle stations the country was just dry savannah woodland.

After crossing the Haughton River (dry sand) the road went southwest for a few kilometres before curving west again past the entrance to Maidavale Station. The bivouac was mostly being conducted on Maidavale and that reminded Major Wickham he needed to draft a letter of thanks and to try to find time to drop in and say hello to the landowners. He had seen them a couple of months before to get permission and had phoned them the previous night to remind them that the cadets were coming that weekend. Keeping on good terms with the landowners who allowed the cadets to use their land was one of his priorities.

After the Maidavale turn-off the Flinders Highway turns south and climbs up through a line of very rugged little hills, the Mingela Range. The Mingela Range is not high, only a hundred metres, but it consists of thousands of small, rocky hills and gullies, most of which are not accurately portrayed on the military topographic maps because they are smaller than the contour interval. It is a very interesting piece of country and an awkward area to navigate in.

But the training area to be used for the next day and night was on top of the range and was mostly flat or gently undulating and also mostly quite open, with short grass or even no grass amid a scattering of eucalyptus trees and other bushes. The bivouac site was in a fenced paddock next to the main road and only a kilometre east of the tiny township of Mingela.[1]

The highway climbed up through the dark hills via several sweeping curves. At the top it turned right and went almost due west for 2 kilometres. Just after the last curve Major Wickham made out the faint silhouette of a radio tower on his left. The road went down a slight dip and then up to a road junction. A bitumen road went off to the left, the signs informing travellers that the side road led to Mingela, Ravenswood and the Burdekin Falls Dam.

Major Wickham slowed down and turned left onto the side road. Almost immediately he did a U-turn and pulled over onto a bare stretch of gravel on the side of the road and parked. On the other side of the road was another stretch of bare gravel beside the bitumen. This was where the coaches would stop to unload the cadets. After switching off the engine

---

[1] Population 7. Refer to Map 1.

Major Wickham climbed out and stretched, savouring the cool, fresh air and the relaxing silence of the bush. A kilometre away the few lights of the tiny township twinkled in the darkness.

Ah well, here we are again, he thought. *Let's hope everything goes well!*

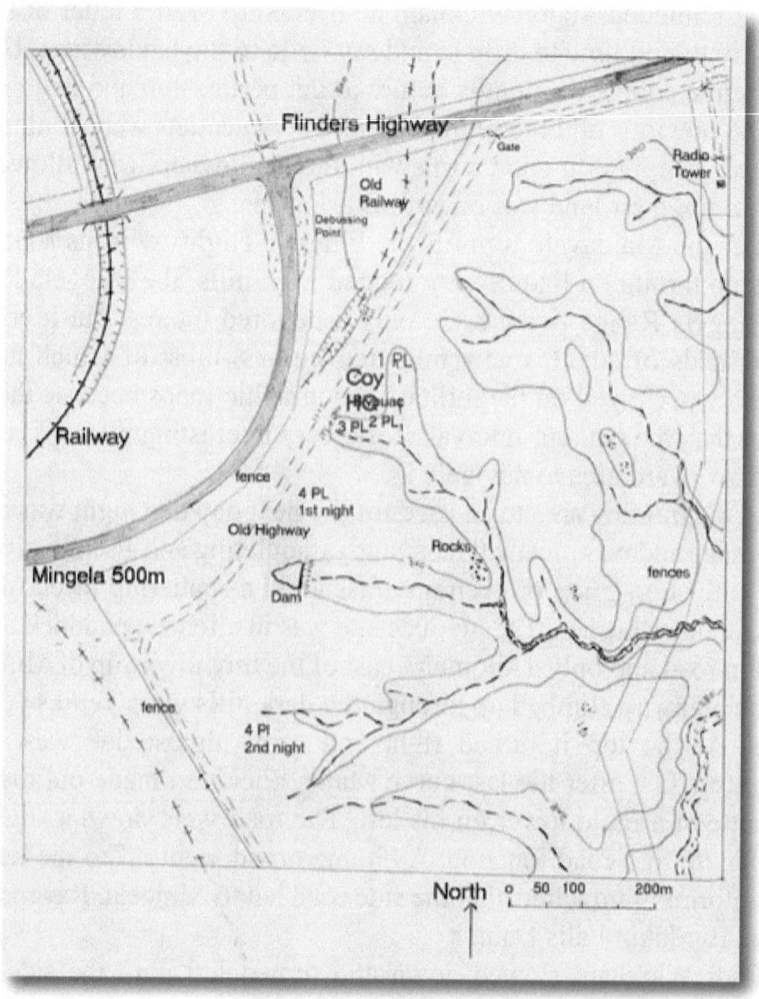

Map 2: Bivouac Area

Chapter 2

BIVOUAC

At 2015hrs the coaches pulled to a stop on the side of the road at the place indicated by Major Wickham. The Company Sergeant Major, Cadet Warrant Officer Class 2 Glenn, growled to the cadets to remain seated until the coach had stopped. Sgt Lepson had half raised himself but at once slid back into his seat, blushing at the rebuke. He had been on a dozen coach trips with the unit and knew the rules. Now he silently cursed his forgetfulness.

I hope nobody noticed, he thought as he waited for the coach to come to a standstill.

When it had and the door had hissed open he stood up and ordered his platoon to get off. "Form a line at the door and unload the gear," he bellowed above the excited hubbub of voices.

Outside the coach it was organised chaos for a few minutes with the CSM and sergeants organising the unloading. Sgt Lepson pushed his way through the milling throng and yelled to 4 Platoon to form a line. As he got things moving he shook his head with annoyance when he realised that he had not remembered to keep his torch ready.

Damn! It is in my webbing, he thought, and then he swore again when he saw how hard it might be to identify his webbing in the poor light. Apart from the lights inside the coach and in its cargo bins there was only the flicker of an occasional torch.

130ACU had a standard drill for unloading coaches. Major Wickham believed that using a chain to pass things from hand to hand was very inefficient and also dangerous as it resulted in a big pile of gear. It was then hard for the cadets to find their packs and webbing. Instead he had trained the unit to unload by using a walking oval pattern of movement, each cadet taking just one item and walking back to where a sergeant indicated it should be put down. The item was placed number up on the end of the growing line. The person then walked around the circle and joined the line again to collect a second item. This way the packs and webbing ended up in long lines beside the road with the numbers indicating ownership clearly visible. It was a fast and efficient system and had everyone moving in the same direction.

As the packs and webbing were passed out of the cargo bays by HQ cadets the CSM came along, torch in hand and snapped, "Sgt Lepson, don't let them take more than one piece of gear. It just slows things down when they have to turn it so that the number is up."

"Yes CSM," Sgt Lepson replied, biting back his anger as he noted several cadets look at him with what he imagined were mocking looks.

It took more frustrated growling to stop the cadets from stacking the gear in a huge pile. With an effort he got them to start laying it out in a long line. As he did cadets began grabbing their own gear and leaving the line.

"Hey! Get back in line and go and get more gear Cadet Arthur," Sgt Lepson snapped.

For a second he thought Arthur was going to disobey him and his anger and determination surged. This must have transmitted it to Arthur as he reluctantly rejoined the line. Sgt Lepson knew that he had trouble getting cadets to do what he said when there were no authority figures around to bolster him and the weakness rankled and made him even more anxious.

It annoyed him even more when he saw Chloe point and say to Arthur, "Put that there Cadet Arthur."

Arthur immediately did as he was told. Irritated by her easy manner Sgt Lepson snapped, "Keep your mouth shut Cummings and stop giving orders. You don't have any stripes, and you never will have if I can help it."

Chloe looked surprised and then angry. She straightened up and looked back at him. By then her face was blank and she said, "Cadet Cummings sergeant."

Her publicly correcting his military etiquette in front of other cadets sent another spurt of anger through Sgt Lepson. He struggled to think up a crushing rejoinder but as he opened his mouth to shout at her the CSM appeared beside him.

"Hurry up Sgt Lepson. We don't want to be here all night."

"No CSM. Come on 4 Platoon, get your gear and move over there," Sgt Lepson replied, his frustration seething inside him.

He moved to the line of gear and began searching for his own pack and webbing. As he did the coach driver moved along closing the bins. This reduced the amount of light and caused more curses. To add to Sgt Lepson's annoyance he saw that both Chloe and Jane had small pocket torches that they were using to check names on the gear.

"Here Rachel," Chloe called, passing a set of webbing back to another girl. Then she shone her torch on the name tag of another set of webbing. She pulled it free of the pile and turned. "Sgt Lepson, here is your webbing."

Sgt Lepson found his emotions in turmoil. He wanted to give her a blast but found himself feeling foolish and also thankful.

Now I can find my pack, he thought.

"Thanks," he grunted, taking the webbing. Swinging it on he undid the left basic pouch and dug out his torch.

But then it wouldn't work. After clicking the switch a few times he swore and then unscrewed end of the torch and slid the first battery out. He had been expecting to find it reversed as that was normal procedure in the unit, to turn the first battery around when the webbing was stored so that the batteries would not go flat if the torch was accidentally turned on. But now he found he had neglected to do that and the torch had obviously been on until the batteries were drained.

Muttering with annoyance Sgt Lepson moved aside and dug in the pouch for his spare batteries. Luckily there were a couple, so he took out the flat batteries and flicked them aside then inserted the new batteries. After quickly screwing up the torch he clicked the switch. To his relief it came on at once and he was able to move back into the throng to find his pack.

Luckily it was near the end of the line and he was able to elbow his way in and drag it clear. Holding the pack by its carry strap he moved around the milling group to near the front of the coach and started shouting.

"Here 4 Platoon! 4 Platoon, move over here!"

Cadets began moving to him and he shone his torch on the ground and said, "Sit on your packs there in your sections."

As the first cadets seated themselves and Sgt Lepson began to feel that he was getting a grip on the situation the CSM again came along.

"What are you doing there Sgt Lepson? That is in between 2 Platoon and 3 Platoon. Move your platoon down past the back of the bus."

"Yes CSM," Sgt Lepson replied. Embarrassment flamed and he swore again, then shouted, "Come on 4 Platoon, down to the back of the bus."

From out of the darkness nearby came the mocking voice of Sgt Kramer, platoon sergeant of 3 Platoon.

"The troublemakers are always at the back of the bus!"

"Get stuffed Kramer!" Sgt Lepson retorted.

He and Kramer had been enemies and rivals for years and he did not feel like being taunted by him in front of the platoon.

Another voice called from nearby, Lt Peter's, "Stop that bad language Sgt Lepson!"

"Yes Ma'am," Sgt Lepson replied, while silently seething and blushing.

He moved away, elbowing several First Year cadets aside as he went. When he was past the group that he now saw must be 3 Platoon he stopped and again went about seating 4 Platoon in section lines. But it wasn't happening easily.

"Bloody corporals!" he muttered, "Where are they?" He saw that only Cpl Callan was seated in front of his section.

"Hurry up Hankin! Get a move on Lang!" he called.

This time Major Wickham's voice came out of the darkness, "Corporal Hankin, Cpl Lang, get a move on."

While the major had not actually publicly rebuked him for not using the correct military courtesies and titles Sgt Lepson knew that it was meant as a reminder to him and he burned with embarrassment and annoyance.

Damn! I must watch that. If I get into the OC's bad books I may not get promoted, he thought.

To remind him of his possible problems Chloe and Jane made their way past and dropped their packs where 12 Section would line up. "Over here Cadet MacDonald," Jane called. As she showed MacDonald where to sit Chloe came over to Sgt Lepson.

"Excuse me sergeant, but I need to go to the toilet," she said.

Sgt Lepson was tempted to tell her to do it in her pants but he knew that the officers were very strong against any sort of sexual harassment, so he snapped, "So hurry up and go."

"Which way?" Chloe asked.

Sgt Lepson pointed across the road, "Over there, and be quick about it. We have to move."

Across the road beyond the major's car was a large flat area of grass and a wide gravel parking place where trucks often pulled up. In the darkness it was just visible. As Chloe hurried across the road Cadet Stevens from 11 Section called after her, "Don't get bitten on the bum by a snake."

Chloe just snorted and hurried on. Cadet Kane, also from 11 Section, then called, "It's the one-eyed trouser snakes she wants to watch out for!"

There was a titter of laughter, instantly stilled by Major Wickham's voice and the blinding beam of his 'Big Jim' torch. "It will be me you want to watch out for Cadet Kane, if I hear any more talk like that!"

"Yes sir," mumbled a sheepish Kane, who was pinned in the beam.

The torch clicked off and Sgt Lepson shook his head.

Silly bugger! he thought.

By this time almost all of the cadets had found their gear. The coaches both started up and drove off, leaving a sense of relief and peace behind. The coaches did not try to turn around but instead drove off towards the town of Mingela. Sgt Lepson knew that there was a second road which circled back to rejoin the highway about another kilometre to the west and guessed the drivers would go that way.

Major Wickham now called in the platoon commanders and CSM to give orders for the move to the bivouac area which Sgt Lepson knew was a couple of hundred metres away.

I had better get the platoon ready, he thought anxiously.

He moved to the front of the platoon and bellowed at them to hurry up and sit. One cadet kept dithering and walking around. Sgt Lepson shone his torch on him and saw it was Cadet Flegel.

"Hurry up Flegel and sit down!" he snapped.

"I can't find my webbing," Cadet Flegel wailed in reply.

"Did you put it on the bus?" Sgt Lepson asked.

"Yes, I did," Cadet Flegel answered in a tone of injured dignity.

"Blast!" Sgt Lepson said under his breath. "Cpl Lang, help Flegel find his bloody webbing."

Reluctantly Cpl Lang got up and did as he was told, using his torch to search the grass and around where the other platoons were. Sgt Lepson heard him castigating Cadet Flegel for not having a torch.

"I have!" Cadet Flegel wailed. "But it's in my webbing."

It took five minutes to find Cadet Flegel's webbing. It was in among

3 Platoon with some of their gear. By then the OC had finished and CUO Roach had returned. "Are they ready to go sergeant?" he asked.

"As soon as Carson and Cummings are back," Sgt Lepson replied.

Chloe's voice came from among the seated group. "I am here sergeant."

Sgt Lepson grunted, pleased she was because it meant the platoon was ready to go but also irritated that she was as it gave him no opportunity to discipline her.

As Cpl Lang and Cadet Flegel seated themselves the CSM came along. "Are they all here Sgt Lepson?"

"Yes sir," Sgt Lepson replied automatically, while berating himself for not checking.

"How many are there?" the CSM asked.

"Twe... er... nine... er not sure sir," Sgt Lepson answered.

CSM Glenn snorted. "So count them right now. And make sure you count them when they arrive."

"Yes sir," Sgt Lepson replied, burning with embarrassment at having made such an elementary mistake.

He ordered the corporals to count their sections and while they did he counted the whole platoon. Then he called for the corporals to report and added them up. During all of this the CSM stood beside him.

"Nineteen CSM, including CUO Roach."

"Good. Thank you CUO Roach, your platoon may move now," he said.

CUO Roach stood up and swung on his pack. "Thanks CSM. OK 4 Platoon, stand up, packs on. Ten Section, lead section behind me, then Eleven Section followed by Twelve," he ordered.

There was a couple of minutes hustle while packs were hoisted on. Sgt Lepson then ordered them into a long line, one section behind the other. He then counted forward, snarling at cadets to stand still and to stand in line.

"All here sir," he reported to CUO Roach.

CUO Roach then led them along the bitumen side road, following 3 Platoon. They marched for about a hundred metres and then turned left into the long grass beside the road. Within 10 paces they had come to a barbed wire fence. "Packs off! Crawl under. Each section take its own panel," CUO Roach ordered.

This was normal drill for the unit. They always rolled or crawled under barbed wire fences after passing their packs over first. There was more organised confusion. As the platoon made its way under the fence Sgt Lepson heard Jane say, "On your back Chloe, so you can see the barbed wire."

"I don't want to snag my tits," Chloe replied.

There were sniggers and Cadet Kane called, "She should be used to being on her back!"

Chloe snapped back, "You want to watch out you don't have your nuts torn off!"

"Big talk!" Kane blustered, but he shut up.

Sgt Lepson could just see the group in the darkness, but he did not go and intervene. His mind had filled with lustful images of Chloe's breasts and he felt a savage surge of desire to touch them. Shaking his head at his own confusion he crawled under, managing to spike his hand on a prickle as he did. After standing up and dusting himself he swung on his pack and urged the cadets to hurry.

The platoon now walked through open bush over ground that was quite bumpy. There was almost no grass and the trees were few and far between. After about 50 paces they came to an old railway cutting. This was a couple of metres deep with sloping sandy sides. They slid down into the cutting and then scrabbled up the other side. Another hundred paces through ground almost bare of grass but dotted with waist high prickly bushes brought them to the Old Highway.

The OC and CSM were waiting there and as the platoon arrived CSM Glenn shone a torch and indicated where 4 Platoon was to sit. This was in 'section lines' behind their corporals on the left of 3 Platoon. Within minutes the entire company was seated on their packs in a tight mass but in orderly rows in platoon groups. Once CSM Glenn had checked with the sergeants that all were present, he handed over to the OC. Major Wickham handed over to Lt Cavendish. She had a torch, but she mostly stood in the darkness in front of them and only used it to point when she described places in a short Ground Orientation and Safety Brief.

Sgt Lepson had heard it all before a dozen times, so he just sat and looked at the cadets or studied the masses of stars that were showing. During the briefing a car came from the direction of the Mingela. Its headlights shone over their heads and it went racing round the curved side road towards the highway, its driver obviously unaware the cadets were there. Behind them there was an almost constant sound of vehicles on the Flinders Highway. By turning his head Sgt Lepson was able to watch the vehicle headlights and the red sidelights on the large trucks as they went racing by 300 metres away.

The safety briefing over Major Wickham told the CUOs to take their platoons to their designated areas. For 4 Platoon this was 200 metres southwest along the Old Highway. CUO Roach got them up and moving and Sgt Lepson just hoisted on his pack and trudged along at the rear.

By tradition 4 Platoon, as the 'Senior' platoon, normally camped a bit apart from the remainder of the company and Sgt Lepson was glad of that. It meant that the CSM and officers did not bother them so much. The route took them across a small depression via an embankment and then across a hundred-metre-wide, flat, open ridge almost bare of trees. On the far side of this open area, on the left of the Old Highway, was a nice stand of trees, just right for a platoon bivouac. Across the Old Highway from the bivouac site was a belt of long grass and thorn bushes and then the curved side road leading to Mingela. The few lights of the small township were clearly visible about a kilometre away to the west.

CUO Roach took the three section commanders into the trees and allocated section areas to them. They then came back out and called their sections to follow them. Sgt Lepson made his way to where CUO Roach was standing between two trees. CUO Roach pointed to them and said, "These trees will do us Ryan. Get your hutchie out."

Sgt Lepson would much rather have camped on his own as he did not particularly like CUO Roach, thinking he was a not very capable bully, but instead he just agreed and set to work. Within five minutes he and the CUO had clipped their two plastic shelters together and tied the centre to trees at each end. The four corners were then pegged down to make an 'A' frame tent. The ground was sandy and soft and the thin steel tent pegs slid in easily.

That done CUO Roach went off to check on the cadets. Sgt Lepson wanted to sit down and have something to eat but knew he had better look like he was making an effort. So he also walked around, helping and criticizing the shelters.

Almost at once he found problems. Cadet Dipkins, in Cpl Hankin's section, did not have a 'Shelter Individual'.

"Where's your hutchie Dipkins?" Sgt Lepson growled.

"Didn't get issued with one," Cadet Dipkins replied.

"Sergeant!"

"Eh?"

"Sergeant. You call me sergeant," Sgt Lepson snapped. "Now why didn't you get issued with one?"

Cadet Dipkins shrugged. "Nobody told me to get one," he answered.

"Sergeant!"

"Eh?"

"Bloody hell! Cpl Hankin, why didn't you make sure Dipkins had a hutchie?"

Cpl Hankin muttered and made evasive answers. Sgt Lepson shook his head. *What a drongo! How did he ever get to be a corporal?* But he thought he knew how: he was a mate of CUO Roach's.

"Well, you will have to make sure he is sharing with someone," he said.

He left Cpl Hankin muttering and telling Cadet MacDonald to share. Sgt Lepson only walked five paces and found another problem. Two hutchies were secured to the same tree with no gap to walk between them.

"Whose is this?" he asked.

From inside one hutchie Jane's voice answered. "Ours, mine and Chloe's."

Sgt Lepson bent and looked in the other hutchie and shone his torch. "And who is in here?" he asked. He saw it was two boys from 11 Section: Cadets Davidson and Grey. As the implications of the arrangement sank in Sgt Lepson straightened up and swore softly. "Cummings, you and Carson can't have your hutchie here. These boys will be able to see right in."

"Lucky them!" came Chloe's reply.

Her flippant, teasing tone angered Sgt Lepson. "You will have to shift." He shone his torch around. As he did he could not help thinking about being able to see into the girl's hutchie.

If they shift if to those two trees over there, I might be able to get a look in, he thought, noting two nearby trees that were almost in line with his hutchie. Then a wave of guilt and anger at his own weakness and lewd thoughts made him snap at the girls and point to two other trees further away.

Jane objected. "But we've already put up our hutchie!"

"Too bad! Get it moved," Sgt Lepson snapped.

Reluctantly Jane crawled out and began to unite the knots. Sgt Lepson opened his mouth to shout at Chloe but as he did she appeared at the other end and began quickly untying the cord. He then stood and watched as they moved the shelter and re-erected it.

This move caused trouble with Kim Keeler, who was putting up a shelter with Cadet Chantelle Sandilands nearby. "Oh, go away! We don't want you near us," Kim cried.

"The sergeant said we had to," Jane answered, plainly angry and struggling to control her tongue.

Kim turned and called, "Oh Sgt Lepson! Get them to move further away."

Sgt Lepson shook his head and said no. He did not want to appear weak and that made him stubborn. After asking again Kim fell to soft grumbling. Sgt Lepson moved off before there was more trouble. The fact that it was his duty to inspect all the cadet's shelters eased his conscience. But as he walked slowly from group to group his mind kept going back to Chloe and her friend.

They are going to be trouble, he told himself. Then a niggling worry added the thought, *I wonder what mischief they are getting up to now?*

Hoping to catch them doing the wrong thing he set off to find out.

Chapter 3

FIRST NIGHT

Jane straightened up from pushing in the last peg on her side of the hutchie.

"Phew! Now, what about something to eat?" she said to Chloe, who was working on the other side.

"Good idea. I'm as hungry as a horse," Chloe answered.

From out of the darkness came Kim Keeler's voice. "You smell like one!"

Jane tensed, ready to help Chloe but hoping for peace. To her relief Chloe just stood up and glared into the darkness but did not say anything.

Shaking her head, she said quietly, "Where will we sit?"

"With our section," Jane answered, hoping to steer Chloe from thoughts of mischief.

"No, with Davo and Grey," Chloe answered. Davo was Cadet Mark Davidson and he was a good looking, dark-haired Year 10. Grey was a cheerful Year 9 with a chubby face and nice eyes. Reluctantly Jane nodded.

The two girls picked up their webbing and packs and moved to beside the two boys. As they placed their packs down Jane saw Kim Keeler look up and scowl. In the flickering light of Grey's hexamine stove the hostile glint in her eyes was unmistakeable.

Kim met her gaze. "You two should stay with your own section," she snapped.

"Who are you to tell us where to sit? You aren't a corporal. We will sit where we like," Chloe replied evenly. She smiled down at Davo and he grinned back and moved to make room for her.

On hearing Kim's statement Jane was both offended and annoyed. Her anger made her stubborn and she also sat down, between Grey and Davo. This put her next to Shona Newman, a quiet Year 11 girl. She was in the same section as Kim and Chantelle but had obviously been excluded from their group. Shona looked a bit anxious but then gave a hesitant smile back.

As Jane unpacked her stove and food, she noted Chloe place her hand on Davo's arm while she talked. *Bugger Chloe! She is flirting and that could cause trouble,* she mused. Shaking her head and hoping for peace she settled to cooking and joined in the general conversation.

As usual the conversation in 4 Platoon was fairly 'blue' and risqué. Every second sentence seemed to have some sort of innuendo or double meaning. That did not bother Jane in the slightest and she laughed heartily at several 'off' jokes which made Shona frown with disapproval.

Others came to join them and the circle had to move out. In the process Jane noted Chloe leaning on both Grey and Davo and she saw Chloe several times place her hand on Davo's knee.

Poor bugger! He will be getting horny and hopeful, she thought.

Among the others were several people Jane disliked immensely. These included Cpl Hankin and Cadets Kane and Stevenson. CUO Roach and Sgt Lepson also joined the group. The conversation became even more sexual in content.

This did not amuse Shona, who finally objected. "You don't have to keep talking like that," she said.

Cpl Hankin answered her, sneering and saying, "Huh! If you don't like it then piss off! You can transfer to another platoon."

Cpl Lang chipped in to add, "Yeah, remember the platoon motto: 'Go hard or go home!'." He then sniggered, as did most of the others.

Shona bristled. "That's not what it means," she retorted, adding, "And if you say things like that again I will tell on you."

Jane looked up and watched the expressions on the faces of CUO Roach and Sgt Lepson.

You weaklings should be controlling this, she thought.

Then she noted Lepson's eyes. They seemed to be following every move Chloe made.

He has his eye on her, the slimy mongrel, she thought.

The arrival of CSM Glenn from out of the darkness ended the dispute. He took firm control by saying, "That's enough arguing. It is time for bed. Start packing up. Sgt Lepson, put them to bed. CUO Roach sir, the OC wants you for an O Group."

By then Jane had heated a drink of Milo so she drank this quickly and then rinsed the cup before placing it in a water bottle carrier on her webbing. As she did she noted that Kim had drawn Sgt Lepson and

Chantelle aside. Kim was holding Lepson's sleeve and talking quickly while glancing towards Chantelle as she did.

I wonder what they are discussing? Jane thought.

Whatever it was Sgt Lepson did not look happy and he shook his head. Kim's reaction was to lean closer and hiss at him. Jane bent to pick up her webbing, frowning as she did.

Lepson doesn't like whatever Kim just told him, she observed.

As she turned to walk to her hutchie she saw Lepson swallow nervously and nod then glance towards Chloe. That caused a prickle of unease to go up Jane's back but then Sgt Lepson turned away and Kim and Chantelle walked off into the darkness.

Jane stood and watched them until they had vanished into the night then walked back through the darkness to her hutchie. When she got there she looked around, wondering where Chloe was. To her concern she saw her talking to Cpl Callan over near his hutchie.

Then she noticed Sgt Lepson also watching. He was standing to one side in the shadows and was not aware that Jane was also watching.

He is trying to catch Chloe out, Jane thought.

She wondered what to do that was not obvious to get Chloe to move away from Cpl Callan but before she could think of anything Chloe turned and headed for her hutchie.

As she passed between Hankin's hutchie and Davo's, Sgt Lepson stepped forward. "You behave yourself tonight Cummings, or else."

Chloe glanced at him and nodded, then kept on walking. When she joined Jane she was simmering with anger.

"That bastard has been perving on me all night! He just threatened me!" she muttered indignantly.

"I know. I heard," Jane whispered, lowering herself behind the hutchie to be out of sight of Sgt Lepson.

Chloe was really peeved. "I haven't done anything, and I wasn't planning to, although the boys just hinted they'd like a bit," she said. "But now I think I will. He is making it a challenge."

Jane was dismayed. She knew how stubborn and wrongheaded Chloe could be. "Chloe don't! I think he is just trying to set you up for a trap. Please don't."

Chloe shook her head and the anger showed on her face in a flicker of torchlight. "He's not that smart," she said contemptuously.

"Oh Chloe, don't please! It isn't worth it. He isn't worth it."

Chloe made a face and turned to sneer in Sgt Lepson's direction. "You are right there. But it still gets right up my nose," Chloe replied.

"I know, but I think we need to be careful," Jane answered.

Chloe knelt down to undo her pack. As she did she chuckled and said, "That's what my Mum says: If you can't be good, then be careful!"

Jane laughed. "So does mine. Oh Chloe, please don't do anything silly."

"But I'm now feeling really horny," Chloe whispered.

"So I will look after you," Jane answered.

Suddenly a torch came on, catching them in its beam. Sgt Lepson's voice called, "You two stop talking and get to bed!"

It was obvious to Jane that Sgt Lepson had moved right around the other hutchies so that none blocked his view and that annoyed her.

We could have been undressing, she thought angrily.

"Yes sergeant," she replied as coolly as she could.

The torch went out and Sgt Lepson moved away to deal with noisy people over in 10 Section. Jane unrolled her groundsheet and sleeping bag and then crawled into the hutchie. Chloe did likewise beside her. Both sat to unlace boots. Jane tugged hers off and then the socks. It was quite a warm night, so she decided to sleep nude as she usually did. Chloe, she knew, definitely would.

Within minutes both girls were naked. Jane carefully placed her clothes to one side while Chloe just tossed hers off. "Careful Chloe, you will never find things in the morning," she said.

Chloe chuckled. "Be like last year," she replied. On her first ever weekend bivouac she had taken quite literally the call to go on check parade with boots and hat.

Jane smiled at the memory as she knelt to tidy up her gear. By now her eyes had adjusted to the darkness and she saw that it was quite light outside. Taking one of the strings of her mosquito net she crawled to the back end of the hutchie and looked up.

Half-moon, she noted, seeing that it was almost vertically overhead.

With deft fingers she threaded the string through a loop in the end of the hutchie and pulled it taut before tying a slip knot. Quickly she found the other corner string for that end and tied it up.

Now for the other end, she told herself.

As she turned, she encountered Chloe's bare rump. Chloe was kneeling on her sleeping bag, facing the other way, while she tied up the other end of her mosquito net.

"Chloe! That's my face you are poking your bum into," she complained.

Chloe giggled and called back, "Well kiss my butt!"

Jane twisted and did so. At the same time, she gave her a light smack. Chloe giggled again and wriggled her bottom. Suddenly a light came on. The torch was over beyond the next hutchie but its beam shone straight in, lighting up Chloe.

Sgt Lepson's voice called, "You girls stop your noise and get to sleep."

"Turn that torch off and have some manners," Chloe snarled back. "We haven't got any clothes on."

"Well you should have," Sgt Lepson retorted.

The torch stayed on. Jane felt Chloe stiffen so she moved to look. She was mostly hidden behind Chloe and stayed in her shadow.

"Rot! This is our bedroom and we are entitled to privacy," Chloe cried angrily. "Now turn the torch off or I will complain to the major."

From the next hutchie Davo's voice called, "Keep it on! Keep it on!" But the torch went off. Jane held Chloe, as much to restrain and calm her as anything. She did not mind that the boys in the next hutchie had been able to see but she resented Sgt Lepson doing what he did.

So did Chloe. "Bloody perve!" she muttered. "I should report him to the officers."

"Forget him," Jane said.

She did not feel like the aggravation such a complaint would cause. "He could quite legitimately say he was just checking who was in the hutchies. And Major Wickham will be annoyed. Don't forget that he has often said we should be decently dressed so that nobody gets offended."

"I don't get offended if people see me nude," Chloe answered.

Jane sighed. "Yes, but he will answer that the person who sees you might be offended."

Chloe grumbled that it was stupid world. "This is how God made me. Why should we be ashamed of that?"

"Because most men can't cope," Jane answered. "They are too insecure and need to keep it all under wraps to hide their inadequacies."

"You are right there," Chloe agreed.

Jane finished tying up her mosquito net. "I actually need to do a pee," she commented.

"Me too," Chloe agreed. She tied a last slip knot for her mosquito net, then groped for her boots. Jane found hers and pulled them on. By the time she had done so Chloe had crawled out of the hutchie into the moonlight and stood up.

Heavens, it is bright! You can see everything, Jane thought, seeing how Chloe's nude form shone in the bright moonlight.

For a moment she was struck by admiration. She thought Chloe had the most perfect female form she had ever seen and noted how the shadows from the moonlight accentuated her curves. Jane knew she had a good body too, and she was proud to show it off, but there were times when she was more than a little jealous of Chloe.

Watching Chloe cover her breasts with her hands as she looked around, she said, "Chloe, the boys will be able to see."

"Lucky them," Chloe answered, stretching and looking towards Davo's hutchie as she did. Their hutchie was on the outside of the circle with one end facing diagonally out. It was open in the direction of the distant company bivouac.

Jane smiled but felt anxious. "Get dressed," she said. "We don't want to get caught by Lepson."

Chloe sighed. "I'd rather go in the nude," she said.

It was Jane's turn to sigh. "No. Not tonight. We can't take the risk of getting caught," she cautioned.

Chloe snorted. "Huh! I may as well go out with a bang!" she said. "Get it Janie Babe? Bang?"

Jane gave a low laugh at the feeble joke, but then said, "Please don't Chloe."

"Aren't you game?" Chloe retorted.

"You know I am!" Jane snapped back. "But I don't want either of us getting chucked out of Cadets."

"I don't care! I'm sick of this!" Chloe replied. "I'll give them something to talk about."

Jane felt a stab of concern and knew she had to win this struggle of wills. "Please Chloe. You are my friend and I want us both to be in Cadets."

"You can stay," Chloe replied.

"I could but I want you here too. Please, if you are my friend don't do anything foolish," Jane pleaded.

"That's not fair!" Chloe cried softly.

"It is! I care about you mate! I don't want you getting into trouble," Jane answered.

She was determined now. Then she heard Chloe begin to snuffle and saw her slump. She sat down again and Jane heard what could only be the sound of crying. Immediately she moved in and put her arm around her.

"It's alright Chlo Babe. You are my friend and we hang together."

She patted Chloe's shoulder and found herself in a fierce embrace. For a few minutes the two girls clung together while Chloe sobbed quietly.

"They all hate me! They've all got it in for me," Chloe whimpered, "Peters and Cavendish and the CSM and Lepson."

"Don't let them win! Don't give them the satisfaction," Jane replied, patting and then stroking her as she trembled in her embrace.

"Sometimes I just want it to end," Chloe said between sniffles.

That really got Jane worried. *Is Chloe hinting that she wants to end it all? Is she thinking of suicide?* she worried.

"It's alright mate. I will help you. Now dry those peepers and let's get dressed and go and do a pee."

To her relief Chloe let go of her. "Sorry Janie Babe," she said. "Life's been getting me down a bit lately."

"You just hang in there," Jane answered, "If you need a shoulder to cry on use mine. And if you need a bit of a cuddle, I'll give you one. You don't have to go looking for some hairy, smelly male."

At that Chloe gave a soft chuckle. "Now that sounds good!"

"Chloe! Please!" Jane answered, giving her a last comforting squeeze and moving apart.

"I'm fine now. Thanks," Chloe said. She began to struggle into her trousers as she sat on her sleeping bag.

Jane heaved a mental sigh of relief and moved to put her own clothes on. She quickly pulled on trousers and shirt without underwear and then socks and unlaced boots, the laces tucked in the tops. "Now let's check that shitface Lepson isn't watching."

Chloe nodded her head and peeked out to stare intently around the bivouac area. "Can't see him," she whispered.

Jane did up one button on her shirt then snatched up her torch and crawled out to join Chloe. For a minute she stood beside her and they studied the silent hutchies. There was no sign of any movement.

Chloe whispered, "No sign of him. They are all asleep. Let's go."

She turned and started walking away from the hutchie towards the Old Highway. Jane followed, walking as quietly as she could manage. Neither girl turned their torch on, preferring to use their night vision. The going was easy with almost no grass cover and only a light sprinkling of deadfall on the sandy ground.

After they reached the Old Highway and turned right and were walking along it, Jane said, "This is far enough. They won't hear us here."

Chloe chuckled and pointed along the brightly moonlit clearing. "I thought the girl's latrine was along the road past HQ."

Jane nodded. "It is, but I only need a pee and I don't feel like walking hundreds of metres just for that. If we nip into the bushes across the road no-one at our platoon can see us."

Chloe nodded so the two girls made their way in among the bushes on the other side of the road. As she pushed in between two bushes Chloe let out a little yelp.

"Yikes! These are prickly," she whispered.

"I thought you liked a bit of a prickle," Jane replied, smiling as she did. She had remembered that these particular bushes were prickly and had avoided them.

Chloe gave a low snort and then chuckled. "I need a lot more than that," she answered.

Both girls found places out of each other's sight a few paces in and squatted. As she did Jane got a fright. Lights had suddenly illuminated the tops of the trees and the bushes. For a moment she went tense with anxiety but then she relaxed. It was only a car coming along the curving access road from Mingela.

The driver won't see us down here in these bushes, she reasoned.

And she was right. The car raced past, its headlights flickering through the trees and bushes and passed only 25 metres away.

A minute later she was back out on the Old Highway, buttoning up her trousers. Chloe joined her, chuckling as she did.

"I thought we'd been sprung then," she muttered.

Jane nodded and started walking back towards their bivouac. She felt tired now and just wanted to get to bed. The two girls walked quietly back along the Old Highway, their boots crunching softly on the sand and patches of bitumen. As they approached the platoon area Jane anxiously scanned the bush around her. She could plainly see the shelters dotted among the trees and suckers. The hutchies stood out as dark blobs from one side but the plastic shone in the moonlight after they had passed them.

"I hope they are all asleep," she whispered to Chloe as they approached their own hutchie. It seemed they were. No sound other than the ones they made came to her ears and thankfully she reached the hutchie and knelt to crawl inside. Chloe followed.

Boots and socks were pulled off and placed handy inside the mosquito net. For a moment Jane considered undressing but it just felt like too much effort, so she slid down into her sleeping bag.

"Goodnight Bub," she whispered.

"Goodnight Janie Babe," Chloe answered.

Jane tucked her mosquito net carefully in under the edges of her groundsheet and then lay back and stretched.

Will I strip off? she wondered.

At home she always slept nude. From the wriggling sounds next to her she deduced that Chloe was removing at least some of her clothing. Jane knew that Chloe nearly always slept naked but some niggling concern caused Jane to decide not to. She rolled on her side, wriggled her hip into her 'hip hole' and composed herself to sleep.

Chapter 4

MAJOR WICKHAM

By the time Lt Cavendish finished giving the Safety Brief Major Wickham was feeling exhausted. He had worked all week and Friday had been a particularly trying day for a teacher. One of the Year 11 classes had caused more discipline problems than usual, and he felt drained out. All he really wanted to do was lie down. But he forced himself to stay functioning.

I'm getting a bit too bloody old for this caper! he thought ruefully as he walked to where he had unloaded his gear.

One of the items was a red plastic Eski. This had originally been purchased for family picnics but for the last few years he had used it as a waterproof container to hold paperwork and other items. It was also just the right height to sit on and he thankfully eased himself down onto it, groaning at the stiffness of his joints and muscles as he did. He was in his mid-fifties and felt it.

Then he softly swore and made himself get up. He knew there were things he needed to organise. Stiffly he walked back the 25 metres to his car and opened the back door. For the next few minutes he busied himself with filling and lighting a kerosene hurricane lantern. This was then hung in a tree near where he was to sleep. The lantern was not so much to give light but to help guide cadets to him in an emergency.

With this moon there is plenty of light, he thought.

That done he collected his pack, webbing and briefcase and carried them to where he was going to set up his hutchie. He then trudged back to his car and rummaged in a box to collect food and the makings for coffee. With these he returned to his red box and again sat down. Sighing with relief he pulled his basic webbing to where he could easily reach it and set to work preparing a meal. That at least was something relaxing. First, he laid everything out close handy and opened the tin of meat. Coffee and sugar were placed in his steel cup canteen ready for the hot water. Then he opened his folding metal stove and took out the box of hexamine, the white chemical that burned as solid fuel

Lighting the hexamine with a match also lifted his mood. Ever since he had been a cadet himself forty years earlier, he had enjoyed the smell of burning hexamine. At the same time the small flame gave a cheery glow. After pouring water from a water bottle into one of his aluminium mess tins he placed this on the stove and then sat back to wait for the water to heat.

He was joined by the other five officers; Capt Mel Buchan, Capt Hamilton, Lt Barker, Lt Cavendish and Lt Peters. They all seated themselves on their packs and also began preparing hot drinks of food.

After a few minutes Capt Buchan said, "Our numbers are badly down this weekend."

"Yes, they are," Major Wickham agreed. "A couple of the platoons are barely strong enough to do tomorrow night's exercise."

"The usual platoon against platoon, isn't it?" Lt Cavendish asked.

"Yes," Major Wickham agreed. For nearly twenty years the unit had done weekend bivouacs at Mingela every May and the night fieldcraft exercise was one of their standard activities.

"We could maybe combine a couple," Capt Buchan suggested. "What are the numbers?"

Major Wickham listed them: "HQ has ten; 1 Platoon has twelve; 2 Platoon has eighteen; 3 Platoon has seventeen and 4 Platoon has nineteen."

"So 4 Platoon is our strongest platoon?" Lt Peters said.

"Yes, and our weakest," Capt Hamilton added.

Capt Buchan nodded and said, "Yes, if there are going to be real problems then it will be in 4 Platoon."

"Chloe and Jane," Lt Cavendish commented.

"Yes!" sighed Major Wickham. "But not just them. We seem to have a particularly weak team of leaders this year."

Capt Hamilton nodded vigorously. "You are right there. Only one of the platoon commanders is worth anything. The other three, Roach, Lewis and Summers, are as weak as water."

"Lewis and Summers have good sergeants though," said Lt Cavendish.

Lt Peters looked up from stirring her coffee. "How many girls came this weekend?"

"Twenty-eight of them, about a third of our numbers," Major Wickham replied. "There are eight of them in 1 Platoon, eight out of twelve!"

Capt Buchan shook his head and the others laughed. Major Wickham spooned coffee and sugar into his cup canteen, then poured the hot water in. After stirring it for a few seconds he left that and reached down to place his second mess tin, now containing 'spaghetti and meatballs', onto the hexamine stove. He then added condensed milk to the coffee and stirred that in.

For the next twenty minutes the OOCs ate and drank and talked. The conversation was a mixture of discussing the activities planned for the next day and reminiscences about previous Mingela bivouacs.

Having eaten his food and washed it down with coffee Major Wickham washed up his mess gear and packed it away. After picking up his 'Big Jim' torch he stood up.

"I will just have a look around the platoons," he said as he walked off towards 1 Platoon.

For the next 45 minutes he walked around in the darkness visiting the 'First Year' platoons. At the edge of his consciousness was a desire to visit 4 Platoon as well but he got so tied up inspecting hutchies and advising platoon commanders and sergeants on getting their new cadets properly set up and looked after that he never found the time. By 2150 he was back at the OOCs camp. There was a briefing for the Coy Orders Group (O Group) due and he needed to prepare for that.

Now that he knew exactly who had turned up Major Wickham was able to plan with certainty and he quickly pencilled names or postings against the lessons on the next day's training program. As he worked on this part of his mind kept a note of what was going on around the company. He was pleased to hear CSM Glenn's voice telling the platoon sergeants to get their cadets to bed.

At least I have a good CSM this year, he thought.

This was in contrast to the worry that his platoon commanders were not the best. That they were not became more obvious as 2215hrs arrived but not the platoon commanders for the O Group. Major Wickham held the small UHF radio he had hung by a cord around his neck and called. There was no response, even though each of the CUOs had been issued a radio. More minutes ticked by. CUO Joy Randall from 2 Platoon arrived but none of the others.

Major Wickham tried calling again and then sent CUO Randall to get 1 Platoon commander, CUO Natalie Summers. The CQMS, Sgt Karen

Harvey, was there so he sent her to get CUO Lewis from 3 Platoon and Sgt Moyle, the signals sergeant, to get 4 Platoon commander. Even then it was another fifteen minutes before the last (CUO Roach) arrived. By then CSM Glenn had reported that all platoons were now in bed.

As CUO Roach seated himself Major Wickham said, "You CUOs keep your radios turned on, especially you 4 Platoon commander." As he said this Major Wickham noted CUO Roach look guilty and try to surreptitiously turn his radio on. Major Wickham then said, "Right, take out your training programs."

CUO Summers, CUO Randall and the CSM all extracted theirs from trouser map pocket. CUO Roach and CUO Lewis both looked uncomfortable and Major Wickham felt a spurt of irritation.

"Do you have it?" he asked.

They shook their heads and Major Wickham bit back a savage and sarcastic retort that flashed into his mind. Instead he bent to his briefcase and extracted two more copies of the program and handed them over. But then he noted that CUO Roach did not have either a pen or a pencil.

Irritation boiled over. "I expect all NCOs to have a pencil and paper at all times," he growled. "And CUOs are cadet officers, so they should be even better prepared."

CUO Roach looked hurt and blushed. CUO Summers passed him her spare pencil and Major Wickham noted that Roach did not even have the good manners to thank her.

Why did I pick Roach to be 4 Platoon commander? he wondered. But he knew why. Of the four Roach had seemed the best for the independent, rough and tough 'senior' platoon.

For the next half hour Major Wickham detailed who was to teach each of the 40-minute lessons the next day. He also laid down times for a Coy O Group and for Platoon and Section O Groups.

That done he said, "Now, platoon commanders, the unit is a bit weak at the moment and it is important we have a good bivouac. Numbers are down and we need to make sure the cadets really enjoy the weekend and feel like they have learnt a lot and done useful training. We need to make sure there is no mischief. I don't want any problems to spoil the weekend."

As he said this Major Wickham looked at CUO Roach and images of a nude Chloe floated in his consciousness. Twice in the last year Major

Wickham had seen Chloe totally nude: a glimpse at the school swimming carnival; and on the day she and Jane had escaped from the smugglers at Bamfield Beach. On that occasion she had run towards him along the beach and he had been awestruck by her sheer animal sexuality and the perfection of her female form. Just thinking about the scene caused him to feel very uncomfortable.

CUO Roach looked worried and nodded. "I will keep an eye on those two girls sir. Sgt Lepson is watching them."

CUO Lewis snickered and muttered, "I'll bet he is!"

"That's enough of that thank you CUO Lewis," Major Wickham reproached him. "I did not name any individuals."

CUO Lewis looked abashed but Capt Hamilton commented, "You didn't need to sir. If there is going to be any mischief, then Chloe and Jane will be in it."

Lt Cavendish nodded vigorously. "They will wish they had never been born if I catch them up to any of their usual tricks! I will see them chucked out on their ear if they do," she added.

As she said this, she looked at Major Wickham for confirmation and he was both shocked by the vicious tone of her voice and by the implication that he would act on her wishes. In truth he found himself torn and could only nod.

"That will be all commanders. Back to your platoons and get to bed."

The cadets all stood and moved away, leaving the officers to talk for a while longer. By then it was 2300hrs and Capt Buchan yawned. "Bed for me," he said.

This started a general movement. Major Wickham stood up and groaned, then began to put up his hutchie. The other OOCs had already done so and soon moved off to them. The five OOCs had their hutchies in a small cluster at the top of a small slope between their vehicles and a shallow, grassy re-entrant. 1 Platoon was to the east straddling the top end of the dip, 2 Platoon to the south in the triangle where the shallow re-entrant joined another similar feature to the west. Beside them, camped on the low rise leading to the low embankment of the Old Highway, was 3 Platoon. HQ Platoon was fitted in between the officers and 3 Platoon.

The OOCs had set up three hutchies in one line, each a few metres apart and set up so that the occupants could not see into each other's shelter. Captain Buchan and Lt Peters were nearest to 2 PL and HQ. Major

Wickham set his up next. Capt Hamilton, Lt Barker and Lt Cavendish each had hutchies between him and 1 PL.

It only took a few minutes for Major Wickham to set up his shelter. He used the same two trees each year and had a double hutchie he kept clipped together. First, he brushed aside the twigs. Next, he used his boot heel to scrape out a 'hip hole'. Then he tied the shelter between the two trees. The work of pegging down the four corners took only a minute or so. When it was done, he placed his gear inside and crawled in to unroll his bedding. The erection of a mosquito net, tied up at four points with slip knots, took another couple of minutes. Once that was done, he sat on his sleeping bag and unlaced his boots and took them off, then carefully placed them aside with his hat on top of them and his glasses on top of that. His torch he placed beside his pack. Thankfully he lay down and stretched out.

For a few minutes he just lay and let the strain ease out. The air was still pleasantly warm, and he did not feel the need to put on a pullover or pull his sleeping bag up. As always, he felt a sense of relief that the unit had deployed to the field without incident and was ready to begin training.

But then sleep would not come. He lay there fretting about all the things he should have done to improve morale and to increase recruiting, while knowing he was being unreasonable with himself. Running a cadet unit was not his job. It was something he did as a volunteer in his spare time. His full-time job was teaching and that was enough to tire him out most days. He was also divorced and had his three young children stay with him on most weekends.

Oh, I hope we don't have any problems this weekend, he thought. He really just wanted a weekend off.

The soft crunch of boots on the Old Highway came to his ears. *Some girls going to the latrine,* he thought.

But it was just too much effort required to roll over and crawl to the end of his hutchie to look so he didn't bother. Instead he closed his eyes and tried to sleep.

The sounds of more boots, this time approaching his hutchie, caused him a spurt of irritation. *Bloody hell! Who is this?* he wondered.

A cadet's voice, Cadet Sergeant Trevor Lynes, the Intelligence Sgt, came from just outside.

"Sir! OC sir. Major Wickham."

"Yes, what is it?" Major Wickham replied.

"Two naked girls just walked past sir," Sgt Lynes replied.

Oh bloody hell! If it's that bloody Chloe up to her tricks that will be the end of her, Major Wickham thought.

Groaning with fatigue and irritation he rolled over and crawled out of his hutchie, getting caught up in the mosquito net as he did.

"Who were they? What did they do?"

Sgt Lynes appeared to be both excited and apprehensive. "They just walked past sir, starkers, I mean with nothing on."

"They wore joggers," added another cadet.

Major Wickham squinted in the moonlight and saw that it was Cpl Bailey from 3 PL. That did not surprise him as the nightly 'Fire and Security' piquet always had two cadets rostered on at the same time on staggered shifts of one hour. As the CSM organised that and as each platoon took it in turn it was obviously 3 PL's turn.

"Who was it?" Major Wickham queried as he got stiffly to his feet.

Sgt Lynes shrugged. "Don't know sir. I couldn't see properly in the dark. They had their hands over their faces."

Major Wickham noted the bright moonlight and pursed his lips. *Lacking moral courage this one? Or is he trying to protect a friend?*

Cpl Bailey stepped closer. "I reckon it was Chloe and her friend sir," he added.

"Are you sure? Why do you say that?" Major Wickham queried. He could hear other officers stirring around him as the talking disturbed their sleep.

"One was a big blonde sir," Bailey replied. He started to use his hands to indicate large breasts then realised what he was doing and stopped.

"Where are they now? Which way did they go?" Major Wickham asked.

Sgt Lynes pointed eastwards along the Old Highway. "That way sir. They came from the direction of 4 Platoon and went towards the girl's latrine."

Major Wickham shook his head in exasperation. *Oh blast! I'll have to do something.* He was amazed that Chloe and Jane could be so brazen.

"And they haven't come back?"

"No sir."

"OK, thank you. Go back on piquet," Major Wickham directed. He then turned and knelt to go back into his hutchie knowing that he needed his boots on and also that he would have to take action, however much he privately regretted it. The two cadets returned to their sentry post which was at the 'Q' hutchie beside the road at the left end of the row of parked vehicles.

On hands and knees Major Wickham pushed in under his mosquito net. "Oh bugger!" he muttered.

Testily he groped around and found his glasses and slid them into his pocket then placed his hat aside and dragged his boots and socks out. His glasses he did not put on because he had found over many years that his night vision was above average and that wearing glasses tended to make it harder, not easier to see clearly in the dark. After tugging his socks on he tucked the boot laces into his boots and then slid his feet into them.

Surely those girls can't be so stupid as to think they could pull off a prank like this and get away with it? he told himself. *Not after the formal warning they got a few weeks ago!*

He could only assume it was some sort of a dare or a silly attempt at defiance. Now thoroughly annoyed and even a bit upset he crawled out and stood up.

Plenty of light, he thought, again noting how bright the moonlight was. *Those boys must have got a real eyeful.*

Taking hold of the broom handle he always used as a staff in the bush he reluctantly walked over to Lt Peter's hutchie and quietly called out to her. It took another call to get her to mumble a response.

"What is it?" she asked sleepily.

"An incident involving two girls," Major Wickham answered. "I need you and Caitlin awake and in uniform."

Lt Peters groaned and muttered her annoyance as well. Major Wickham turned to go and said, "I will be up on the road."

As he walked through the knee-high grass towards the vehicles Major Wickham passed Capt Buchan's hutchie. From out of it came that officer's voice. "What is it?' he asked.

"Two girls running around in the nuddy. We will have to investigate," Major Wickham replied. He now conceded that he could not hope to keep this quiet and that he needed all the staff. "Wake Warwick and Ashley and join me up on the road please."

Major Wickham walked the twenty paces to where the two cadets on piquet stood near the end vehicle. The cadets were staring along the road towards where the girl's latrine had been sited. "Can you see them?"

"No sir," they replied.

Major Wickham moved out a few paces onto the Old Highway to get a clear view along it. Nothing moved in the moonlight and he reckoned he could see clearly for several hundred metres. He began to turn away when movement along to his right caught his eye. Two figures, black with the moon behind them, were visible about 50 metres away. Even as he turned back, he saw them scuttle off to the other side of the road.

"The Devil taken them! The piquet were right. I wonder who that is?" he muttered.

For a few seconds he hesitated. His first thoughts were to hurry along the road to catch the girls but then he decided that was not a good idea.

I had better get the female officers to do that, he thought.

So he stood there watching intently for any further signs of movement. He was joined by Capt Buchan who wanted to know the details. As quickly as he could Major Wickham told him. Then he had to repeat the information twice over as first Capt Hamilton and Lt Barker joined him and then the two lady officers.

Lt Cavendish was irritable but sparked up noticeably when told who the girls might be. "Chloe and Jane? Oh good! This might give us just the reason we need to get rid of those two troublemakers," she commented.

Capt Buchan frowned and shook his head. "Are we sure it is Chloe and Jane? Surely they aren't that stupid?"

Lt Barker chuckled. "How many blondes with big tits do we have who run around in the nuddy?" he commented.

"Lieutenant Barker!" Major Wickham snapped, not amused by the levity in the young officer's voice.

Capt Buchan took a look along the Old Highway and then turned to Major Wickham. "What are we going to do?"

"Try to catch them first," Major Wickham replied. "Jenny, you and Caitlin walk along the Old Highway and search the area around the girl's latrine. Mel, you get written statements from the two cadets on piquet. Warwick, you and Ash go back down the slope and watch the rear of the camp in case they try to circle back through the bush to 4 Platoon's area. I will go over onto the high ground on the other side."

With that he turned and walked across the road while the two female lieutenants walked along it towards where he had seen the two figures. In the still night air the sound of their boots crunching on the sand and old bitumen sounded very loud.

I wish they'd try to walk more quietly, Major Wickham thought.

He climbed up the low rise on the north side of the Old Highway and stood looking eastwards along it. The two female officers were quite visible in the moonlight. They made their way east for about a hundred metres and then looked into the bushes beside the road. There was a stand of young saplings there with several thorn trees on the down slope beyond. Then the lady officers turned and walked on further along the road.

Major Wickham looked in all directions but no-one else was visible, so he stood and listened. Puzzled and a bit concerned he walked a few more paces and peered into the shadows under the nearest prickly bushes.

Knowing that the cutting of the Old Railway could provide a covered route he made his way across the flat area covered with small, spiky bushes of about waist height. On his left was a Chinese apple tree and to his right a mound of earth. Twenty-five metres across this flat area was the Old Railway cutting. At the point where Major Wickham reached the cutting it was about two metres deep, with sloping, sandy sides lined with clumps of the spiky shrubbery.

Once again, he paused to listen and to look around. Off to his left were the distant lights of Mingela township. In front of him three hundred metres away was the highway and even as he stood watching the lights of a road train went rushing by, each trailer outlined by rows of red lights.

Once the road train had vanished down the range silence settled again. There was not even a rustle of breeze in the tall gun trees beyond the cutting. Major Wickham looked around at the moon-dappled landscape and shivered. Then he noticed an anomaly in the pattern of shadows and moonlight. Unable to get a clear view from where he was, he took three steps to his right and peered down into the shadowy cutting.

As he did two figures erupted from the shadows just below him. They gave him such a fright he stepped hastily back, notions of wild pigs and bulls flitting across his mind. But then he realised he was looking at two human beings who were both running away from him westwards along the bottom of the cutting. And not just any human beings! In the bright moonlight he could clearly see the gleam of bare skin and female shapes. Blonde hair waved bright in the moonlight and showed clearly.

"Stop! Stop!" Major Wickham shouted.

But the two naked girls didn't. They kept on running. Major Wickham set off after them, calling to the other officers as he did.

At his age and level of fitness he was no match for the two girls who quickly drew ahead and then vanished among the bushes. Major Wickham slowed to a gasping trot.

They are heading for 4 Platoon. It must be Chloe and Jane, he thought.

Chapter 5

ACCUSATIONS

"**G**et up! Get out here!" called a loud and angry voice.

Jane tried to ignore the voice. She had only just slipped into a deep sleep and did not want to wake up. But the voice was insistent, and she recognized it as Major Wickham's.

"Wake up and get out of that hutchie!" he called. Reluctantly Jane rolled on her back and opened her eyes.

Another voice joined in: Lieutenant Cavendish's. "Get out here at once you girls!" she snapped. A torch came on and shone into the hutchie.

Jane blinked and rolled away from the light as it hurt her eyes. Then she struggled to a sitting position, remembering just in time that she had undone her waistband before going to bed. Hastily she clutched the sleeping bag to her front.

What on earth is going on? she wondered.

There were more voices outside and the tramp of boots on the dead leaves. Muttering and voices came from the hutchies nearby. Lt Cavendish called again, louder and sounding more annoyed this time. "Get up Cummings! Carson, get out here!"

Jane mumbled a yes and began groping for the waist of her trousers. Chloe let out a groan and rolled on her back beside her. As she did her sleeping bag was dragged down to expose her left breast. That did not surprise Jane as she knew Chloe liked to sleep nude but the torch shining in annoyed her.

"Turn the torch off! We have to get dressed," she cried.

"You should be dressed!" Lt Cavendish retorted, the torch beam shifting to Jane's face.

Jane shielded her face and swore under her breath. She was going to call out again when the torch was switched off. She reached across and nudged Chloe's arm.

"Wake up Chlo Babe. We have to get up," she said.

Chloe groaned again and muttered but then opened her eyes and sat up. As she did her sleeping bag fell down, revealing she wore no top.

Another torch came on outside and while it did not shine directly into the hutchie it provided enough light to make Chloe's nakedness very visible.

That annoyed Jane even more and she called, "Turn the torches off while we get dressed."

Outside she heard Major Wickham say, "So they haven't got any clothes on?"

Lt Cavendish bent to look in and then said, "Carson has but Cummings hasn't."

Jane saw red. "Stop looking! Give us some privacy or I will complain to my mum."

"You should be decent," Lt Cavendish retorted, but she moved away so that all Jane could see in the torchlight outside were trouser legs and boots. More voices told her that all of the adult staff were there and so were CUO Roach and Sgt Lepson.

While Jane struggled to do up the zip on her trousers, she heard Major Wickham say, "Did either of you see Cadets Cummings or Carson walking or running around the area a few minutes ago?"

CUO Roach answered. "No sir, but I did hear people running."

Sgt Lepson spoke next. "I heard people running and I looked out and saw two people run to these hutchies here sir."

Jane was both angry and mystified. As she zipped up her trousers her mind raced. *What is this all about? All we have done is go to bed.*

Chloe rubbed her eyes and began untangling a shirt. "What's going on?" she whispered to Jane.

Jane shook her head. "No idea," she whispered back.

"Stop that whispering and get out here at once!" Lt Cavendish snapped.

Chloe did not worry about a bra but just pulled on her shirt and began hastily buttoning it up. Jane pulled on her right sock. Outside many voices were now talking, most asking questions about what was happening and others muttering what sounded like accusations.

Major Wickham said, "Sgt Lepson, check that all of the platoon are here. Use your torch."

"Yes sir."

Jane saw Lepson's torch beam move to the next hutchie as he began walking around the platoon area. Next, he bent and shone his torch into Kim and Chantelle's hutchie.

He shouldn't be shining a torch into a girl's hutchie, Jane thought.

She could not see into that hutchie from were she sat but she heard Lepson talking to the two girls, explaining that he had to do a bed check. In reply there was some angry muttering and hissing. Then he moved on to the next hutchie.

Jane pulled on her left sock and then began to pull on her boots. As she did Lt Cavendish bent down and snapped, "Hurry up and get out!"

"But we aren't dressed yet," Chloe answered.

"I don't care! Just make sure you are covered and get out here!" Lt Cavendish shouted back.

Feeling both mystified and annoyed Jane tugged on her second boot and crawled out, not bothering to do up the laces. Next to her Chloe stopped looking for her trousers and just tugged on her boots and followed. Seeing that Chloe only wore her shirt Jane paused to whisper, "You need your duds Chlo."

"Covered," Chloe hissed back. She pulled on her second boot and began crawling out as well.

Oh dear, Chloe is being silly Jane thought. *Just wearing her shirt is going to light another fuze.*

She wasn't wrong. As Chloe stood up Lt Cavendish switched her torch on and shone it on Chloe's legs. "Where are your trousers Cummings?" she snapped.

Jane saw Chloe's lovely long legs glowing in the torchlight and tensed for the explosion. Chloe gestured back at the hutchie.

"In there miss, but you said to get out and make sure we were covered."

Only just! Jane thought, noting how short Chloe's shirt was.

Lt Cavendish obviously thought so too. "Put your trousers on!" she ordered. Jane was sure she also muttered some insulting words but wasn't sure. The torch clicked off.

Chloe turned and bent over into the hutchie to find her trousers. As she did her shirt rode up over her buttocks, exposing the fact that she was not wearing undies. At the same moment a torch came on, lighting her bare bum for all to see.

Major Wickham snapped angrily: "Turn that torch off!"

The torch went off but Jane had noted that it was held by CUO Roach. *The bastard!* she thought. *What a perve.*

"Sorry sir. I thought she might need some light," CUO Roach replied.

Chloe had called out in annoyance but now found her trousers but she had to sit to take her boots off so she could pull them on. Another minute went by. As they waited Jane looked around. She saw that all the adult staff was there and so was half the platoon. Sgt Lepson was still moving from shelter to shelter checking people.

"Where are Grey and Davidson?" he called.

"Here," called Grey from just nearby.

Major Wickham turned on them. "All you people from 4 Platoon get back into your hutchies. Move!"

They moved. He was so obviously angry nobody felt like being slow or last. Sgt Lepson continued with his bed check while Chloe finished dressing and stood up.

"Ready now?" Lt Cavendish snapped.

"Yes Ma'am," Chloe replied.

"You should sleep dressed," Lt Cavendish went on.

"I do when it is a tactical exercise Ma'am," Chloe replied.

"You should at least wear pyjamas."

"I don't own any Ma'am," Chloe answered, causing a ripple of whispering and snickering from the nearby hutchies.

"What about at home? What does your mother think of that?" Lt Cavendish went on.

"She doesn't wear any either," Chloe replied.

"Then your mother..." Lt Cavendish began.

But Major Wickham cut her off. "We will leave home out of this thank you Lt Cavendish. OK, Cadets Cummings and Carson, did either of you walk to the female latrine up past headquarters a few minutes ago?"

"No sir," Jane answered. "We were in bed and were asleep."

"Cummings?"

"No sir."

"So you didn't go to the latrine?"

Jane blushed and felt guilty. Reluctantly she admitted they had. "We did sir. Before we went to bed."

Chloe nodded. "But not at the proper latrine sir. It was too far so we just went in the bushes over the road there." She pointed towards the place.

Major Wickham looked doubtful and frowned. "So you did not walk along the road past headquarters?"

"No sir," Jane replied.

"Too far to walk sir," Chloe added.

Lt Cavendish hissed. "You are not supposed to just go anywhere. That is bad hygiene."

Before Jane or Chloe could respond Major Wickham cut in. "Perhaps 4 Platoon needs its own latrines if it is so far away. Now, Cadet Carson, did you see or hear anyone running past here a few minutes ago?"

"No sir. I was asleep."

"Cadet Cummings?"

"No sir."

Major Wickham turned to the others. "Did anyone else see or hear people running in this area?"

"I did sir," Sgt Lepson replied.

You lying bastard! Jane thought. But she knew she had been asleep so couldn't be sure.

"You say you saw people running to these hutchies. Where were you and exactly what did you see?" Major Wickham queried.

Sgt Lepson pointed to his own hutchie. "I was in there sir. Some noises woke me, and I heard people running. I knew the cadets should all be in bed, so I stuck my head out to look."

"And what exactly did you see?"

"I saw two people run to one of these hutchies and crawl in sir," Sgt Lepson replied.

As he was pointing at her hutchie Jane was appalled. She also thought she noted a very strained note in Sgt Lepson's voice. *He is lying, but why?*

"To this hutchie?" Major Wickham asked, pointing Chloe and Janes'.

Sgt Lepson hesitated and swallowed. "Er.. I think so sir," he said.

"Did you identify either of the people?"

"No sir."

"What were the people wearing?"

Again, Sgt Lepson hesitated. "Er.. er.. I ..it was dark sir so I'm not sure but it looked like they weren't wearing anything."

"Naked you mean?"

"Could have been sir."

"And how long before we arrived was this?" Major Wickham queried.

"Only a minute or so sir," Sgt Lepson answered.

Major Wickham turned to CUO Roach. "Did you see these people CUO Roach?"

"No sir. I was asleep but I did hear people running. That's what woke me up."

Major Wickham turned to the officers. "Go and ask at each of these hutchies if they heard or saw anything."

As the officers dispersed to do this Major Wickham turned back to Sgt Lepson. "And you say the people ran to this hutchie?"

"Er... er... maybe sir. I thought so."

"But you aren't sure?"

"It was dark sir and I was half asleep," Sgt Lepson replied.

Major Wickham then waited till the officers all returned. Each gave a negative report.

"Nobody saw or heard anything," Capt Buchan said.

Major Wickham again turned to Jane and Chloe. "And you girls deny running around just before we arrived?"

"Yes sir," Jane and Chloe chorused.

Jane was angry now. *I don't understand what is going on but it all sounds odd to me,* she thought.

She said, "It wasn't us sir. We were asleep."

There was strained silence while Major Wickham looked hard at them. "Yes, well. Something happened and I want to know what. You two girls are under suspicion. I can't prove you have done anything, but be warned; if I find out you have been up to mischief, I will chuck you both out on your ear, no ifs or buts. Do you understand?"

"Yes sir," Chloe replied.

Jane had to get control of her temper before she could answer. Gritting her teeth, she muttered "Yes sir."

Major Wickham stared hard at Chloe. "And in future Cadet Cummings make sure you are decently dressed all of the time so that nobody is offended if they have to wake you. Do you understand?"

"Yes sir," Chloe replied.

"Then everyone get to bed. We will investigate further in the morning," Major Wickham said. With that he turned and began walking away. The other officers followed. CUO Roach and Sgt Lepson waited a few moments before also leaving.

As they did Jane heard CUO Roach mutter to Sgt Lepson, "What was that all about?"

She didn't hear Sgt Lepson's reply but the exchange heightened her suspicions even more.

Lepson is up to something. I wonder if he tried to set us up?

This was the theory she put to Chloe when the two of them were again lying in their sleeping bags but she got no opportunity to elaborate as Sgt Lepson called, "You girls stop talking and get to sleep!"

Bastard! Jane thought.

So she obeyed. But sleep did not immediately come. For quite a while she lay awake, puzzling over what had happened and why. She had to wait until after check parade the next morning to get the outline and that started badly. As Sgt Lepson began calling them out with the traditional: "Check parade! Boots and hat!" several other boys also began calling.

Kane called loudly: "Boots and hat Chloe, boots and hat!"

It was such an obvious jibe at the famous incident the previous year that Chloe bristled, and Jane began to get angry again. She opened her mouth to protest but Sgt Lepson beat her too it.

"Stop that sort of talk!" he snapped. "Just get out on parade."

That also mystified Jane. *For once Lepson is doing the right thing, but what was that all about last night?*

The platoon lined up out on the Old Highway and Sgt Lepson formed them up in three ranks and marched them along to where the rest of the company was waiting. It was obvious to Jane that Sgt Lepson was not organised and that they were late as twice CSM Glenn called to them to hurry up.

Good! Serves the hypocritical prick right, she thought.

Then Sgt Lepson made more obvious mistakes in moving the platoon into line on the left of HQ instead of its proper position between 3 Platoon and HQ. This gave Jane some more malicious pleasure.

I wouldn't mind him so much if he was good at his job, she told herself.

But it was the looks and behind–the–hand whispering from cadets in the platoons on either side that got Jane bothered again. It was obvious to her that the story about what she and Chloe had allegedly done was widely known and believed. The embarrassment and unfairness of the situation caused tears to prickle in Jane's eyes, but she made herself stand tall and with a poker face.

CSM Glenn proceeded to Right Dress the company and then told the sergeants to call the roll. During the parade Jane remained very conscious that she and Chloe were the centre of attention. Other cadets kept glancing at them and there was a lot of whispering and sniggering.

What the bloody hell happened? Jane thought, worrying now that some secret enemy was trying to get at them.

She soon found out, courtesy of Cpl Callan and Cadet Grey. They came over as the girls packed away their bedding.

"You know what everyone reckons you chicks done last night?" Cpl Callan queried.

"No, what?" Chloe asked.

"They reckon that you walked over past headquarters and on along the road in the nuddy and that the major nearly caught you and chased you back here," Callan replied.

Jane was appalled. "Who is they?" she asked.

"Sgt Lynes and Cpl Bailey. They were the piquet," Callan answered.

"Why do they think it was us?" Jane demanded to know.

Callan shrugged. "Two naked sheilas running around and one of 'em a big blonde? How many big blondes do we have in the unit?" he said, looking at Chloe as he did.

Jane was again appalled. *Our reputations are certainly coming back to hurt us,* she thought. But Callan was right. The only other blonde she could think of was Megan Smith, a thin little First Year. *And she certainly doesn't have Chloe's build.*

Chloe was also very annoyed. "Well it wasn't us! Did Lynes say it was?"

"He thought it was you. Who else could it have been?" Callan replied.

Who else indeed? Jane thought. It was certainly a mystery and it left her feeling quite sick. *I suppose we deserve it from the way we have behaved in the past,* she thought ruefully. But it all seemed somehow unfair. *We have really tried to be good this year, at least at Cadets, and even at school.*

I hope there is no more trouble, Jane thought as she unpacked her mess gear.

Breakfast followed. Jane deliberately sat on the other side of the hutchie and did not try to join a group. Chloe sat with her, their backs to the platoon. But then Lepson annoyed Jane even more by picking Chloe to go and join the work party to dig the girl's latrine. For a second, she feared that Chloe might argue and refuse, but she just smiled and went off, apparently cheerful. Lepson then rebuking Jane for Chloe's unpacked gear did not help her mood.

It was a resentful girl that stood in the ranks during the morning parade. After the OC posted the officers and the sergeants had moved to the rear Jane was very conscious of Lepson being behind her. Even though she did not know if he was looking at her or not her skin seemed to crawl and she prickled with dislike.

After the 0800 company parade the whole unit was seated in section lines in the shade. Jane sat behind Chloe and tried to make herself comfortable. Once again, she was hotly aware of cadets casting looks at her and Chloe. The smirking and whispering was what really irked her and she boiled inside.

When I find out who set us up they will be sorry! she told herself.

Major Wickham had maps distributed and Capt Buchan began the full Ground Orientation and Safety Brief. The maps were photocopies on a 1:25 000 scale and Jane had seen them before. As Capt Buchan pointed out the main features she studied the map and was confident she was familiar with the area.

Several times during the Safety Brief Jane glanced around. Each time she caught Sgt Lepson looking at her and Chloe. That caused her to feel irritated and slightly threatened.

He is such a creep! she thought.

Following the briefing there was a 10-minute break followed by a lesson on stretchers and the improvised movement of casualties. This was revision of lessons taught previously at Home Training. At the beginning of the lesson each section commander and 2ic was issued with a broom handle to quickly make improvised stretchers if needed. Webbing was looped and buckled around the broom handles for the casualty to lie on.

This caused Jane more irritation as Cpl Hankin selected Cadet MacDonald to be the acting section 2ic. He was not given any rank, promotions to lance corporal usually being done much later in the year before annual camp. What annoyed Jane was that both she and Chloe had been in Cadets at least six months longer than MacDonald and she felt quite sure she was more capable than him.

During the lesson they also practised moving casualties without a stretcher, by making 'chairs' with people's arms. That was something Jane had done before and she and Chloe quickly worked out how to cross their arms at right angles to make a 'seat'. The problem was who to practise with as the unit policy was that girls did not lift boys and boys did not lift girls. That meant they had to group with Renee Moss and Shona.

Shona was fine with it and they all took turns at lifts with two people. Moss did not want to but Cpl Hankin made her join in. To show what she thought Moss curled her lip into a sneer of distaste. Jane felt a sharp stab of anger, but she managed to control herself.

Then the boys annoyed her again. As Chloe and Shona went to lift Moss Chloe stumbled and nearly fell. Kane, who was standing beside her, grabbed her and held her up, but in the process he gripped her left arm so that the back of his fingers touched her breast. He then made the mistake of holding on a millisecond longer than he needed to once she had regained her balance.

Chloe turned a Basilisk-like glare on him and hissed, "Keep your hands off me or I will break your face!"

Kane let go at once and tried to bluster. "Just trying to help!" he replied.

"Then don't!" Chloe retorted.

Kane went white and then red and turned away, muttering and his lips forming the word 'bitch'. Jane pursed her lips and then noted that Sgt Lepson was again watching Chloe's every move.

Creepy bugger! I will report him for stalking or harassment, she thought. She was now thoroughly annoyed.

There was another 10-minute break and they moved on to a revision lesson by the section corporals of silent 'Field Signals' and then patrol formations.

Chapter 6

MORNING ROUTINE

Sgt Lepson woke up as he nearly always did feeling aroused. As he stirred to consciousness, he was very aware of his condition, having unbuttoned his waistband and unzipped his fly for comfort while he slept. He was also very conscious that he had been having an erotic dream and that it involved Chloe. Wisps of memory told him that in the dream he had been about to have sex with Chloe. Erotic images rose to torment him. The images held an extra edge as he knew that he subconsciously did want to have sex with her, while consciously despising her. To add to his mental discomfiture was the searing heat of jealousy as he knew several other boys who claimed to have had sex with her, or who claimed to have witnessed her with other males.

Sgt Lepson saw that it was still dark but that there were the beginnings of a greyness off to the east. He also became aware that he had been woken by CSM Glenn, who again nudged at his feet. Luckily it was dark and cool so that Sgt Lepson was inside his sleeping bag and his aroused state was not obvious.

"Yeah, I'm awake," he grumbled as CSM Glenn told him to get up and get moving.

The CSM grunted and walked off back towards the company bivouac. Sgt Lepson swore softly as he watched the CSM's departing shape. He knew he was a bit afraid of the CSM and that rankled.

Then memories of the previous night's events flooded in and Sgt Lepson experienced a sharp sense of emotional discomfort. He knew he had tried to harm Chloe and that knowledge made his conscience feel distinctly uneasy. Then other memories returned: of shining his torch into Chantelle and Kim's hutchie and of finding them hastily dressing and of them hissing at him not to say anything or he would regret it.

That really bothered Sgt Lepson. Earlier in the day Kim had told him to point to Chloe's hutchie when he was asked by the officers and she had made it very clear that she would accuse him of doing improper things to her if he did not, or if he mentioned them doing anything. The threat had made him go cold with fear. He knew his father would explode with wrath if such an accusation was made.

But what exactly had Kim and Sandilands done? he wondered.

He distinctly remembered being woken by calling voices and by the sound of people running through the bush. And he had stuck his head out and seen two naked girls in the moonlight. But they had not run to Chloe and Jane's hutchie, but to Kim and Sandilands'.

And when he had gone to check and shone his torch in it was obvious that both girls were trying to get quickly dressed. He had even glimpsed Chantelle's right tit so had no doubt she had been naked. The image had helped torment him with erotic fantasies and dreams far into the night.

But what were they up to? Were they trying to get Chloe and Jane into trouble? he wondered. *Well, if that was their plan they have succeeded,* he decided.

A check of his watch showed Sgt Lepson that it was 0545. Reluctantly he did his trousers up. Then he crawled out of the sleeping bag and pulled on his boots. As he did desire ebbed away and his body returned to normal, until he realised he was able to see into Chloe's hutchie.

Even in the shadows he was able to discern that there appeared to be two heads in one sleeping bag. His heart leapt with a spurt of triumph, even as his prurient interest was sparked.

Got the bitch! Caught her in bed with someone, he thought.

Snatching up his torch he strode across to the hutchie and bent down. The beam of the torch was directed in. Then his emotions went into turmoil again. There were two heads close together and under one sleeping bag but they were both female: Chloe's and Jane's. The two girls appeared to be sleeping as 'spoons'; Chloe behind Jane and both facing the same way. For a few seconds Sgt Lepson pondered what to do. He also wondered whether the girls were dressed or not. He was sorely tempted to lift the sleeping bag to check but fear held his hands.

They could complain and even if I got them into trouble I could be in even more, he thought.

Besides, what should he do about two girls snuggling up to each other in the cold? After a moment's reflection he realised it could make him look both silly and vindictive if he tried to blow it up as an incident. As he stood there, Jane stirred and Sgt Lepson quickly retreated, clicking off the torch as he did.

He withdrew to the cover of his hutchie and resumed lacing up his boots. To his annoyance and surprise, he found he had become fully aroused again and that his heart was hammering rapidly. It hurt his pride to find that the girls he despised had so much influence on him. Knowing that he was being hypocritical made him even angrier with himself.

After doing a quick pee behind a nearby bush Sgt Lepson positioned himself where he could see into Chloe's hutchie. By then it was 0555 and the half-light of dawn was making it easier to see. Sgt Lepson looked around to check that no-one was watching him but was satisfied that all members of the platoon were still asleep.

At 0600 CSM Glenn's voice reached him through the still morning air. Sgt Lepson at once began calling, "Wake up 4 Platoon! All out! Get out for Check Parade! Wake up! Get out! Boots and hat and get on parade."

There were groans and curses and people began stirring in the hutchies. Then Kane began calling: "Boots and hat Chloe! Boots and hat!"

Sgt Lepson knew it was a reference to an incident the previous year but it nettled his tender conscience. Ashamed of his part in the previous incident he snapped back: "Stop that sort of talk!" he snapped. "Just get out on parade."

Sgt Lepson knew he should go to each hutchie and make sure the cadets were awake but he felt compelled to stand and watch Chloe's hutchie. So instead he stood and yelled.

But his stand was not rewarded. When Chloe and Jane stirred and then rolled apart before sitting up the sleeping bag slid off them to reveal that both were fully dressed. Sgt Lepson felt a stab of disappointment and quickly turned side on, to pretend that he wasn't looking, but out of the corner of his eye he kept watching.

At that moment Jane looked up and he quickly looked away and moved to shout at Kane and Stevenson, to get them moving. But he wasn't quite quick enough, and he saw the beginnings of a scowl on Jane's face. That caused him a twinge of anxiety so he moved right away.

To mask his interest Sgt Lepson walked over to a boy's hutchie. "Hurry up Dipkins!" he snapped. Then he walked across to near the Old Highway and called loudly, "Get a move on 4 Platoon! Out on the road, move!"

While he waited Sgt Lepson found his mind filled with images of

Kim and Chantelle and of Chloe and he stiffened up. Being aroused in front of the platoon was a new and very embarrassing experience for Sgt Lepson. He began to pace up and down and kept glancing down to check whether it was at all visible through the camouflage uniform.

Go down! he thought, trying to will his body to relax.

But it seemed the more he thought about it the stiffer it got. Sgt Lepson began to sweat and his breathing and heart rate shot up. By then cadets were straggling out to stand in a group nearby.

"Hurry up! Stop your chattering and get on parade," he yelled.

Chantelle and Kim came walking past. As Kim walked past she met his eye. "Remember to keep your mouth shut, or else!" she hissed.

Sgt Lepson was shocked. A spear of fear stabbed through him but he tried to pretend he wasn't bothered. All he managed to do was keep his face from showing too much and to nod.

What are those two up to? he wondered, ashamed that he should feel so afraid of them.

As he stood there waiting, Sgt Lepson found his desire ebb. That it was from fear was something he did not want to admit, even to himself. To take his mind off his condition he strode off into the bivouac and began yelling at Flegel who was looking for his hat amidst a jumble of gear and then at Arthur, who was still in his sleeping bag.

Once they were out Sgt Lepson chivvied them out to join the others. Feeling distinctly anxious about possibly being late he then looked along the road. A hundred metres away he could just see the company forming up in the semi darkness. Then he was embarrassed even more by CSM Glenn calling, "Hurry up 4 Platoon!"

Sgt Lepson realised he had not even formed the platoon up in three ranks. Hastily he nominated Cpl Callan as the Right Marker, then ordered the others to form three ranks. That done he moved them to the right in threes and started them marching.

As they marched along the old road towards the company Sgt Lepson was able to see that all of the other platoons were standing in position and obviously waiting. From his position out to the side and rear he could also see Chloe marching. The sight was enough to keep him aroused. Even in the shapeless camouflage uniform her rounded buttocks and hips were very obvious and she moved with a sensuous grace that made his mouth go dry just to watch. Then CSM Glenn again called on them to hurry up, causing Sgt Lepson to blush in shame and to feel angry.

We have the furthest to go, he thought, his feelings hurt by the apparent injustice.

The CSM then added to it by calling out, "And get them in step!"

Being publicly rebuked added to Sgt Lepson's sense of grievance. *He shouldn't do that in front of the troops. He's picking on me,* he fumed.

And it did not help his feelings any to note that at least half of the platoon were out of step. "Get in step Arthur! Dipkins! Flegel, get in step!" he snarled.

As the platoon approached the waiting company Sgt Lepson began to fluster. In his panic he decided to go for the easiest option he could and he called 'Halt!' just before they collided with the end of HQ Platoon.

More pubic humiliation instantly followed. CSM Glenn shook his head. "In their proper position between Headquarters and 3 Platoon Sgt Lepson," he called.

Blushing at the audible snickers, Sgt Lepson stepped aside so he could study what to do. It was very apparent that to get them into position between HQ PL and 3 Pl while marching would need skill and timing. For a few seconds he dithered about whether to march in front of HQ or behind, but Cpl Callan made the choice for him by leading over to the rear of HQ. As he did not feel up to the rapid sequence of orders to turn the platoon smartly into the gap Sgt Lepson called to Cpl Callan to wheel into position. But then his view was blocked, and he miscalculated when to give the order to halt. By the time he could see and did give the command he saw that Cpl Callan had started marking time only a pace from the end of 3 Platoon. Flushing with shame Sgt Lepson ordered the platoon to halt and do a left turn.

CSM Glenn glowered at him and then called the company to attention and ordered a 'right dress'. Now the positioning of the platoon caused Sgt Lepson more embarrassment as there was not sufficient room for him to stand to the right of his own marker. After correcting this, with the resulting shuffling and movement of the cadets to their left, he completed lining the platoon up.

CSM Glenn then gave the order to the platoon sergeants to mark their roll books. Sgt Lepson faced the platoon and pulled his notebook and pen out of his pocket. Then he got another embarrassing shock. When he opened the book and tried to read the names, he found it was still too dark to be able to do so.

Burning with embarrassment he said, "Does anyone have a torch?"

Several did, among them Chloe and Jane and also Cpl Callan. There were also snickers which caused Sgt Lepson to writhe inside in hurt at the contempt obvious in their tone.

"Cpl Callan, hold your torch for me please," he called softly.

As Cpl Callan made his way to join him CSM Glenn called, "What is the delay Sgt Lepson?"

"Just getting a torch sir," Sgt Lepson replied, blushing even more.

He steeled himself for another rebuke and could imagine what the CSM was thinking. However CSM Glenn remained silent and Sgt Lepson was able to complete the roll marking. By the time he had done this all desire had ebbed from his body and he felt tired.

After the roll marking CSM Glenn called for reports and then detailed administrative tasks and timings. That done he ordered the platoon sergeants to take their platoons back to their areas for breakfast.

Sgt Lepson marched the platoon back along the Old Highway to the platoon bivouac. Once there he ordered them to fall out and carry out their morning routine. Feeling quite dejected Sgt Lepson walked back to his hutchie. As he approached it he was surprised to hear a radio calling. It sounded like the OC's voice. On reaching the hutchie he knelt and looked in. To his surprise he saw that CUO Roach was still in his sleeping bag. The radio crackled again and it was the OC.

"Two Four, this is Sunray, over," called Major Wickham.

Sgt Lepson reached in and shook CUO Roach by the shoulder. "Roachy, sir, wake up!"

CUO Roach groaned and stirred and then open bleary eyes to look up at him. "Wha... what?"

"Wake up Sir. The OC is calling on the radio," Sgt Lepson replied.

"OC? Radio? What.. what bloody time is it?" CUO Roach asked as he struggled to sit up.

"Six twenty," Sgt Lepson answered.

"Six... Bloody hell! Have you had check parade?" CUO Roach queried.

"Yes. We just got back," Sgt Lepson answered. By now he was feeling uneasy because he realised he should have woken his platoon commander just before six so that he could report to the OC. This was something Major Wickham insisted on.

CUO Roach swore then glared at him. "Bloody hell! You didn't wake me you bastard! Now I will be in the shit."

As CUO Roach struggled to pull on his boots the radio crackled again. This time he answered it and Sgt Lepson saw that his face did not look happy as the OC replied. CUO Roach said, "Yes sir, Yes sir. Right away sir. Five minutes sir. Yes, two minutes sir, over."

He then resumed lacing up his boots and as he stood up he snapped, "Have some breakfast cooked for me when I get back." Then he strode off.

Sgt Lepson swore softly but he was angry with himself for forgetting to check that the CUO was awake. With a guilty start he realised he had been too taken up with watching Chloe and Jane.

Bloody molls! They will pay, he vowed.

Now he had extra work and knew it would not be a good idea to delegate it. So he settled to cooking two meals at once.

On his return CUO Roach was grumpy and said that the OC had torn strips off him. He took the meal without any thanks and sat eating it. Sgt Lepson tried to act as though nothing had happened but his attempts at normal conversation were snubbed and he was left to eat in sulky silence.

Once he had eaten his breakfast Sgt Lepson heated more water to shave. Shaving made him feel very grown up and he glanced across to see if Chloe had noticed. To his irritation it seemed she had not. All he could see was her back and he decided that she and Jane were deliberately sitting on the far side of their hutchie.

He tried to push thoughts of Chloe out of his mind but found it hard to do. The more he tried it seemed the more he found himself glancing in her direction. He noted her go into her hutchie and then surreptitiously watched as she took off her shirt. She had her back to him and he could only see part of her back but he did get a glimpse of the side of her right breast. His body reacted and he became aroused again, to his own annoyance.

But he kept sneaking glances and watched with prurient interest as she clipped on her bra. His mouth went dry with lust. Then he noticed Jane looking in his direction. Blushing with shame he hastily looked away.

To appease his guilt and anger Sgt Lepson ordered Chloe to be part of the work party being sent to dig the girl's latrine. That earned him another scowl from Jane.

And I'll get even with you too, you snooty bitch! he thought angrily.

The morning routine ground on. Sgt Lepson finished his own by packing his bedding. Then he walked around chivvying the cadets to get them packed up and ready. By 0745 he had checked all were ready, taking pleasure in rebuking Jane because Chloe's area was not neat and tidy. "This should have been clean and tidy by now," he snapped.

"She's on a work party digging latrines, sergeant," Jane explained.

"No excuse! Get it cleaned up, quickly," Sgt Lepson ordered.

A few minutes later he called the platoon out to form up for parade. He was hoping Chloe would be late for parade, but she hurried in just as he called the platoon to attention.

"Hurry up Cadet Cummings. Don't make the platoon late," he snapped.

"Yes sergeant," Chloe replied, her eyes flashing but her face a mask of normality. She ran to get her webbing and joined the end of the back rank as the platoon began marching.

Sgt Lepson thought that was a good place for her stand because, once he had handed over to CUO Roach on the company parade and taken his position three paces to the rear of the platoon, he could stand and admire her shape without her knowing.

And it is a nice shape, he noted, admiring the curve of her buttocks and thighs and the full front of her shirt.

Once again lust warred with morality and he became confused and aroused.

Chapter 7

TIME SPENT ON RECONNAISSANCE

During Check Parade Major Wickham stood and greeted the platoon commanders. When they had all appeared, except CUO Roach, he reminded them of the morning timings and sent them away to prepare. By then the other adult staff were awake and packing up. Annoyed that CUO Roach had not reported he called him on the radio, becoming more annoyed by the minute because of the delay.

While he waited he was joined by the other adult staff. Capt Buchan and Capt Hamilton arrived first then Lt Barker. After the usual good mornings Capt Buchan raised an eyebrow and asked, "What are you going to do about Chloe and her mate?"

That was something Major Wickham had been thinking hard about for hours. "Nothing yet," he replied. "I don't think we have enough evidence to act on."

Lt Cavendish heard this as she joined them. "Oh you have! She and that Carson should be sent home at once. You should call their parents and tell them to come and get them."

Lt Peters nodded. "I agree. And tell the parents to bring civilian clothes so we can take their uniforms off them. They are both a bad influence and we would be well rid of them. That nonsense last night was just sheer provocation."

Major Wickham pursed his lips. "It was, but I am not certain it was them," he replied.

"Oh it was so! What other girls would run around naked like that," Lt Peters cried.

Quite a few, Major Wickham thought, remembering back to his uni days, but had the good sense not to say it.

"Something didn't look right," he answered.

Lt Barker chuckled. "That's right, they didn't have any clothes on!"

"Not that," Major Wickham replied. "Even though it was dark, now that I think about it, I don't think the big girl with the blonde hair was Chloe."

"Oh, how many big girls with blonde hair do we have in the unit!" Lt Cavendish cried. "She is the only one."

Major Wickham did not answer but still shook his head. Through his mind he replayed what he had seen the previous night and tried to match it up with images of Chloe from previous incidents. He did not want to indicate big breasts to the ladies but that was what was bothering him.

That girl last night didn't have big boobs, or not as big as Chloe's anyway, he thought.

"But we must do something," Lt Peters insisted. "If we don't, they will laugh at us behind our backs and the cadets will think we are weak. It will just encourage them to taunt us even more."

"When we have some solid evidence we will act," Major Wickham insisted. "Now excuse me while I have a word with CUO Roach."

He left the officers arguing and moved to intercept Roach. After rebuking the CUO for not reporting earlier he sent him away and then returned to join the officers who were still grumbling but had accepted his position. They settled in a circle to have breakfast and to carry out their morning routine. Major Wickham was left feeling that they were not happy with his decision.

I'm not happy either, he thought. *But something isn't ringing true.*

Still nettled and mystified he settled to preparing his breakfast. Company Parade followed and during it he made a point of studying the cadet's faces to see if they were smirking or in any way rebellious. But they looked quite normal and all he could do was shake his head and shrug. Even Chloe and Jane appeared normal, if not very happy.

During the lesson by Capt Hamilton on stretchers Major Wickham stood to one side and watched. It was one of the lessons he was most anxious be done, and done well. Thus, he was a witness to Kane grabbing Chloe. As she stood up and snapped at Kane Major Wickham felt a mix of emotions.

She is beautiful when she is angry, he thought, then felt guilty at having such thoughts about one of the cadets.

At that moment CUO Roach sidled up beside him and said, "That Chloe, she is causing trouble again."

Major Wickham gave a non-committal grunt. "Again?"

"Yes sir. After Check Parade she took off her shirt where people could see her."

Inwardly Major Wickham groaned and at the same time his mind filled with images of a nude Chloe. "What happened? Where did this happen? Was she out in the open and who saw her?" he questioned.

CUO Roach hesitated, then shook his head. "No, she was in her hutchie. Sgt Lepson saw her sir."

At the mention of Sgt Lepson Major Wickham winced. "Did he complain?" he asked.

"Er… well, er… no, not really. He just commented to me," CUO Roach replied.

"OK, thanks for telling me. Now, you should be supervising your cadets for safety CUO Roach," Major Wickham replied, inwardly sighing with relief.

As CUO Roach walked away Lt Barker joined Major Wickham. "I'm ready to go now sir," he said. Lt Barker was acting as QM and had been sorting stores.

Major Wickham had previously arranged for him to walk with him while he did a reconnaissance of the area. The old army adage that time spent on reconnaissance was seldom wasted was one he worked by.

"I want to check over the area we are using for the exercise tomorrow. I haven't been there for two years and I want to check that nothing has changed," he explained as the two officers set off. Both wore basic webbing and carried small UHF radios and Major Wickham had the stout walking stick he habitually used in the bush.

It was 0945 when they left the bivouac area and Major Wickham walked fast. As Lt Barker was also a corporal in the active Army Reserve, he had no difficulty in keeping up with him. Although in his mid-fifties Major Wickham was very fit and did a lot of hiking. The pair went east along the Old Highway to the entrance gate at the Flinders Highway. Here they paused and discussed whether that end of the paddock could be safely used for the night exercise.

To the east of the gate was the top end of a small valley about 300 metres across. Both sides of the valley and the upper end were quite rocky and the grass was waist high. Only a scatter of trees, many dead from the drought, gave any shade. On the far side of the valley was a very prominent Radio Tower for mobile phone use.

Major Wickham pointed to the tower. "At least it makes a good navigation reference," he said. From experience he knew that the tower was visible from almost anywhere in the paddock except when down in the creeks.

Lt Barker shook his head. "Won't stop them from getting lost."

Major Wickham laughed. On many previous exercises, patrols had roamed the whole paddock for hours while trying to find their platoons. He led the way Southeast along the spine of a rough ridge. There were places where he could position a platoon for the night exercise but the fact that patrols had to cross the ridge in the dark bothered him. He did not want a cadet injured on the rough ground.

They crossed a rocky knoll and came down onto easier going. Down to the right was another valley, smaller but smoother. This was nicknamed Grassy Valley. In its bed was a small rocky rise with a flat top 50 metres long and 25 metres wide. The rise was covered in ironbarks and grass.

"A platoon can go there," he said, pointing to the area he had in mind.

A hundred metres further on he and Lt Barker came to a lane formed by two barbed wire cattle fences with a vehicle track between them. This lane led from the highway near the Radio Tower and ran southwards for over a kilometre to a windmill named the No1 Top Mill. The lane's purpose was to allow beef cattle to get water and to move from the flat country below the ranges to the gentler country above without getting injured or lost in the rugged hills and gullies of the range country.

The two officers turned right and followed the fences southwards. This led them down across the small dry creek in the bottom of the valley and then across some small rises before coming to Bivouac Creek. Bivouac Creek started in the shallow dip right near where the officers had their shelters and ran South and then Southeast to pass under the fence and into a very rugged little gorge before joining Sullivan Creek. Like all the creeks in the area at that time of year it was dry, its bed a mixture of sand and rocks.

The area between Grassy Valley and Bivouac Creek was mostly taken up by a wide, gentle ridge nicknamed Grassy Ridge. This ended in a rocky down slope 50 metres from the fences. From there Major Wickham and Lt Barker crossed Bivouac Creek and walked on along the fence southwards, crossing a wide flat ridge covered with sparse clumps of bushes and a short grass with occasional outcrops of rock and a scattering of gum trees. This was nicknamed Centre Ridge. Major Wickham decided that another platoon could be deployed onto the eastern end of it.

By then both officers were perspiring freely. The sky was clear and there was no sign of any cloud formation. That suited Major Wickham. He did not want rain. The previous year's night exercise had been cancelled because of un-seasonal rain and drizzle.

Ten minutes fast walk took the pair across two small dry gullies and brought them on to a low rise overlooking No1 Top Mill. For a few minutes Major Wickham studied the area around the mill, his mouth curling in distaste. The windmill and a white painted water tank stood in the middle of a flat area on the west bank of Sullivan Creek.

From there the two officers walked West along the fence until they came to a wire gate about 300 metres from the mill. Here a dirt vehicle track came in from the North and then branched, one track going to the mill and the other in the opposite direction. According to the map it went to No 2 Top Mill but the trees along Sullivans Creek hid this from view.

Major Wickham now led the way northwards along the vehicle track. It was hot and the track was dusty, and he had several drinks from a water bottle as he walked along. After about half a kilometre Major Wickham pointed to his left.

"Those earthworks are what's left of the railway to Ravenswood," he explained.

From a low earth mound they were able to look both ways along what remained of the permanent way. To the South this was a shallow cutting and then bushes and to the North an overgrown strip of gravel and rotting wooden sleepers. These were grey with age and many were missing. A few rusty dog spikes lay on the ground or protruded from the sleepers. The Old Railway ran through a fence near a corner post and went up a gentle rise. From there the town of Mingela was just out of view, hidden by the slope. Just on the other side of the fence on the crest stood a set of buffers.

"That is the end of a siding," Major Wickham explained. "There used to be a large set of cattle yards and a loading ramp. I'm not sure what remains now."

Turning right at the corner post he led the way northwards along the dirt vehicle track. One section of the fence went West and the other North. "That goes across to the Ravenswood Road," Major Wickham said, pointing west.

Northwards about 200 metres they came to where the old cattle yards had stood. All that remained were two uprights with a cross bar to mark where the gate had been. The yards were all gone and in their place stood a field overgrown with long grass and prickly bushes.

They were now at the top end of the Centre Ridge and he decided that a platoon could be placed among a thicket of small suckers and trees at the top of the creek line that went East from the north side of the ridge. That creek went Northeast and joined with Bivouac Creek 500 metres away, at a kink in the creek near Ironbark Knoll.

On the north side of the small creek was an area of almost flat land which was covered with numerous thick clumps of the prickly, waist high bushes and stands of trees. The area was bordered on the West by the fence and on the North by the fence beside the Mingela Access Road. The town of Mingela was clearly visible half a kilometre away to the West. To the East the ground sloped off down a gentle ridge covered with bushes and a thick stand of eucalypts.

"4 Platoon can go here," Major Wickham commented.

The two officers walked across the area, following a cattle pad that wound between clumps of the prickly bush. As they made their way across it an earth dam became visible and then 4 Platoon's bivouac area. In the distance beyond the next flat rise was the company bivouac and vehicles. The pair walked down to the earth dam which was in a small dip near where 4 Platoon had its shelters. The dam wall was only three metres high and 50 metres across and the water in the dam looked like a muddy sludge.

"That shouldn't be a safety problem," Major Wickham said, indicating the water.

Lt Barker shook his head. "Not deep enough. It will serve them right if they are stupid enough to walk into it. There will be a moon won't there?"

"Not really. There is only a half moon and it will set at about nineteen hundred." Major Wickham answered.

He led the way across the top of the dam and then turned right to make his way down the low ridge that ran southwards from 4 Platoon's area to Bivouac Creek. This brought him to rocky outcrop and then to a nicely wooded area where three creeks; the one from the dam, Bivouac Creek, and the one from the yards all came together. This was the centre of the exercise area.

At this point Bivouac Creek did a sharp kink from South to East and then back again to Southeast. The area around the bends was well sheltered by trees, mostly she-oaks, and there were thick clumps of rubber vines along the banks. On the eastern side the ground rose to a gentle, well-timbered extension of Grassy Ridge. A major cattle pad came in from the direction of the No1 Top Mill, crossed Bivouac Creek and went through a gap in the ruber vine before continuing on up over the low, wooded rise and on across Grassy Ridge. From the creek junction Ironbark Knoll was only 100 metres away to the East.

From there the two officers went up along the cattle pad over the low, wooded rise and onto Grassy Ridge. By then the company bivouac area and vehicles were clearly visible. But instead of going there Major Wickham walked across Grassy Ridge until he could look down into Grassy Valley at the small rocky rise.

At that point they could see across to the rough ridge and stony knoll. On their left were a dip and then a small hill that was just as high as Stony Knoll. They went to this and Major Wickham indicted a bowl about 100 metres across at the top end of Grassy Valley. The ground in the bowl was almost bare earth and the cattle pad ran across it and on towards the front gate. There was plenty of shade as numerous small gum trees grew in and around the depression.

To the north about 100 metres was a huge Chinese apple tree growing in a bulldozer scrape. In previous years this had been the location of the girl's latrine but this year Major Wickham had ordered it to be dug on the other side of the Old Highway in the area where he had seen the two people the night before.

By walking west 100 paces the pair came onto the gentle top of Grassy Ridge and were able to see the company bivouac area across the shallow dip at the top of Bivouac Creek. As they did they heard yelling over to their right along the Old Highway. Major Wickham again led the way and they came to where Capt Hamilton was conducting a lesson on section movement.

At that moment the sections were scattered and doing a practice. Major Wickham stood and watched, noting how various corporals went about their work. By chance the closest section was 12 Section and the first person to catch Major Wickham's eye was Chloe. On command she sprang up and dashed forward, then did a perfect demonstration of how to go safely to ground so that her knees were not injured: stop, hand down, bend and take the weight, kick the feet back and then lower the body.

Lt Barker watched from beside him and shook his head in admiration. "God almighty she is amazing!" he muttered.

Major Wickham could only agree. He watched her pretend to give covering fire and then again spring up on command. As she dashed forward ten paces her boobs bounced inside her shirt and he felt his mouth go dry with lust.

She certainly is amazing, he thought, guilt niggling at him. Once again he was assailed by doubts that the person he had seen the night before was her.

Once again Chloe went to ground in textbook style. The next group to move included Cpl Hankin and he seemed weak and indecisive. In addition, he dropped to his knees as he went to ground. Major Wickham felt a spurt of anger. The last thing he needed was a cadet inflicting a permanent injury on himself by doing the wrong thing.

"Cpl Hankin, go to ground correctly!" he roared.

Cpl Hankin looked sheepish and went red. Then he got all flustered and began to shout at his section, sending two groups running at once without giving any fire control orders to the group still theoretically providing covering fire.

Not a good corporal, Major Wickham thought.

Lt Barker again shook his head and muttered, "She is certainly a handful that girl."

"I hope you don't know that from personal experience," Major Wickham grunted anxiously.

"No, only from rumour and hearsay," Lt Barker answered. "And heaven only knows there is enough of that. The latest word is that her current boyfriend is a regular army soldier at Lavarack Barracks and that she did a strip in the barracks one night."

Major Wickham was genuinely shocked. "Oh, I hope there is no substance to that rumour," he muttered, eyeing Chloe thoughtfully.

"That's the word among the boys at Thirty-One," Lt Barker replied, naming his Army Reserve battalion. "She is real trouble. We should probably discharge her before she does something that causes real harm to the unit's reputation."

Hearing that put Major Wickham into even more distress. He was torn, knowing that he had an unhealthy regard and affection for Chloe, and that what he was being told was right. But he still would not admit it.

"She is on a warning," he replied. "One more thing and she is out."

Having said that he turned left and made his way along the Old Highway back to HQ. Seating himself on his red box he took out his folder and began checking the written orders for the night exercise. Now that he had checked that the ground was unchanged and that he knew exactly how many in each platoon he was able to amend his plans and write orders with some certainty.

For the next forty minutes he wrote orders for the night exercise and then drew overlays to the map showing each platoon where its night location was. That done he went to watch the training. After checking that everything was going OK he got Sgt Lynes and Cpl Brandt and told them to get a radio and come with him. He led them down Bivouac Creek to near the creek junctions and gave them instructions for a First Aid exercise. That done he walked back to the company bivouac area and organised 4 Platoon and HQ, plus the OOCs for a practice of the unit's Emergency Procedures.

This was done as an SOP by the unit, the procedure being laid down on a printed form. Practising the emergency casualty evacuation was something Major Wickham had a particular passion for. The last thing he ever wanted was a dead cadet on his conscience because he had neglected to have things properly organised. He also insisted that all of the officers regularly practised as well. On this occasion he had Lt Cavendish as the Duty Officer in the Command Post (CP) which was a shelter erected near his own and equipped with the CP box (as a table), a map board, two radios, map, protractor, clipboards with rosters and the emergency procedure form and a light for night use.

Lt Peters was designated as the OOC to go with the rescue party and stood to one side. Capt Buchan took the remainder of the company for training. When all members of HQ and 4 Platoon were present Major Wickham organised three HQ members as a duty signaller, duty Intelligence person and one as HQ runner. Satisfied all was ready he then explained why they needed to practice and then read through the headings on the form, explaining why and how to do each part of it.

As he did this Major Wickham found his eyes continually straying to

Chloe. She sat in line behind Jane Carson and Cpl Hankin. Her attitude was attentive and interested but he found her very distracting.

Stop looking at her! It isn't right, Major Wickham told himself angrily.

When he had explained the procedures to be followed Major Wickham unhooked his small radio from his shirt and called the codeword 'Mango'. Almost at once Sgt Lynes came on the radio, calling HQ. He reported that Cpl Brandt had fallen down a gully and broken his leg, that the bone was sticking out and that there was a lot of blood. He then gave his estimated Grid Reference.

The CP team went to work. Lt Cavendish sent the 'runner' to tell Major Wickham and then Capt Hamilton (as the Duty Driver). Lt Peters was sent to get the cadet's Medical and Next-of-Kin Form. The CSM was called to assemble the First Aid party. These comprised the CUO of 4 Pl, plus two sections, a signaller from HQ and a medic from the medical section. Lt Cavendish then walked along, getting the First Aid party to stand in one straight line while she wrote down their names and checked their equipment.

This included basic webbing for all cadets, radios for the commander and signaller, a mobile phone, whistle, torch, First Aid kit, Litter Folding (a proper army medic stretcher), rope, spare hutchie (in case of rain), spare sleeping bag and compass. While this was being done Major Wickham kept timing with his stopwatch. He also made sure that the relevant timings were written down: when the first report came in, when the First Aid party was despatched, time the Ambulance was called, etc. All this preparation took nearly 10 minutes, but Major Wickham had learned from hard experience that they were minutes well spent.

"Don't forget the old five 'Ps', that prior preparation prevents poor performance," he said.

Once all was ready the group set off, walking on a compass bearing calculated by the Duty Officer on the map board in the CP. Major Wickham went with them to monitor the exercise and to take photos. It was an easy walk for 500 metres and the compass bearing took them almost straight to where the two cadets waited.

Here he had to intervene to get the stretcher party to stand to one side while the medic and OOC did an assessment and then carried out basic First Aid. Once that was done Lt Peters radioed a report and called the stretcher party in to pick the 'casualty' up. Both CUO Roach and

Sgt Lepson began to give contradictory orders and the stretcher bearers milled around in confusion.

Major Wickham forced himself to stand back and not interfere. *They must learn to organise themselves,* he told himself. Then, when CUO Roach got all the stretcher bearers in a bunch on the wrong side of the stretcher he groaned and thought, *Thank heavens this is only a practice. I'd hate Roach to be trying to cope with a real emergency; and Lepson is even worse!*

It was Jane Carson who pointed out the mistake and then quietly told people what to do. This earned her embarrassed glares from both Roach and Lepson but Major Wickham noted it.

She is a natural leader, he thought. *People listen to her and do what she says.*

She even instructed Cpl Hankin to take the correct corner of the stretcher and reminded him that while a normal adult stretcher party is only four the unit policy was to have eight cadets to carry it. This was for safety so that if one tired and let go or if their hand slipped the stretcher was not dropped. Thus four went on each side, all using both hands.

Chloe now took over, telling cadets where to stand. When she had marshalled seven other cadets into position Chloe knelt at the back of the stretcher and called quietly, "Hands on! Prepare to left! Lift!"

Major Wickham watched with interest, noting that both Roach and Lepson did nothing. The others just did as they were told, even Cpl Hankin. He looked unsure and flustered and once again it was Chloe who gave the order to 'quick march!'

Roach and Hankin are both useless! Major Wickham told himself. *And so is Sgt Lepson,* he added, noting the sergeant just standing at the rear.

Major Wickham stood back and left it to Lt Cavendish to get things moving. The stretcher party set off back towards the camp while others were detailed by Jane to pick up the casualty's webbing and other items left lying around. Once all were moving Major Wickham followed. He was pleased they had done the practice but was not happy with how it had gone. *Maybe we should do another one,* he mused as he walked back through the bush behind the group.

It was 1130 by the time the practice was over. Major Wickham did a short debrief on the activity. He then called for a company O Group.

This included the other OOCs, who sat at the rear, the CUOs, who sat at the front, and the CSM and HQ Sgts, who sat behind the CUOs. It was a standard army set of Verbal Orders, those present writing notes on the relevant sections. At the end there were questions.

Major Wickham then took each CUO aside and showed them the map overlay he had drawn showing them where their platoon was to be that night. As they moved back to join their platoons for lunch, he was very thoughtful.

CUO Roach is not very clever. Should I re-plan tomorrow's exercise for 4 Platoon? he wondered.

Chapter 8

AFTERNOON

Sgt Lepson ate his lunch in moody silence, his eyes continually flicking to look at Chloe. He was really bothered by the mischief the night before and found he was unable to meet the eyes of Chantelle and Kim.

I wonder what their game is? he thought, puzzled and more than a little worried lest it somehow come back to hurt him.

But so far no whisper or rumour had reached him from his usual toadies Stevenson and Hankin. All morning Sgt Lepson had watched Chloe and Jane, telling himself he was checking for some clue to their plans to misbehave so he could prevent them. But in his heart he knew he was being a hypocrite and the knowledge made him angry with self-loathing.

He was also angry with his CUO and the section commanders. There seemed to be one little problem after another, each attributable to some neglect or silly decision by one of them. Then his jealous interest and anger were aroused even more by overhearing snatches of the conversation among the boys of 11 Section, who were seated nearby. They were discussing stories about some girl and her behaviour and Cpl Callan even boasted he had done it with her.

Sgt Lepson was both aroused and seething with a mixture of envy and irritation. *Is that Chloe they are talking about?* he wondered.

He could not think of any other girl in the cadet unit, or even at their school, who might act in such a way. But he was afraid to admit any interest, so he did not ask. Nor did he ever find out. The conversation shifted to things that had happened during the morning's training.

Ten minutes later, while Sgt Lepson was packing away his mess gear, he saw Kane walk over to where Chloe and Jane sat. He said something to Chloe, but Sgt Lepson was too far away to hear what he said. But he did hear part of Chloe's answer. He saw her frown and then her lip curl before she snapped, "No!" Then she hissed, "Piss off!"

Kane swore at her and blustered but did as he was told. Sgt Lepson felt sure that Kane had either made a suggestive comment to Chloe or even asked her directly for some sort of sexual favours, but Kane walked away and did not return. A minute later Chloe stood up and hurried off into the bush. Jane looked anxious and hurried up her wiping up and packing, then set off after her.

Something wrong, Sgt Lepson decided.

But he did not know what to do and just shrugged. His conscience vaguely niggled at him when the thought that as platoon sergeant he should make some attempt to find out.

No, he rationalized. *If she wants to complain to me she will.*

The next time he saw Chloe was just before training resumed. She came walking back out of the bush with Jane and he thought that it looked as though she had been crying. Once again he shrugged.

Serves her right, the way she carries on, he thought.

He was then jerked out of his speculations about whether he had any chance of winning Chloe's favours or not by CUO Roach looking at his watch and saying, "Holy shit! We are supposed to have everything packed and ready to march in five minutes. What are you doing Sgt Lepson? Get them moving!"

Sgt Lepson felt a wave of shock as the realization that he had been so absorbed by Chloe that he had quite forgotten the orders to pack up. He began to shout at the platoon and snapped at them to hurry up. As he did he set to work pulling down his own hutchie.

After hastily stuffing his own gear into his pack Sgt Lepson walked around chivvying the others to get a move on. This led to many resentful looks and some rebellious muttering. Knowing that he was being unjust and that it was his own forgetfulness that had led to the situation did not help. That just made Sgt Lepson angrier.

CUO Roach fuelled this by calling out, "Hurry them up Lepson! Major Wickham is going to use this area for his lesson, and he wants to use the platoon for a demo squad."

That got Sgt Lepson even more anxious and annoyed. Because he had ambitions to be a CUO he did not want Major Wickham to see the platoon disorganised. That got him walking around and snapping even more.

This led to another incident. He came upon Chloe and Jane rolling up their hutchies. Both were kneeling to tuck in cords and to dust the plastic as they rolled. What instantly struck Sgt Lepson was how desirable Chloe looked. The sight of her shirt front sagging open set him aflame. Lust fed his anger.

"Get a move on you two!" he snarled, adding, "And do your shirt up Cummings."

Chloe looked up, then glanced down at her front, then looked up again. Hastily clutching her shirt front she met his eye with a defiant look and replied, "We are going as fast as we can sergeant. And you don't have to look."

"Don't back answer," Sgt Lepson snarled, his eyes still feasting on her bulging bosom.

"You can stop perving on me," Chloe retorted.

Sgt Lepson felt both his anger and his desire rise and he struggled to control his temper. "It's hard not to look when you make such a spectacle of yourself." he snapped.

Chloe stood up and dusted her hands, deliberately letting go of her shirt as she did. She glared defiantly at him and for a moment he felt scared, fearing she would complain. But instead she curled her lip slightly before turning her back. Without another word she knelt to help Jane.

Sgt Lepson felt his temper boil. Her defiance made him almost incoherent with anger. Bitter and harsh words formed in his mind, but then stayed unsaid as he noted Major Wickham and CSM Glenn walking towards the platoon area.

"I'll deal with you later!" he hissed, before hurrying across to get 11 Section sorted out.

As Major Wickham arrived, he looked around with a frown. Turning to CUO Roach, who had hurried across to meet him, he said, "I thought I said we were using your platoon for the demo squad."

"Yes sir, you did," CUO Roach replied. Sgt Lepson saw him swallow and then dart an angry glance at him.

Major Wickham's face showed that he was not impressed. He also glanced at Sgt Lepson, then said to CUO Roach, "Well, we will be late now. Here come the remainder of the company."

Sgt Lepson glanced along the Old Highway and saw a long line of cadets walking in their direction. The rebuke made him both angry and nervous.

"Get a move on!" he shouted angrily.

But that also earned him a frown from Major Wickham. Major

Wickham said to CUO Roach, but loud enough for Sgt Lepson to hear, "I want you to move your platoon to the right hand end of the company. They are to sit in section lines and on their packs. When I tell you to move you are to walk away to the west for one hundred metres, then circle left into the scrub and lead them back to that tree just there. Move in single file. Now, get your platoon moving please."

Sgt Lepson didn't wait. He shouted, "OK 4 Platoon, put on your webbing and put your packs on."

As the cadets began hauling on webbing and packs CSM Glenn called out, "Sgt Lepson, don't get them to put on their packs. They will only have to take them off again."

Sgt Lepson blushed. He knew it was one of the unit's SOPs. If they were only getting on a vehicle or going a short distance they were to carry their packs by the strap on top, to avoid the wasted time and energy of getting it on and off.

"Carry your packs," he countermanded. This earned him several glares from cadets who had already hoisted their packs on.

CSM Glenn moved out to the Old Highway and began directing the sections where to sit. Sgt Lepson continued to hector 4 Platoon, trying to get them ready.

"Hurry up Arthur!" he snarled, noting that Cadet Arthur was still folding his shelter. To his dismay the ground was covered in litter; empty tins, pieces of paper, torn packets which had contained food.

I hope the OC doesn't notice, he thought.

But he did. As the cadets moved to stand in line more and more bare earth and rubbish became visible. Sgt Lepson saw Major Wickham look at it and frown.

"CUO Roach, this platoon area is a pigsty. Make sure it is cleaned up before you move this afternoon."

"Yes sir," CUO Roach replied, going red and flicking another resentful glance at Sgt Lepson as he did.

Sgt Lepson swallowed and felt angry, knowing it was his fault. It made him even more snappy and flustered. "Get a move on! Get in line!" he yelled. Knowing that most of the company was now sitting and watching made Sgt Lepson even more embarrassed and flustered. He looked along the line that was forming and met Chloe's eyes. Her face was neutral but her eyes suggested a scornful look before she quickly turned away. Sgt

Lepson noted that she had done up the front of her shirt and that annoyed him too as it did not give him any reason to reprimand her.

When Cadet Arthur had scurried into line Sgt Lepson led the platoon across to where the company now sat in section lines facing the bivouac area. As the platoon approached CSM Glenn frowned and pointed, "Lead them around the back! Come in from behind!" he ordered.

Once again Sgt Lepson blushed and felt angry. It was a drill they often did and he knew it was easier and safer to file the sections in from the rear to sit behind their section commanders but in his flustered state he had forgotten. Seeing the smirks and looks of contempt on the faces of the company added to his feeling of hurt. Burning with embarrassment he led them around to the rear of the company.

When 4 Platoon was at last seated CSM Glenn called them to attention and handed over to Major Wickham. For the next 40 minutes the OC taught a lesson on how platoons formed a 'harbour' in the jungle. He explained that they were learning in open country but those of the unit who were going on the unit's annual 'Senior Exercise' in the June school holidays would be exercising in tropical rain forest somewhere near Cairns so they would use the drill then. It was also made clear that a 'harbour' was a temporary defensive bivouac that was only used in close country and when contact with troops from an opposing force was not considered imminent.

"If it is likely you will encounter opposing force troops then the platoon commander deploys the platoon in a proper defensive layout, siting the weapons to best effect. As cadets are not allowed to be taught proper tactics we will not be covering that," Major Wickham explained.

The drill involved a platoon arriving at the selected area in single file and then deploying the first section to cover a third of a circle by going to the right and the second section covering another third by going to the left from a designated point. The third section filled in the rear third. The troops then lay down and faced out while the platoon and section commanders checked and adjusted their positions to enure there were no gaps and that the circle linked up.

Once that was done ropes were tied to trees around the outside to mark the perimeter. The ropes were tied at waist height from a tree in front of each pair of cadets to the next on their right. Other ropes, nicknamed 'tramlines', were tied from the section sentry post to the section commander's hutchie site and then in to platoon HQ in the centre.

"It can be so dark in the jungle at night," Major Wickham explained, "That you cannot see your hand in front of your face."

Some of the younger cadets looked sceptical at hearing this but Sgt Lepson, who had done the 'Senior Ex' the previous year, knew from experience that this was true.

Major Wickham got 4 Platoon to walk around and deploy, talking them into position a group at a time and then explaining each step. Sgt Lepson had little to do other than sit in the centre and then make sure that cadets were using clove hitches to tie the perimeter cord and tramlines.

At the conclusion of the lesson Major Wickham ordered the platoons to move back to their own areas for a lesson by the platoon sergeant on 'Field Routine'. While this was being done the CUOs were to go with their corporals to reconnoitre their new night location.

As the other platoons got up to move away CSM Glenn came over to Sgt Lepson and said quietly, "And make sure this area is clean before you move Sgt Lepson."

"Yes CSM," Sgt Lepson replied.

He managed to keep a straight face but inside he seethed with resentment. Several of the cadets, including Cpl Callan and Cpl Hankin, had overheard the CSM and that rankled as well.

He shouldn't tell me off in front of the troops, he thought.

As CUO Roach planned his reconnaissance, Sgt Lepson ordered 4 Platoon to untie the ropes and roll them up. Once this was done, he told the corporals to clean up their section areas. He then stood and badgered them until all the litter was picked up. That led to another small battle. In defiance of unit policy Cpl Hankin had all of his section's litter placed in one garbage bag. Sgt Lepson only noticed this when a dispute broke out.

Cpl Hankin held out the bag and said, "Cummings, you carry this."

"No. It's not mine," Chloe objected. "None of that rubbish belongs to either Jane or me. It was all yours or Dipkins'. You carry your own garbage. That's the unit policy."

"You do what I say!" Cpl Hankin yelled.

Sgt Lepson knew that Chloe was in the right about the policy and he was also reasonably sure that the rubbish was actually Hankin's and Dipkins' but he felt a surge of malicious pleasure.

She is disobeying an NCO. Maybe I can use that to get her into trouble?

With that thought he made his way over to where the angry confrontation was taking place. As he approached Cpl Hankin snapped angrily.

"Do what you are told. You carry the rubbish."

"It's not fair! Why should I?" Chloe cried angrily. Sgt Lepson saw her friend Jane looking anxious and tugging at her sleeve.

Cpl Hankin sneered and yelled back, "Because I said so! And because that's all you are good for!"

"What do you mean by that?" Chloe demanded, her eyes sparkling with anger.

"Because you are just trash," Cpl Hankin retorted.

Chloe's face went even redder and her eyes widened in fury. "Better than you!" she snapped.

"You are just a cheap slut!" Cpl Hankin snarled. "Now take the rubbish, you piece of garbage." He held the bag towards her.

"How dare you!" Chloe snarled. Her hand shot out and swept the plastic bag aside, hurling it to the ground and scattering its contents.

By then Sgt Lepson had arrived. "Now pick it all up!" he ordered.

"No! Not till he apologises," Chloe shouted back.

Sgt Lepson noted that she had her clenched fists on her hips and that she was breathing fast, each breath lifting her breasts so that they strained at her shirt. The sight got him even more aroused. He felt sure he now had her for disobeying orders.

"You were ordered by Cpl Hankin to do it. Now I am telling you to. If you don't obey I will report you to Major Wickham," he said.

Chloe's face went white and she seemed to gulp. Jane grabbed at her right arm. Sgt Lepson felt a twinge of fear, thinking she might strike him. Instead she gulped again and said, "Good! And I will report Cpl Hankin for sexual harassment; and you for not taking action to prevent it. And you can stop leering at my breasts!"

To Sgt Lepson it was as though he had been walking across firm ground and then suddenly found himself on quicksand. Knowing that the big 'political' push in the Army Cadets at present was the eradication of sexual harassment and bullying sent a spasm of alarm through him. This rapidly turned to fear as the consequences of her statement sank in. He had the awful suspicion that there was more to the story than he knew and that he might be blundering in. He shrugged and struggled to control his emotions and his eyes.

Then he said, "If you pick up the rubbish I will forget that you were being disobedient."

The moment he uttered the words he despised himself for being weak. He saw a look of scorn in Chloe's face and that made him flush with shame and get angrier. Torn by conflicting emotions of lust, jealousy, anger and impotence at his lack of authority he wondered anxiously what to do next.

But nothing came to him. To his horror he felt desperation well up. All he could do was bluster and threaten. Again he told her to do what Cpl Hankin had ordered. A stubborn look settled on Chloe's face and Sgt Lepson felt another spurt of triumph.

Good! She is going to defy me as well, he thought. *That will give us an excuse to get rid of the useless trollop.*

Chloe gritted her teeth for a moment and Sgt Lepson saw tears forming in the corners of her eyes. That gave him even more satisfaction, but he tried to hide it. He opened his mouth to reprimand her over her body language, words like 'threatening' and 'insubordinate' flitting across his mind. But even as he went to speak, she took her hands off her hips and stood to attention.

With an obvious effort of will she said, "Yes sergeant, but I want an apology from Cpl Hankin."

Sgt Lepson experienced a spurt of relief, mostly that she had not demanded an apology from him. He turned to Cpl Hankin and said, "Apologize Cpl Hankin."

For a few seconds Hankin stood with rebellion written on his face and Sgt Lepson feared he was going to have another challenge to his authority. By this time most of the platoon members were standing watching and he was hotly aware that if he failed to impose his will it would be a very public humiliation.

Cpl Hankin met his eyes defiantly but then he muttered indignantly and said in a surly tone, "Sorry."

Sgt Lepson nodded and tried to change the subject, glossing over the incident. "Good, now corporals, get your sections sitting over in that patch of shade, move!"

As he walked towards the place he had indicated he was hotly aware that the rubbish still lay on the ground and he mentally groaned, fearing he would have to have another battle to get it picked up. To his relief Jane tugged at Chloe's sleeve and the two girls moved to start picking it up, resentment plain in every line of their bodies. Out of the corner of his eye Sgt Lepson saw Chloe place the bag of rubbish beside Dipkin's pack and he had to hide a grin. Rather than make an issue of it he turned and called on Cpl Lang to hurry his section up. The three corporals then went with CUO Roach while he did his reconnaissance.

When the cadets were all seated in a group in the shade Sgt Lepson took out the information sheet he had been given on Field Routine and began to read from it. He knew he should have the knowledge but there were so many little details that he did not trust his memory. Knowing that he was not well prepared and that the cadets could tell that made him feel ashamed and also annoyed.

Particularly irritating was Chloe's contemptuous facial expression. She sat at the back of her section behind Jane and looked bored and unhappy. Several times Sgt Lepson tried to put her on a spot by asking her questions but to his annoyance she always knew the answer and he could not catch her out.

At the end as the cadets moved back to their areas he watched her go. *I'll get you yet, you snooty slut,* he vowed.

Chapter 9

REDEPLOYMENT

Jane sighed with relief when Chloe kept her cool. For a few seconds she had feared she would lash out and slap or punch Lepson or Hankin. But she hadn't. Instead she had bent to pick up the rubbish. Jane seethed with anger at the injustice of it but she wasn't sure what else she could do to remedy that. All she could do was move to help Chloe. With that in mind she knelt and started picking up rubbish. As she did Jane half-feared that Lepson would tell her to keep out of it.

She glanced up and met Lepson's eye but he just sneered and turned away. Jane relaxed a little.

He doesn't know how to handle this either, she thought.

The incident lowered still further her already low opinion of Lepson. As quickly as possible she helped Chloe, who gave her a teary smile and whispered thanks. Then, when Chloe walked over and placed the rubbish bag next to Dipkins' pack, Jane had to hide a smile.

Good old Chloe! she thought as she moved to pick up her webbing.

She was now very worried about Chloe and moved close to her as they lined up. What she was particularly worried about was Chloe losing her temper and saying something that could end up with her being chucked out of Cadets. It had come close to that at lunch time when Kane had sidled over and hinted that he would like to have sex with Chloe. Chloe had been very frosty but even then Kane had been too thick skinned to get the hint.

Chloe had got all fierce and told him to 'Piss off!' Jane had feared she would say more but had not been particularly worried as Kane was clearly breaking the regulations. But then Chloe had broken down and wept. She had managed to hold back the tears until she was out of sight of the camp but by the time Jane had caught up with her she was sobbing miserably.

"They all think I am just the cheapest, easiest slut!" Chloe had wailed.

That had put Jane on the spot because she was sure that was what they did think. But she did not say so and did not quite know how to respond. Instead it was Chloe who answered herself by adding, "It is my own fault. I have behaved like a real moll and everyone knows. I am just so slack."

"We both have," Jane said as she hugged and patted her friend.

"Yeah, but you have a boyfriend who can look after you and I haven't," Chloe answered.

"Hush! Sssh! You will be alright. You will find a good boy," Jane had replied.

But that had not calmed Chloe at all. She had burst into tears again and cried, "Oh no I won't! All the good ones think I am just a cheap tart and won't have anything to do with me!"

All Jane could think to say was that there were plenty of nice boys. That hadn't helped. Chloe had sniffed and wailed, "Nice boys! I need a man! Anyway, nice boys are all scared of me and won't even speak to me."

Jane thought that was probably true and wasn't sure how to respond. But she was very worried. Chloe saying that she just itched for sex every day did not reassure her. Then Chloe had resumed sobbing and said she was just useless.

"I'm no good at anything!" she cried.

"Oh Chloe, you are!" Jane said, her anxiety for her friend increasing. "You are clever and pretty and can do lots of things," she said.

Chloe wasn't reassured but did eventually calm down and stop crying. Drying her eyes, she had held her head up and walked back to re-join the platoon, acting as though nothing had happened.

All through the lesson by Sgt Lepson Jane fumed about how Chloe had been treated. It also irritated her to see how Lepson's eyes continually flicked to Chloe. Chloe did not seem to be aware of it and sat with her face set in a mask or with her head down. For some weeks now Jane had been seriously worried about Chloe becoming depressed and possibly doing even more foolish things. That Chloe might be contemplating suicide was her gravest worry. So she sat there wracking her brains and wondering how she could help.

The need to do something seemed to become even more urgent during the next period. During this the cadets were sent back to their section areas while CUO Roach, who had returned from his recon, gave a platoon Orders Group to the three section commanders and Sgt Lepson.

Chloe carried her pack and webbing back to where their hutchie had been and sat down facing away from the platoon.

Jane joined her, stretching out and putting her feet up on a tree. "Get some rest Chloe. It is going to be a long night," she said.

"It will be," Chloe agreed. Then she alarmed Jane by saying, "I might root all night."

"Chlo! Don't think things like that. If you get caught you will be chucked out of cadets."

Chloe shrugged and said, "I don't care. That seems to be the only thing I am any good for. I may as well make it my profession."

Jane became even more alarmed and struggled into a sitting position and looked anxiously at her friend. "Chloe, don't say things like that. You are just so capable. Don't throw it all away."

"I'm no good at anything else," Chloe wailed. "I'm useless. I can't do anything right. I can't make friends. I get into trouble all the time. People are always saying horrible things about me. All the other girls are jealous of me and hate me."

Jane felt hurt by that and wanted to say that she was her friend, but it seemed inadequate at that moment. She saw a tear trickle out of Chloe's right eye and she worried even more.

"You are not going to be a prostitute," she said in a fierce whisper.

"Why not? We've done sex for money or favours before," Chloe challenged.

They had too and Jane blushed fiercely at the memories. A wave of bitter regret engulfed her but was then tempered by an almost as strong flood of erotic memoires that got her breathing fast and her heat racing.

She said, "We were just young and silly then. We didn't understand what we were doing."

To her surprise and relief Chloe chuckled and then said, "Yes Grandma."

"Oh, you know what I mean!" Jane retorted.

Chloe smiled at her and nodded. "I do, and it was mostly great fun. But I have done myself terrible damage by it. I have a reputation that is dragging me down into the gutter and it is starting to really hurt."

"You could change schools," Jane suggested.

Chloe gave a bitter laugh and shook her head. "What good would that do? My reputation would go with me. There are cadets from the unit in all the schools in town. It won't even help to move to another town. Sooner or later I will run into someone who knows, and the pain will all start over again."

Jane suspected that what Chloe had said was all too true. In her exasperation she almost said, 'Then change countries' but she knew that would sound all wrong. "Then you will have to hope you meet a man who really loves you for you," she said.

Chloe nodded and more tears came. Jane sat with her in silence for a few minutes, then said, "But please promise me you won't play up tonight."

"I will if I want to," Chloe answered. "I just don't care anymore. If they are going to chuck me out I may as well go out with a bang!"

"Please Chloe! For my sake at least," Jane pleaded. She was now really worried but could not think of what else to say. In any case she did not get time to say it as they were both called in by Cpl Hankin for the section Orders Group.

Cpl Hankin's orders were a shambles. It was painfully obvious to Jane that he had not written down the notes he should have during the Platoon O Group and was trying to do it from memory. As a Second Year she had heard some good sets of orders from other NCOs and had a clear idea of what they should be like. She also knew that they should be delivered in a set sequence with headings and sub-headings so that nothing important was forgotten. But Cpl Hankin just rambled, giving them bits of information and all out of sequence so that Jane wondered what they really had to do.

Chloe obviously thought the same thing because when Cpl Hankin finished and asked if there were any questions she said, "What is the password tonight?"

Cpl Hankin blushed and glared at her, then tried to bluster, "Oh, you will be told that later."

"Why not now?" Chloe challenged.

"For security," Cpl Hankin replied angrily. "So you don't get a chance to tell anyone from another platoon."

Chloe bristled. "Are you suggesting I am not loyal to my own platoon?" she snapped.

"No, no!" Cpl Hankin answered. "It is just in case someone accidentally lets it slip."

Jane could tell from Chloe's face that she did not believe him and at that moment she heard Cpl Callan, who was conducting his own section's O Group nearby, say, "Password. The password tonight is Deadly Wombat."

Cpl Hankin heard this too and went red. Then he said, "OK, I may as well tell you. The password is Deadly Wombat."

You are a wombat! thought Jane. Annoyed she said, "What time do we go out on patrol?"

Again, Cpl Hankin looked flustered and angry. He said, "CUO Roach will tell us when."

Realizing there was nothing to be gained by baiting Cpl Hankin Jane just shook her head in disgust and sat quietly. She and Chloe exchanged looks and Chloe gave a wry grin. The two girls sat and whispered to each other until CUO Roach came around to check that all of the section commanders had finished giving their orders.

Satisfied that they had he gave the order 'Packs on!' and then stood ready to lead them. Sgt Lepson began to fuss and snap to get people up and moving. Both Chloe and Jane stood up immediately and swung on their webbing. Jane then hoisted on her pack and moved to help Chloe, whose shirt sleeves had caught in the straps. As Chloe's pack slid on she jumped and jiggled to get the straps to fit comfortably.

"My tits are too big!" Chloe said with a giggle as she tugged at her shirt and at the straps.

Dipkins heard this and said, "Not possible."

"Shut up Dipstick," Chloe snapped back.

"My name's Dipkins, not Dipstick," Dipkins replied angrily.

"Then don't act like one," Chloe said before turning her back and jumping up and down to settle the pack more comfortably.

But Jane could only agree. The webbing harness and packs straps forced Chloe's boobs together and outwards, making them very noticeable.

This became another cause for Jane to feel annoyed when Sgt Lepson walked along the platoon while lining them up. The way his eyes scanned Chloe's front caused Jane a spurt of intense irritation.

He doesn't have to ogle her like that, the creepy perv! she thought.

Once the platoon was standing in line, each section led by its corporal and with CUO Roach at the front Sgt Lepson walked back along the line and reported that all were present. CUO Roach nodded and started walking. Sgt Lepson waited, counting them a second time. Once again his eyes seemed to swivel and feast on Chloe's bosom. Jane avoided his eyes but still felt a sour taste in her mouth. Sgt Lepson joined the end of the line.

It was while she was looking away that Jane noted the bag of rubbish that Chloe had placed against Dipkins' pack. It had been left lying in the middle of a patch of bare dirt. Obviously Dipkins had not picked it up and equally obviously Sgt Lepson was going to do nothing about it, even if he had noticed it. For a few seconds, until they were past the rubbish bag, Jane held her breath, worrying that Chloe might be ordered to pick it up. This did not happen, so she relaxed and concentrated on where they were going.

After leaving the bivouac area the platoon walked west through the open bush to the earth dam. CUO Roach led them across the top of the dam and on across the flat area covered by waist high prickly bushes and a few trees. Most of the time they followed a cattle pad until they came to a vehicle track beside a fence. From there Jane had a good view out across a few hundred metres of waist high dry grass to the scattered buildings of Mingela township.

CUO Roach led them south along the vehicle track. They plodded past a gate with two high posts and a cross bar and then through the top of end of a small gully. By then Jane was sweating and starting to feel the weight of her pack. She wasn't used to carrying it and the straps began to cut in and hurt.

Suddenly CUO Roach stopped. It was so unexpected that several cadets, Jane included, walked into the pack of the person in front of them. There were grumbles and muttering and then the platoon stood in the afternoon heat while CUO Roach studied his map and looked around.

Without any explanation CUO Roach began walking back the way they had come, telling the section commanders to follow. There were a lot of muttered, 'What the...?' and 'Where are we going now?' It was obvious to Jane that CUO Roach had gone past the place they were supposed to stop at.

Bloody drongo! she thought, knowing he had been to the place on his reconnaissance.

Two hundred metres back, just opposite the gateway with the posts,

CUO Roach turned right and led them 50 paces to a small, flat-topped spur about 50 paces wide and 100 paces long. It had a shallow gully on two sides, the gullies coming together to form a larger creek line which led east down towards the centre of the training area. There was a fair coverage of small bushes and thin trees on the ridge but almost no grass or ground cover.

CUO Roach stopped the platoon and moved to the centre of the flat spur. Here he dropped his pack and called the section commanders and Sgt Lepson to him. He then pointed out the section areas. The section commanders then called out to their sections to join them.

At that Jane shook her head. "They shouldn't be calling out," she muttered to Chloe.

Chloe nodded in agreement. "You are right. I thought the whole idea was for us to sneak away to a place where the other platoons don't know. I'll bet they can hear us right now," she said.

The two girls walked over to Cpl Hankin, along with Dipkins and MacDonald. Cpl Hankin pointed to a large ironbark in the middle of the spur opposite the gate and 25 metres from it.

"That is where our section joins up with Ten Section on our left. We are on the right between the tree and the gully over there." He pointed to a large rock about 30 metres away on the bank of the small gully. "Eleven Section is on our right and faces east down the gully."

Jane studied the ground and frowned. *This is not good,* she thought. *We are facing the most likely approach for any enemy patrols and we are the weakest section in both numbers and leadership. Cpl Callan's section is the best. They should be here.*

But she knew there was no point in arguing. That would only make CUO Roach resent her even more. So she went to the two smaller trees just to the right of the big iron bark, which was where Cpl Hankin indicated she and Chloe should be. That had them almost facing the old gate and towards the Mingela Township. The dirt vehicle track was only 50 paces away.

Cpl Hankin placed himself twenty paces to Jane's right and indicated that MacDonald and Dipkins were to take up a position just near the rock on the bank of the small dry gully, another twenty paces or so to his right. Once the members of the section were in position Cpl Hankin ordered packs off and told them to lie down facing out.

Jane and Chloe did so. As she made herself comfortable, lying on her front and facing towards the track, Chloe said, "I don't like this. We are right at the most likely point of contact, and we have Arthur and Flegel on our left."

Jane, who was lying on Chloe's right, turned her head and glanced across to her left past the big iron bark. She saw that Chloe was right. Arthur and Flegel were both lying down about twenty-five paces away and facing the old gateway. Cpl Lang and Cadet Leece were twenty paces beyond them on their left rear.

That is a big gap between them and us, Jane thought, having some experience of these sorts of exercises.

About twenty paces behind her were CUO Roach and Sgt Lepson. She saw Sgt Lepson drop his pack and then sit on it, looking bored. That did not impress her either. CUO Roach walked around, checking that the platoon formed an 'all-round defence'. As he walked past behind her Jane cringed, feeling sure that his gaze was raking up and down hers and Chloe's bodies.

Once he was satisfied the platoon was deployed in a circle CUO Roach called in the section commanders and gave quick instructions, then sent them back to their sections. Jane saw Cpl Hankin walking towards them and just knew what he was going to say. She was right. Cpl Hankin stopped and said,

"You two are to be the day sentries. Cummings, you go back along the track to that big dead tree and keep watch towards camp. Carson, you swap with her in twenty minutes. Then I will send Dipkins to take over from you."

"What do I do in the meantime corporal?" Jane asked in a controlled but annoyed sounding voice.

"Cook your tea and get ready for the night," Cpl Hankin answered.

"What about putting up our hutchie?" Chloe asked.

Cpl Hankin shook his head. "We aren't putting up hutchies."

At that Jane spoke. "But it was in the exercise orders. To make it fair and so that patrols can find platoons everyone is to put up a hutchie."

Cpl Hankin curled is lip. "Nah! Roachy ain't that dumb! We aren't gunna put up hutchies. We don't want anyone to find us."

Jane had to bite her lip lest she sneer. All she could do was shake her head and lower her opinion of CUO Roach even more.

He is going to be unfair and is going to disobey the OC's orders, she thought sadly.

Chloe thought the same thing. She got up and dusted herself as Cpl Hankin walked over towards Dipkins and MacDonald. "That is cheating," Chloe hissed indignantly.

"It is," agreed Jane. "I hope we never have to depend on this bunch of leaders in a real crisis."

"The other patrols will find it a lot harder to find us," Chloe added.

Jane nodded and said, "Then we might get a quiet night."

"Oh poo!" Chloe said. "I wanted a bit of action."

"What sort of action?" Jane queried cheekily.

"That too," Chloe answered, a mischievous grin spreading across her face. "I told Miles and Ashwood that if they can sneak in properly without getting caught then I will give them a reward."

Jane felt a stab of thrill and alarm. "Oh Chloe! Don't you dare play up."

Chloe shrugged. "What have I got to lose? They've all got it in for me anyway. I may as well be hung for a sheep as for a lamb."

She then shrugged and gave a wry grin and walked off towards her designated sentry post. Jane got up and dusted her front, then sat on her pack and began digging out her stove and food.

Oh I hope Chloe doesn't do anything silly tonight, she worried.

Chapter 10

WORRIES

When he had finished teaching the lesson on harbouring Major Wickham walked back to HQ with CSM Glenn. The major was not feeling happy. After watching 4 Platoon's performance he was worried about how well they might do on the exercise he had planned for the next day.

I could change the exercise, he mused.

Over the years 4 Platoon had done several different exercises while the junior platoons were trained at platoon movement.

But they need this training for Senior Ex, he thought.

Senior Exercise was a one-week activity the unit did each year and it was always in a different place each year, requiring a high standard of navigation by the participants. It always involved a lot of walking and also had a story which was different every year.

Senior Ex was now only 6 weeks away. *We could do some sort of training in three weeks' time instead of doing a hike,* Major Wickham considered.

In three weeks' time the unit was scheduled to do a 20 kilometre hike with packs to toughen the cadets up for Senior Ex. But after some more thought he shook his head. The paperwork to get army approval for activities had to be submitted at least eight weeks ahead and the hike had already been planned and approved. While it was possible to change it he knew it would involve a lot of extra work in his already limited spare time.

"They need the navigation and recon training," he muttered.

Having decided to go ahead with the exercise he organised Capt Buchan and two from HQ to man the radios in the CP. Then he collected Sgt Grey from HQ, with an army RTF200 radio, plus Capt Hamilton, Lt Barker and Lt Peters. After filling their water bottles the group set off. Major Wickham led them across the low mound to the cutting of the Old Railway, then along it to the Flinders Highway. Even though that was only about 300 metres all were perspiring by the time they reached it.

The highway was busy with traffic and they had to wait for a safe gap before crossing. This necessitated crawling under the barbed wire fences on both sides. It was one of the unit's rules that nobody climbed over a fence or through it but instead rolled under in the best infantry style.

As he crawled under the second fence through a waist high stand of spear grass Major Wickham found he was hurting and puffing.

Oh bugger! I am getting too old for this sort of thing, he thought ruefully. Puffing and groaning at the pains in his joints he stood up and dusted himself.

When the others were all through he set off again, still following the line of the Old Railway. This had been constructed back in the 1880s and pulled up in the 1960s when the railway was re-aligned. It was easy to walk along because of a cattle pad and because it was flat and level, the gradient so small that it was all but unnoticed by a walking person. The old line was easy to see, the small embankments and shallow cuttings being obvious, as were the thousands of weathered grey sleepers still lying in place after the rails had been removed. An occasional metal dog spike or rail joint and a few pieces of coal added historical interest to the scene.

This section of the Old Railway ran northwards along the bottom of a shallow valley. The small dry creek was on the right and had almost no trees along its bed. The hills on both sides were low and rocky and also almost bare of trees, being covered mainly in the waist high spear grass.

After about half a kilometre they came to where a rough dirt vehicle track came down the slope from the left. Major Wickham pointed to it and said to Capt Hamilton, "This is where the safety vehicle will move to when the cadets withdraw. The track comes in from the front gate opposite the Mingela Turn-off."

Capt Hamilton nodded and replied, "I remember it from that Senior Ex we did a few years ago."

Major Wickham smiled at the memory. "That was a really good Senior Ex," he said.

At that Sgt Grey asked, "Sir, where is this year's Senior?"

Major Wickham looked back and grinned. "You will find out when you go."

"Aw sir!" Sgt Grey said. "You can tell us. We can be trusted to keep our mouth shut."

At that Major Wickham laughed. "Sorry. It remains a secret. No cadets ever get to find out until they arrive at the exercise start point," he answered.

Which was true. In nearly 20 years of planning and running such exercises Major Wickham had never yet let slip the secret. He firmly believed that the mystery was half the fun for the cadets, turning it into a real adventure. Not even the parents were told. Of course, the whole activity had to be meticulously planned for safety and had to be approved by the army HQ but they also kept the secret.

The annual Senior Exercise was for 'Second Year' cadets and above and was one of Major Wickham's favourite activities. He and the other staff spent nearly six months preparing starting with a series of preliminary reconnaissances in January and then a walk-through for key staff members in the Easter holidays. He also thought up the story line and wrote all of the hundreds of pages of orders, instructions and clues to make the 'One-sided' exercise seem very real to the 'Friendly' team.

This year's Senior Exercise was to start in the town of Herberton in the mountains 350 kilometres further north and was to end a week later at the town of Ravenshoe on the Evelyn Tableland. The story was set in 1919 and involved trying to rescue a Russian princess from the Communist 'Red Army'. It involved a lot of small patrols in fairly open forest and also a lot of walking along an old railway line so this weekend was direct training for that.

At that point Capt Hamilton left them to go and went back to get his Land Rover. The others continued walking. They now came to a change in the country. The line passed to the right of a steep little ridge which then ran parallel to it for a hundred metres. The valley narrowed and the railway crossed the creek line on a high embankment. To allow floodwaters to flow clear the builders of the railway had constructed a large concrete culvert in the embankment. The cadets had often used this for a hideout during previous exercises but not during the time that Sgt Grey had been in the cadets. After doing a radio check with the CP Major Wickham led the way down under a large thorn tree and took them into the culvert. It was large enough to stand upright in and was about 25 metres long.

"Just letting you know this is here," he explained.

From there Major Wickham led the group on along the railway. This now had a steep drop to the dry creek bed on the left. The creek line changed its nature to resemble a small gorge filled with large rocks. On their right they still had the line of rocky hills. A powerline passed overhead, the wires running NE, SW. Major Wickham pointed to the rough vehicle track following the powerline.

"That goes over this hill to the highway," he explained to the two cadets.

A hundred metres further north the Old Railway curved sharply to the right into a steep, rock-sided cutting. On the left an animal pad went on along the ridge above the dry creek. Major Wickham stopped and did a radio check with his UHF hand-held and told Sgt Grey to do the same with the Army 200 set. Both managed to get coms so he left the railway and went down the animal pad. It was rougher going and they had to be careful not to trip. The pad wound its way downhill, crossing a low saddle to the right-hand side of a stony ridge. After two hundred metres of sweaty plodding downhill the group reached the bottom at a windmill located among a dense stand of timber.

"This is the Number One Bottom Mill," Major Wickham explained, indicating its location on the map. The mill stood on a small flat area where the dry creek came around the end of the steep, rocky ridge to join a much smaller dry sandy creek which came from the right rear. The flat area was an unpleasant dusty waste covered in cattle droppings, particularly around a water trough. Surrounding the area grew quite a dense stand of tall trees and numerous thorn bushes forming a thicket. A rough vehicle track and cattle pad came in from the north beside the dry creek and then went up a steep slope on their right to where the Old Railway ran around the hillside.

Because of the heat and dust Major Wickham did not linger there. After trying without success to raise HQ on the radios he led them up the steep vehicle track to the Old Railway. Here he came to a panting stop and took out his water bottle. While they got their breath back and had a drink he pointed out how the Old Railway came around in a big curve, first to the east, then to the north and then to the west. It ran through a series of cuttings and along a bench cut around the side of Hill 288.

"This hill on the right, Hill 288, is the highest hill in the area and we will be positioning a radio relay station on top. We will give it the nickname 'Railway Hill'. Sgt Grey, you will drop that team off on your way to your start point," he explained. Once again he tried to contact the CP on the radio but got no response. Nor could Sgt Grey get in touch. That only served to confirm in Major Wickham's mind the need to have a radio relay station on the hill.

After checking his watch Major Wickham resumed walking. He followed the Old Railway to the left. It was easy to walk on, just being a bench cut with a few small rocks littering it. A cattle pad along it made it easy to see where to put their feet. The railway slowly curved around to the right until it ran north through a small gorge with a similar but lower rocky hill across the dry creek to their left.

As they reached the northern end of the gorge the view improved dramatically. Here the Old Railway curved right again to run east. At that point the cattle pad left it and went down a dry, open spur northwards. The group stopped for another drink as it was very hot. They could now see for many kilometres out over the dry bush of the upper Haughton Valley.

Major Wickham pointed to a peculiar hill two kilometres away. It was almost the original perfect conical hill. "That is Mt Square Post," he said. "This land all belongs to 'Square Post' cattle station. And down there below us is the New Railway. That is where you are going Sgt Grey."

He took five minutes to ensure that Sgt Grey knew where he was on the map and then indicated a dirt vehicle track that ran along beside the New Railway, running east-west. Sgt Grey's start point was a ridge 2 kilometres to the NW of where they stood and was clearly visible. Once he was sure that Sgt Grey understood clearly Major Wickham made another attempt to contact the CP or Capt Buchan by radio. Once again he was unsuccessful but a call to Capt Hamilton was answered almost at once. The reception was weak and crackly but adequate.

"He is parked beside the New Railway near the bottom of this spur," Major Wickham explained as he resumed walking along the Old Railway. They walked for another hundred paces and then turned left to follow a cattle pad down a long, gentle spur leading down from the NW slope of Hill 288. The spur was covered with a scattering of trees but very little undergrowth. After about half a kilometre they came to the dirt vehicle track beside the New Railway, here very obvious on a long, high embankment.

By then they had been walking for just over an hour and Major

Wickham was starting to feel quite tired. He was also suffering from some chafe. Anxiety about the others kept him glancing back to check on them. He was worrying about heat stress but to his relief they all seemed to be coping alright.

As he walked, he kept glancing down to his left where 4 Platoon was planned to deploy in patrols along the dirt vehicle track.

I hope that isn't too far for the cadets, he mused.

The exercise was only to last four hours and two of those were allowed for the walking. All the way he worried about what would happen if there was an accident or a snake bite or if it was too hard on the cadets. In his imagination he conjured up all the worst things that might go wrong: snake bite, heat stroke, a cadet falling on the rocks and breaking a leg, or his back, or sustaining a serious head injury.

They will get lost too, he thought.

But that had been taken into account. The whole exercise was being conducted inside the curve of the New Railway and the highway. The exercise area was only 2 kilometres by 2 kilometres, although there were many hills and gullies and it was rough country.

We must be able to find them quickly, he reasoned. Having imagined the possible problems he again weighed the distances and rough ground. Then he shook his head.

No, we have vehicle access, a safety vehicle with extra water, radio relays, adult staff at check points. It is safe enough, and if it isn't a bit tough what is the point? It is supposed to get them ready for Senior Ex.

He decided to go ahead with the plan. By then they could see where the Old Railway curved left through smaller cuttings and hills to run beside the Flinders Highway. At the dirt road Major Wickham turned left and led the group down to where it crossed a dry creek. On the right the New Railway loomed above them on its embankment, the dry creek passing through the embankment via a large culvert.

"This is the creek we have been following all the way down," he explained, "The one that flows past Number One Bottom Mill."

He led the way puffing up the next slope and they found Capt Hamilton's Land Rover parked there. "This is where the Safety Vehicle will be and Sgt Grey, your patrol will start from the next hill to the north," Major Wickham explained, pointing to where the dirt vehicle track went up a larger hill about a kilometre away.

Major Wickham had arranged for Capt Hamilton to do a reconnaissance along the road and then to RV with them. "We go back by vehicle," Major Wickham explained.

At that there were audible sighs of relief from the others. Major Wickham could only agree.

I have done enough walking today, he thought, ruefully aware of aching leg muscles and sore feet.

They placed their webbing in the back and then seated themselves in the vehicle. Lt Hamilton then drove them back along the dirt road to the highway. The road went over several small but steep little hills with Railway Hill and the bench cut of the Old Railway on their right. After a kilometre or so the two joined and turned sharp left just below the Flinders Highway. Major Wickham noted the traffic whizzing along the highway in both directions and was glad they didn't have to walk back up it.

The dirt road now ran along the formwork of the Old Railway northwards for a hundred metres to where it turned sharp right off the Old Railway at the base of an obvious, steep-sided, razor, backed ridge. The Old Railway went to the left of this ridge, to run beside the New Railway northwards for another 2 kilometres.

There was a gate just before the Flinders Highway and then the problem of having to turn left onto the busy highway even though they wanted to go uphill to the right. This was because of double white lines. Only when they were right at the bottom of the range another kilometre further down the highway could they safely do a U-turn and proceed back up.

A few minutes later they were back at the bivouac area. It was 1545 by the time they reached the HQ area and Major Wickham noted section O Groups going on in the platoon areas. Once again, as he climbed out of the vehicle, he was reminded of his age. Sitting still for 10 minutes had allowed his joints and muscles to stiffen up and he was unable to stifle the groan that came to his lips as he straightened up.

Taking his webbing in his left-hand and swinging it over his left shoulder he hobbled over to his hutchie and thankfully eased himself down onto his red box. For a couple of minutes he just sat and relaxed. Then he had another drink and dug out his stove and mess gear. After lighting some hexamine and putting water on to heat he looked around.

The bivouac area now looked quite deserted as the platoons had all taken down their hutchies and packed everything. Only the officers and HQ still had their shelters up. Even as Major Wickham looked the first platoon began to move. 2 Platoon stood up and began pulling on packs and webbing. CUO Joy Randall came on the radio to do a radio check. There was no response from the CP. Irritably Major Wickham looked across to HQ and saw that they were all busy talking. He opened his mouth to yell at them but Capt Buchan beat him to it.

"Headquarters! Keep listening to the radio!" he called.

Major Wickham looked across and met CUO Randall's gaze as she was answered by the CP, Sgt Moyle.

Joy is the best of the CUOs this year, he decided.

As soon as she had completed the radio check CUO Randall informed the CP she was leaving and she led 2 Platoon off south down Bivouac Creek. Their movement sent a flurry through the other 2 Platoons and also drew some smart comments from 3 Platoon. Major Wickham smiled.

Good! We need some platoon pride and rivalry, he thought.

He made up a cup of coffee and sat sipping it and chatting to the other OOCs while the sun sank lower in the west. Nearby 1 Platoon kept having annoying little personality clashes and discipline problems. Major Wickham shook his head.

Eight girls and only four boys, he thought.

That meant that five boys and one girl had not come to the bivouac. None of Cpl Zanek's boys had attended and all of Cpl Forster's section, five girls, had. Cpl Hungerford had only one girl in her section. Major Wickham had not made any attempt to interfere in how CUO Summers had organised the platoon.

That is her business, he thought.

2 Platoon had vanished from sight down the creek before 3 Platoon began moving. Soon after that 4 Platoon called up and said they were also moving. 3 Platoon went east past the OOCs and across the dip below 1 Platoon. Because he knew where the platoons were supposed to end up Major Wickham had to smile.

"They will run into 2 Platoon along the way," he said to the other OOCs. "2 Platoon's position is just over the other side of Grassy Ridge from here."

1 Platoon finally moved off after 3 Platoon had vanished from sight.

They went the same direction and also went out of sight over the crest of Grassy Ridge. With the departure of the platoons the area suddenly seemed quite empty and a peaceful hush settled on the bush, broken only by the chatter of HQ and an occasional radio message.

It was already 1700hrs by then and the sun was well down. Major Wickham sipped his coffee and looked at the silent bush. A stab of intense worry suddenly gripped him. He was deeply conscious that he had sent all those cadets off into the bush and that there would be many walking around in the bush during the night. The Duty of Care lay heavily on his conscience.

Oh, I hope no-one gets hurt, he thought anxiously.

The worry over safety was then replaced by worries about behaviour when Lt Barker said, "I wonder if that bloody Chloe will get up to any mischief tonight?"

Major Wickham looked up and frowned. "Do you have any reason to suspect she might?" he asked.

Lt Barker grinned. "I heard a rumour at HQ that she has dared some of the boys, saying that if they can sneak in without being seen she will reward them," he said.

"She had better not!" Lt Peters spat.

Capt Buchan chuckled and said, "It might not be a bad thing. It might actually induce some of the cadets to use proper fieldcraft rather than just running around like the silly buggers they usually are."

Despite his worry Major Wickham had to smile. Over the years the most common action of the patrols when they located another platoon's position was to run around shouting 'Bang! Bang!' with no serious attempt at trying to creep in.

"We certainly need to improve our attitude to proper fieldcraft," he agreed.

With nothing else to do he settled to cooking his evening meal as dusk brought a tinge of rust to the surrounding bush. As he cooked, he sighed. There was nothing more to be done now, other than calling off the exercise.

And if I do that we may as well not have Army Cadets at all, he mused. *There has to be some inherent degree of risk to achieve any character building or training at all.*

Knowing that the platoons had no adult with them added to his concerns, but he knew it was part of his plan to develop the leadership and character of the cadet leaders. Even though the platoons were barely out of sight, in fact 1, 2 and 3 Platoons were all within voice distance and vehicles could drive to within a few metres of their positions, he was still worried.

As darkness set in, he lit his kerosene lantern and hung it from a nearby tree as a navigation marker for lost cadets and in an emergency. That done he sent off Capt Hamilton and Lt Cavendish with a safety vehicle. They were to park at the corner of the paddock closest to Mingela township to support 4 Platoon and any patrols from other platoons that were in that area.

Then all there was to do was sit and talk to the other officers , and worry.

Chapter 11

FIELD ROUTINE

Sgt Lepson was left seething with a mixture of annoyance and satisfaction as he watched Chloe walk off to do her sentry duty. Part of him had been hoping for her to argue and even to defy him, which would have given him a chance to report her for disobedience or at least insolence. But he also had the satisfaction of upsetting her and making her do an onerous duty at a time when all people wanted to do was sit and cook their evening meal.

Serves the snooty bitch right! he thought maliciously. *With a bit of luck Carson will forget to relieve her until too late so she will miss out on a hot meal.*

But that was finally no comfort as he still found himself simultaneously attracted and repelled by her. Jealousy warred with lust and he found his hands were twitching at the thought of touching her, of grasping those….

"Stop it!" he told himself, angry for such lewd thoughts and weakness. "She is not worth it."

To take his mind off Chloe he hurried on to Cpl Callan's section and passed on the order for a sentry to be put out by that section. Then he went to Cpl Lang's section to do the same thing. Once he had given the orders for the sentries to move out Sgt Lepson returned to Pl HQ. There he found CUO Roach sitting on his pack cooking. Sgt Lepson looked at him with distaste for a moment as resentment smouldered.

Organising the sentries is the platoon commander's job, he thought.

On the edge of being in a bad mood, he sat down and began preparing his own evening meal. It was 1715 so he had 45 minutes to cook and eat before the practice 'Stand-to' they were scheduled to conduct.

After heating some water and making a cup of coffee, Sgt Lepson felt the need to do a pee. Leaving the unwashed mess tins on his stove he stood up and wandered across to the 'edge' of the platoon area. There he paused and looked around. It now occurred to him that he had not nominated where the male and female latrines were to be and had taken no action to organise work parties to dig them.

Too bad! It's only for one night, he told himself.

But there was a niggle of anxiety and even some guilt as he knew it was the platoon sergeant's responsibility.

Again he looked around and saw that neither Chloe nor Jane were at their packs. His first thought was that they were both out at the sentry post but another look around showed him Chloe. She was walking away from the platoon area in the direction of the Mingela corner.

On an impulse he set off after her. *This might be a chance to catch her out. I can pretend I haven't seen her and didn't know she was there,* he thought. The idea instantly got him aroused and his breathing became rapid and his palms sweaty.

As he walked quickly through the waist-high bushes he glanced back several times to check that no-one at the platoon area was looking. As far as he could tell nobody had noticed and he was quickly out of sight of them. He became even more excited and wiped his sweaty palms on his trousers and began to press and rub at the front of them. When he saw Chloe stop behind a large clump of bushes a hundred paces away he started to work out a plan to walk to one side where he could get the best view.

Just as he had made that decision a girl's voice spoke from close beside him. It was Jane Carson and she said, "Don't go over there. Chloe is going to the toilet."

Sgt Lepson came to an embarrassed stop. He looked around and saw that Jane was standing amongst a clump of trees and bushes. From there she could see nearly all the way back to the company bivouac site.

"Oh! Oh, I didn't know," he replied, while trying to pretend he wasn't surprised. "I was just checking that the sentry post was in a good position."

He saw a look of disbelief on Jane's face, but she made no reply that he could take obvious offence to. But he was so ashamed and angry that he nearly said, 'It won't be anything Chloe hasn't seen before,' but he managed to hold his tongue.

Carson is just the sort of bitch to tell her and to complain. And she will twist my words, he thought angrily. For something to say he asked if Jane had seen any enemy.

Jane shook her head and then turned away to ostentatiously pretend to be scanning the distant bush. There was nothing Sgt Lepson could do but turn and walk back towards the platoon area. As he made his way between the clumps of spiky bush he was in turmoil. His body seethed with emotions: lust, shame, anger, self-loathing. Part of his mind was still gripped by an intense desire to expose himself to Chloe, the fantasy running on so that she was so impressed that she willingly gave in to his desires. But another part of his consciousness was filled with disgust and fear.

What a weak fool I am! he berated himself. *I could have got myself into real trouble and she isn't worth it.*

But even as he said this to himself, he knew in his heart that he was weak and that if there was the slightest chance he would fall. Images of Chloe's naked body swirled in his mind to tempt and taunt him.

And then he had to walk a hundred paces past the platoon in the other direction to find some bushes to pee behind. The extra walking hurt his feet and he seethed with frustration and annoyance.

He found it a relief to re-join CUO Roach at PL HQ. Roach looked up from cooking and said, "Where have you been?"

"Just checking the sentries," Sgt Lepson replied, trying to sound as casual as he could.

He lowered himself onto his pack and began preparing his own meal. This was tinned spaghetti and he heated it in the tin, even though he knew the OC did not approve of the method. To his annoyance Sgt Lepson discovered that what the OC repeatedly said was true: the food in the bottom of the can was burnt and the food at the top was still cold. Worse still the heating had caused it to expand and greasy residue had oozed out and down the side of the can, making it slippery. His attempts to stir the food only spilled more.

By the time he had finished scraping the unappetizing mess out of the can and getting it down his throat he felt slightly ill and distinctly unsatisfied. Then he made himself angrier by being lazy and shoving the can under a bush. Knowing it was exactly what he was supposed to prevent nagged at his conscience, but he convinced himself there was no way he was going to try to carry the greasy can in his pack.

Not even in a garbage bag, he thought.

As he packed away his hexamine stove Sgt Lepson saw Chloe walk back to her pack and sit down. Once again guilt and lust stirred, and he made a point of turning to face away from her. By then it was time for patrol orders and CUO Roach called the three section commanders in. He then began giving fairly detailed Verbal Orders to the three corporals. During this Sgt Lepson took his coffee and sat to one side sipping it. This earned him a few irritated glances from CUO Roach and a couple of reproachful looks from Cpl Callan, but they served only to annoy him. He knew very well that, as the platoon second-in-command, he should write all the orders down, particularly the timings and Grid References and so on, but he took no notes.

Why should I bother? he rationalized. *I'm not going out with any patrols. I will be stuck here all night.*

When the O Group was over the section commanders moved back to their section areas and called their sections together to give their own orders. CUO Roach lay down with his head on his pack and Sgt Lepson stood up and strolled over to the fence to look around. As he did he saw Cpl Lang signalling Cadet Shepherd to come in for orders.

He shouldn't do that. The sentries should stay on duty and he should tell them later, Sgt Lepson thought. Then he shrugged. *Anyway, it doesn't matter. It's only a silly exercise and it doesn't start until after dark.*

So he stood leaning on a fence post while staring at the empty bush in the quiet of the evening. Satisfied there were no enemy around he strolled back, to find Cpl Lang almost finished his orders and CUO Roach asleep with his hat over his face. Feeling tired Sgt Lepson dropped his webbing and sat down beside him and leaned back on his pack, his mind still active with fantasies about Chloe.

Time passed. The sun sank lower over beyond the tiny township. The evening hush settled on the bush and Sgt Lepson found his eyes sliding closed. But then the sound of an approaching vehicle caused them to jerk open.

Vehicle coming! Where is it? he wondered. Then he thought about who it might be. *This could be the OC coming to check our Stand-to.*

Stand-to!

It was nearly dark and CUO Roach was sound asleep and nothing was happening. Sgt Lepson stood up and stared anxiously towards the sound of the vehicle. Even as he did it stopped but he was just able to make out a Land Rover in the gloom. It was about 200 metres away, over at the point where the Old Highway reached the boundary fence of the paddock.

Only the Safety Vehicle getting into position, Sgt Lepson decided with relief. But he also decided that they had better carry out the practice 'Stand-to', just in case.

Nudging CUO Roach with his boot he told him what he thought. CUO Roach opened his eyes and then looked alarmed. He squinted at his watch in the gloom and then sprang to his feet.

"Bloody hell! 1830! We should have stood to half an hour ago. Why didn't you wake me, you stupid drongo!" he snarled. "Go and tell the corporals to get their sections standing to and to bring in the day sentries."

It was on the tip of his tongue to say: 'You do it!' but Sgt Lepson just grunted. Seething with resentment at being called a drongo he strode over to Cpl Callan. To his pleased surprise he found that Cpl Callan's section were already standing to, seated on their packs and staring out over the bushes facing their allotted front.

"Good!" Sgt Lepson grudgingly conceded. He turned and strode over to Cpl Hankin's section. As he expected they were not standing to. There was gear everywhere and Hankin was not even there. "Where is he?" Sgt Lepson asked Cadet Dipkins.

"Over talkin' ter Lang," Dipkins replied.

"You people get your webbing on, pack up all this cooking gear and rubbish and stand to," Sgt Lepson snapped.

CUO Roach's voice carried loudly to him. "Don't call out so loudly Sgt Lepson," he reprimanded.

Sgt Lepson swore under his breath, both at his own forgetfulness and at the public reprimand.

Pot calling the bloody kettle black! he thought disrespectfully.

Then he noted that both Carson and Cummings were sitting on their packs facing out and that they had everything packed and their webbing on. That caused him a twinge of grudging respect but also annoyance as it gave him no reason to speak to them.

Instead he made his way over to Cpl Lang's section. They were all sitting in a bunch chatting, exactly what they had been trained not to do, and the two corporals were both in the group.

"You two section commanders get you sections standing to and silent!" Sgt Lepson snapped. "And get all this gear packed and rubbish picked up!" he hissed.

The cadets moved and Sgt Lepson stood and watched until they appeared to be more or less ready. Then he strolled along in the twilight checking each person.

"Get your webbing on Cadet Flegel!" he snapped.

"You haven't got yours on!" Flegel replied in an insolent tone.

Sgt Lepson flushed with both anger and embarrassment. He knew he was setting a bad example and that Major Wickham had repeatedly told the leaders to set a good example and not to be hypocrites. "Lead by example," was what the major said.

"Just do what you are told Flegel!" Sgt Lepson retorted. Angry he turned away and walked on to the next pair. This was Chantelle and Kim and he would have avoided them if he had thought about it. But it was too late, and he peered in the semi-darkness to check if they were ready.

To his surprise Chantelle beckoned him to come closer. "Don't you see anything again tonight," she whispered.

"Yeah," Kim added, "And if you say we were with you and doing the right thing all the time you might even get a bit of a reward."

Bit of a reward! Sgt Lepson's mind cavorted.

He had heard that both Chantelle and Kim were hot goers and his fantasies exploded, the surge of lust smothering the spasm of concern over what they intended to do.

His thoughts were interrupted by CUO Roach. "Where are the people for my patrol? Where's Cadet Leece?" he hissed.

He had Cadet Davidson with him. Sgt Lepson then remembered that CUO Roach was supposed to be leading the first patrol and that it was supposed to have gone out at 1830! A glance at the illuminated face of his watch revealed that it was now 1845. Already fifteen minutes late!

CUO Roach collected one cadet from each section and took them to Cpl Callan's section area to brief them. Sgt Lepson continued walking around the platoon defensive perimeter. He found Cadet Dipkins was now with Cpl Hankin in the centre of that section area and when he wandered on he found a big gap with only McDonald's pack to show it was part of the section.

I need to spread this section out a bit more, he thought, anxiety stabbing into him.

He stared into the night and then hurried across to speak to CUO Roach about it. But when he got there he could not find him.

"Where's CUO Roach?" he asked Cpl Callan.

Cpl Callan pointed off towards the east. "He and his patrol headed off that way a few minutes ago," he replied.

Oh great! The lazy bugger didn't even tell me he was going, Sgt Lepson thought angrily. But the anger was almost immediately replaced by anxiety. *That means I am in charge.*

The idea that he had to take control if something went wrong momentarily stunned Sgt Lepson and he stood there shaking his head.

Oh gawd! I hope nothing happens!

Sgt Lepson suddenly felt very lonely and anxious. *Patrols from the other platoons will be out now looking for us and they could attack at any time,* he thought.

That notion got him quite panicky and he quite forgot that the aim of the exercise was to practice good fieldcraft and not that the patrols should attack. They were supposed to sneak in. His anxiety received a sudden boost when voices began calling 'Bang! Bang!' somewhere to his left out in the darkness.

Two patrols have run into each other, he reasoned. *Or is there another platoon camped that close?*

For the first time he wished he had paid more attention to the orders and that he knew where the other platoons were. Licking suddenly dry lips he stood and listened until the 'contact' died away to the odd shout and some laughter and then to silence.

Is there an enemy patrol on their way here now? he wondered.

That got him worrying about the platoon so he walked on around the perimeter to check that all the cadets were awake and alert. They weren't. Within a minute he found Cadets Kane and Stevenson lying back with their heads on their packs. "Sit up and stay on guard you two!" he snarled.

Fear added to his anger as he strode on around to where dark bumps in the undergrowth indicated the three girls, except that there were four dark bumps.

"Who's that person on the end?" Sgt Lepson hissed angrily.

"Me, Corporal Lang," replied the last person.

"What are you doing here Lang?" Sgt Lepson queried. "You should be in the middle of your section."

"Just checking on the girls," Cpl Lang replied, getting to his feet.

You were not! Sgt Lepson thought, but he bit off the comment and walked with Lang back to where his pack was.

Cpl Lang sat down alone and Sgt Lepson walked on, all the time casting anxious glances out to his left to try to detect any patrols that might be approaching.

He came to two packs in the trampled grass. *Where are Arthur and Flegel?* he wondered.

His first thought was that they had gone to talk to Chloe and Jane who were somewhere over on their right so he strode quickly over that way. To his surprise both Chloe and Jane were crouching behind bushes.

"Sssh!" hissed Chloe.

"W... What? Where are Arthur and Flegel?" he replied.

"Quiet sergeant. There is someone out there," Chloe whispered, pointing off towards the right of the township's lights.

"Probably Arthur and Flegel. They aren't where they are supposed to be," Sgt Lepson replied testily. He did not like being told what to do by Chloe and was in no mood to listen.

"It's not them," Chloe whispered back. "We heard them go off the other way, to the south."

Jane pointed. "There are at least four people there. Look, you can see them against the lights of the town," she said quietly.

And Sgt Lepson could. He glimpsed a dark figure flit across the lights but found it hard to see any more. He found his heart hammering and his mouth dry.

Oh no! The enemy! What will I do?

Wild notions of leading a counterattack or of trying to just hide flitted across his mind. By then the 'enemy' patrol were due west of them and only about 50 metres away.

Chloe nudged him and leaned over to whisper in his ear. "They are out on the vehicle track beside the fence," she said. "If we are very quiet they might just miss us and go past."

Sgt Lepson earnestly hoped so. But almost immediately his hopes were dashed when one of the three girls in Cpl Lang's section let out a giggle and the mutter of voices carried across on the faint breeze. The four dark figures near the fence at once went into a crouch and then huddled to whisper to each other.

Blast! They've heard us, Sgt Lepson thought.

But he still could not decide what to do and he found he was trembling with anxiety. Then the four dark figures spread out and began moving slowly towards him in extended line and he swallowed as the anxiety rose towards panic.

They are coming this way!

They were. Sgt Lepson could now hear the soft swish of their boots through the long grass but they moved very slowly, frequently halting to listen and to stare into the darkness. He found his own heart noise and breathing seemed to drown out the sounds of the enemy.

I must do something.

"They are going to miss us and go into Lang's area," Chloe whispered, pointing as she did. She was so close that Sgt Lepson could now smell her and the sweet scent of her person further confused his emotions and thoughts.

She is right, he realised.

Then it dawned on him that there was a big gap because Arthur and Flegel were missing. To make matters worse the sound of the girls talking and giggling sounded quiet loudly.

Oh shut up you silly bitches! he thought angrily.

The enemy patrol crouched for a few seconds and then began moving towards the sound, spreading out as they did. They moved into the area where Arthur and Flegel should have been.

Oh, what will I do?

"Challenge them sergeant," Chloe whispered

How dare she tell me what to do! Sgt Lepson thought, his status and dignity both affronted.

He was about to retort that he would give the orders at the right moment, even though the closest member of the enemy patrol was now only ten paces to his left front when voices sounded from the darkness over behind the patrol.

Sgt Lepson had just been recovering from the shock of realizing that he could not challenge because he could not remember the platoon password when he heard the voices.

Who are they? he wondered. *Oh, what will I do?*

Chapter 12

NIGHT PATROL

Jane crouched in the darkness behind a spiky bush. She was now thoroughly enjoying herself. The night exercise was developing more or less the way she expected it to, and she and Chloe had detected the approaching 'enemy' patrol and warned Sgt Lepson.

And he's all in a dither over what to do! she thought with malicious satisfaction. Even in the dark Lepson's voice and body language revealed his uncertainty.

At that moment the voices came from the darkness to the south, from behind the 'enemy' patrol. The patrol members crouched down and Jane's heart rate went up.

That will be Flegel and Arthur coming back. We've got the patrol between two groups, she thought.

But Sgt Lepson just stood and did nothing. Instead he muttered, "What is going on? Who are the new people?"

It was Flegel and Arthur. Jane distinctly heard Arthur say, "The platoon is just here somewhere."

"Yeah but where?" Flegel replied loudly. "I can't see them. We are lost. We'd better call out."

At that moment the patrol member closest to them suddenly stood up and called, "Gotcha! You are our prisoners. Hands up!"

"Shit! W... Who are you?" cried Arthur.

"Bang! Bang! Gotcha! Hands up! Surrender!" called another member of the enemy patrol.

Cpl Ellery from 2 Platoon, Jane recognized.

She tensed, ready to act. But Sgt Lepson still did nothing although he had obviously heard it all.

Not so Chloe. She stood up. "Jane, you hold here," she called. Then she dashed across towards the enemy shouting "Bang! Bang!"

Jane joined in the pretend firing but obeyed Chloe and stayed at her post. Next to her, Sgt Lepson stood and appeared to hop from foot to foot.

Go on you useless jerk! Lead the counterattack, Jane thought.

Other voices now joined in and Jane noted that Cpl Lang was firing and the girls near him. Then pretend firing began behind her and she turned to look, then swore. It was Cpl Hankin and Cadet Dipkins. Jane shook her head.

They are shooting at this enemy patrol. If they had real bullets, they would be blasting the middle of the platoon.

"Hoy! Stop firing Cpl Hankin. We are here," she shouted.

Hankin did but Dikins didn't until the main action had died down to confused shouting and scuffles. Jane turned back to see what was going on and saw two figures struggling against each other in the darkness.

What's going on there? she wondered.

Chloe's voice sounded loud and clear. She was one of the two people. "Arthur, come and help me hold your pack. Let go Klein, you aren't supposed to take things," she yelled.

Jane now realised that what she was looking at was two people wrestling over the possession of a pack. Klein shouted angrily, "Let go, you stupid moll!"

Next thing Chloe suddenly stopped pulling and instead sprang forward and pushed. Klein went tumbling over backwards and Chloe leapt forward and reefed the pack from his grasp. Klein cried out in pain and Chloe dashed back into the platoon area with the pack.

"Ow!" Klein cried. "She hit me!"

Still Sgt Lepson did nothing. Jane shook her head in contempt. "They are fighting Sgt Lepson. You should stop them."

Chloe called back, "You call me names again and I will really hit you. Now surrender. We have you surrounded."

At that Cpl Ellery's voice sounded: "Pull back 4 Section, pull back! Bang! Bang! Tat-at-atat!"

Chloe stood her ground and also fired, in between yelling, "Arthur, Flegel, attack them! Open fire!"

Arthur and Flegel didn't attack but they did open fire and there were a few more moments of confused action. Figures ran across from the left and Jane heard Kim and Chantelle yelling and then Cpl Lang. They lined up beside Chloe and also joined in the battle. The patrol members scampered back through the scrub, ducking and weaving and shouting until they were near the fence.

Jane watched them and then looked to her right to check that no more enemy were visible. But all she could see in the dark were the bumps that indicated Cpl Hankin and Dipkins.

Arthur went to follow the retreating enemy but Chloe yelled to him. "Arthur, stop! Stand fast!"

Arthur did but continued to shout loudly. Chloe held her arms out. "OK 4 Platoon, cease fire!" she called.

At that Sgt Lepson at last spoke. "4 Platoon, get back into your proper places! Get back! Cummings, come here!"

Jane was astounded. *Chloe just did what he should have done, the useless bugger,* she thought angrily.

"She was saving Arthur and Flegel," she said.

"And you be quiet! I am in charge here," Sgt Lepson yelled angrily.

Jane opened her mouth to retort that he hadn't done anything but instead swallowed the injustice and waited. Chloe came strolling back, chuckling and obviously pleased with herself. "That showed them," she said.

Sgt Lepson was furious. "How dare you give orders! You gave away or position then," he snapped.

Chloe chortled, the amusement clear in her voice. "I think they knew we were here. They were stealing Arthur's and Flegel's packs."

"Be quiet! Who do you think you are! You haven't got any stripes. You aren't an NCO! And you never will be if I have anything to do with it," Sgt Lepson shouted.

Jane stiffened, ready to jump to Chloe's aid. But to her astonishment Chloe did not retort. Instead she very meekly answered: "Yes sergeant."

Sgt Lepson muttered and huffed but the reply obviously wasn't what he wanted to hear. Jane bit her lip and shook her head.

He is trying to goad Chloe into arguing back, she thought. Sgt Lepson pointed to where Jane was.

"Get back on guard," he ordered. "There may be more of them out there. And you two be quiet."

The injustice of this really rankled with Jane but she also bit back the sarcastic retort that rose to her lips. Instead she just patted Chloe on the sleeve when she arrived and whispered, "Well done Chloe Babe!"

The two girls sat back down on their packs and faced their front while Sgt Lepson marched off to berate Arthur and Flegel. Jane had already worked out what had occurred and their answers to Sgt Lepson's angry questions merely confirmed it. They had both gone to the toilet without telling their corporal and had then got lost.

"You bloody idiots!" Sgt Lepson snarled. "You left a big gap in the defences. You could have let the whole platoon be overrun."

Again, Jane shook her head. "Sgt Lepson said to be quiet," she whispered to Chloe, "But he must be audible a kilometre away!"

Chloe pursed her lips. "He's a weak bastard," she muttered. "But I'm not going to give him the satisfaction of catching me out."

"Good girl!" Jane replied, again patting her sleeve.

The two girls then sat and stared into the darkness. For some time they heard noises made by the 2 Platoon patrol but these were moving away so they relaxed. The members of the platoon returned to their places and Sgt Lepson stood in the centre. Relative silence settled.

This was broken by yelling far off to the east as a patrol found another platoon position. Jane usually really enjoyed such night exercises but this time she was annoyed at the poor leadership they were getting.

And more was to come. She heard movement to her right rear and noted Cpl Hankin walk across to Sgt Lepson. "What do you want?" Lepson asked, far too loudly for the situation.

"Time for my patrol got go out," Cpl Hankin answered.

"Oh alright. Get them ready," Sgt Lepson sulkily agreed.

Cpl Hankin came over to Jane and Chloe. "Get up and put your webbing on. Time for our patrol," he said.

"We've got our webbing on," Jane pointed out.

Cpl Hankin just shrugged and grunted to follow him, then moved to collect Dipkins. Chloe and Jane went with him. Jane was puzzled. "Corporal, who is going to guard our section area when we go out?" she asked.

Cpl Hankin obviously hadn't thought of that and nor, equally obviously, had Sgt Lepson who was nearby. Cpl Hankin just snapped back.

"Not your problem, now let's get going."

But it is our problem, Jane thought.

She remembered the careful lessons by Major Wickham on how platoons had to thin and spread out to cover such gaps and how patrols should not move out until relieved. But there was nothing for it but to follow Cpl Hankin.

She expected him to appoint a scout and to get them moving slowly in some sort of patrol formation but instead he just pulled out his compass, looked at it and set off walking. For lack of instructions the others just followed in single file. Jane shook her head as she stepped into line behind Chloe.

Hankin thinks this is a Navex, she reasoned. *We should be doing a proper night patrol.*

But being only a cadet there was nothing she could do so she just walked along behind the others, Dipkins at the rear. Luckily it was fairly easy going. After about a hundred paces they left the area of spiky bushes and big trees and entered a stand of small trees. The ground was mostly flat with plenty of thin trees but very little undergrowth. But they were just walking, not creeping or patrolling so they were making a lot of noise as they trod on dry sticks and other deadfall.

This is dumb! Jane thought. *We will just get ambushed.*

And then, seconds later, they were. Out of the darkness to their left front came the challenge, "Halt! Hands up!"

Cpl Hankin halted and put his hands up. Chloe crouched down behind a bush and so did Jane. But Dipkins ran to the left side and began yelling, "Bang! Bang!"

"Shut up Dipkins! Stop firing!" Cpl Hankin yelled. But it was too late. Whoever had challenged them began firing back. Now Jane and Chloe joined in.

Jane 'fired' several times before she recognized one of the voices. *That is McDonald. We are fighting our own platoon,* she thought.

"Cpl Hankin, that is CUO Roach's patrol," she called.

Chloe stopped firing as well but both Hankin and Dipkins continued firing until CUO Roach shouted from the darkness.

"Cease fire! Cease fire!"

They did. CUO Roach then called, "Is that you Cpl Hankin?"

"Yes sir," Cpl Hankin replied.

CUO Roach and his patrol stood up and moved into view. "Bloody hell! What are you doing out here now? You are supposed to wait until we get back," he snapped.

Cpl Hankin shrugged, "You told me to go out at twenty hundred so I did," he answered.

"I also told you to wait until my patrol was back," CUO Roach hissed.

There was a painful silence. Then CUO Roach turned on Cadet Dipkins and began to rebuke him for just opening fire without waiting to find out who they had encountered.

As he did this there was a sudden outburst of yelling, firing and then jeering laughter from back at the 4 Platoon position. Jane winced.

That sounds like another patrol has found our platoon position and got right in. Oh, how embarrassing!

CUO Roach obviously thought so too as he began calling on his radio. He kept calling Sgt Lepson and got no reply. Jane shook her head.

"Sir, Sgt Lepson hasn't got a radio. Only the corporals have them."

CUO Roach cast Jane a venomous glance and changed to calling the corporals.

Cpl Callan answered at once. "Two Four, this is One One, over."

"One One, this is Two Four. What's going on? Over."

"Two Four, Cpl Forster's patrol has snuck in and captured Sgt Lepson, over," Cpl Callan replied.

"Bloody hell!" CUO Roach swore. "One One, I will be back in two minutes. Hold them off, Over."

"Two Four, too late. They have gone. Over," Cpl Callan replied.

CUO Roach swore again. He turned to Cpl Hankin. "Get on with your patrol. 3 Platoon are just ahead on the low rise the other side of the creek," he snarled. Then he strode off into the darkness.

His patrol followed. As they did McDonald whispered as he passed, "Hope you have better luck than us!"

"Why?" Jane asked.

"Because we have been all over the place and the only platoon we found is Three," McDonald answered. "We've been lost half the time, just blundering around and getting ambushed."

Jane could only shake her head. *I wish we had a more capable platoon commander,* she thought.

For a few seconds she thought that Major Wickham had made a serious error putting CUO Roach in charge of 4 Platoon, the 'senior' platoon, but then she shrugged.

Roach is a 'Show Pony'. He can make himself look good when he's not under pressure.

She started walking, but this time Cpl Hankin slowed down and they spaced out so that there were ten paces between people. But they still didn't stop and listen every ten paces as they had been taught to do. And Hankin still led with no scout in front of him. Half the time he had his head bent forward as he looked at the compass. Jane knew the patrol was being poorly done and shook her head.

A few minutes later they came to a dry creek. Jane was expecting this from her study of the map and she knew that there were smaller creeks coming in on both sides of her to join that creek.

We have just walked down the ridge between the creeks, she reasoned.

They halted at the dry creek and then began looking for a safe place to cross as even in the starlight she could see that it had vertical sides and that there was a drop of at least a metre to the bottom. This appeared to be dry sand and rocks but turned out to include some mud which clung to their boots.

Jane was peering at the low, wooded ridge a hundred paces ahead when she heard what sounded like a groan over to her left.

The groan sounded again and then a girl's voice called, "Help! Help!"

Jane stiffened and turned to look. So did the others. "Someone in trouble," Chloe commented.

"Help! Help!" came the voice again.

Chloe began moving that way, but Cpl Hankin stopped her. "Where are you going?" he hissed.

"To help," Chloe replied.

"Sssh! They don't know we are here. You will give our patrol away," Cpl Hankin replied in a hoarse whisper.

Chloe snorted. "Oh crap! Someone is in trouble. The exercise doesn't matter," she said.

"But it might be a trick," Cpl Hankin said, his voice rising and cracking with anxiety.

Jane was astonished. "Bull! Major will tear strips off anyone who tries silly games like that. Let's go and see what the problem is."

Chloe nodded. "I agree. That is a patrol with a medical problem. They need help. We must go."

"I'm the corporal. I say what we do," Cpl Hankin.

At that moment the girl called again, groaning loudly this time. "Help! Help me!"

"This is ridiculous!" Chloe snapped. "There is someone hurt just over there. We must go and help."

Cpl Hankin still hesitated. He looked anxiously around and appeared to shake his head. Jane was exasperated. "It is just over at those rocks back there. We can be there in one minute. I think we should go."

Chloe nodded. "We must, and if you won't then I am going anyway," she said firmly to Cpl Hankin.

"Oh alright," Cpl Hankin muttered, his voice full of resentment.

Chloe didn't wait. She slid back down into the dry creek bed and hurried across. A few seconds later she had scrambled out and was striding towards the sound. Jane followed, taking care not to trip or sprain her ankle on the rocks in the dry creek bed. Behind her Cpl Hankin swore but she heard his boots on the rocks and knew he was following and then she heard Dipkins slither back down into the creek bed as well.

There was enough starlight and so little grass that walking was easy and safe but after thirty paces they came to where the side creek joined the main creek from the left.

This is the creek that comes down from the dam, Jane reasoned.

The side creek was only a tiny, shallow gully so narrow it could be stepped over, but this was in the bottom of wide, gentle-sided and shallow dip about 50 paces across. In the angle between that creek and the one coming down from the bivouac area was a small rise topped by a rough pile of rocks and a few ironbarks. The girl sounded to be on the left side of that. Jane studied the rocks in the darkness and nodded.

The place where we bivouacked last night is just up past these rocks.

Chloe began moving up over the rocks. "Hello! Where are you?" she called.

"Here! Oh here!" the girl cried out again, the relief very evident in her voice. "I've hurt myself."

Natalie from 3 Platoon, Jane thought, recognizing the voice.

She joined Chloe who was now standing over Natalie. She lay on the lower edge of the rock pile and even in the starlight Jane could see the scared look on her face.

Chloe knelt. "Where?" What happened?"

"We had a contact and Cpl Tedforth said to run so we did and I tripped. I... I... think I hit my head and my leg hurts," Natalie replied.

"Where is your patrol?" Chloe asked, looking around.

"They... They (sniff) left me," Natalie blubbered. Then she began crying.

Jane was aghast. "Left you!" she cried. "Boy, I wouldn't want to be Tedforth when the major finds out!" She joined Chloe and knelt. "Where does it hurt?"

"My head and my left leg," Natalie replied.

"Can I help you? I know First Aid," Jane asked.

"Yes please," Natalie sobbed.

Jane very gingerly felt along Natalie's left leg but could not find any obvious break and Natalie did not wince or cry out in pain when she did.

Jane frowned. "Can you move your leg?"

Natalie tried. "Yes, but my hip hurts a bit."

That worried Jane but not as much as Natalie's statement that she thought she had hit her head. Taking out her small pocket torch she moved behind Chloe to get near Natalie's head.

"I'm going to shine a torch into your face Natalie," she informed her.

At that Cpl Hankin interrupted. "You can't use a torch! The enemy might see it!"

"Oh baloney!" Jane snapped. "Our Safety Briefs always tell us that safety comes first and that if there is a real accident we stop any exercises and deal with the situation. Now Natalie, I am going to shine the light into your eyes so don't close them or look away please," she instructed.

She turned her small pocket on, taking care to point it to the side to begin with. Then she slowly moved the beam across onto Natalie's face. Natalie blinked and squinted and moved to shield her eyes. Jane gently held her hand away.

"I need to check your pupils Natalie. Now, does anything look blurry? How many fingers am I holding up?"

She held up three and moved the torch beam onto them. Natalie blinked, squinted and shook her head. "Three, but they do look a bit blurry."

"Did you get knocked out?" Jane asked.

"I… I'm not sure," Natalie replied.

"Did you see your patrol go? Do you remember the battle?" Jane asked. She was more concerned now because she thought one of Natalie's pupils looked dilated.

Or at least unfocused. I think she has hit her head.

Natalie shook her head. "I don't remember. I just know it was suddenly all quiet and dark. That's when I heard you."

Jane turned to Cpl Hankin. "Get on the radio and call the CP. It is a 'Noduff'."

"A what?"

"A Noduff, a real accident, not a drill," Jane replied, not caring to hide her contempt for his ignorance in her tone. "Now call headquarters."

"Aw, do you think we should?" Cpl Hankin objected.

Jane was annoyed. "Natalie has been unconscious. She may have a head injury, and a back or hip injury, now call HQ!" she snapped.

Cpl Hankin began calling and Jane told Chloe to move to pillow the casualty's head. "Natalie, Chloe will help you get more comfortable. We aren't going to move you but it is alright if you move yourself to get more comfortable," she advised.

Cpl Hankin made contact with the CP at the first call. Then he listened before turning to Natalie. "What's yer name and what's wrong with yer?"

Jane was again astounded. *She's been in the unit all year and he still doesn't know who she is!*

Worried now that the medical situation might be serious, she continued to carefully feel along Natalie's limbs.

If she's got concussion she needs to get to hospital, she thought, remembering her First Aid lessons about bleeding inside the brain or skull.

Then Cpl Hankin astonished her even more by saying, "Grid Reference? Uh... Er... um... I'm not sure. Wait."

Looking to be all in a fluster he knelt and pulled out his map. After unfolding it and placing it on the ground he fumbled out a torch and then got all confused as he tried to hold the radio as well. Chloe sniffed and pulled out her own torch. Clicking this on she shone the beam on the badly crumpled piece of paper.

Cpl Hankin stared at the map, muttering as he did. Then he turned the paper the other way around and again stared at it, frowning and mumbling to himself.

Jane watched this with concern. *He had the map orientated. Now he's turned it upside down. He hasn't got a clue.*

Hankin obviously hadn't as he turned the map again then shook his head and muttered, "Does anyone know where we are?"

Chloe at once stabbed her finger down. "We are here, just down this little dry creek from the dam," she said, her voice sounding scornful.

Jane looked and agreed. She said, "If you walked up onto the top of these rocks you could see the camp. It's only a couple of hundred metres away. We are just down from where we were camped last night."

Cpl Hankin flicked her a surly glance and put his finger on the map. He then ran it back and forth across the map to find the grid lines and grid numbers. "Er... um... Er, HQ this is Twelve Section... I mean One Two, we are at Grid Reference... er... Zero One... er..."

At that Chloe snorted and called out, "No it isn't! You are giving the Northing. You should always start with the Easting."

"Oh is that so!" Cpl Hankin snapped, stung by the correction. "Well if you are so smart you do it." With that he shoved the radio towards Chloe.

In the torchlight Jane was able to see Cpl Hankin's face clearly and she noted that he was sweating and that his lips were trembling.

Hankin is in a real state, she thought. *He can't navigate and now he doesn't know how to cope with this.*

Chloe took the radio, which Jane noted wasn't looped onto Cpl Hankin by its lanyard as unit SOPs said it should have been. Chloe then bent her head to study the map. As she did the CP called again. "One Two, what is your Grid Reference? Over."

Chloe held the radio close to her mouth and pressed the 'Press to talk;' button. "Hotel, this is One Two. Our location is Grid Reference six two four, zero one seven; I say again six two four, zero one seven, over."

The CP acknowledged this and Chloe then went on, "We are one hundred metres Southeast of the Dam and will have people with torches on the rocks nearby to guide you here. We require medical assistance, over."

As the CP acknowledged the radio crackled again. "One Two, this is Sunray, over." It was Major Wickham.

"Sunray, this is One Two, send over," Chloe answered.

Major Wickham came on again. "We will be there in five minutes. Do not attempt to move the casualty, over,"

"Roger Sunray, over," Chloe replied.

Jane looked up and nodded. *Good! Major Wickham knows and is on his way. Things should be alright now.*

Chapter 13

MIDNIGHT INVESTIGATIONS

Major Wickham was speaking to Sgt Lepson when the radio message telling him that there was a 'Noduff' was received.

"Alright Sgt Lepson, just wait over at the CP, and next time when someone tells you that you have been captured just tell them where to go, especially if you are a higher rank."

"Yes sir," Sgt Lepson muttered.

He was obviously upset but Major Wickham was so annoyed that he wasn't in any mood to give him sympathy. He had left a platoon on its own without either the commander or the sergeant.

And all because Cpl Forster told him he had been captured!

Then Major Wickham heard the 'Noduff' and immediately lifted his radio up to his ear. The CP answered the call and he then monitored the whole exchange. As he did he felt sick in the stomach. It was just what he really fretted about, an accident.

Bloody hell! Just what I didn't want.

Then his concern and annoyance dramatically increased when he heard Cpl Hankin's failed attempt to send a Grid Reference.

Oh bloody hell! Hankin doesn't know how to find a Grid Reference! It was just what he dreaded, a patrol in trouble and they didn't know where they were.

Then his concern changed to puzzlement when he heard a female voice take over on the patrol radio. *Who is that? Is that Cadet Cummings?* he wondered. After listening to the next exchange, he decided it was. *She has taken over the radio from Cpl Hankin,* he decided.

The CP acknowledged the location and Major Wickham heard Chloe say, "We are one hundred metres Southeast of the Dam and will have people with torches on the rocks nearby to guide you here. We require medical assistance, over."

As the CP acknowledged Major Wickham decided to intervene. He waited till the CP had signed off and then pressed the 'transmit' button and said, "One Two, this is Sunray, over."

"Sunray, this is One Two, send over," Chloe answered.

Major Wickham came on again. "We will be there in five minutes. Do not attempt to move the casualty, over,"

"Roger Sunray, over," Chloe replied.

She hasn't just taken over the radio she has taken over the patrol, Major Wickham thought. Suddenly he felt quite comforted. *Now to get things organised.*

Quickly he told other patrols to stay off the radio and then called up Capt Hamilton. "Playtime, move the Safety Vehicle to where 4 Platoon were camped last night," he ordered.

"Wilco, Over," Capt Hamilton replied.

Major Wickham next got Lt Cavendish to assemble a stretcher party from the HQ Platoon members who were not out on patrol or in the CP.

"Work out the compass bearing," he instructed.

Now all that training and preparation paid off. Lt Cavendish began filling out the Emergency Checklist the unit had developed and Major Wickham quickly put on his webbing, collected his large torch and his walking stick and called Capt Buchan to take over the CP. Lt Cavendish was told to accompany the First Aid party.

"The casualty is a girl, so I need a female officer," he explained. He then walked over to the CP. As he did he called the patrol. "One Two, this is Sunray, how is the casualty? Over."

Chloe answered, clear and lucid. "She is conscious and calm. She says she is sore but not in any real pain. Over."

"Roger that. The First Aid party is getting ready now. We will be with you in a few minutes. Out," Major Wickham replied.

By then he was at the CP and saw that Sgt Lynes was busy with protractor and pencil and that Cpl Pretzel was leaning over watching. Lt Cavendish had three HQ cadets standing in a line with a stretcher, First Aid kit and a pack containing water, sleeping bag and other items. Lt Barker stood ready with them and his presence greatly eased Major Wickham's worries.

"Come with us Ashley," he said.

Sgt Lynes looked up. "Three thousand five hundred mils ma'am."

That sounds about right, Major Wickham thought.

He had walked around that bit of country dozens of times over the last twenty years and was confident he could just walk to the location but decided to let the procedures go through. While he waited for the last checks to be made and the names of the First Aid party to be recorded, he took out his mobile phone and checked its signal.

I hope I don't have to call the ambulance, he thought.

Next he looked at who was lined up as the First Aid Party. There were only three and he glanced towards the CP, thinking to take another cadet from there. His gaze detected a person standing nearby.

"Sgt Lepson, you come with us," he instructed.

Lt Cavendish set her compass and then shone her torch into the top to brighten the luminosity. "Ready to go sir," she said.

"Right Caitlin, you lead. I will come with you. Let's go."

The group headed off down slope through the 2 Platoon bivouac area and across a gentle depression at the head of the Bivouac Creek. As they did the headlights of the Land Rover became visible moving along the Old Highway towards the camp. It then turned right, the beams of its headlights sweeping over the heads of the First Aid party before the vehicle began to move slowly through the bush off to their right. The vehicle drove down the gentle ridge there for about 50 metres and then stopped.

Major Wickham was about to radio Capt Hamilton to tell him to wait when he spotted a torch flashing from about a hundred metres ahead.

"Oh well done!" he muttered.

From then on the navigation was easy, the First Aid Party being met on the end of the low rise by Chloe. She pointed to their right. "She is just behind this pile of rocks sir," she said.

She then led the party around the rocks and a minute later they reached the casualty. Major Wickham noted Jane Carson kneeling with the girl and Cpl Hankin and Cadet Dipkins standing back to one side. He then told Sgt Moyle to radio the CP to let them know they had reached the casualty. He then turned to the casualty.

Cadet Swanson, he noted.

Major Wickham knelt to examine her and as he did Jane Carson gave him a succinct description of the situation. At the end she said, "I think she has been unconscious sir. There may be a head injury."

Bugger! Major Wickham thought, his mind racing to cover all the complications that might flow from that. *But that has been good First Aid by Cadet Carson.*

"Thanks, Cadet Carson. That is good. Now Cadet Swanson how do you feel? Do you have a headache?"

"Bit sore sir but not really," Natalie replied.

"What about your head, do you have any sore spots of bumps?"

Natalie frowned and used her left-hand to feel around the top and back of her skull. "Not really sir."

"But you said your vision was a bit blurry. Is it still?" Major Wickham asked.

"Not sure sir. It is too dark."

"OK, what about your back? Can you feel your legs and feet?"

"Yes sir."

"Can you move them?"

"Yes sir." To demonstrate, Natalie lifted her right leg and lowered it.

Thank God! Major Wickham thought.

He didn't want all the dramas of bringing the Emergency Services to that spot in the dark but was prepared to call them if there was any hint of a back injury.

"Can you get up?" he asked.

Natalie nodded and moved to roll over. Major Wickham stopped her. "No need to try just yet. Let's get the stretcher in position beside you."

The stretcher was unfolded and locked and then placed right next to Natalie. Major Wickham then shone his torch on the stretcher.

"Now Cadet Swanson I would like you to move yourself onto the stretcher, but if you feel even the slightest twinge you stop. Got that?"

"Yes sir," Natalie replied, moving to do so. Helped by Lt Cavendish, Jane and Chloe she then sat up and eased herself across onto the stretcher.

At that Major Wickham sighed with relief. He opened his mouth to organise people around the stretcher, but Chloe beat him to it.

"Cpl Hankin, you go at the right front," she instructed, "And Dipkins, you go behind him on the side of the stretcher. Cpl Brandt you take the right rear and I will take the left. Cpl Reppington, you go in the middle on this side. Sir (This to Lt Barker) would you take the left front?"

The cadets named moved to obey without comment or protest. Jane picked up Natalie's webbing and placed it on the stretcher for her to use as a pillow and then stepped out of the way.

Chloe knelt and called, "Hands on! Prepare to lift! Lift! Use your legs Dipkins, not your back!" she called.

Well that was well done, Major Wickham thought, noting the way Sgt Lepson had just stood there and not moved to take command. *Maybe Chloe is a natural leader?*

Jane now led, using her torch to show rocks and small logs in the long grass. Major Wickham hurried to get ahead of her and pointed to the left. "Go up this ridge. The Safety Vehicle is just up there."

"I know sir, I saw its headlights," Jane replied.

Once again Major Wickham was impressed. *She is pretty switched on too,* he mused.

After stumbling on a rock in the long grass he switched on his own torch and then radioed the CP to inform them that they were moving the casualty.

Two minutes later the stretcher party reached the Safety Vehicle and Lt Hamilton and Lt Peters took over, lifting and directing to get the stretcher into the back of the Land Rover. As they adjusted and secured it Major Wickham relaxed a little. Believing the worst was over he began to question to determine the cause of the accident.

Natalie explained again how her section had been ambushed and had run away. It was only then, when she mentioned Cpl Tedforth that Major Wickham remembered that Natalie was not in Cpl Hankin's section.

Of course! She is in 3 Platoon, not Four, he thought.

"So where is Cpl Tedforth?" he asked.

"Don't know sir."

Major Wickham felt his astonishment and anger begin to grow. He turned to Cpl Hankin. "Do you know where he is Cpl Hankin?"

"No sir," Hankin mumbled.

"Any of you others?"

Chloe answered. "No sir. His section wasn't in this area when we arrived."

Bloody hell! A section commander has lost one of his cadets and he hasn't let us know.

It was obvious to him that the accident had happened some time before. A stab of chill went through him as the enormity of the situation hit him. Shaking his head he turned to Capt Hamilton.

"OK Warwick, drive her up to camp. She will have to be taken to hospital so I will phone the parents and then the army. Caitlin, you go with her. We will look into this later."

Capt Hamilton and Lt Peters got into the vehicle and it was started up and driven away. Major Wickham then turned to the section. "OK Cpl Hankin, you get on with your patrol. Sgt Lepson, you go with them back to your platoon. You others in the First Aid Party come back to HQ with me."

"Sir!"

Major Wickham, Lt Cavendish and Lt Barker set off cross-country towards the bivouac area, the three HQ cadets following. As they walked across the gentle ridge Lt Barker said, "Do you want me to go and find Cpl Tedforth boss?"

Major Wickham was about to say yes when he changed his mind. "No, we will radio and find out where he is," he said.

"I'll do that," Lt Barker answered. He proceeded to call 3 Platoon commander. CUO Lewis replied after the second call and said that Cpl Tedforth was in the platoon position.

Major Wickham monitored this and then said, "Tell 3 Platoon commander to get Cpl Tedforth and his patrol to come to HQ. They are to bring Cadet Swanson's pack."

This message was relayed and by then the group were back in the bivouac area. Major Wickham then spent an unhappy quarter of an hour organising Lt Cavendish and a female cadet to go with Natalie in Capt Buchan's car. The parents were phoned and also the Executive Officer at the Cadet Brigade HQ in Townsville. During all of this Natalie was continually monitored and while she kept saying she was alright Major Wickham was insistent she be taken to hospital for a proper medical assessment.

"She might have bleeding inside the skull or any of those problems that come from knocks on the head," he said.

So as soon as Cpl Tedforth and two other cadets arrived with Natalie's pack the car set off. Major Wickham then seated himself away from the CP, making sure that he had Lt Barker and Capt Buchan with him. Once he was ready with a lantern and the Incident Book on a folding table he sent Lt Barker to get the CSM to bring Cpl Telford. A visibly nervous Cpl Tedforth and CSM Glenn appeared out of the darkness. As they did there was an outburst of shouting and pretend firing over in the 2 Platoon area.

Major Wickham waited until this had died down and then looked hard at the unhappy section commander.

"Well Cpl Tedforth, what happened?"

Cpl Tedforth gave his version of the encounter with another patrol. "And we withdrew sir and then we discovered that Natalie wasn't with us."

"We?"

"Cadet Norris noticed sir," Cpl Tedforth admitted.

"So what did you do then?" Major Wickham asked, noting the admission that it had not been the section commander who had checked who was present when they regrouped.

"We yelled out sir and we looked for her but we couldn't find her and then we went back to the platoon area thinking she might be there."

"Did you inform your platoon commander?"

Cpl Tedforth bit his lip and hung his head. "No sir," he admitted.

"Bloody hell! A cadet is missing and you don't think to tell anyone?" Major Wickham cried. He found he was so angry and astonished that he was almost speechless for a few seconds.

Lt Barker leaned across. "Obviously his platoon sergeant did not do a check of who had returned from patrol either," he commented.

"No," Major Wickham replied.

That will be two people who are going to have to work hard to convince me to ever promote them, he thought.

There was another burst of firing, this time over in the 1 Platoon area and then another at 2 Platoon. *At least some of the patrols are finding their objectives,* he thought.

Looking up he met Cpl Tedforth's gaze. "Did your patrol achieve its mission?"

"Er... don't know sir.

"What was your mission?" Major Wickham asked, the anger strong he had trouble keeping it out of his voice.

"To find 4 Platoon and raid them sir," Cpl Tedforth replied.

"You weren't supposed to raid anyone. You were supposed to creep in and leave a note," Major Wickham cried, pounding his fist on the table.

What did his platoon commander say in his orders? he wondered. Once again his opinion of CUO Lewis was lowered.

After more questioning Cpl Tedforth was sent to sit under Lt Barker's supervision to write out his version of the incident. The two cadets were both questioned and it was from them that Major Wickham learned that it had been a good twenty minutes before the patrol had realised they were missing a member. Major Wickham was aghast.

Cadet Swanson must have been lying there injured and unconscious all that time, he reasoned.

One of the cadets, Stone, let slip that in fact Cpl Tedforth had no idea where they were at the time; they had just wandered around for another twenty minutes before stumbling upon their own platoon position.

"Bloody lucky," Cadet Stone added, "Or we'd still be blundering around in the dark."

Maybe I'm getting too old for this? Major Wickham thought.

After sighing he ordered the cadets to sit with Capt Buchan and to write out their accounts of the incident. He then stood up and stretched, rubbing his aching back. As he did there was another patrol 'battle' off to the southeast near the dam. That prompted him to check the time and he saw that it was only 2150.

Should be the second wave of patrols. It's going to be a long night.

The reports were written and handed in and the patrol sent back to its platoon. The CSM and three HQ cadets went with them to make sure they got back safely and to continue the action. The officers then stood and discussed the incident. Major Wickham felt quite depressed.

"Now I have to work out what to do with Cpl Tedforth," he said.

"I'd sack the idiot," Lt Barker replied.

Major Wickham could only nod. Another burst of firing and yelling off in the distance to the south caught his attention and he lifted his head and stared gloomily into the darkness.

"I just hope Cadet Swanson hasn't suffered a serious injury," he commented.

More time crept by. There were more 'battles' out in the night and each time Major Wickham realised he was now dreading more radio calls of possible casualties. None came but he remained tense. 2200hrs passed and he got up to go and do a pee then he walked around for a bit to ease his cramped leg and back muscles.

As Major Wickham strolled around the HQ area the radio again came to life in the CP. As he did not hear the message he frowned, then remembered he had turned his radio down while he had been talking to Cpl Tedforth. He lifted the radio and adjusted the volume control. As he did CUO Lewis's voice came through loudly.

"HQ, tell the OC that there are two naked girls running through our platoon area. We think it is Chloe and Jane, over."

Major Wickham silently cursed, then his emotions boiled. "Oh blast! They'd better not be," he muttered.

Chapter 14

SCARED

Sgt Lepson sat beside CUO Roach feeling quite upset. He knew he had not managed the platoon well while the platoon commander had been away. The memory of being captured by Cpl Forster's patrol now burned as a deep humiliation. At the time, he rationalized, it had seemed reasonable.

There were five of them and I was surrounded, he told himself.

Then the resentful thought crossed his mind that Cpl Lang and his section had not come to his aid. Only now did he see his mistake of not repositioning some of Lang's section to fill the gap left when Cpl Hankin's section had gone out on patrol. The knowledge burned.

CUO Roach was no help. "You could have at least died heroically defending the position," he commented.

And get stuffed to you too! Sgt Lepson thought resentfully.

It took all his willpower not to make an insubordinate retort to the CUO. His only consolation was that things had gone no better when Roach was back. Twice patrols from other platoons had snuck in and raided them and Roach had just run around yelling and could not seem to give any sensible orders.

He's a real turkey, Sgt Lepson thought angrily. *I'd hate to be with him if something really happened.*

For something to do he got up and walked around the platoon perimeter. He started walking towards Cpl Hankin's section but the memory of how Chloe and Jane had taken over during the casevac caused him another little spurt of resentment and he veered away to his right, intending to visit Cpl Callan's section. But then he remembered that Cpl Callan's section was out on patrol, so he went to his left. At that moment all was quiet and he was annoyed to find a couple of cadets asleep, including Cpl Lang. Angrily he woke him and told him to make sure his cadets were alert.

The next two on the perimeter were Cadets Leece and Shephard. For a boy-girl pair they were sitting very close together and even appeared to move apart when he approached but as they were sitting up and looking alert he said nothing. Instead he muttered and walked on to the next pair. This was Kim and Chantelle.

As he approached, Chantelle looked over her shoulder. "Oh it's you."

"Thanks!" Sgt Lepson retorted, hurt by her sneering tone. "You just keep a good lookout."

"You too," Kim whispered. "When you are asked later if Chloe and Jane are here then say no."

"What?"

"You heard me. If the officers want to know if Chloe and Jane are here then say no and deny it until the officers turn up."

"Why should the officers turn up?" Sgt Lepson asked. He was puzzled but he also felt a chill of anxiety start to grip his stomach.

What is going on? he wondered.

"Because we are going out and we are going to get Chloe and Jane into trouble and you are going to say we were here all the time and that they weren't," Kim replied.

There was a hard undertone in her voice that alarmed Sgt Lepson but he tried to ignore it. "But that could get me into trouble," he protested.

"Not nearly as much trouble as when I say you have sexually assaulted me," Kim answered.

For a moment the import of what she had said did not register and then it swept through Sgt Lepson like a douche of icy water. "But... but that's... that's..." he groped for the right words and looked anxiously around to see who might be listening.

"Blackmail?" Kim hissed in a mocking tone. "Too right it is. We are going to set those two snooty molls up and you are going to help, whether you like it or not."

Chantelle now spoke, her voice all seductive honey. "And if you do we will give you a nice reward," she whispered.

Sgt Lepson was so stunned he could not answer for a few seconds. Then his pride kicked in. *I don't want this pair to think I am scared of them,* he told himself.

With an effort of willpower he mastered his dry mouth and racing thoughts to gabble, "What... what are you going to do?"

Chantelle curled her lip. "You'll see. As soon as you hear about it you will understand,"

Kim sniggered then added, "And you will agree it is a good plan. Now piss off and make sure you do what we say."

Sgt Lepson wanted to snap back to tell her she couldn't speak to a sergeant like that but he felt so scared that all he could do was walk quickly away.

Oh my God! he thought. *What are they going to do? What have I gotten myself into?*

He was diverted from these thoughts by hearing Cpl Lang's radio. Quickly he moved over to join him, wishing that platoon sergeants also had radios. Finding Cpl Lang sitting up he queried, "What is it?"

Cpl Lang put his finger to his lips to indicate silence. "Some sort of incident between two patrols," he answered. But Sgt Lepson wasn't really interested. His mind was a squirming maggot's nest of fear and doubt over Kim's threat.

They wouldn't, would they? he told himself.

But he also knew he was not game to put that to the test. And he knew even a false accusation could cause massive harm. When he had been a First Year cadet a girl had complained after a night Navex that a male cadet had touched her and it had all snowballed so that the police became involved and the boy had gone to court. The boy had left Cadets so Sgt Lepson never did find out the details but the whisper among the other cadets was that the girl had just made it up to teach the boy a lesson but had then not had the courage to admit it.

It was very sobering food for thought and as he pictured the angry and upset faces of his parents if that happened Sgt Lepson mentally winced. Into his already seething thoughts crept images he conjured up of the humiliation and shame as the police arrested him and of how his friends and family would look at him.

While he was brooding over this Cpl Lang touched his sleeve and pointed to their left.

"Someone moving over there," he whispered.

There was. The faint sounds of breaking twigs and occasional rustle of bushes sounded on the still night air but it was at least 50 metres away and grew fainter.

"Maybe an enemy patrol but they've missed us?" he suggested, but at the back of his mind was another awful notion.

Is that Kim and Chantelle? he wondered.

It was. When he walked back around Cpl Lang's section a few minutes later he saw that the two girls were gone. He knew he should question Lang but when he went back he saw he was lying down and appeared to be asleep again. Despite knowing he should not be weak Sgt Lepson did not wake him but walked on, noting that Leece and Shephard were also lying down, and quite close together. For a minute or so he stood there, dithering and afraid. He knew that cadets were not supposed to go off without permission and that the unit policy was a minimum of four when out in the bush. He was surprised that Kim and Chantelle were even game to do that and wondered what he would say if they got lost.

Then he shook his head and felt both angry and depressed. *They will just say they got lost going to the latrine,* he thought.

It was all very distressing but he felt so gripped by indecision and what he did not like to name as fear that he just went back to platoon HQ. When he got there he found that CUO Roach was also asleep. That annoyed Sgt Lepson even more.

The fearless leader setting a good example as usual! he thought.

For a few moments he was tempted to do the same thing but then he realised someone had to stay awake or the platoon would possibly be shamed even more.

Not that I will be able to sleep, he told himself. His mind was now a swirling fog of fear and worries. *What are those girls going to do?* he wondered.

He soon found out. A few minutes later he heard CUO Roach's radio crackle and quite clearly over it came the radio message from CUO Lewis. "HQ, tell the OC that there are two naked girls running through our platoon area. We think it is Chloe and Jane, over."

Sgt Lepson was stunned. *Is that Kim and Chantelle?* he thought.

To check if it really was Chloe and Jane he stood up and walked ten paces to where he could see Cpl Hankin's section. Quite clearly in the starlight he could make out two dark humps where Chloe and Jane were positioned. They appeared to be sitting up facing out as they were supposed to until the exercise was over.

Is that them? Or have they just made their sleeping bags up to look like they are in them? he wondered. But he did not dare go over to check. *If they see me and I have to say they aren't here they will be sure I am lying,* he thought.

The whole situation now had him under great stress and he felt sick. Deep down he hoped he would not have to say anything.

But then he heard CUO Roach's radio so he turned and quickly walked back to where the CUO lay. He was sound asleep and snoring and the radio was calling him.

"Two Four, this is Sunray, over," it said.

The major, wanting CUO Roach, Sgt Lepson thought.

A rush of fear almost paralysed him, but he knew he had to act, if only to save himself. Hastily he knelt and picked up the radio which lay beside the CUO's head. Pressing the 'Press to Talk' button he said, "Sunray, this is Two Four, over."

Major Wickham's angry voice came straight back at him. "Is that you Sunray Minor?"

"Yes sir," Sgt Lepson replied, forgetting his correct RATEL procedure in his fluster.

"Get your Sunray and at the same time go and check if Cadets Cummings and Carson are in your platoon area, over."

"Yes sir. I mean Wilco, over."

"Sunray waiting. Out."

By now Sgt Lepson was so scared he could hardly think straight and he found, to his private shame, that he was shaking.

What do I do? he fretted.

His first decision was to delay things so he stood up and walked over to where he could just see Cpl Hankin and the dark bumps he assumed were Chloe and Jane. Cpl Hankin was lying down and appeared to be curled up with his head on his pack.

He should be awake and keeping his cadets alert, Sgt Lepson thought resentfully. And then he despised himself even more as he did not have the courage to go over and wake the corporal up. *If he is asleep he can't contradict my story,* he thought.

At that moment the radio came to life. Sgt Lepson got such a fright he almost dropped it. It felt like a burning hot, live thing in his hand. It was Major Wickham.

"Sunray Minor Two Four, this is Sunray. Report, over."

Sgt Lepson stared at the radio on horror as his mind raced. *What do I say? What do I do?* he thought.

Desperation rose up to gag him and he felt he wanted to throw up. He began to tremble. This wasn't helped by Major Wickham again calling, annoyance and frustration clear in his tone.

"Two Four answer, over!"

Kim's and Chantelle's threats and promises rose up in his mind to engulf his ability to reason. Gasping for breath he held the radio up and pressed the button.

"Sunray, this is Sunray Minor Two Four. No, over."

"NO what? Over"

"Cadets Cummings and Carson are not here, over." As soon as he said that Sgt Lepson began to shiver uncontrollably. He knew he had acted dishonourably and in a cowardly way and he despised himself so much he felt sick.

"Are you sure? Over."

Sgt Lepson had to swallow and calm himself. "Yes over," he lied. "I have been to their section area to check, over."

"Where is your platoon commander? Put him on."

"Roger over." Sgt Lepson felt his desperation mount even higher.

With sickening certainty he saw that having lied once he must lie again. He began to prepare his answers to justify making a mistake. Slowly he walked over to where CUO Roach lay snoring.

How do I stop Roach going to check? What will I say if he does? he wondered, perspiration breaking out on his brow and the palms of his hands.

After a few deep breaths to calm himself, he bent down and shook the CUO's shoulder. "CUO Roach, wake up. The major wants you."

"Huh! Humpf. Wha... What?"

"The major wants you," Sgt Lepson said, holding the radio in front of the CUO's obviously bleary eyes.

"Wha... What for. Oh bugger!"

CUO Roach rolled over and sat up, rubbing his eyes and yawning. As he did Major Wickham called again, wanting to know what the delay was. As a response Sgt Lepson thrust the radio into the CUO's hand. As he did he heard distant sounds of people hurrying through the bush on the south side of the platoon area.

Who is that? he wondered. Was it Cpl Callan's patrol returning? *Or an enemy patrol?* Then another idea came to him: Was it Kim and Chantelle returning?

CUO Roach took the radio and replied to the OC. In response Major Wickham snapped at him, "Were you asleep platoon commander?"

CUO Roach tried to bluff and bluster and that only made the major angrier. "We will talk about this later," he went on. "Now confirm that Cadets Cummings and Carson are not in your platoon area."

"Cummings, Carson?" Roach replied, obviously mystified.

"Get your sergeant to explain and then get back to me ASAP, over!" exploded Major Wickham.

"Roger... er... Wilco, over," CUO Roach mumbled.

During this exchange Sgt Lepson had heard the noises getting closer and then a soft challenge from Cpl Lang. There was a whispered exchange and the sound of people pushing through bushes. In the starlight Sgt Lepson could just discern two people walking into Cpl Lang's area. They then sat down and the sounds stopped.

Was that Kim and Chantelle? Sgt Lepson worried.

CUO Roach got grumpily to his feet and snapped. "What the buggery's going on Lepson?"

As quickly as he could Sgt Lepson outlined the request to check on Chloe and Jane. CUO Roach was astounded. "Chloe and Jane? Running around 3 Platoon area in the nuddy? I don't believe it. So, are they here?"

Sgt Lepson swallowed and forced himself to lie. "No. I just checked," he croaked, his mouth now dry with fear.

CUO Roach called Major Wickham and relayed this information. To Sgt Lepson's dismay Major said what he had been dreading to hear. "Have you seen them with your own eyes?"

"Er... Er... no Sunray. Sgt Lepson went to check, over."

"You go and check!" Major Wickham snarled, his anger evident. Then he finished by saying, "Sunray out!"

CUO Roach swore and then stood up. "OK, let's go and check," he said, obviously annoyed and puzzled. With that he turned and walked toward Cpl Hankin's section.

This was what Sgt Lepson had been dreading but he could not think of any ploy to delay or prevent the check. CUO Roach walked straight over to Cpl Hankin and kicked his recumbent form in the kidneys.

"Get up Hankin you slug! You are supposed to stay awake during the exercise, "he snapped.

You bloody hypocrite! Sgt Lepson thought.

But he was now so scared he wanted to vomit. Reluctantly he moved with CUO Roach towards the two heads that were swivelled to look in their direction. As he had feared the dark bumps did belong to Chloe and Jane and even a casual glance showed they were both fully dressed. They were even wearing their webbing.

"Yes sir?" Chloe whispered.

"HQ wanted to know if you were here," CUO Roach replied. "Have you been here all the time?"

Chloe was obviously puzzled. Even in the starlight Sgt Lepson saw her frown. "Yes sir, except when we went on patrol."

"So you haven't been over to 3 Platoon?"

"No. What's this about?" Chloe asked.

"HQ wants to know," CUO Roach replied.

Jane now spoke. "Why? What are supposed to have done now?"

That hit right into the nub of the matter and Sgt Lepson winced. Luckily CUO Roach had enough sense not to tell her but he did turn on Cpl Hankin, who had now stumbled sleepily over.

"Hankin, have Chloe and Jane been here all the time?"

Hankin looked and sounded resentful. "As far as I know," he replied.

At that moment the radio started again, Major Wickham. After CUO Roach acknowledged Major Wickham went on: "Are they there?"

"Yes sir,"

"Good. Keep them there. I will be there in 10 minutes. And check everyone else is there, over."

"Roger sir, Wilco, over," CUO Roach replied.

"You mean 'This is Sunray Two Four, Wilco, over,'. Sunray out."

The public rebuke about radio voice procedure caused Sgt Lepson to wince, but the order to check all the others also caused him doubts.

Does the OC suspect that it might not have been Chloe and Jane? he wondered. Anxiety about possible repercussions began to well up in his already nauseous stomach.

CUO Roach turned and said, "Hankin, check your people!" Then he turned to Sgt Lepson and leaned close. "What the hell! You said they weren't here," he hissed.

Sgt Lepson swallowed but managed to answer immediately. "They weren't. But I did hear two people come back into the area while I was waking you. You heard them too."

CUO Roach looked doubtful and Sgt Lepson saw him frown in the starlight. CUO Roach shook his head and mumbled something then said, "You go and check Lang's section and I will check Callan's."

Sgt Lepson wasn't impressed by the poor military etiquette of just calling people with rank by their surnames and it gave him some malicious satisfaction to say, "Callan's section is on patrol."

"When are they due back?" CUO Roach queried.

Useless bugger! You made the plan and gave the timings, Sgt Lepson thought.

He said, "2230." But even as he said this, he heard sounds which indicated that the patrol might be returning. CUO Roach heard it too. He glanced at his watch and then said, "That might be them now. I will go and check. You get moving."

Sgt Lepson mentally sighed with relief but all he did was mutter. *If Roach had checked Lang's section he might have found Kim and Chantelle missing,* he thought.

To his dismay and shame, he found he was shaking and sweating at the same time. With difficulty he calmed himself and walked back towards Cpl Lang's area, ignoring a call from Jane to explain what was going on.

To his relief he found that Leece and Shephard were sitting up again and then noted three people over to the left where Kim and Chantelle were supposed to be. They were just an indistinct huddle in the darkness. As he walked towards them, he saw that two were very close together and he could not work out what they were doing. Then he saw heads turn to look and he heard Kim's voice called softly.

"It's OK, it's only Lepson."

That annoyed Sgt Lepson but also relieved him. *They are there. Good!*

Sgt Lepson came to a halt beside Cpl Lang and the two girls. They were seated facing out as though diligently defending the position.

Kim now spoke. "Remember what to say Lepson, or else."

"I... I will," Sgt :Lepson croaked back, his mouth and throat now dry with fear. Anxiously he looked in all directions to check that no-one else could see.

"Did you do what we said?" Kim demanded to know.

"I told the OC that they weren't here," Sgt Lepson croaked back.

"Good!"

To add to his emotional turmoil, Kim suddenly opened the front of her unbuttoned shirt. Even in the starlight Sgt Lepson could clearly see, confirming his long-held conviction, that they were nice big breasts, and they quivered tantalizingly!

She smiled and said: "Would you like a little play?"

Sgt Lepson was almost overcome with disbelief. But he was also even more scared. *If I touch her in front of witnesses then I will be really in their grip,* he thought.

Instant fantasies of being in Kim's grip flooded his mind. But to his dismay and secret shame, Sgt Lepson found that he had no actual desire at all.

Almost paralysed by fear he gestured into the night and said, "Get organised. You are supposed to be going on patrol and the officers are coming."

Kim stood up and began buttoning up her shirt. "Have to be later then. And remember, stick to your story Lepson."

"I will," Sgt Lepson croaked as he was again swamped by a mixture of hopeful lust and fear.

Chapter 15

DISMAY AND SUSPICION

Jane stared after Sgt Lepson's retreating back and then turned to Chloe. "What was that about? I wonder what we are being accused of now?"

Chloe also stared hard and then called to Cpl Hankin as he came back towards them. "Hey Corporal Hankin, what is going on?"

"Dunno," Cpl Hankin answered. "They didn't say. They just said I have to make sure you two stay here until the officers arrive."

Hearing that sent sudden chills of apprehension through Jane and she felt both dismay and suspicion. "Something has happened and we are being accused of doing it," she muttered.

"But what? And how? We've been here all along," Chloe replied.

"I don't know but there is some sort of bastardry afoot," Jane replied.

She began to feel sick with dread. The worst thing was the knowledge that there was someone who hated them so much they wanted to hurt them.

"I'm going to find out," Chloe replied. She stood up.

Cpl Hankin at once stepped forward. "Sit down Cummings! You were told to stay here," he said, his voice quavering with evident anxiety.

"Get stuffed Hankin!" Chloe retorted. "If I'm being accused of something I have a right to know what it is." She began walking towards Cpl Callan's section area.

Jane opened her mouth to caution Chloe but then closed it. *I agree,* she thought. But she did not want Chloe to get into more trouble.

At that moment CUO Roach appeared from the other direction. "Who's that? Cummings! You go back and sit down," he snarled.

"I want to know what is going on," Chloe replied.

"You'll be told when the major gets here. Now go back and sit down," CUO Roach replied, his voice full of what Jane felt sure was malicious satisfaction.

Muttering and with obvious reluctance Chloe did what she was told. She sat down beside Jane and muttered, "There's something bad going on and we are being blamed for it."

"I agree," Jane replied.

CUO Roach stood over them. "Shut up the pair of you. Just sit there and wait," he snapped.

"What are we, prisoners?" Chloe retorted.

"Sir!" CUO Roach snapped.

Jane thought he was speaking to Major Wickham but then realised he was rebuking Chloe for not addressing him as sir. She nudged Chloe, not wanting her to make things worse by insubordination. But Chloe did not respond, and to add to Jane's already low opinion of CUO Roach he did not follow up to try to make her.

You weak, hypocritical bastard! she thought.

Radios began to crackle and Jane heard Major Wickham telling all the platoon commanders and section commanders that the exercise was now finished and all patrols were to return to their platoons.

That means it must be serious, she decided, her apprehension deepening.

Then she overheard CUO Roach being called. "Sunray Two Four, have a guide out on the vehicle track in five minutes, over," Major Wickham said.

"Wilco Sunray, over," CUO Roach replied. He then turned to Cpl Hankin. "Get one of your cadets and go over to the vehicle track near the fence," he said.

"What vehicle track?" Cpl Hankin asked.

Jane was astonished. *You useless prick!* she thought.

The vehicle track beside the boundary fence was clearly marked on the map they had all been given and she knew that Cpl Hankin had even walked along it the previous year.

CUO Roach obviously thought the same but did not say it. "Over there beside the fence," he snapped, pointing towards the lights of Mingela township.

"West," Chloe added.

"Shut up Cummings!" CUO Roach snarled.

"Cadet Cummings, sir," Chloe answered, her voice calm and without a hint of dumb insolence.

CUO Roach made no reply and Cpl Hankin went off to get Cadet McDonald. As he did Jane heard a vehicle's engine start back at camp and then saw the glow of its headlights light up the trees.

This is not going to be enjoyable, she thought unhappily.

A few minutes later the vehicle stopped about 50 metres to the west and its headlights and motor were switched off. A group of people walked from it through the bushes and Jane was dismayed at how many there appeared to be. When they arrived, she saw that it included four of the officers as well as CSM Glenn and Cpl Hankin and Cadet McDonald.

CUO Roach went to meet them. "They are over here sir," he said.

Major Wickham stopped nearby. For a few seconds he shone a torch that lit up Chloe and then Jane, but he was careful to keep the beam away from their eyes. Then he directed the beam towards the vehicle and said, "Alright. Thank you CUO Roach. Now, Cadet Cummings, you go with Lt Peters. Cadet Carson, you go with Capt Hamilton and CSM Glenn. Sgt Lepson. Where is Sgt Lepson?"

"Here sir," came Sgt Lepson's response from 25 metres away in the darkness.

"You go with Lt Barker and mark your platoon roll book. Check that every cadet is here. CUO Roach, are all of your sections here?"

"Yes sir, but Cpl Lang's section was about to go out on patrol."

"The exercise is cancelled so stop them. They won't be going. You come with me. I want to check all of your sections. Now lead me around the area, move!" Major Wickham snapped. He then turned and began walking with CUO Roach over to where Cadets Flegel and Arthur sat watching.

Jane and Chloe both stood up. As they did Chloe called, "Excuse me sir, what is going on?"

Major Wickham stopped and turned to face her. "You don't know?"

"No sir," Chloe replied. "We haven't been told anything, other than to sit here and to shut up."

Major Wickham let out a snort of exasperation. Then he shrugged. "You and Cadet Carson have been accused of running naked through 3 Platoon's position."

Jane was astonished. Her mind went into an instant ferment of speculation and suspicion even as Chloe asked who had made the accusation.

Major Wickham answered. "CUO Lewis radioed in that two girls were running around naked in their area and he believed that they were you and Cadet Carson."

"Oh, why us?" Chloe cried.

Jane bit her lip and shook her head but knew why. Major Wickham confirmed her suspicion. "Probably because you pair have done things like that before," he answered.

"Well it wasn't us sir," Chloe replied, anger in her tone. "And it wasn't us last night either," she added.

Several pieces of the mental jigsaw clicked into place in Jane's mind. *Kim and Chantelle,* she thought, remembering the sounds she had heard of people moving through the bush.

Chloe persisted. "But we've been here the whole time on guard!" she protested. "Ask Cpl Hankin."

"We will," Major Wickham answered, "But we were told you were not here at a critical time."

"Oh, what a lie! Who by?" Chloe cried, anger and astonishment clear in her voice.

CUO Roach now spoke. "Sgt Lepson reported you were not here just after the time when the incident happened," he said.

"Oh, that's a lie!" Chloe cried angrily. She turned towards Sgt Lepson. "We were there!"

"You weren't. I checked," Sgt Lepson replied, his voice faltering with emotion.

"We were so! Ask Cpl Hankin," Chloe retorted.

Sgt Lepson again answered her. "Hankin was asleep. He wouldn't know," he said.

Major Wickham cut in loudly. "That will do! Be quiet all of you. We will investigate this properly. You are all to write statements and we will make enquiries to try to determine exactly what happened. Now walk over to the vehicle and do as you are told."

They began walking again. As they did Jane's mind raced. *Hankin probably was asleep. But why is Lepson lying? What's causing this?* she wondered.

She was now certain that she and Chloe were being 'fitted up' but did not have enough information to work out by whom or to prove anything. By now her apprehension had congealed into a nauseating mixture of anxiety and anger. It took her an effort of will power to hold her tongue and not to voice her suspicions.

Instead she walked quietly over to the vehicle. Here several lanterns were lit and Capt Hamilton took one and told her to follow him. He and CSM Glenn led her 50 paces along the fence southwards and then the lantern was hung on a fence post. "OK Cadet Carson, write down your account of everything that you know has happened since your section returned from patrol this evening," he instructed.

"Sir," Jane replied.

Still trying to act calm and innocent she took off her webbing and placed it aside then took the offered clipboard and pen and sat herself down where the light from the lantern allowed her to see the writing paper secured to the clipboard. For a few minutes she just sat, her mind racing and her emotions in gut-churning turmoil, while she organised her thoughts. Capt Hamilton and CSM sat nearby in silence and watched. Back near the vehicle Major Wickham and Capt Buchan were just visible in the light of another lantern, the major leaning on the engine cover while he wrote something. Jane saw that he was busy questioning CUO Roach.

Knowing that she and Chloe were in real trouble helped clarify Jane's thoughts. She decided to be very thorough and to make sure she wasn't going to be criticised for poor work or for avoiding anything she pedantically wrote a heading and addressed her statement like a formal letter with her full rank and name and the date, time and place. Then she began to write in short, clear paragraphs.

Not that there was much to write. She and Chloe had just sat there in relative silence for nearly two hours. *Neither of us even went to the latrine or had anything to eat,* she remembered.

Then she paused and chewed the end of the pen. *If we are going to be hung I'd better put in everything that will sow doubt or get our enemies to reveal themselves,* she decided. Gnawing at her was why Sgt Lepson should so blatantly lie. *What's his game?* she wondered. She hadn't thought he had the courage to do anything.

Still speculating on this she resumed writing, adding details of when she and Chloe had heard people moving around, mentioning details of patrols that she had heard or seen trying to sneak in or which had gone walking past.

And those noises we heard of people walking off through the bush, she added, wishing she had noted the times. She even included a note about Sgt Lepson walking over to near Cpl Hankin just before the drama had all begun. *He was looking to see if we were here, I'm sure,* she thought. *So why is he so blatantly lying?*

When she had finished, she signed the statement and handed it to Capt Hamilton. Then she sat there, her thoughts now icy calm and logical even though her stomach felt so upset she felt like throwing up.

If they want a fight then we will give them one! she vowed.

Looking around she saw that Sgt Lepson was being questioned by Major Wickham. Seeing Sgt Lepson added to her rising sense of injustice and anger.

Why is that bastard lying? she thought.

She had always thought him a sanctimonious hypocrite and was sure he secretly lusted to have sex with Chloe (Jealousy now adding a honed sense of being wronged to her emotions!). But what was driving him to take such a drastic action?

If the major finds out he has lied he is finished, she told herself.

Which made her think that he must have some very powerful inducement to take such a potentially disastrous action. It certainly had her puzzled.

Jane saw Lt Barker direct Sgt Lepson to sit in the darkness north of the vehicle while Capt Hamilton took her statement to Major Wickham. Ten more minutes of anxious waiting crept by while it was read and while the officers conferred. Then Capt Hamilton came back and indicated she should come with him.

"The OC will see you now," he said.

For the next twenty minutes Jane endured a rigorous questioning by Major Wickham. The hardest aspect for her was to keep her emotions in check so that she did not make angry accusations or counter claims. By an effort of willpower she kept her voice calm and managed to answer every question without hesitating. Major Wickham, Capt Hamilton and Capt Buchan all asked questions and she managed to keep herself under control even though all three were studying her intently.

Major Wickham then glanced at his watch and shook his head. Holding up her statement he said, "So you stand by this as a true and accurate account of what you and Cadet Cummings did during this period of time?"

"Yes sir."

"And what about this reference to Sgt Lepson?"

"That's exactly what he did sir," Jane replied as calmly as she could, even though she wanted to scream that Lepson was a lying turd. "Chloe and I were sitting on guard facing out and we heard movement behind us so we both looked back. I clearly saw Sgt Lepson stop and look down at Cpl Hankin and then he looked directly at us. He must have seen us because there is plenty of light, even without the moon."

"It is possible he did not see you or that he mistook you for someone else," Major Wickham replied.

Jane gave a snort of derision. "Only if he needs glasses or if he is useless in the bush at night! There were only two small sections in this area, and he had been around the perimeter a dozen times," she replied.

Once again, she had to reign in her fury and almost had to literally bite her tongue to hold back the angry accusations she itched to make.

"So you deny that you and Cadet Cummings left the area?"

"Yes sir."

"And you deny that you took your clothes off."

"Yes sir. Chloe and I want to do well at Cadets sir, so we are making a big effort to do the right thing," Jane answered. She was going to add that she and Chloe both wanted to be promoted but she held that back.

"But you have done it in the past," Major Wickham said.

"Yes sir, you know we have. You've seen us. But we have behaved on this bivouac and now our past is being used against us," Jane replied some of her anger loosening her tongue.

Major Wickham nodded. "That may well be. That's the problem with doing the wrong thing, it can come back to cause you more trouble later on.

"I know sir," Jane replied, quiet unable to keep some of the bitterness out of her voice.

Major Wickham pointed back into the platoon area. "Alright, go back to your place and sit down. We still have other people to question. Don't wander around and don't talk to other people about this. And certainly don't start arguing or making accusations. We will inform you when we are finished."

That was what Jane had expected as Chloe hadn't been interviewed yet. "Thank you sir," she said. Then she turned and started walking back south along the fence.

Capt Hamilton called to her, "Where are you going Cadet Carson?"

"To get my webbing and to go to the latrine sir," Jane answered.

She was annoyed by the peremptory nature of the question but was perversely pleased as it emphasized that she and Chloe really had been doing the right thing by having their webbing on while 'Standing To'.

Nothing more was said so she kept walking. Having collected her webbing, she swung it on and resumed walking south along the fence, even though the girl's latrine was the other way. There was no way she was going anywhere near Lepson or Roach!

Five minutes later, after having done a pee in the long grass beside the track, she walked back towards the lights at the vehicle. As she got closer, she saw that Chloe was now being questioned. Rather than go too close Jane detoured to her right and that took her into the platoon area past Arthur and Flegel.

They were both awake and watching and Flegel called on her to halt. Jane curled her lip. "The exercise is finished Flegel," she replied.

"So what's with all the questioning by the officers? Who's in trouble?" Flegel asked.

Jane was sorely tempted to explain to try to get them on her side but managed to hold her tongue. "I'm not allowed to say until the OC has spoken to everyone," she replied.

"Are we in trouble?" Arthur asked in an alarmed tone.

Jane had to smile at the guilty sound in his voice. "They'll let you know," she answered. With that she walked on, passing behind Cpl Hankin who gave her a curious stare. Jane ignored him and sat down on her pack. From there she could just see Chloe being interrogated and she could only shake her head at the trouble they were in.

We could be chucked out of Cadets if the officers believe this story, she thought sadly. *And I was just starting to really enjoy it.*

She glanced at her watch and was surprised to see that it was almost midnight. *Oh, this is going to be a long night,* she decided.

But there was nothing she could do but sit there and think. She had a drink and then brooded over what was happening, her paranoia growing as she listed her possible rivals and enemies. But each time it came back to Kim and Chantelle.

It has to be them. None of the other girls is big enough or curvy enough to be mistaken for Chloe and me, even in the dark, she decided.

Once again, she pictured each female cadet and tried to image why they might have it in for her and Chloe so badly they would do such a thing.

It was nearly 0030hrs when Chloe walked over to join her, pointedly ignoring Cpl Hankin as she passed him. She dropped her webbing and slumped down beside Jane. "Well, that wasn't very pleasant," she said. "What did they ask you?"

Jane recounted the questions she had been asked and her answers and then described how she had described Sgt Lepson's action.

Chloe nodded. "So did I. That slimy mongrel is up to something," she said.

"I agree, but what? He hasn't got the guts to start a stunt like this. Someone has put him up to it and he is really scared. You can see it," Jane replied.

"So who is our enemy?" Chloe speculated.

Jane had now done a lot of thinking about this and answered at once. "Kim and Chantelle," she said.

Chloe looked thoughtful and nodded. "But why would Lepson do what they say? Do you think they have offered him a bit if he will co-operate?"

Jane snorted. "They might have, but he hasn't got the guts to take advantage of that sort of an offer. He's not only a hypocrite, he's all messed up by religion and he's a coward."

"You are right there," Chloe replied. "He's been fantasizing about me for years, but if I offered it to him on a plate he'd run a mile."

Jane smiled and agreed. The image of a naked Chloe offering herself to Lepson on a plate helped ease her feelings, even though she was niggled by Chloe's egotistical assumption that it was herself and not Jane who was the object of Lepson's fantasies. Then she became serious.

"So they have to have some hold over him. I reckon they have threatened him about something and he has caved in," she said.

"You might be right," Chloe agreed. "But what?"

Jane had no answer to that but it was the only theory that made sense. "And how do we find out and then prove it?" she added.

The two girls sat quietly talking, watching while first Cadet Arthur and then Cadet Flegel were questioned. Then corporals Callan and Lang were taken one at a time to the officers. Time dragged slowly on and Jane noted that 0130 had passed. After the corporals CUO Roach and

Sgt Lepson were brought back for more questions and then stood to one side. To Jane's surprise the lanterns and torches were all turned off and the whole group came walking over. Jane tense with anticipatory dread but Major Wickham pleased and surprised her when he told everyone to go to their places in the platoon layout.

"Is this where you were?" he asked.

"Yes sir," Chloe answered.

"Where are your hutchies?"

Jane answered. "We were told not to put them up sir," she said.

Major Wickham turned to CUO Roach. "Did you order that platoon commander?"

Roach shifted from one foot to the other and hesitated then mumbled yes. Major Wickham let out an audible breath.

"Why was that?" he queried.

"Er... er... to make the platoon harder to find sir," he replied, an anxious quaver sounding in his voice.

"I thought my orders for the exercise were clear: platoons were to be easy to find by having the hutchies up as an obvious objective. Isn't that so?"

"Er... Yes sir," CUO Roach mumbled.

"We will speak about this later CUO. Now, Cadet Cummings, you and Cadet Carson sit where you were during the exercise. Cpl Hankin you go to your place and everyone else come with me," Major Wickham instructed.

Jane nearly chortled with glee at hearing the rebuke to CUO Roach but she resisted the urge to nudge Chloe until the others had moved away. "That got the mongrel!" she whispered. Sitting down she looked back and was pleased to hear Major Wickham tell Sgt Lepson to stand where he had been when he checked if Chloe and Jane were there. Sgt Lepson moved to near Cpl Hankin and Major Wickham stood beside him. They were clearly visible in the starlight.

Oh good! Jane thought. *That will cast doubt on Lepson's story.* She was now hopeful the truth would come out.

Major Wickham and the other officers and CUO Roach then went on a short tour around the platoon position. When they came back, they made their way to the vehicles. CSM Glenn made his way past and told Sgt Lepson and Cpl Hankin to join the group and then walked over to

Jane and Chloe and told them to come to the vehicle. That sent Jane's heart a-flutter and once again the apprehension churned in her stomach. Almost trembling with anxiety over what she was about to be told she walked across with Chloe and stood facing the four officers.

Major Wickham looked tired and strained. He studied them for a minute and then said, "We have not decided yet. There are a few more people we need to question to get a clearer picture of what went on so you are all to go back to your platoon area. You will just act normally and there will be no accusations or recriminations or any sort of trouble from any of you until we have resolved the issue. Is that clear?"

He looked first at CUO Roach and Sgt Lepson and then at Chloe and Jane. They all chorused yes. Jane was relieved and pleased at the inconclusive outcome but was then further dismayed when Major Wickham said, "Capt Hamilton, you and Lt Barker sleep here tonight just to keep an eye on things. Lt Peters and the CSM and I will now go and do some more digging at 3 Platoon."

They aren't going to question Kim or Chantelle or any other cadets here, Jane thought.

Now she regretted not having stated her suspicions but decided that this was not the moment to do so. Chloe let out a little gasp and looked as though she might have been about to say something, but when Major Wickham looked at her she shook her head and looked down.

Jane took hold of Chloe's sleeve. "Come on Chlo," she said softly. To her relief Chloe turned and walked with her and a scene was avoided.

"They aren't going to question Kim and Chantelle!" Chloe hissed.

"If we need to state our suspicions we will, but I don't think now is the time to say it," Jane replied.

"Why not?"

"Because I think the major can smell a rat and he might just sus them out on his own, which will be even better. Now let's get to bed and try to get some sleep."

Chapter 16

DOUBTS

Jane was right. Major Wickham found he was full of doubts. Even after questioning half a dozen people in 3 Platoon he was still unsure of who had done what.

"Something isn't gelling here. I have lots of doubts" he said to Capt Buchan as the pair walked back through the bush towards HQ. Lt Peters and CSM Glenn walked behind but made no comment.

Capt Buchan nodded. "I agree. Particularly as the two girls seen at 3 Platoon wore some sort of cloth covering over their lower face. About the only thing that isn't in doubt is that two naked girls ran through the 3 Platoon position, and that one of them was a big blonde."

"Yes, but none of the other blondes in the unit had that platinum shade of Chloe's," Major Wickham replied.

"Oh sir!" Capt Buchan replied. "These are females we are taking about! They dye their hair all sorts of shades."

Lt Peters spoke from behind. "Yes, they do. But there aren't any other girls in the unit that have hair that colour or length right now," she said. "It just doesn't make sense."

"So, are we going to question anyone in One Platoon and 2 Platoon?" Capt Buchan queried.

Major Wickham looked at his watch and then groaned. "Bloody hell! It's after three o'clock. No. Maybe tomorrow we will. I think we need a bit of sleep. I don't want to commit an injustice by making a hasty decision while I'm tired," he said.

So the group returned to HQ and separated to their hutchies. Major Wickham first checked that the HQ cadets were maintaining a radio piquet in the CP and then went to his hutchie.

This whole situation has got me beat, he mused. *Something is going on but what?*

Not even bothering to take off his boots he unrolled his sleeping bag and lay down. The night was not cold so he did not bother to get into it. But then sleep would not come. For the next three hours he lay there, his mind turning over all the information he had collected and then speculating on what was actually happening.

One of the things that bothered him was that Sgt Lepson had reported that Chloe and Jane were not there yet CUO Roach had said they were only a few minutes later.

That is a very small time window but I suppose they could have done something at 3 Platoon and then run back to their own platoon, Major Wickham thought. *But they must have gotten dressed very quickly.*

Images of Chloe and Jane standing in the beam of his torch fully dressed and with their webbing on flitted across his mind. He also remembered noting that they had not looked breathless and weren't perspiring. These thoughts were followed by images of the naked girls who had run away from him the previous night along the railway cutting. He pondered this for a few minutes and decided that the nude runners of the first night could have easily and safely run back to the 4 Platoon position, but when he thought about the current locations of 3 Platoon and 4 Platoon he had real doubts.

There is some pretty thick scrub between the two and they would not want to run through that with nothing on. So they must have stripped near 3 Platoon and then got dressed again before returning to their own area, he decided.

He was sure they had not detoured up past HQ and along the Old Highway. He was also reasonably certain that no-one from 1 Platoon or 2 Platoon was involved.

Then other memories came into his mind to bother him. He clearly remembered other images of nude Chloe and realised, with a sharp stab of guilt, that he found them both arousing and disturbing. Once again, his conscience nagged at him and he flushed with secret shame.

But it was those very images that added to his doubts. The images of the naked blonde on the first night somehow did not seem to match them. He could not quite decide exactly why but he was sure it was something to do with the curves: the shape of the hips and buttocks and the size and movement of the breasts.

But if it wasn't Chloe who was it? he wondered. *And why is this person acting that way; what is her game?*

The doubts still nagged at him when he got up at 0545 to go to the latrine. By the time had made his way back in the half-light pre-dawn the platoons were moving in from their night locations. 1 Platoon was first, and they dropped their packs and moved to Check Parade. 3 Platoon was next and then 2 Platoon. 4 Platoon was last, and he did not see them because they were at the far end of the company and by then he was talking to the other CUOs.

A tired and surly looking CUO Roach joined them. "4 Platoon here now sir," he reported.

"Good," Major Wickham replied, noting the curious glances from the other CUOs. They obviously knew that there had been some drama in the night but not the details.

They will soon know. It will be all over the company in five minutes, he mused.

Quickly he gave orders for the day, reminding them of the exercises they planned to do and then sent them to organise their platoons for their morning routine.

As soon as the Check Parade was over CSM Glenn reported, also looking tired but still cheerful. "All present except for Cadet Swanson sir," he said.

"Good," Major Wickham replied. He had been a little bit worried that either Chloe or Jane or both might have absconded in the dark. He saw the CSM waiting, looking worried and expectant. "You go on with your personal admin CSM. If there is any more questioning to do I will let you know."

"Sir!"

The CSM turned and walked away. Lt Peters arrived, clearly having been to the latrine while the cadets were on Check Parade. "So what are we going to do sir?" she asked.

Major Wickham shook his head. "I haven't decided. I need a bit more time to think this through. We will discuss it when the others get here," he answered.

Capt Hamilton and Lt Barker arrived by vehicle and joined them. As they sat down another vehicle drove in from the other direction. It was Capt Buchan and Lt Cavendish returning. Major Wickham placed his pack down and then his webbing and then sat on the pack while waiting for them.

"How is Cadet Swanson?" he asked Lt Cavendish as she joined the group.

"Fine. She is home now. The hospital X-rayed her and found no damage."

Lt Barker chuckled. "Hard to find brain damage when there isn't one!" he said.

"Ash! Be nice," Major Wickham said.

Lt Cavendish got her gear and sat down. "You all look very serious. What's happened?"

The others all looked at Major Wickham. He sighed. "The case of the naked girls," he answered.

"Chloe and Jane? Oh good! Now we can chuck the little troublemakers out," Lt Cavendish cried.

Major Wickham was a bit nettled that there was no presumption of innocence but then he shook his head. "We don't know if it was them," he answered.

"Oh, who else would it be?" Lt Cavendish said.

"I think that is the assumption their enemies are working on," Major Wickham replied. They all looked at him again. "The more I look at this the more it doesn't make sense. We haven't had any trouble from that pair so far this year. In fact they have been model cadets."

"Yes, but there have been endless stories of what they have been getting up to at parties and so on," Capt Buchan put in.

"Yes, but that is their private lives, not Cadets. No, something doesn't add up here," Major Wickham answered.

"What happened?" Lt Cavendish asked.

Major Wickham described the incident as reported and then the subsequent investigation.

"And I'm still not sure what happened," he concluded.

"But surely it must have been them!" Lt Cavendish cried. "They've been in enough trouble at other times. Now is our chance to be rid of them!"

Her willingness to use any excuse even if the girls were innocent disturbed Major Wickham but he hid this and shook his head. "There are too many doubts. Whole chunks of the story don't fit together. To start with I don't think the blonde girl the first night was Chloe. She just didn't... er.... didn't look right."

"How?" Capt Hamilton queried.

"Well... she looked more gangly and less, well, less graceful. You've all seen Chloe run, and she has a sort of animal grace to her. And that girl just didn't look er... didn't; er... look rounded enough in the buttocks and her er... her front wasn't as big as..." Major Wickham blushed and stopped speaking.

Lt Barker grinned. "Chloe's certainly big up front," he commented.

"That will do Lt Barker!" Major Wickham rebuked, noting the distasteful glances from the two female lieutenants.

"So why don't you think it was them, apart from a perception based on a fleeting glimpse in the dark?" Lt Peters asked. Her tone indicated she also wanted the pair gone from the unit.

"Sgt Lepson's story is very thin. He said that they weren't in the platoon area only a few minutes after the incident was reported by 3 Platoon. Yet both girls claim they were there and when we stood at the spot Sgt Lepson indicated I could quite clearly see them, even in the dark."

"And they even had their webbing on," Capt Hamilton added.

"Yes. And CUO Roach radioed that they were there a few minutes later. So, if it was them, they must have run back from 3 Platoon, nearly a kilometre in the dark, and at some stage got dressed. Yet they didn't look hot or puffed or even worried," Major Wickham said.

"But that means that either Sgt Lepson or CUO Roach are lying," Capt Buchan pointed out.

"Yes."

Capt Buchan went on: "And Lepson did change his story and admit he might have made a mistake."

"Yes, and he looked really anxious at that stage," Major Wickham agreed. "So I am doubtful. I know he doesn't like Cadet Cummings. So I am wondering if he was telling the truth."

"You mean he deliberately lied?" Capt Hamilton suggested.

"Yes."

"But..." Lt Cavendish frowned. "Why would he do that?"

"I don't know. But I intend to find out. Something is going on and it has the potential to do great harm to the unit. We must find out what it is," Major Wickham said.

"So what about this exercise today? Does it go ahead?" Capt Hamilton queried.

Major Wickham nodded. "Yes."

"What about Carson and Cummings, do they get suspended or separated or something?" Lt Peters asked.

Major Wickham shook his head. "No. They can stay with their platoon. We haven't proved anything and until we do I don't think we should be singling them out. It could be construed as victimization."

The others were silent for a minute or so while they considered this. Lt Cavendish was plainly unhappy with the decision and Lt Peters looked doubtful but Major Wickham was determined.

"Besides, it might upset the plans of whoever is orchestrating this mischief and might provoke them into another action that could reveal who they are and why they are doing it," he said.

"Why is easy," Capt Buchan commented. "They hate Chloe and Jane and want to hurt them."

"Probably," Major Wickham conceded.

"But who?" Lt Peters asked.

"Either a male who has been rejected and is acting out of hurt pride or a female who is jealous," suggested Lt Barker.

They left it at that and settled to their morning routine. But it was a very subdued group who cooked and ate breakfast. Major Wickham felt very uneasy and this sense lingered during the morning. Having completed his own morning routine he prepared for orders and then sent runners from the CP to collect the people he wanted. Capt Buchan did likewise. He was running a Day Navex for the three 'First Year' platoons and needed to brief the checkpoints.

The exercise for 4 Platoon was to be on the other side of the highway and HQ was to provide the 'Control Group' for it: the Opposing Force to be observed and a radio relay station and medics for safety. 4 Platoon was to establish four Observation Posts. The OPs were to be along the road at the bottom of the range between the Old railway and the New Railway. HQ, minus Cpl Pretzel and a cadet, who were detached to the Dav Navex as a check point, was seated in a group by Major Wickham who issued new maps and then read out the orders he had prepared for the activities. This took until 0730 and as soon as he had finished the HQ people hurried off to get ready.

"Not you CSM," Major Wickham called. "You are with me and first I want to you to get CUO Roach."

The CSM hurried off and Major Wickham stood and watched as the platoon sergeants began organising their platoons for an inspection. He called Capt Hamilton to join him. He wanted a reliable witness when he spoke to the cadets. And what he said to CUO Roach when he arrived was scathing. "You are performing at a very low level. Your platoon is a rabble and they should be the best in the company."

"It's Sgt Lepson sir, he..." Roach began.

"Don't you blame your sergeant! You are responsible. You set the example. You make sure he is doing his job. And you do the right thing yourself. Make sure you are awake if they are supposed to be awake," he snapped. Anger surged in him and he really wondered how he could have read a person so wrong to choose Roach for such an important position. Then an image of Chloe and Jane in his torch beam the previous night flitted across his mind. "And make sure you have your webbing on if that is what is required. As I said, set the example and set the standards. Now, you will carry out exactly the orders today. No short cuts or changing the plan to make it easier or to suit yourself. Got that?"

"Yes sir."

"And make sure there is no bullying, harassment or trouble related to last night. Understand?"

"Yes sir."

"Good. Now, here are your exercise orders. Read them and then come and clear up any doubtful points with me. Then give your platoon a proper O Group." He handed five pages of typed orders in the SMEAC Format to the CUO.

"Sir."

"Now get the CSM to bring me Sgt Lepson."

CUO Roach stalked off, his stiff bearing indicating his unhappiness. While Major Wickham waited, he watched the platoon commanders of 1 Platoon and 2 Platoon do an inspection of their platoons, hygiene and dress. HQ got itself organised and began filling water bottles and pulling on webbing. Radios were tested and the teams who were supporting the 4 Platoon exercise did radio checks and then set off.

As they did CSM Glenn and a very nervous looking Sgt Lepson arrived. "You sent for me sir?" Sgt Lepson asked.

Major Wickham studied Sgt Lepson and noted that he was looking very tired and that he was perspiring and trembling. *This guy is in a real state,* he thought with concern.

Maybe I should not send him out?

But then he shook his head. Sgt Lepson obviously misinterpreted this as he looked even more anxious. Major Wickham met his gaze and said, "I don't know what happened last night, but I do know I haven't got all the facts. There seems to be some doubt as to whether Cadets Carson and Cummings were absent from your platoon area or not and you seem unsure yourself."

Major Wickham left the doubt hanging and saw Sgt Lepson lick his lips. "Maybe... er... maybe I went to the wrong place in the dark sir. But I thought they weren't there."

"So you said. Now, you need to lift your game and get a better grip on your platoon. They were very slack last night, most had no webbing on when they were supposed to be defending their position and that included you."

"Yes sir."

"So set a good example. You can't reprimand people if you are a hypocrite! And make sure there is no trouble today: no bullying, no teasing, no hurtful comments, no follow-on from last night. We will continue to investigate what happened after the exercise, but we aren't going to stop it and disadvantage all those cadets who have been training for it. So make sure things go well."

"Yes sir."

"Good! Now go. CSM, you go and bring me Cadets Carson and Cummings."

"Sir."

Sgt Lepson and CSM Glenn turned and hurried away. Capt Hamilton shook his head. "He looked bloody guilty then," he commented.

"Yes. And he went an odd colour too. I am sure he is involved somehow," Major Wickham replied.

"He was certainly the colour of bad shit when he arrived and the blood quite drained out of his face when you got up him," Capt Hamilton added.

Major Wickham almost laughed at the colourful description, but he was too strained and upset to really feel like humour. Instead he asked Warwick to stay and called over Lt Peters.

"I want a lady officer present while I speak to these two girls," he explained.

A few minutes later CSM Glenn appeared leading Chloe and Jane. Chloe had a tight, almost defiant look on her face but Jane's was set and respectful. CSM Glenn was starting to turn away but Major Wickham stopped him. "You stay CSM. You need to hear this."

"I was just going to seat the First Years for Capt Buchan sir," CSM Glenn explained, gesturing to where 1 Platoon was filing past ready for their exercise briefing.

"Just tell One Platoon sergeant to seat her people and the others will go where they normally go," Major Wickham replied.

CSM Glenn did this and then stood just behind Chloe and Jane. The three officers stood side by side facing them. Major Wickham studied the two girls for a moment and could not help but admire them.

They are good cadets, he thought.

He cleared his throat. "We have not yet completed our investigation into what went on last night, but I personally have some doubts about what I have been told by some people. I want to find out exactly what happened."

Jane nodded. "So do we sir," she said.

"But I am not going to stop the training for eighty people just to do that, so the exercise is going ahead and you are allowed to go on it. But you are going to promise me you will do the right thing and behave, no matter what others say or who provokes you. Got that?"

"Yes sir," both girls chorused.

"And if there is any trouble, I want you to report it, not try to solve it yourselves, understand?"

"Yes sir."

"Right, go back to your platoon and stay out of mischief."

"Sir."

The two girls did an about turn and hurried away, exchanging glances as they did. Lt Peters shook her head.

"I hope that isn't a mistake," she said. "What if there is another incident while they are out there on the exercise?"

"Then we will deal with that when it happens," Major Wickham replied grimly. He was a bit annoyed at the apparent vendetta the lady officers were conducting and was niggled by the fact that they were openly stating his private fears.

I hope there isn't any trouble today, he thought.

As he did the roar of motorbikes out on the highway came to his ears. When the sounds moved onto the Mingela Road he glanced that way and saw five leather-jacketed bikies roar past.

Capt Hamilton gestured to them and chuckled. "They look like bikies to me. I thought it was against the law for more then three motorcyclists to ride together?"

Major Wickham agreed. A few years before the Queensland government had passed legislation banning Outlaw Motorcycle Gangs and restricting such groups in an attempt to combat organised crime. A later government had eased up on the restrictions but, as far as he knew, the law still stood. He watched the last bikie vanish towards Mingela and shrugged.

"He certainly looks like a bikie," he commented. "So you go and tell them to stop it," he added.

"Pigs! No fear! Not me," Capt Hamilton replied. They both smiled, being well aware of the reputation bikies had for extreme violence.

Major Wickham said: "OK Warwick, if you are happy you can get to your check point?"

"No problem," Capt Hamilton replied. "I'll get an army radio and get going."

"I'll see you around mid-morning when I come to check how things are going."

"Right you are. Have a good day boss."

Capt Hamilton walked over to the CP and began talking to the signals corporal. The signallers were busy doing radio checks with check points and platoon commanders. Major Wickham turned to Lt Peters. "You are Duty Officer in the CP for the morning Jenny. You can have more excitement this afternoon."

"Suits me. I'm happy with that," Lt Peters replied.

Major Wickham nodded and glanced at his watch. It was now 0830 and movement across the Old Highway caught his eye. It was 4 Platoon heading off on their exercise.

CUO Roach didn't come to check anything. I hope he understands it all, Major Wickham thought. *And I hope there isn't any trouble out there!*

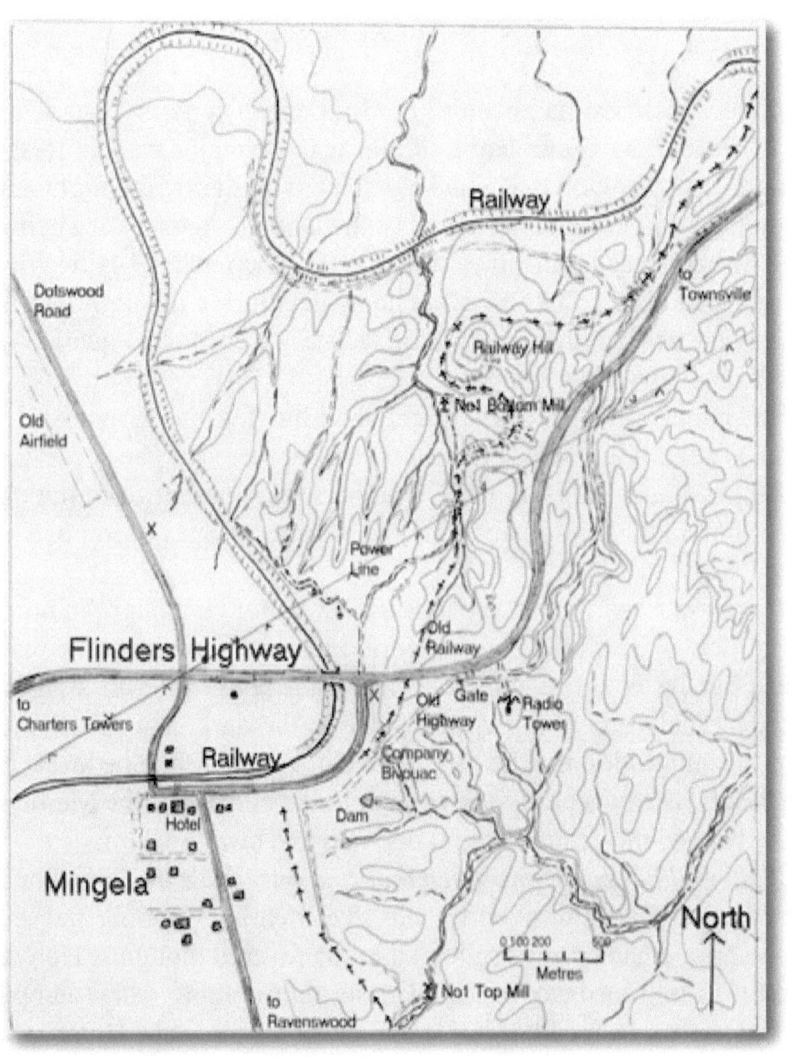

Map 3 Exercise Area

Chapter 17

FIELD EXERCISE

Major Wickham had been right. Sgt Lepson certainly was in a state. When CSM Glenn had told him that the major wanted to see him he had nearly thrown up. He had not slept at all during the night and was now almost quivering with nervous exhaustion. Almost overwhelmed by dread he had forced himself to walk to HQ. Then, when Major Wickham had said that he didn't know what happened during the night but that he also knew that he didn't have all the facts Sgt Lepson had quailed inside.

This isn't over! he thought.

He managed to keep a straight face but felt nauseous. And it got worse. When Major Wickham said that there seemed to be some doubt as to whether Cadets Carson and Cummings were absent from the platoon area or not and that he seemed unsure of himself Sgt Lepson had almost fainted.

He doesn't believe me! He thinks I am lying! he thought in horror.

Sgt Lepson's mind raced as he tried to come up with some plausible excuse but he could not think of anything better than to suggest that maybe he had gone to the wrong place in the dark. But the moment he made the suggestion that he might have made a mistake he knew he had blundered. He saw a hard look come into the corners of the Major's eyes and he wished the ground would open up and swallow him.

What will happen to me when they find out I have lied? he wondered.

After that the major's reprimands over wearing webbing and setting a good example had barely registered in his fevered thoughts. He was just thankful to be sent back to the platoon with nothing worse happening. But that wasn't then end of it. He had to walk with CSM Glenn who had been tasked with parading Carson and Cummings to the major and that added to his emotional turmoil.

Is he just going to speak to them? Or are they being thrown out? he wondered.

Back at the platoon when the CSM called the two girls to go with him they had both looked hard at him and he had shivered at their icy stares.

Deep down Sgt Lepson was now certain that none of his fantasies about Chloe would ever come true.

She will hate me now, he thought unhappily. *And she will really have it in for me if she ever learns the truth.*

He was so unfocused and upset that CUO Roach had to twice rebuke him for not doing his duties as a platoon sergeant. With an effort he tried to concentrate on what felt to him like the trivia of making sure water bottles were filled and that everyone had a spare meal and so on.

If they are so dumb to forget to fill their water bottles they can just go bloody thirsty! he thought angrily.

He was then thrown into a fluster when the female medical corporal from HQ, Rachel Reppington, and the Signals lance corporal, Travis, arrived and asked where they were to go.

"What are you doing here?" he asked.

Rachel pointed to the litter folding she and Travis were carrying and said, "We are attached for your exercise."

"I don't know anything about that. You'd better ask CUO Roach," Sgt Lepson had said.

But even as he did CUO Roach called to him. "Sgt Lepson! I said to have the platoon seated for a briefing by zero eight hundred. Get them here!"

Sgt Lepson blushed and bit his lip but then began to shout at the cadets to get seated in their sections. He was still organising this when he saw Chloe and Jane return. They both gave him a hard look that set his emotions churning again but neither said anything. They just sat in their section. Sgt Lepson had been hoping they would not be allowed to take part in the exercise but now his doubts returned and he began to fret.

What has the major said to them? he worried.

Seeing Kim and Chantelle whispering and glancing at Chloe and Jane was no help. Sgt Lepson knew he should tell the two girls to stop talking but he did not want to antagonize them. His state of mind was not helped when Kim turned to look at him and gave him what he took to be an accusing look.

God, how can I get out of this mess? he wondered.

CUO Roach now called on the platoon to be silent and began to give orders. He read these from printed sheets and they were a full set of Patrol Verbal Orders. Only after CUO Roach had been reading for five minutes did Sgt Lepson notice the corporals and some of the cadets writing the orders into their notebooks.

I should be doing that too, he thought.

He knew he was the platoon 2ic and that theoretically it was his responsibility to take over if something happened to the platoon commander. But he did not really believe it was necessary. Such a situation had never happened in the three years he had been a cadet.

Then he realised he had missed some of the important bits of information at the beginning and that the exercise was to be in a new bit of country where he had never been. A glance at his map reassured him.

It is in between the Old Railway and the new one. How could we get lost in there? he told himself.

When the orders were complete the platoon began its final preparations. CUO Roach called out: "OK section commanders, place your packs in line over under that tree and then line up, Ten, Eleven and Twelve. Sgt Lepson, supervise the packs. Move!"

Sgt Lepson hurried over to the tree indicated and stood there supervising while the sections came over to put their packs in a neat line. As they did he got another jolt. Kim bent over near him to put her pack down then, as she straightened up she looked hard at him and hissed, "Don't you change your story Lepson, or you'll regret it."

Then she was gone, leaving Sgt Lepson trembling and bitterly regretting his weakness. Then he realised he had left his own pack some distance away and he had to hurry across to get it to add it to the row. By then the platoon was standing in a long single file on the Old Highway near where the company did morning parades while people with radios did radio checks. Each section corporal and CUO Roach had their hand-held UHF CB radios and these Sgt Lepson now learned were on a different channel so as not to interfere with the First Year's Day Navex. Lance Cpl Travis had a big army RTF200 Radio set which he wore on his back like a pack and he also did a radio check with the CP. Then he called a Call Sign named 'Hotel Two'.

"Who is that?" Sgt Lepson queried.

LCpl Travis gave him a reproachful look indicating he should have listened to the 'Command and Signals' paragraphs of the orders. Then Travis shrugged and said, "They are an OP and radio relay station. That is the one we have to avoid being seen while getting into the area."

"Where are they?"

"On a feature nicknamed Railway Hill," LCpl Travis replied, but he did not make any attempt to explain further.

Sgt Lepson shrugged it out of his mind and began checking webbing. His efforts were only half-hearted, and he did only a perfunctory glance at the webbing of both Kim and Chantelle, being hotly aware that they were also giving him sour looks. He did not even go near Chloe and Jane and despised himself for not having the courage to do so.

CUO Roach then called on the platoon to line up and Sgt Lepson still had his wits sufficiently about him to follow the unit SOP of counting them to get the number present at the start of the exercise. "Twenty-one present sir," he reported to CUO Roach.

CUO Roach frowned. "I thought we had only nineteen in the platoon."

"We have a medic and sig attached from HQ," Sgt Lepson replied, mentally kicking himself for not telling the CUO.

CUO Roach scowled. "Why wasn't I told?"

Sgt Lepson was about to retort that it was in the written orders that the CUO had read out but he held his tongue. Instead he said, "They arrived just as you were starting your orders."

"Where are they?"

Sgt Lepson pointed to the two at the back of the platoon. CUO Roach nodded. "OK, let's get moving." He started walking and the platoon followed in single file. Their route led them across the front of where Capt Buchan was briefing the First Years for their Day Navex, but the captain's scowl of disapproval did not really register. Nor did the roar of motorcycles racing past on the Mingela Road although several of the cadets pointed at them and made comments.

The platoon was strung out in a long single file on the small rise between the Old Highway and the cutting of the Old Railway when CUO Roach's radio crackled. It was Major Wickham. "Sunray Two Four, you are supposed to be patrolling, over."

CUO Roach swore and picked up his radio. "Yes sir... Er roger, over. I was going to start after we had crossed the highway, over."

"Start now, and cross by sections when it is safe. Don't be seen by civilians driving past, over."

"Wilco, over."

"Sunray out."

CUO Roach swore again. "Bloody major! All this military bull! OK, Cpl Lang, get your section leading in 'arrowhead'," he called.

It took a couple of minutes to get the first section spaced out. Because of the restrictions on warlike training for cadets it wasn't something they did very much of and there was confusion. CUO Roach didn't help by not making it clear what the platoon formation was to be so the sections stayed one behind the other.

As Cpl Lang's section began moving again, the cadets spaced 25 paces apart, CUO Roach turned to Sgt Lepson. "This is a tactical exercise so you should be back between the second and third sections. Move there and send that signaller up to me," he ordered.

Sgt Lepson mentally kicked himself for not having remembered where the platoon sergeant moved in a tactical platoon formation but he also resented the CUO's way of telling him.

I could have just waited here until Callan's section passed me, he thought. But rather than risk another rebuke he walked back past Cpl Callan's section.

That gave him another unpleasant experience as Chloe and Jane were the scouts for the last section and he carefully avoided eye contact with either, while being hotly aware of their hostile stares. But then he had to walk further back because the HQ signaller and medic were right at the rear of the platoon. He explained where they had to go and then had to hurry forward with them to get in between the second and third sections.

That put him directly in front of Jane and he felt very uneasy, imagining her angry gaze boring its way through his shirt!

Bitches! We must get rid of them, he told himself.

By then the platoon had passed over the low rise and past the big mound of earth and the scouts of the lead section were approaching the Flinders Highway. Suddenly the scouts signalled and lay down in the long grass. The whole section vanished and then CUO Roach and the second section.

What are they doing? Sgt Lepson wondered.

The roar of motorcycles came to his ears and he saw them out to his right as they came around the bend at the top of the range. From behind him Sgt Lepson heard Jane's voice saying, "Our orders are to hide from all civilian vehicles."

Is she talking to me? Sgt Lepson wondered.

Angrily he spun round but then he saw that the medic was starting to lie down and that all of the section behind was already under cover. He realised he was the only person in the platoon still standing and that he was right out in the open and the motorcycles were already passing across his front two hundred metres away. Quickly he lay down, an action he instantly regretted as there were prickles and a scattering of sharp little rocks.

The motorcycles slowed and then turned left onto the Mingela Road on his left. From behind him he heard Cpl Hankin say, "More bikies."

Sgt Lepson glanced and was just able to glimpse through the scatter of trees on the edge of the paddock four leather clad people riding motorcycles. One looked like she might be a female but with the helmets, gloves and leather jackets on it was hard to tell. The four vanished to the left rear towards Mingela.

Cpl Lang's section stood up and continued moving, only to go to ground after another twenty paces as a car went past. Sgt Lepson had just risen to his feet and cursed. Once again, he went to ground. A minute later and ten paces on the same thing happened again, this time because a road train loaded with cattle came from the direction of Charters Towers.

"This is bloody stupid!" he muttered angrily.

Some of the others thought so too because it took them 15 minutes to get to the highway. During that time they went to ground eight times for cars and trucks going in both directions. At CUO Roach's direction they began crawling under the fence beside the highway as they reached it and then started to cross one or two at a time, scuttling across between vehicles. This took another 10 minutes and Sgt Lepson hated it. He was terrified of snakes and having to crawl in the weeds and long grass under the fence and in the ditch beside the highway had him worrying continually.

When his turn came he stood up, keeping low up the low embankment and then glanced both ways before hurrying across. He only just made it before a truck sped into view over the rise from the Charters Towers direction. The medic also just made it in time and flopped down in the long grass with the stretcher.

Then there was another fence and this time Sgt Lepson ignored the major's instructions and went under face down. The result was that his webbing got snagged on the bottom strand of the barbed wire and then, when he tried to wriggle free, he caught his trousers. "Give me a hand," he snapped at the medic, who was already under.

She looked resentful but came over and grabbed the strand of wire. "You are supposed to take your webbing off and go under on your back," she commented.

Sgt Lepson's temper boiled and he was about to shout angrily that he was the sergeant and she wasn't to speak to him like that when Jane appeared on the highway. She crossed at the run and scrambled down close to him, giving him a hard look as she did. Sgt Lepson freed himself and stood up.

"Get moving," he muttered.

The medic pursed her lips. "You could have said thanks. And it would be nice if you got a section to help me carry this stretcher," she commented.

Sgt Lepson knew that was normal procedure as the medic also had a large First Aid kit slung on her back. He glanced around and noted Chloe coming across the road. Jerking his thumb towards her and Jane he said, "Get them to help you."

"Down!" called Jane.

Sgt Lepson was about to snap 'don't you tell me what to do' when he heard the roar of engines. Reluctantly he crouched down behind a large tree. From the direction of Townsville came more motorcycles; six of them this time.

More bikies, he thought.

But then he noted that two of the motorcycles were ridden by females in jeans and short, skimpy tops, their long hair streaming behind their crash helmets. There were two more females seated behind two of the bikies.

The group vanished towards Mingela and Sgt Lepson stood up and resumed walking. As he did he looked around and saw that the leading two sections were now a good couple of hundred paces ahead.

Roach should slow down or the platoon will split in half, he thought.

But rather than initiate that he just growled at Cpl Hankin, who arrived at that moment, to get his section to hurry up. He then strode off to catch up with the second section.

It was getting hot by then and Sgt Lepson began to perspire. After taking a quick drink from his right-hand water bottle he glanced back and noted that all of Cpl Hankin's section was now across the highway and the last two were crawling under the fence. Chloe and Jane were carrying the stretcher between them and the medic was hurrying to catch up with him. Then he noted Jane point and Chloe nod. For a few seconds Sgt Lepson wondered what Jane was pointing at but then he realised it was the overgrown remains of the Old Railway. There beside him, running across the gentle slope near the bottom of a wide, shallow valley, was the remains of the earthworks. There were even a few rotten sleepers visible, now grey with age.

At least I know where I am, Sgt Lepson thought.

For a moment he considered taking out his map to check but then he shrugged. The highway was just behind them, so he thought that was good enough. He had heard that they only had about 2.5 kilometres to go and estimated that they had already gone nearly one.

We have until 1100hrs to be in position, he thought, glancing at his watch and noting that it was nearly 1000hrs.

The last section began moving but then the sound of a large vehicle climbing the range caused the last section to throw themselves into the long grass. Sgt Lepson did not bother, judging himself far enough from the highway so unlikely to be seen by a truck driver. So he stood and watched as a large fuel tanker growled across the embankment behind the last section. Only then did he note Jane staring hard at him, her lip curled in what looked uncomfortably to him like an expression of contempt. Flushing angrily Sgt Lepson ordered the section to its feet as the tanker vanished from view. Then he turned and strode after the platoon.

Five minutes of steady walking brought them to a point where a rough vehicle track, just two-wheel ruts in the grass, came down the slope from their left. The vehicle track then ran along the top of the old permanent way. Patrolling became more difficult as the ground began to change to small hills and steeper gullies. The lead section found itself split across a deep, steep sided creekline and it took five minutes for them to all get across onto the railway track.

CUO Roach did not wait but told them to become the rear section and moved Cpl Callan's section up to lead. The CUO then indicated they should just walk along the Old Railway in single file.

That's because we are out of sight of the major, Sgt Lepson decided, half admiring and half despising the CUO's decision.

He now stopped and waited till Cpl Hankin's section had passed him, telling the medic to stay with him. She recovered her stretcher from Chloe and Jane as they did so. As Chloe and Jane walked past Sgt Lepson they both curled their lips but did not look directly at him. Once again, he flushed with shame and then felt a sense of relief. At least they were not behind him, studying his every action!

The platoon crossed the small creek on an embankment which Sgt Lepson realised must have a culvert under it. As he walked across the embankment Sgt Lepson saw Chloe pointing up and, to his surprise, he saw that they were passing under a major set of powerlines. This made him take out his map and look at it. He noted that the powerlines ran right across the map. He was now able to pinpoint his position and felt more confident. At the back of his mind was the lurking concern that CUO Roach would get them lost and that he might have to work out where to go.

Sitting against the bank on his right were Cpl Lang, Kim and Chantelle. Cadets Leece and Shephard were still scrambling, puffing and sweating, up out of the steep creek line. Sgt Lepson tried to act cool and nonchalant as he passed Kim and Chantelle, grinning and giving them a friendly nod but inside his stomach churned with anxiety. To his relief they seemed friendly enough but did not look like they were enjoying the walking in the heat. After that he had a low hill on the right and the deep creekline on his left and then another small rocky hill.

There was another delay a hundred metres on while Cpl Callan argued with CUO Roach about which way to go. CUO Roach insisted they follow the Old Railway but Cpl Callan and the sig both disagreed. Sgt Lepson overheard the tail end of the dispute when he walked forward to find out what the problem was. It seemed that the Radio Relay Station they were supposed to avoid, because it was acting as an Opposing Force OP, was on the big hill he could just see through the steep cutting ahead.

Cpl Callan then pointed to a cattle pad going off on the left. It went along the side of the creek line they had been following.

"This goes the way we want to go. It leads down to the Number One Bottom Mill and then to the creek we should follow," he said.

"Oh alright! You lead then," CUO Roach cried in an exasperated tone.

You weakling! Sgt Lepson thought. He told himself he would have made the corporal do as he was ordered.

So they plodded down the cattle pad in single file, all perspiring now and taking it slow over the rocky sections of track. But Sgt Lepson had to concede Callan was right. The track went down behind a ridge and then in among a dense stand of trees so that they were quite hidden from the OP on Railway Hill.

At the bottom they came out into an area of dust and bare earth under the trees. In the middle was a windmill and drinking trough for cattle. The area was thick with fresh cow droppings and the reek of the dung made it quite unpleasant to Sgt Lepson but CUO Roach ordered a halt. At Cpl Callan's suggestion his section was deployed for protection while the others just stopped in line and sat down beside the track.

Sgt Lepson was glad to rest. He drank another few gulps of water and noted that he had drunk about half a water bottle. That didn't bother him. The exercise was planned to finish by 1500hrs and a glance at his watch showed him it was already 1025.

But we'd better hurry. We've still got about a kilometre to go and we are supposed to be in position by 1100hrs, he thought.

At 1030 CUO Roach got the platoon moving again, this time sending Cpl Hankin's section to lead and telling Cpl Callan to become the last section. Sgt Lepson waited until Cpl Lang's section had moved and then followed on, this time remembering to help the medic by telling Cpl Callan to have his section carry the stretcher.

The route now led down along a dry creek bed. This ran in a small gorge with steep rocky sides and the bed was a mixture of boulders, rocks and sand. It was not easy to walk along and there was a need to do a lot of clambering and stepping from rock to rock. Worse still the sun was blazing down directly into the valley and there was no breeze to cool them.

This is dumb! Sgt Lepson thought. *Bugger the silly exercise. We could have walked half the way along the Old Railway instead of doing this mountain goat stuff!*

He began to worry what they would do if one of the cadets tripped and injured themselves. *Be a real bugger getting a stretcher along this creek bed,* he decided. He paused to get his balance and had another drink, almost emptying his right water bottle.

Half a kilometre later and twenty minutes on in time the platoon emerged from the gorge. They were still in the dry creek bed with a fairly steep rocky slope on both sides but the hills on each side were now much smaller. The hills were very rocky and covered with yellow dry grass but with very few trees. Sgt Lepson saw that it was 1050hrs and he curled his lip.

We are going to be late. Bloody Roach! The fool should have taken an easier route.

The movement along the creek bed went on, around a curve to the left and along for 200 paces then around a big curve to the right. Sgt Lepson glanced at his map and wondered when the platoon was going to split into its four OP groups.

I thought it was somewhere like this bend, he thought.

Cpl Callan obviously thought so too as he came up and queried the location with Sgt Lepson. Sgt Lepson just shrugged.

"The platoon commander is up the front," he answered.

Shaking his head and muttering a frowning Cpl Callan stopped and waited for his section to come forward. Sgt Lepson plodded on, stepping carefully over rocks and finding that the dry creek bed, which was now about ten paces wide and with a bed mostly of sand, was hard going.

The platoon rounded a curve to the left and Sgt Lepson found himself looking along a straight section of about 50 paces. Ahead of him he saw that the first two sections had stopped and were crouching or sitting against the banks of the creek bed. There was no sign of the platoon commander, so he signalled for Cpl Callan's section to halt and walked forward to find him.

At the next bend Sgt Lepson found CUO Roach and Cpl Hankin standing behind a small tree on the side of the creek. They were arguing over a map. Standing beside them was the signaller and just ahead, crouched against the bank on either side of the creek, were Chloe and Jane who were obviously the scouts. Sgt Lepson avoided their eyes and moved to join CUO Roach and Cpl Hankin.

Cpl Hankin pointed down the creek. "That big mound of earth you can see is the railway embankment of the New Railway and there, just in front of my scouts, is a vehicle track. I reckon we have gone too far," he said.

Just as Sgt Lepson reached CUO Roach he heard the roar of motorcycles. The sound was coming from the right and echoing in the low hills.

More motorbikes, he thought. *What are they doing here? We aren't near the highway.*

Into view down the creek came two motorcycles and at that moment Sgt Lepson saw that a third one was parked beside the creek on the right. The bikes came to a stop and their engines were switched off. Two men dressed as bikies got off and hauled the bikes onto their stands. One was a big hulking man wearing full leathers and knee length boots. The other was a thin man who wore a sleeveless leather jacket over a denim shirt. The two men took off their helmets and looked around. Sgt Lepson realised that he and the others hadn't taken cover but before he could move or suggest it there was a sudden burst of gunfire.

Before his astonished gaze both bikies went down, obviously hit by bullets. Then the big man sprang up and began running up the creek bed towards him. The thin man rolled over and then back again and struggled to his hands and knees. As he did three more men, also bikies, sprang up from behind rocks and bushes further down the creek and began shooting at the man running away. Bullets began to snap and crack past Sgt Lepson, who was frozen by disbelief and then fear.

They are shooting this way! They are real bullets. I could be killed! he thought. He turned and ran.

Chapter 18

SUDDEN DEATH

For the last half hour Jane had been feeling exhausted. The cross-country walking coming on top of a stressful and sleepless night was taking its toll. She crouched against the eroded vertical bank of the dry creek and licked her lips, conscious of her thirst and the heat. Weariness seemed to engulf her. Five paces to her right front crouched Chloe. She was close against the other bank of the creek which in this area was about two metres high and almost vertical. Like Jane Chloe was in a small washout and in behind a rocky outcrop.

The two girls were the scouts for their section and had been leading the platoon since the windmill. But now they had come to a dirt vehicle track which crossed the creek ten metres ahead of them and Chloe had signalled Cpl Hankin that they had reached a tactical obstacle and called him forward to have a look. As Chloe talked and pointed Cpl Hankin had frowned and nodded and then called CUO Roach on the radio.

While they waited Jane blinked in the glare and shook her head. Chloe also shook her head and indicated by her facial expression that there was a problem. Jane nodded.

This is the vehicle track our patrols are supposed to be spread along watching, she thought. *We have come too far.*

Chloe pointed down the creek and Jane leaned out to look. She saw that there was a sort of flat basin 50 paces across and then a fence line. Beyond the fence was a large mound of earth that blocked all vision further down the creek. Her eyes scanned it briefly and she noted that the mound had a surprisingly regular flat top. Only then did its meaning click in her mind.

That is the railway line up there, she told herself.

Her gaze then took in something even more surprising. A shiny, new motorcycle, all gleaming chrome and polished black steel, was parked on the right of the creek on a small flat area just across the vehicle track.

What is that doing here? she wondered.

CUO Roach came forward with the signaller to talk to Cpl Hankin.

The group stood over on the other side of the creek with a small tree providing cover from further down the creek. Cpl Hankin took out his map and pointed.

"We are here, at this vehicle track. We should have stopped back at that big bend a few hundred paces back."

"I don't think so," CUO Roach replied. "I think we are only at this point."

Cpl Hankin did not agree. "That's this vehicle track just here and there is the railway embankment," he said, pointing as he did. "Look, you can even see the culvert where this creek goes under the railway."

Jane hadn't noticed the culvert but now that it was pointed out to her she wondered how she could have missed it. It was a very obvious black semi-circle, the bottom half hidden by the ground where the creek bed curved first left and then right on the other side of the parked motorcycle. The sound of boots crunching on sand made her glance back and she saw it was Sgt Lepson. Curling her lip with distaste she looked away from him. Her eyes met Chloe's. Chloe also curled her lips in contempt and gave a wry grin then focused her gaze down the creek.

Just as Sgt Lepson reached CUO Roach the roar of approaching motorcycles sounded loudly. The sound was coming from the right and echoing in the low hills.

More motorbikes, Jane thought. *What are they doing here? What's going on? Have they got anything to do with our exercise?*

Into view came two motorcycles. They were ridden by men dressed as bikies. The bikes were brought to a stop and were switched off. The two men got off and hauled the bikes up onto their stands. Jane now saw that one of the bikies was a big hulking man wearing full leathers and knee length boots. The other was a thin man who wore a sleeveless leather jacket over a denim shirt. The two men took off their helmets and looked around. As they did Jane got a good look at the back of their jackets and saw that they had a horned helmet embroidered on it along with a crossed sword and axe. The words ATTILA'S AXEMEN were emblazoned above the image.

Real bikies, Jane decided. *I thought they had been outlawed.*

Feeling just a little bit unsure and scared Jane pressed herself further back into her niche in the rocky outcrop. As she did she heard the big man say, "OK Peewee, where's this bloke I have to meet?"

As the man called Peewee opened his mouth to reply there was a sudden burst of gunfire.

Before Jane's astonished gaze both bikies fell down, obviously hit by bullets. Then the big man sprang up and began running up the creek bed. Jane could only gape in disbelief and growing horror. She saw the thin man, Peewee, roll over in apparent agony and then back again. He then struggled to his hands and knees as the big man dashed across the vehicle track. As he did three men, also bikies, sprang up from behind rocks and bushes down near the railway embankment. They began shooting at the man running away. He was hit again, obviously in the back of his right leg. He almost fell but then continued running, limping painfully. Bullets snapped and cracked past Jane and she flinched and pressed herself against the rocks, still frozen by disbelief. It was a bullet striking a rock near her and screeching off as a ricochet that jerked her mind into action.

They are shooting real bullets! This isn't an exercise! her shocked mind thought.

Another bullet struck the rocks near her and she gasped and flinched and crouched even lower. By then the big man was across the road and running up the bed of the creek towards her. He was gasping and labouring hard in the soft sand. But as he passed Chloe he was hit again and fell heavily on his face. He went down so hard that Jane felt sure he had been killed and she almost choked with apprehension. Fear began to well up and she tensed ready to run.

Through eyes now blurred by fright she saw that two of the ambushers were also running towards her. One, a big hulking man with a goatee beard, shouted, "Get Harley Slasher." Then he stopped behind the shaking Peewee, who was still crouched on his hands and knees. With cold deliberation that froze Jane with disbelief and horror he raised the pistol he was carrying and aimed it at the back of Peewee's head.

He's going to shoot him! He won't, surely? her numbed mind cried.

Bang!

The man fired and, to Jane's horror, a red mist of blood sprang out of Peewee's skull. Peewee twitched and flopped down, obviously dead. Jane's mouth hung open in shocked horror.

He killed him! He shot him dead! her mind cried, as it tried to grapple with the awful reality she was witnessing.

But the second bikie, the one nicknamed 'Slasher', now took her attention. He was running fast towards her and he also had a gun in his hand. Slasher was a tall, black-haired man with a pony tail and a hard face. His eyes were fixed on the big man lying on the sand beside Jane.

Oh my God! He's going to kill him, Jane thought. And then the fear hit her as she realised she was also in deadly danger.

Slasher skidded to a halt near the big man's boots and raised his gun to aim it. Jane was appalled and felt impelled to act. Instinctively she knew she could not just let another person be killed while doing nothing to prevent it. Through her mind flashed the notion that the man would stop once he saw how many people were watching.

"No!" she cried.

The moment she called out Jane knew she had done a foolish thing. She saw Slasher turn and look at her, his eyes widening in astonishment. Then he swung the gun to aim it at her. Jane's mind raced but she could not seem to make her muscles move as she was still gripped by disbelief.

He's going to shoot me! Move! Move! she told herself.

In desperation Jane acted. Her right-hand grabbed a handful of stones and sand and she flung it in an underarm throw. The move caught Slasher by surprise, and he stepped back and flung up his left arm to shield himself from the shower of pebbles and grit. But then his face clouded with anger and his eyes blazed and Jane knew she was in deadly danger. She scrabbled to grab a larger stone but, in her heart, sensed she would be too late. Slasher raised the pistol again.

Now Chloe acted. Just as Slasher's pistol came up to point directly at Jane Chloe sprang out and chopped down at Slasher's right wrist with her left-hand. The pistol was knocked from his surprised grasp and as he turned his head to see what was happening Chloe smashed him in the face with a large rock held in her right-hand. There was an audible 'thunk!' and Slasher collapsed. To Jane's astonished mind it looked like a puppet that had had its strings cut. Down he went in a crumpled heap.

Instantly Chloe raised the rock to strike again but Slasher lay still. Chloe glanced to her right down the creek as she stood out in the open. Dropping the rock, she bent down to snatch up the gun. As she did a commotion on Jane's right attracted her gaze. She saw that CUO Roach had shoved the signaller aside and was running away up the creek. Sgt Lepson was also turning to run but he was in CUO Roach's way and the CUO just pushed him. Sgt Lepson tripped on a rock and fell hard on his bum and CUO Roach kept running. Cpl Hankin followed him and then a dazed Sgt Lepson scrambled to his feet and, after casting a terrified glance over his shoulder, bolted as well.

Bloody cowards! Jane thought. Her gaze shifted back to Chloe and she cried, "Thanks!"

Chloe nodded then looked down at the pistol. She touched something on it with her left-hand and then nodded and looked down the creek. Jane also looked. She was appalled to see that the bikie with the goatee beard was staring at Chloe in astonishment. He had been looking down at the dead Peewee but had heard the scuffle and jerked his head around to look. But even as Jane looked, she saw the look of astonishment get replaced by angry determination. The man swung up his pistol.

Horrified Jane cried out, "Chloe, take cover!" but it came out as a strangled croak from her dry and constricted throat.

Chloe had seen her peril. Even as Goatee fired she sprang aside and her own pistol came up.

Bang!

Bang!

Both fired again and Goatee jerked and then looked down at his left arm in astonishment and then jumped sideways. The man again aimed his pistol and Chloe swung hers towards him.

Bang!

Crack!

Jane saw sand and dust fly from near the man's feet. She cried out, "Chloe!" What she wanted to say was 'Aim! Go slower!' but she did not want to interrupt Chloe as she acted. Chloe was now dancing sideways on the soft sand, her pistol still raised. The bikie also ran sideways, firing as he did. Jane heard the snap of a bullet passing close to her head. It struck the creek bank somewhere behind her and she heard cadets cry out in fear. Or maybe it was herself. She was now so focused she wasn't sure. Through a narrow tunnel of blurred vision she glimpsed Chloe spring aside, back into the cover of the rocks on her side of the creek.

There was the sound of scuffling and the thud of running boots and Jane glanced and saw that it was the signaller running away up the creek.

Bang! Bang! Bang!

The bikie, now under cover down the creek, fired twice and the third bikie also fired. Jane heard a sharp cry of pain and swung her head to see the signaller throw up his arms and fall forward on his face in the middle of the creek bed.

Oh my God! He's hit! she thought.

It seemed to be just stunning horror piled on horror but now her mind was accepting the situation and was racing with options.

We must get him to cover, she thought.

"Chloe, cover me while I get the sig," Jane shouted.

Chloe glanced over her shoulder and nodded. "Take care kiddo!" she called. Then she levelled the pistol across her forearm and braced her left-hand against the rocks. After sighting carefully, she squeezed the shot.

"Go!" she shouted.

Jane was filled with admiration. *I couldn't do that,* she thought.

But she was already up and running. She scurried out into the open creek bed and back the ten paces to where the sig lay face down on the sand. To her relief she saw that he was squirming and trying to get up. Reaching down she grabbed the radio harness at the back and lifted.

"Get up! Run!" she cried.

The sig managed to scramble to his feet and with Jane's help got his legs moving. Then she saw Dipkins and McDonald huddled wide-eyed against the bank.

"Take care of him," she yelled at them, pushing the sig towards them.

From behind her she heard Chloe's gun go off again and she flinched but knew she had to get back to her friend. As she turned, she saw Cpl Callan come hurrying around the corner.

"What's going on?" he called.

"Help me!" Jane replied. As she ran back towards Chloe her racing mind calculated that she was safer on the other side of the creek. All those fieldcraft lessons over the last year had given her that much knowledge and she now acted on it. Within twenty seconds she was back crouched under cover opposite Chloe.

Chloe glanced at her and grinned. "Nearly got the bastard," she said.

"You be careful," Jane replied, shaking her head in wonder.

She knew that Chloe did Medieval Martial Arts as a hobby on Tuesday nights and some weekends but had not known she was so adept with an automatic pistol.

Chloe gestured to the big man lying on the sand between them. "Grab this guy and get him under cover," she said. "I'll cover you."

Jane looked at the big man, noting blood on the side of his head and on his back. She nodded. "What about this other bloke?" she asked, pointing to the unconscious Slasher.

"Leave the mongrel," Chloe replied. She then looked back over her shoulder to see who was coming. It was Cpl Callan.

"Callan, help Jane. I'll cover you."

Cpl Callan, eyes wide with shocked amazement, took in the scene and nodded.

Jane turned to him. "I'll grab his left arm. You go this side and we will drag him back around the bend," she said. She found that she was just able to speak despite her rapid heartbeats and gasping breath. But her throat felt dry and raspy and she had to wipe sweaty palms.

Chloe called, "Ready? Go!" She faced back down the creek, pistol ready.

Jane's whole body was now tingling with fear and excitement but she nerved herself to act. After taking a deep breath she sprang out and jumped over the big man then knelt to grasp his sleeves and collar. As she did her whole body seemed to cringe and flinch in anticipation of a bullet hitting her. Without waiting for Cpl Callan she began to haul. To her dismay the wounded man was dreadfully heavy and she had trouble dragging him even a metre.

But then Cpl Callan joined her and grabbed the man's other sleeve and between them they were able to get the inert man moving. Fear added a surge of adrenalin and with the extra strength Jane found they were able to hurry along.

Crack! Wheeeeee!

Jane heard the bullet snap past her and then ricochet off the rocks ahead of her. This was followed by screams of fear and the bang of Chloe's return fire. Jane nearly wet herself and was tempted to let go but some shred of pride and determination made her keep dragging the wounded man along the sandy creek bed. She and Cpl Callan hurried past Dipkins and McDonald and the stunned looking signaller.

As they reached the bend Jane saw three cadets kneeling over another cadet lying on the sand.

Oh no! What's happened here? she wondered.

She kept going for five paces past them until she was sure they were around the bend and then let go of the big man.

"Look after him," she snapped at Cadets Flegel and Arthur who were crouching there looking terrified.

Heart in mouth from dread Jane turned to the group behind her. They included a weeping and near hysterical Chantelle and a sobbing and shaking Cadet Shephard. Cpl Lang was standing flapping his hands and looking distraught.

It was Kim. She had been shot and a glance showed Jane that it was serious. There was a lot of blood on the front of her shirt, low down near the belt. Chantelle, Cpl Lang and Cadet Shephard were with her but not doing much, just flustering. Jane pushed her way in and bent to look. "What's happened?" she asked.

"She's been shot!" Chantelle wailed. "Oh save her! Save her! Do something!"

"I can see that," Jane retorted waspishly. She felt like screaming at them to do something, but she restrained herself. Her gaze took in that it was a stomach wound rather than a chest wound but her knowledge of First Aid was not good enough to let her decide if that was better or not.

Kim was gasping and wide-eyed with terror. "Help me! Help me!" she cried.

For a few seconds Jane felt utterly helpless and could only stare in horror at the dark red blood staining Kim's uniform.

We must do something, she thought. But what?

Frantically she looked around. At first all she saw were terrified cadets crouching under cover or edging back up the creek bed. Then she saw CUO Roach, Sgt Lepson and Cpl Hankin standing behind some trees. CUO Roach was looking very pale and drawn and was talking on his CB radio. Sgt Lepson just stood there looking stunned, blood smearing his lips and jaw. Cpl Hankin was fidgeting and continually glancing up and down the creek.

Jane hurried over to CUO Roach. "Sir, get stretchers organised," she called. But CUO Roach just glanced at her and kept calling on the radio, his eyes also flicking continually to look down the creek. Jane felt suddenly helpless and then frustrated. "CUO Roach, help us!" she cried.

CUO Roach glanced towards her. "We have to get away from here," he cried.

"We can't leave Kim and this man," Jane said, quite shocked at his suggestion but feeling the same fear and understanding the urge to flee.

"We must get away from here," CUO Roach repeated. Then he looked away and began calling on his CB radio again.

Jane trembled with emotion and clenched her fists as the fear and anxiety shook her. "Sgt Lepson, can you organise a stretcher party?" she queried, her desperation adding a sharp edge to her voice.

But Sgt Lepson just stared at her, his mouth working but no words coming out.

Useless mongrel! Jane thought.

She was so shocked that for several seconds she could not think straight. Disgusted she shook her head and then had to control her own urge to run. But then she saw the medic from HQ huddled behind a tree.

"Rachel! Get over here with that First Aid Kit," Jane snapped, her fear and rising anger making her voice even sharper.

The medic nodded and scuttled out from cover. Reluctantly she knelt and began to examine Kim. Jane was about to help her unbutton Kim's shirt but at that moment she remembered a bit of advice she had overheard Major Wickham give to the NCOs once. 'If you are in charge do not do the First Aid. Do not touch the patient. The moment you have skin on skin contact your emotions become more involved and you find it harder to make the right decisions. You have to stay in command of yourself to stay in control of the situation.'

But I'm not in charge, Jane thought. *I'm only a cadet and CUO Roach and Sgt Lepson are here, and all these corporals and lance corporals.*

But she found the cadets and corporals were all looking at her. Still in stunned disbelief and near shock she shook her head and then said, "Cpl Lang, find the stretcher and get Kim onto it. Cpl Callan, make another stretcher for this wounded man."

At that moment Jane heard yelling back down the creek. *Chloe might be in trouble,* she thought.

"Get the stretchers ready. I'm going to help Chloe."

Determined to be with her friend Jane hurried back to the bend and glanced around. She met Dipkins, McDonald and the signaller crawling along beside the bank towards her. She stopped the signaller.

"Are you OK? Where were you hit?"

Travis shook his head and looked hurt. "I wasn't!" he explained. "The bullet hit the radio and the radio hit me in the back of the head when I fell over. It knocked me out."

Jane nodded with relief. "You are lucky then. OK, you lot get around the corner and then keep watch back down the creek," she snapped.

They nodded and she scurried past them. As she did, she saw that Slasher was moving, shaking his head and groaning. Further down the creek she could just see the shiny motorcycle but no sign of the man with the goatee. Chloe was still crouched under cover with her pistol ready, looking down towards where she thought the bikies were.

"Chloe, be careful!" Jane called, her heart in her mouth.

Chloe nodded but then yelled down the creek. "No! You go away."

Jane scuttled across to crouch just opposite her, glancing fearfully at Slasher as she did.

"What's going on?" she asked.

"That man with the goatee beard wants us to give him the wounded man. Harley, he called him. I said no."

From down the creek Goatee called again. "If you give me Harley, we will leave you alone. Nobody else will get hurt."

"No!" Chloe shouted. "Go away."

"You do as I say, or you will regret it," Goatee called back. "Even if we don't get you now, we will hunt you down in the future. Now give me Harley."

The threat absolutely chilled Jane and she was sorely tempted to tell Chloe to agree. But Chloe was defiant. "No," she replied.

"There are thirty of us. You can't get all of us."

At that moment Slasher groaned. Jane flinched and looked at him. Slasher sat up and shook his head and then held it. There was blood on his forehead and a livid bruise where Chloe had hit him. Chloe looked at him.

"Lie down and stay there," she ordered.

Slasher glared back at her and then shook his head again. "Or what? You haven't got the guts to shoot me," he snarled.

Chloe pointed the pistol at him. "Come near me and I will," she said, but her voice had a tremble in it.

Slasher stood up and Jane held her breath, dread swamping her emotions.

Oh Chloe don't shoot! she thought, fearing for her friend.

Chloe was shaking now but still held the gun pointing straight at Slasher. "Sit down!" she cried.

"Get stuffed! You'll pay for hurting me, you bitch!" Slasher snarled, rubbing at his bruised and bleeding face. He then turned and began walking back down the creek, staggering slightly as though still half dazed.

Chloe kept her pistol aimed at him. "Stop!" she shrieked. "Stop or I will shoot!"

Jane had her heart in her mouth now from apprehension. "Chloe, don't shoot," she cried. "You will end up in jail."

"I'll claim self-defence," Chloe retorted.

For the first time Jane almost smiled. She snorted and gave a sardonic grin. "Be a bit hard to explain if you shoot him in the back," she said.

Chloe was shaking now, the pistol unsteady in her hands. Her face suddenly crumpled and she looked like she was about to cry. She gave a little sob and then lowered the pistol.

"You are right," she agreed.

So the two friends watched Slasher walk back past the parked motorcycles. To Jane's dismay she saw him stop at the shiny motorcycle and reach into a saddle bag and pull out what looked like a sawn-off shotgun. Then he vanished into the creek line and there was silence. Chloe changed the pistol to her other hand and wiped her face. Jane saw that she was shivering with reaction. Chloe gestured back along the creek.

"What happened back there? How badly hurt is that man?"

That jolted Jane. She shrugged. "I don't know. I didn't get time to examine his wounds. But Kim has been shot."

"Kim! How? Where?"

Jane pointed to her stomach. "Here. I think she just got hit by a stray bullet."

"What about the signaller, Travis?"

Again Jane shook her head. "He's OK. The radio bumped his head and stunned him. We just dragged him to safety. I told Dipkins and McDonald to look after him."

Chloe made a face. "Then he is in trouble!" she said.

This time Jane did smile. She was now trembling and breaking into little fits of shivering as the shock hit her but her mind was clearing as she accepted the reality of the situation.

"I had better check. Let's go."

Chloe nodded but then jerked back to aim the pistol down the creek.

Jane had heard noises too and now saw that the man with the goatee had run out to one of the motorcycles and had jumped astride it. Chloe aimed but did not fire.

"Too far!" she muttered.

Goatee pulled the motorcycle off its stand and kicked the engine into life. A moment later he went roaring up the slope and out of sight. Jane felt her stomach churn with apprehension.

"I think he is going to get more bikies," she said, remembering the groups she had seen riding past.

Chloe nodded. "I agree. It's time we got out of here. Let's go."

Chapter 19

FEAR

Sgt Lepson stood watching CUO Roach as the CUO called on his hand-held radio, but his mind did not seem to be functioning. Through it kept flashing pictures of the man shooting the thin man in the back of the head. Terrifying images of the blood misting and of the thin man flopping down dead seemed to fill his mind. He was scared, and he knew it. His body felt driven by the urge to run and he kept glancing both ways along the creek. Only a shred of pride and sense of duty held him there, hoping the CUO would solve the problem and keep him safe.

As though in a daze he watched Jane and Cpl Callan drag the wounded bikie back and then tell people to make stretchers. A tiny niggle of guilt bothered him at that as he knew that he should be doing those sorts of things. But he could not seem to make his body or mouth function. All he could do was stare and shake.

I must get away from here, he thought, the fear clouding his every thought.

CUO Roach tried again to contact someone. He was almost shouting by this time and looked frightened and pale. "I can't get anyone!" he cried, his voice quavering with fear.

"We should go," Sgt Lepson suggested. Once again he glanced down the creek, terrified of seeing one of the bikies appear.

But it was Jane and Chloe who came around the corner. Sgt Lepson saw Chloe stop and look around then purse her lips and frown. Cadet Shephard called loudly to her, "Chloe, what is going on? What will we do?"

Chloe sucked in a deep breath and then bellowed, "Silence! Shut up all you! Be quiet and stay still!" To Sgt Lepson's surprise the frightened cadets did as they were told.

Turning to Cpl Callan Chloe said, "Cpl Callan, get up on the top of the bank just there where you can see back down the creek and also up the slope. Call me if you see anyone coming."

Cpl Callan nodded and got up and began to climb the steep bank.

Chloe said something to Jane and then came striding over, a pistol gripped in her right-hand.

"CUO Roach, have you contacted the officers?" she asked.

CUO Roach shook his head and held up the small radio. "It.. it doesn't seem to be working."

Chloe frowned. "Have you had the corporals try theirs?" she said.

CUO Roach looked anxious and then shook his head. "Theirs are working. I can hear my signal when I transmit," he said.

"Shouldn't you be using the army radio to contact HQ?" Chloe queried.

A look of surprise crossed CUO Roach's face and he licked his lips and then nodded. "Er... er... yes. Where's that sig from HQ. Travis! Get over here!"

LCpl Travis got up and hurried over from where he and a group of male cadets were huddled unde the bank. "Sir?"

"Use your radio to call HQ," CUO Roach ordered.

"Sir." LCpl Travis took up his handset and began to call. "Hotel, this is Two Four, over. Hotel, this is Two Four, over."

He tried this several times but there was no answer. Then Jane looked up from where she was helping lift Kim onto the stretcher. "I think the radio is damaged," she called.

"How? What did you do Travis, you bloody idiot!" CUO Roach exploded.

Travis blanched then got angry. "I didn't do anything! It got hit by a bullet."

"Sir!"

LCpl Travis frowned. "Sir?" he queried.

"You call me sir!" CUO Roach shouted. "I don't believe you. Where's this bullet?"

LCpl Travis went to take the radio off but Chloe was faster. She grabbed it and lifted so he could slip his arms out of the shoulder harness. Then she swung the radio around and pointed. Sgt Lepson saw a small round hole punched in the top part of the radio. It was a very neat hole, he noted, with some of the dark green paint chipped off to reveal bare metal around the inside.

Seeing that little hole unleashed some of Sgt Lepson's emotions.

"How did you do that, you bloody fool!" he shouted.

"I was trying to get under cover," LCpl Travis replied defensively.

"You useless idiot! Now how do we contact HQ?" Sgt Lepson screamed, his face close to Travis's.

Chloe stepped forwards. "That will do Sgt Lepson! He couldn't help it. It is good that he isn't wounded," she said.

Sgt Lepson was now quivering with emotion. "Stay out of this you dumb bitch! I'm the sergeant!" he screamed at her.

"Then act like it!" Chloe retorted. "Go and get that improvised stretcher organised and get that wounded man onto it."

For a moment rage boiled in Sgt Lepson and he clenched his fists, driven by a fierce desire to smash her face in. But something in her icy stare held him and he swallowed and just glared at her. CUO Roach didn't help by saying, "Yes Sgt Lepson, let's get organised and get out of here. Go and get the wounded on stretchers."

Sgt Lepson turned his gaze on CUO Roach. "We should just get out of here," he cried. "We are wasting time. We need to get away before those men come."

CUO Roach cast a nervous glance down the creek and then looked at Chloe. "What's happening down the creek?" he queried.

Chloe gave him a hard look and then pointed. "There are two bikies there and two motorbikes. The big guy with the goatee beard has ridden off. I presume he has gone to get reinforcements."

"Reinforcements?"

"They are bikies. They go around in gangs. We saw a dozen or more up on the highway earlier," Chloe replied.

"How long will they be?" CUO Roach asked, his voice quavering.

Chloe gave him another appraising look. "How would I know? If they are at Mingela, then maybe twenty minutes to half an hour."

CUO Roach looked alarmed and glanced at his watch. Sgt Lepson also experienced a surge of alarm and cried, "Then we need to get out of here fast."

CUO Roach nodded. "You are right. We can't move these people. We will have to leave them and go and get help," he said.

Chloe shook her head. "We can't! Those bikies will just come and kill this man," she said.

"I don't care! I don't know who he is," CUO Roach replied. "My job is to keep the platoon safe. I say we get moving."

Chloe shook her head and her face went hard. "We can't leave Kim and I won't let this other guy get murdered. You might be able to sleep knowing you let a man die but I don't want his death on my conscience. I say we take them with us."

"It will be quicker to go and get the officers," CUO Roach countered.

Sgt Lepson saw that Jane had been listening. She now left the group crouching or kneeling around Kim and came over. "Kim is seriously wounded. She needs urgent medical help," she said. "We must get her up to where she can be put in a vehicle fast."

"Stay out of this Carson!" CUO Roach shouted. "I say we go."

Chloe gave him a look of contempt. "What about Sgt Grey and his group? We need to warn them too. They are due to walk along that vehicle track soon and they will walk right into those murdering mongrels."

"They have an officer with them. They will be alright," CUO Roach replied.

"And a Safety Vehicle. We could go that way to them," Chloe said.

An argument began. Jane turned to Sgt Lepson. "Sgt Lepson, get the stretcher parties organised please."

By now Sgt Lepson was quivering with fear. He kept glancing at the wounded and down the creek, his heart hammering fast and his vision focused down to a narrow tunnel. He knew he should tell Jane to stop giving orders, but he was just glad someone was. Like a zombie he walked over to the group clustered around Kim. His gaze took in the dark red staining on her lower body and he blanched. The fear hit him with redoubled force. Then his eyes met Kim's.

"Help me Lepson!" she cried, her voice gasping with pain. "Help me! Do something, you useless prick!"

"I... I... I'll go and get help," Sgt Lepson croaked.

"You owe me," Kim cried. "You ... oh! Oh!... Oh help!"

Sgt Lepson again glanced at the blood seeping from the wound and could not take it anymore. He turned and stumbled away. As he re-joined CUO Roach he heard him say, "Well I can't get them on the radio so I am going to get help."

Chloe still objected. "You can send a couple of runners. You are the platoon commander. You don't leave your platoon."

CUO Roach hesitated and Sgt Lepson saw the fear and indecision on his face.

"Who?" he muttered.

"A corporal and one other," Chloe suggested.

At that Cpl Hankin stepped forward. "I'll go," he volunteered.

You bloody weakling! Sgt Lepson thought.

He was tempted to offer to go himself but knew that would look bad. He knew he was supposed to take control, to make things happen.

CUO Roach nodded. "OK. Who else?"

Chloe pointed to LCpl Travis. "The sig. We need everyone else to carry stretchers."

Sgt Lepson saw LCpl Travis nod and look relieved. He bent to pick up the army radio, but Chloe stopped him.

"Leave that," she said.

"But I signed for it. I'll get into trouble if I lose it," LCpl Travis answered.

"Don't be bloody ridiculous!" Chloe snapped. "It doesn't work. Your duty is to run and go fast with the message, not slow yourself down with the weight of a useless radio set. Just leave it and we will collect it later. Get going!"

"Which way?" Cpl Hankin queried.

Chloe gave him a look of contempt. She pointed up the slope to her left. "Up there! There is a radio relay station from HQ on top of that hill. They are closest," she said.

"How do you know that?" Cpl Hankin challenged.

Chloe gave him another withering look. "Because it was in the exercise orders," she replied coldly.

Sgt Lepson saw embarrassed resentment on Cpl Hankin's face. He felt resentment himself at her attitude but also a niggling shame at not having remembered the radio relay station.

Cpl Hankin looked doubtful. "Where?" he queried.

Chloe held the pistol up and glanced at it, then clicked on the safety catch before sliding it into her right trouser pocket. She then reached down into her left map pocket and pulled out the map photocopy they had all been given. She opened the map and smoothed it out, then pointed.

"Here, on top of Railway Hill, this big hill inside the curve of the Old Railway." she said.

CUO Roach cast a nervous glance down the creek and then turned. "I still say we should all go."

"We can't leave the wounded," Chloe insisted.

Resentment showed on CUO Roach's face. "Don't you start telling me what to do! I am the CUO. You are just a cadet. I am the platoon commander and I say we all go. We will get help. Let's go."

"You can't!" Chloe cried.

"Don't you tell me what to do!" CUO Roach blustered. He was now white-faced and trembling, perspiration beading his face. "I'm going."

With that he turned and began walking away up the creek. Sgt Lepson immediately followed and so did several others.

Chloe tried to block him. "You bloody cowards!" she cried. "Stay and do your duty. Lepson, you are a sergeant. You can't just run out on your cadets!"

"Get out of my way! The platoon commander said we are going so I am going," Sgt Lepson yelled back, pushing her aside.

But her words stung and added to his boiling emotions. Deep down he knew he was doing the wrong thing and that knowledge added a spur to his torn emotions. Wanting to get away from the voice making the accusations he broke into a run.

Behind him he heard Chloe's voice. It was like whiplash and full of scorn and anger. "Stay you cadets! Sit down and wait! You can't leave your friends. We need you to help carry the stretchers. Stay!"

Sgt Lepson fled. He was conscious that some cadets were moving with him but he didn't look back to see how many until he rounded the next bend in the creek. When he did glance back he saw that Cpl Hankin and Cadet Flegel were following him. With some surprise he noted that LCpl Travis had not joined them. He had obviously obeyed Chloe and that annoyed him more.

Bitch! I'll make sure she gets chucked out, he vowed.

CUO Roach was going very fast, almost running and Sgt Lepson had to force himself to match this. Several times the CUO got so far ahead he went out of sight around bends in the creek and that got Sgt Lepson very anxious as he did not want to get left behind or lost. The other two followed behind, audibly gasping as they found it hard to keep up.

Five minutes later Sgt Lepson caught up with CUO Roach. The CUO had stopped at a creek junction and was looking both frightened and puzzled.

"Which way?" he cried.

Sgt Lepson tried to remember. It appalled him that the platoon commander did not know.

He's the CUO. He led us here! he thought resentfully.

But the creek to the right looked vaguely familiar and rather than stay and waste more time he pointed up it. CUO Roach at once looked relieved and nodded then turned and led the way along it.

Once again CUO Roach set a cracking pace so that Sgt Lepson and the others were soon gasping for breath. And it was hard going. The creek bed was very rocky and they had to climb up over big rocks and clamber over jumbled piles of loose stones. Sgt Lepson found his vision blurring from the effort and perspiration trickling down into his eyes made it even worse. He found he was gasping for breath and his heart hammering furiously. And he was also beginning to doubt that they were in the right creek.

I don't remember any of this, he thought.

Finding CUO Roach panting to recover his breath at the bottom of a steep section of exposed bedrock confirmed this. Sgt Lepson looked at it and shook his head.

"We have gone up the wrong creek," he said.

"You stupid idiot! You said it was this creek!" CUO Roach cried angrily.

Sgt Lepson felt immediate anger and resentment. "You are the CUO! You've got the map and the compass," he retorted.

Cpl Hankin and Flegel joined them, their chests heaving with exertion. They both looked scared. Cpl Hankin said, "Where are we?"

CUO Roach gave him a reproachful look but then shook his head. With obvious reluctance he took out his map and they crowded around to study it. Finally, CUO Roach put his finger on the creek near the Number One Bottom Mill.

"We are here," he said. "We are in the right creek."

"No, we aren't!" Sgt Lepson disagreed.

"We are!" CUO Roach shouted.

Cpl Hankin looked anxiously around. "Don't yell sir," he suggested.

"Don't tell me what to do!" CUO Roach screamed. "This is the right creek." With that he stood up and continued along it, scaling the bare rock with the speed of a startled baboon. Sgt Lepson stared after him, his mind a whirl of indecision.

I'm sure this is the wrong creek, he thought.

But Cpl Hankin and Flegel had both started climbing and he did not want to be left on his own. Reluctantly he started after them.

A few minutes later they came to another junction. Both creeks were obviously much smaller. CUO Roach started up the right-hand creek. Sgt Lepson stopped to get his breath and shook his head.

"I think we should go left," he said.

"I'm the CUO and I'm going right," CUO Roach replied. He continued on. Even more reluctantly Sgt Lepson followed the others.

And he was right. After another five minutes' walk the creek had become a shallow gully in a dip between rock piles on top of a wide, bare ridge. Out in the distance Sgt Lepson could see more stony hill tops and rocky ridges, and when he turned around he could see out across a wide valley full of trees.

The railway is down there somewhere, he thought.

CUO Roach came to a standstill and looked sheepish. "You must have been right," he admitted. "We will have to go back."

"Why don't we just walk across country on a compass bearing," Sgt Lepson suggested.

"It might be hard work going across the grain of the country," CUO Roach suggested.

"But it will get us to the highway and the camp is just on the other side of that," Sgt Lepson pointed out. Frequent mental images of the thin man flopping down dead made the camp the place he most wanted to be!

CUO Roach looked surly and resentful but now nodded. "OK," he said. He pulled out his compass and held it in the palm of his hand and then turned himself around. Pointing along the compass he said, "That way."

Sgt Lepson felt a niggling doubt but wasn't sure why. But still driven by fear and the urgent desire to get to the camp and safety he did not argue. He began walking behind the others as they made their way up a gentle slope. But it was still awkward for them to move cross-country because, while the grass was short, it concealed hundreds of football sized rocks. That meant taking care and several times Sgt Lepson stumbled or nearly tripped.

As they plodded up to a skyline Sgt Lepson still experienced a nagging feeling that they were not going the right way. While continually looking down to see where he was putting his boots he tried to reason the navigation out.

The sun is on the left side of my face and it comes up in the east so we must be going south, he decided. That cheered him up, knowing that the highway was to the south.

But then they came out on a wide ridge top with two-wheel ruts running up it and a much better view of the surrounding country his doubts returned. CUO Roach had stopped on the vehicle track and taken out his map and was looking puzzled.

"What's the problem?" Sgt Lepson asked.

"I am trying to find this vehicle track on the map," CUO Roach replied.

Sgt Lepson looked around. To his left was higher ground with more low rocky rises and ahead of them was a whole set of parallel rocky ridges barring their path. Out to his right the ground dropped away to the wide valley with a range of rugged mountains on the other side. Then he glimpsed the New Railway.

"Is that the railway I can see?" he queried.

"Yes," Cpl Hankin agreed.

"Shouldn't it be on our left?" Sgt Lepson asked.

CUO Roach turned his map around. "No. We are inside a great big loop. It is on both sides," he said.

Sgt Lepson studied the map. "But the bit on our right should be uphill," he pointed out. Then he pointed to the forested valley and to a very obvious conical hill in the middle of it. "What hill is that?"

Cpl Hankin pointed to the map. "Mount Square Post," he suggested.

Then it hit Sgt Lepson and he looked around. "We are facing north," he said, half accusingly.

"We are not! I was going south," CUO Roach insisted.

"Show me," Sgt Lepson asked.

Reluctantly CUO Roach held out the compass. To Sgt Lepson's horror he saw that the compass was indeed facing north. "You've been going north, you stupid dick!" he snarled, fear again welling up to stir his emotions.

"I have not!" CUO Roach snapped, but with clear doubt in his face. Cpl Hankin then also took out his compass and lined it up. "Yes, you have been," he said.

Then another idea hit Sgt Lepson. He glanced at his watch and was amazed to see that it was 1230.

It is afternoon, he realised with a shock. *So the sun should be on the right if we are going south.*

As the realization that they had been going the wrong way sank in the fear returned with redoubled force.

"You've got us lost, you bloody fool!" he cried.

Chapter 20

CHLOE TAKES COMMAND

Chloe stood in the middle of the creek bed, clenched fists on hips. "Stay you cadets! Sit down and wait! You can't leave your friends. We need you to help carry the stretchers. Stay!"

Stevenson went to move past her, but she reached out and grabbed his arm. "Stop! Stay and help us!" Chloe said very firmly. Stevenson did, casting nervous glances up and down the creek as he did.

Watching her Jane was assailed by a host of emotions: admiration, anxiety and straight out fear being the main ones. She was gripped by a strong urge to run herself but out of loyalty stood her ground. Around her the cadets behaved in a variety of ways. Some sat or stood where they were. Others stood up and moved a few paces and then stopped. A couple began running but then obeyed and a few ran after CUO Roach. All looked scared or at least apprehensive.

Jane was gripped by apprehension. *If they all run away we won't have enough to lift the stretchers,* she worried.

Anxiously she looked around, noting that Cpl Lang was holding Cadet Arthur by the sleeve and that Cadet Leece was blocking Cadet Kane from running. With eyes that seemed blurred by emotion Jane noted that in fact only four people were running up the creek bed: CUO Roach, Sgt Lepson, Cpl Hankin and Cadet Flegel.

Bloody cowards! she thought, echoing Chloe's scathing comment of a few seconds before.

With her lip now curling in contempt Jane watched the four vanish from view around the bend in the creek. Then she shook her head, wondering how a Cadet Under-Officer and a sergeant could just abandon their platoon and run.

Where's their pride? she wondered.

Jane was aware that fear was the trigger to the behaviour, and she knew she was very scared herself but by conscious effort she held herself in check and looked back at Chloe.

Chloe shook her head with evident disgust as she watched the four flee. As they vanished from view, she and turned to face the platoon. "OK Jane, let's get this circus on the road," she said.

"Where are we going?" Jane asked.

Chloe pointed north. "I reckon Captain Hamilton and his Safety Vehicle are our best bet. They are closest. That will save Sgt Grey's team at the same time," Chloe answered.

Jane liked that idea. "I agree. And they will have radios that work," she replied. "OK, who does what?"

"You go scout and navigate. Cpl Lang, get your section to lift this bloke onto that improvised stretcher and you carry him. Cpl Callan, your section is to carry Kim, and I will be rear-guard," she said.

A frightened looking McDonald put his hand up. "What do I do?" he asked, his voice cracking with anxiety.

Chloe glanced at him and then pointed. "You join Cpl Callan's section. Cadet Dipkins, you join Cpl Lang's section. OK, organise six people to each stretcher and get ready to lift."

They began to move. Jane felt a surge of hope and relief. She pulled out her map and began to study it as others moved. Chloe walked over to where Harley was being lifted onto the improvised stretcher made from two broom handles and four sets of webbing clipped together. "Where is this guy hit?" she asked.

Jane had vaguely wondered the same thing and also looked down at the man. The first obvious wound was a big gash on the side of his head, the dried blood matting his hair. A small trickle of blood was still seeping down onto his neck and into his leather jacket. "Put a bandage on that," she ordered. Then she studied his body but couldn't see any other obvious wound.

Cpl Callan now knelt at the back of that stretcher. He pointed. "He's been hit in the back, down here near his kidneys and also in the right thigh," he said.

Chloe nodded. "They may not be all that serious," she commented. "They aren't bleeding much."

The medic, who was crouching nearby answered that. "But there might be serious internal bleeding. Can we get moving please?"

Chloe nodded. "Yes. Sig, you go with Jane and act as runner. Medic, bandage his head and then you go between the two stretchers. Come on people! Get in position. We have to get going!" she snapped.

Cadets scurried to obey, all obviously wanting to be gone from there. Chloe walked over and looked down at Kim.

"Kim, how do you feel?"

Jane saw that Kim looked deathly pale and was shaking. "It doesn't hurt," she replied, her voice quavering. "But it's bad isn't it?"

Chloe nodded. "Might be," she replied.

Jane was glad it wasn't her having to answer as she was not sure what she would have said. *It looks very serious to me,* she thought, the apprehension welling up again to almost choke her.

Kim obviously thought so too as she cried out. "I'm scared. I don't want to die! Please get me to a doctor! Save me Chloe, save me!"

Chloe bent down and gripped her shaking left-hand. "I will. Now just hang in there. OK, Cpl Lang, get the stretcher up and get moving. Your section go first. Come on, get them up and moving!"

Cpl Lang looked nervously around and licked his lips and then gave the orders to "Hands on. Prepare to lift. Lift!"

As the stretcher was lifted up Jane gave a silent thanks for all those lessons Major Wickham had insisted they do on casualty evacuation.

Now is the pay-off, she told herself. She turned and began leading the way up the creek bed.

Chloe called after her, "Jane, what's your plan?"

Jane pointed along the creek bed to the west. "Up the creek for a hundred metres or so then turn right and go up the first side gully we come to and try to find some dead ground to move cross country in," she said.

Chloe glanced at her own map and nodded. "Seems a good plan to me," she agreed. She now took the pistol out of her pocket and checked it.

Seeing the gun sent a shiver through Jane but it also reassured her. Then a worrying thought came to her.

"How many rounds do you have left?" she asked.

Chloe glanced again at the pistol. "I'm not sure. This is a Glock 17 so it should have had seventeen to start with and I have only fired five or six and that Slasher mongrel only fired a couple so I should have at least nine or ten. When we are safely out of here, I will take out the magazine and count them."

Cadet Leece called to her. "What type did you say it was?"

"A Glock Seventeen," Chloe answered. "It is a standard police issue weapon from the look of it. There are Glock Nineteens too."

"How would these bikies have a police gun?" Cadet Arthur asked. "Are they police?"

Chloe gave him a surprised look. "No. These guys are criminals from an Outlaw Motorcycle Gang. This pistol is either stolen or illegal."

"How do you know they are criminals from a gang?" Arthur persisted.

A look of exasperation crossed Chloe's face. "Because of the emblems on the backs of their jackets. Now stop talking and let's get moving." With that Chloe turned to the rear group and growled, "Come on Cpl Callan! Get that stretcher up and moving!"

Cpl Callan gave the orders, but Jane noticed that they had much more trouble. Harley was a big man and obviously weighed a lot more than Kim. Worse still the broom handles weren't very long so his head and lower legs hung down awkwardly.

We have the casualties on the wrong stretchers, she decided.

But now was not the time to try to fix it, she knew. After another anxious glance behind to check that the others were following, and that Chloe was covering the rear, Jane resumed walking.

Within a minute it was obvious that it was going to be a real challenge. After only about 25 paces the cadets carrying the stretchers were puffing and obviously struggling. After 50 Cadet Arthur cried out that he couldn't keep going. The first stretcher was lowered and that meant the second had to be put down as well. Chloe had remained at the bend in the creek looking down it and now turned to look and Jane saw her bite her lip.

This is not going to be easy, she realised.

Her map indicated that it was about a kilometre to Captain Hamilton's vehicle and she again quickly tried to calculate the 'time and space' to determine if she had chosen the best alternative. For a few seconds she wondered if going the other way up onto the Old Railway might not be better. But a glance at the ground and at the map showed her that the cover on that side of the creek was very poor. For hundreds of metres it was a gentle, almost open slope and she felt sure that the bikies would be able to see them.

We need to keep out of sight of them and where they can't just trap us, she worried.

Cpl Lang had his stretcher moving again so Jane kept going along the creek. But the creek bed was already becoming rougher and she knew from the journey down it that the idea of following it all the way up to the Number 1 Bottom Mill and then along the Old Railway would be a very difficult thing to do.

Dread was now clutching at her throat so firmly that she found she was sucking in great big breaths of air and realised she was shaking and that her throat was really dry. When she glanced at her map, she had trouble focusing because her hands were trembling so much. Close behind her Travis was puffing, and a glance at him showed her that he was also perspiring and his chest was heaving as though he had run a race.

After another 25 paces Cpl Lang had the stretcher lowered again.

He should rotate them, Jane thought.

It was something they had been taught to do but obviously Cpl Lang was not remembering that when under stress. She turned to him. "Cpl Lang, have everyone rotate one position each time you stop," she said. She tried to make it sound like a helpful suggestion as she did not want to get his back up.

To her relief Cpl Lang accepted the idea without arguing and directed his team to all move one place clockwise. While they did Jane looked back and saw that Cpl Callan's team with Harley were having an even harder time but Cpl Callan at least was using the medic as an extra person and was not only rotating the places but was swapping one person each time. Chloe still crouched behind some rocks a hundred paces back, alternately watching them and looking down the creek.

The move continued, the cadets struggling in the soft sand. They all now looked hot and were puffing hard, but Jane noted that their initial panic had at least subsided. She continued on, her gaze continually searching for any sign of people ahead or on either side. Ahead she could see the next big bend and the steeper hills.

That big hill on the left front is Railway Hill, she decided. She scanned it intently but could see no sign of the Radio Relay Station that was supposed to be there. That bothered her. *Are they there or not?* she wondered. *And if they are, how come we can't get radio communications with them*

It took the platoon nearly 10 minutes to carry the stretchers 200 paces to the next big bend. By then the going had changed as the creek bed became narrower and rockier. The cadets carrying had to watch carefully where they put their boots and there were frequent slips and stumbles. Only the fact that each stretcher had six people carrying it prevented the casualties being dropped on the rocks and allowed them to progress at all.

LCpl Travis stopped and wiped sweat from his face and then took out his water bottle. "Bloody hell, this is hard going," he muttered.

That annoyed Jane. "You go and change places with Cadet Arthur for a while," she ordered.

LCpl Travis looked resentful, but Cpl Lang heard her and nodded. "Yeah Travis, get here and help!" he snarled.

LCpl Travis looked mutinous for a moment and Jane feared he might refuse or even just walk off, but he had a drink and replaced his water bottle and then did as he was told. Seeing that made Jane realise how dry her own mouth was and she had a drink from her right water bottle. As she screwed the cap back on afterwards, she shook it and was concerned that it felt almost empty.

The slow movement continued; each stretcher only being carried 20 to 25 paces each time before being lowered. Seeing how hard it was Jane went back and took Cadet Shephard's place for a hundred paces the effort causing her to break into a real sweat. It was so slow and so hard that muttering was beginning among the cadets.

"We should just leave the stretchers and go and get help," Cadet Dipkins grumbled.

Jane was stung because she knew she was also very scared and wanted to be gone. "CUO Roach has gone to get help," she replied. "You just help carry the stretcher."

She didn't know why she made any effort to defend the CUO's reputation but felt that anything that encouraged the platoon at that moment was helpful.

When ordered Jane lifted the stretcher, her slippery hands having trouble keeping a safe grip. As she staggered along, she kept looking up to the right. She noted that they were almost past a small rocky rise and after another 25 paces spotted what she was looking for, a gully leading off to the right.

"Go up that," she said.

Cpl Lang looked at the gully and frowned. "Why? That looks bloody steep," he objected.

"Because we need to go north to get to the safety vehicle," Jane replied. "It is just over this rise."

Cpl Lang looked doubtful but reluctantly agreed and the stretcher party swung right and made their way over the rocky creek bed to the narrow, rocky side gully. The first bit was an almost vertical lift of about a metre and took a real effort. Jane led and helped lift and heave, noting that Kim was whimpering and crying as they did. Just seeing Kim's terrified and pale face made Jane feel desperate.

We must get to a doctor and fast, Jane told herself. She tried to push out of her mind thoughts about dying and the fear it must be inducing in Kim.

By the time the first stretcher had been lifted up into the side gully Cpl Callan's stretcher had closed up. "Why are we going up there?" Cpl Callan queried. Jane again explained and then called on Cadet Arthur to take her place.

He also objected. "Why? You've only carried it for a little bit," he objected.

"Because I need to scout up this gully to check the route," Jane snapped. "Now stop whinging and grab hold!"

Still grumbling Cadet Arthur did as he was told and the movement was resumed. Jane studied the narrow, rocky gully and wondered if she had made a mistake but a glance at her map told her this was the best place to turn off, so she began to carefully pick her way upslope, stepping over rocks and pushing long grass aside. Within ten paces she came out from under the shade of the trees growing along the banks of the creek and found herself in blazing sunshine. The air in the gully was stifling and the sun's rays reflected off the sides to make her sweat even more.

This should only be for a bit, she consoled herself. *We should come out into a breeze as we get higher up.*

So she continued on. The gully bent sharply left after another ten paces and then levelled out and became shallower. She saw that it actually did what she hoped; it became just a gentle hollow in between two rocky rises.

Satisfied they could get up the gully Jane turned and made her way back down. She was surprised at how little progress the stretcher parties had made and also at how little of the creek bed she could see through the leaves and branches of the trees. She found Cpl Lang's stretcher party puffing and stumbling just near the bend and Cpl Callan's still struggling up the first steep little section.

Jane at once took Cadet Leece's place. "You have a breather," she said. Tensing her muscles, she took the weight and started walking slowly. Behind her she heard swearing and stumbling and then Chloe's voice, softly encouraging.

Good! Jane thought. *Chloe has caught up.*

She glanced back and noted Chloe scuffing out boot prints in the sand near where they had turned. Jane doubted if that would fool anyone for even a few seconds but conceded it had to be worth the effort.

Anything that makes us safer is a good idea, she told herself.

As the group rounded the bend into the flatter section Jane called softly to Cadet Leece. "Rod, scout up to that crest on the right but don't skyline yourself."

Cadet Leece gave her a thumbs-up and turned to make his way cautiously up the slope to the right. As he got closer to the crest he went to a crouch and then down on his hands and knees before crawling in among the rocks to look over the crest.

That was good fieldcraft! Jane applauded mentally.

The stretcher was put down and Jane moved to the centre position on the right. As they picked the stretcher up again, she muttered, "Chantelle, use both hands."

Chantelle did. She was looking very strained and was perspiring so much that drips of sweat were dripping off her nose and chin. Worse still Kim was looking very stressed and pale. Jane began to worry about the effects of shock.

Or is it from blood loss from internal bleeding? she worried.

That made her glance at the medic who was plodding along between the stretchers. "You can help carry too," she said to her. "Here, take Chantelle's place.

The medic scowled but did as she was told. Jane stayed with the stretcher until they were a hundred paces up the shallow hollow and nearing the crest of the saddle on the north side. Behind them Cpl Callan's stretcher followed and then Chloe. She was again crouched under cover facing the rear.

As she looked back Jane lifted her gaze and noted that she had been right. Now that they were up out of the main creek and on the slopes, she was able to see clearly the ground on the south side of the creek. It was exactly as she had thought: gentle but very open. In a single glance she was able to check that there was no cover for several hundred metres; all the way from the dirt road to the Old Railway. She could not see the dirt road for the treetops but the line of the Old Railway was just visible.

We need to stop and do a recce, she decided. So next time Cpl Lang ordered them to lower the stretcher she said, "Wait here while I do a bit of scouting."

What was nagging at her now was the knowledge that Sgt Grey's squad were due to walk along the dirt road towards where the murder had happened any time after 1100hrs. But the actual timings had not been given in orders. Jane glanced at her watch and got a shock.

1230! That's an hour since this all started, she noted with amazement. *God, I hope they haven't started yet!*

Quickly she strode up the long gentle slope, avoiding rocks in the short grass with practised ease. Like Cadet Leece she went to a crouch as she approached the crest and then got down to her hands and knees. That hurt as the ground was covered with small stones and sharp little rocks. Worse still the grass was waist high spear grass and the sharp little seeds quickly embedded themselves in her shirt as well as her trousers. And it was all hot. But Jane ignored the pain and irritation and made her way up behind some larger rocks on the very crest of the rise on her right.

I might get a view down to the dirt road and New Railway from there, she reasoned.

And she did. As she wriggled up among the rocks next to Cadet Leece she saw that she had a really good view out to the north and the east. Down to her right about 200 metres away she could just see where the dirt road crossed the main creek.

And what she saw chilled her with stunned concern.

Stopped just on the other side of the crossing was Captain Hamilton's Land Rover and standing beside it with his hands above his head was Captain Hamilton. Facing him and pointing guns at him were Slasher and the third bikie.

Oh no! We are too late! Jane thought.

Chapter 21

URGENT ACTION

J ane stared at the drama down on the dirt road with dismay.

Oh no! she thought as her hopes crumbled.

She had been really depending on Captain Hamilton and that Safety Vehicle and its radios to save them.

I'd better tell Chloe before the others find out, she reasoned.

On the edge of her consciousness was the need to maintain morale and keep the frightened cadets going.

After wriggling back a metre or so she turned to look back down into the hollow for Chloe. But she was not in sight. Cpl Callan's stretcher was just coming around the bend so Jane deduced that Chloe was still covering the gully down near where it joined the main creek. Seeing a couple of faces looking in her direction she waved and then through her mind flitted various options for using the silent field signals they had been taught to summon Chloe.

Cadet Leece helped. He looked at her and said, "What do you want?"

"I want Chloe to come and have a look to plan our next move," Jane replied. She was about to ask him if he would go and get her when he nodded and looked at the group at the first stretcher, then put two fingers of his left-hand on his right shoulder and then made a second signal requesting a person to come to them. He did this by placing his hand flat on top of his hat.

That was the signal for platoon commander to come here, Jane thought, knowing that the two fingers represented the two stars of the army lieutenant's rank badge, a lieutenant being the normal rank of a platoon commander.

She saw several cadets and then Cpl Lang all make the same signal and then pass it back. Cpl Callan received it and then turned and made the same signal back down the gully. To Jane it was a bit of a revelation.

CUO Roach isn't here. Are they signalling to Chloe? Is that what they think she is, the platoon commander?

Jane realised it was certainly the role she had mentally fitted Chloe into herself. The others evidently had as well as Chloe appeared a few seconds later. Cpl Callan spoke to her and pointed up towards Jane. Chloe nodded and then ordered Cadet Kane to act as rearguard sentry before hurrying up the slope.

While she waited for Chloe Jane crawled back into position and studied the situation again. She had to wipe perspiration from her face and squint in the glare but then saw that Capt Hamilton still stood with his hands above his head. Then her ears detected the sound of approaching motorcycles and her heart almost stopped beating with dread.

Oh no! Bikie reinforcements, she thought, her fears increasing as her hopes went down.

Into view along the dirt road from the east appeared two motorcycles. These went down to the creek and stopped near the Land Rover.

Only two? Jane thought, her hopes going up one notch. As the bikes were switched off she heard no other engine noises and her hopes went up another. *That looks like Goatee and another bikie,* she decided, although the distance was several hundred metres and she wasn't sure.

To her concern she realised she was having trouble focusing her vision. Little black dots appeared to dance on a fuzzy screen. With a jolt she realised she was gasping in great gulps of air.

I'm hyperventilating, she thought. *Slow the breathing! Calm down! You don't want to be like those hysterical girls.*

With an effort of will power Jane calmed herself. Then, while her mind was still grappling with the implications of yet another bikie, she looked around to her left to see if she could see Sgt Grey. And there he was! Her heart did another leap and her whole chest seemed to be squeezed by concern. About a kilometre away, walking towards her along the dirt road on the downslope to another large creek were four tiny figures in camouflage uniforms.

"Oh no! Here they come!" she muttered as Chloe crawled beside her.

"What is it?" Chloe queried.

"Sgt Grey's patrol. They are heading this way along the dirt road," Jane replied. She pointed to them and then to the right. "I wanted you to see this. Captain Hamilton has been captured by those bikies. We can't go to the safety vehicle now."

Chloe looked, frowned and nodded. "It looks like he has driven along the road and run into them," she commented.

"Probably investigating all the gunfire?" Cadet Leece suggested.

"Maybe," Chloe agreed.

Jane pointed to Sgt Grey's patrol. "But we must do something to save them. We can't just let them walk into danger!" she cried. The thought was so upsetting she almost choked up and her chest felt tight with apprehension.

Chloe looked and again nodded. "You are right. We must try to save them," she agreed.

"But how? Oh bugger! If only the radios worked," Jane said.

"They might from up here on top of the hill," Chloe replied. She turned to Cadet Leece. "Rod, get Cpl Lang up here with his radio, fast!"

Cadet Leece did not argue. He just slid back out of the rocks and began running down the slope. Jane looked back over her right shoulder to watch. Her eyes scanned what she thought was Railway Hill.

"It should be line-of-sight to the Radio Relay Station on Railway Hill too," she said.

Chloe also looked but neither could see anyone. "Either they are well hidden or that isn't Railway Hill," she replied.

Jane squinted in the glare to study the high, bare hill. It was almost completely devoid of trees, just a few small bushes adorning its rugged grassy slopes.

"It is," she said. "You can see the Old Railway cutting around the slope lower down."

A minute later Cpl Lang and Cadet Leece returned. "You wanted a radio?" Cpl Lang asked Chloe.

"Yes," Chloe replied. "Call Sgt Grey, in clear and try to contact him."

In reply Cpl Lang took the radio lanyard from around his neck and passed it to her. "CUO Roach tried," he said.

Chloe took the radio without comment and at once held it in front of her face and pressed the press to talk button. "Sgt Grey, this is Two Four, over."

Nothing. Jane almost held her breath. A glance showed Sgt Grey's small group still patrolling down the distant hill slope.

Oh, answer the radio! she mentally cried, clenching her fists in urgent frustration.

Chloe tried again twice more but there was no response. She then turned the radio to check the settings. "What channel are we on? Ah!

Twenty-Eight. That is our platoon net for the exercise," she muttered. "What is the Control Group channel for this exercise?"

Cpl Lang swallowed and shook his head. "Same as the unit command net, thirty-one," he answered.

Chloe quickly changed the channel setting. "That's probably why CUO Roach didn't get anyone," she said. "He was only calling you guys on the Platoon Net. Sgt Grey, this is Two Four, over."

Jane held her breath while silently cursing CUO Roach. *The bloody idiot! Why didn't he think of that?*

She knew the platoon had been given the army radio to communicate longer distances and to talk to the CP, Relay Station and Control Group if required, but she still thought that a CUO should remember that all those people also had the CB radios for communicating with each other.

The radio crackled and Sgt Grey's voice came back. "This is Hotel Three, use correct voice. Do not use names on the radio, over," he said.

Chloe ignored the rebuke and pressed the press to talk button again. "Sgt Grey, this is Chloe. Never mind that. We have a serious emergency. You are in great danger, over."

"Two Four, this is Hotel Three, say again, over."

"Hotel Three, this is Chloe. You are walking into danger. We have met a gang of bikies and they have shot several of us. You must not walk along the road, over."

"Two Four, is this a wind-up? Put on your sunray, over."

"Sgt Grey, this is Chloe. NO! I am deadly serious. We have dead and wounded people and urgently require medical assistance. But you must stop walking and hide so you don't run into them too."

"Two Four, this is Hotel Three, put on your sunray, over."

Chloe ground her teeth then answered. "Hotel Three he is not here. Please! Believe me! This is not a hoax. I am not making it up. Get off the road and hide, over."

Jane stared hard in the glare and to her relief saw that Sgt Grey's patrol had stopped walking near the bottom of the hill. Then she glanced to her right and went tense. She tapped Chloe and pointed.

"The bikies can hear you! They are listening to you on Captain Hamilton's radio."

Chloe looked and swore. She lifted the radio and said, "Hotel Three, you must hide. Come and join us, over."

"Roger Two Four. Where is that? Over"

Jane felt a sudden jolt of anxiety. She gripped Chloe's forearm. "Chloe! Don't tell them where we are or the bikies will know too. Just tell them to hide and we will come and get them," she cried.

Chloe nodded. "Hotel Three, just turn right and hide where you are. We will come and get you. We cannot tell you anymore as the enemy are listening. They have captured Captain Hamilton and are listening on his radio, over."

Jane had seen the bikies cluster at Captain Hamilton and she now clearly saw one of them hit him and then rip the radio lanyard from around his neck. "They are listening alright," she commented.

Turning her head, she saw with frustration that Sgt Grey's patrol still stood in clear view on the dirt road.

The bikies can't see them because this ridge is in the way, she reasoned.

But if a bikie went along the road he would. She was about to tell Chloe to warn them again when a strange voice came on the radio.

"Two Four, where are you? Over."

"That's him!" Jane hissed, alarm coursing through her as the horrible certainty that they were being listened to swept through her.

Chloe nodded and looked towards the bikies. "Unknown station, this is Two Four, out to you. Hotel Two, this is Two Four, over."

Instantly the radio crackled again. "Two Four, this is Hotel Two, what's going on? Over."

It was the Radio Relay Station. Jane almost wept with relief. "They are there somewhere," she muttered, her eyes scanning Railway Hill again."

"Hotel Two, we have a serious emergency. Get the OC to call the police, over."

"Two... buzzzz... crackle.... buzz.... crackle.... crackle..."

Chloe stared at the radio in bewilderment. Cpl Lang swore softly. "That is jamming. They are jamming the radio by continuous transmission. Try the alternate channel," he said.

Jane had just enough knowledge of radios to understand that but it scared her and she felt her anxiety level rising. Chloe quickly turned the radio and switched channels to 64. Then she tried again but there was no response.

Cadet Leece shook his head. "None of them has thought of that yet."

Chloe turned and looked towards Sgt Grey's patrol. "I wish they'd believe me," she muttered. "I'd better go and get them."

Jane looked and saw that Sgt Grey's patrol was still standing out on the dirt road but were now in a huddle. Shaking her head, she said, "No! You are needed here. I'll go."

"Not on your own," Chloe replied.

Cadet Leece put his hand up. "I'll go with Jane. I'm fit. I can run that in ten minutes."

Chloe again nodded. "OK. But take care you don't get seen or caught," she said.

"We won't," Jane answered. She now felt impelled by an urgent desire to be up and running. She wriggled back and began shrugging off her webbing. "No webbing," she said to Cadet Leece.

She knew that was against unit safety rules and SOPs in the bush, but she also knew she could move much faster without it. Just in case she gulped another drink, draining her right water bottle.

As she slid it back into her webbing Cpl Lang pointed. "Grey's moved off the road at least," he commented.

As she rolled over and stood up below the crest Jane looked north and saw, to her immense relief that Sgt Grey's group were vanishing into the creek line on her side of the road.

"We should be able to find them fairly easily," she said.

Chloe held up the radio. "Give us a call on Channel Six Four when you get to them. Use Grey's radio," she said.

Jane nodded. "Will do. Come on Rod."

Taking care to keep the crest between her and the bikies Jane hurried off down the slope towards the Northwest. She deliberately angled away from her objective to use the dead ground to avoid being seen. She didn't run but hurried as fast as she safely could on such rocky ground.

I don't want to twist an ankle, she thought.

But what was really impelling her was the urgent need to get this done as quickly as possible. She was anxiously aware of Kim lying back there on her stretcher. Dread at the thought of Kim dying so gripped Jane that she had trouble breathing and she let out several small sobs before she recollected herself.

Cadet Leece followed, also glancing continually back and to his right. Jane could just see the dirt road where it appeared three times over low rises in the large, wide ridge they were on. From her study of the map and the ground she was confident she would be able to navigate easily.

Their route took them down into a shallow depression with another small, dry gully at the bottom and then up onto the wide flat part of the big ridge. As she went up onto that crest Jane continually looked to her right and rear to check she wasn't running into view of the bikies. To her relief the swell of the ground hid them. But the dirt road was visible most of the time, slowly curving closer. Beyond it was the New Railway, its tracks very visible, being on top of a large, steep-sided embankment.

As she hurried along Jane tried to calculate how long the journey might take. She agreed with Rod's estimate of 10 minutes.

But that would be on flat, open ground, she decided. She knew that a person could walk a hundred metres in one minute at the 'Quick March' pace and that meant a kilometre in ten. *But this is rocky and up and down,* she reasoned.

She began angling her route to stay a hundred metres from the dirt road. *We don't want to be too close to it,* she reasoned, knowing that they might have to quickly hide if a motorcycle came along it.

The going was fairly easy, but it was hot and there was no obvious breeze so she was soon puffing and sweating. There was another shallow dip to cross and then she went up to another wide, flat crest and came to two wheel ruts in the grass.

"A vehicle track," she called to Cadet Leece.

He joined her. "For one of those quad bikes judging by the width," he said.

"Don't leave any boot prints," Jane warned as she stepped carefully across, making sure her boots went on tufts of grass and bare rock.

Then she hurried on. Next there was a larger re-entrant to cross with another small, dry watercourse and then a steeper, higher ridge barred the route. Jane went over it at a slow plod, continually checking behind her. She was able to see the rise Chloe was on but found it harder to work out which of the larger hills behind her was Railway Hill. The whole range was made up of thousands of small rocky hills which at first glance all looked the same.

Bloody hell! It would be easy to get lost in that, she thought.

But with the dirt road and New Railway close beside her she had no such worries. She went over the ridge top on her hands and knees as they had been trained to do and then paused in among some rocks to study the small valley that had opened up ahead of her. Beyond it was the larger hill that Sgt Grey's patrol had walked down.

This is the creek they should be hiding in, Jane thought, noting that a dry creek similar to the one the bikies were in ran along the bottom of the small valley. Small trees lined the dry creek and studded the slope.

Cadet Leece crawled into position beside her. Jane pointed down. "This is the creek they should be in. Now we have to find them."

In reply Cadet Leece pointed. "There they are."

Jane looked and then swore. She could see an anxious looking face peeking up at them from behind a tree but two other figures in camouflage uniforms were in clear view, sitting out on rocks in the dry creek bed. Scrambling to her feet she hurried down the slope, panting and perspiring but relieved. Cadet Leece followed.

Sgt Grey stood up to meet them. "What's going on? What's all this about bikies and people being shot?"

Cadet Leece voiced what Jane was thinking. "Bloody hell, you want to hide a bit better than this from now on," he commented in a scathing tone. "These guys mean business."

Sgt Grey scowled but again demanded to know what was happening. Jane pointed to his CB radio. "Let me radio first," she replied.

"We tried but it is being jammed," Sgt Grey replied as he passed her the radio.

"We know. We switched to the alternate frequency," she said.

Sgt Grey actually blushed and looked a bit foolish, making Jane shake her head as she quickly changed the channel setting. Then she pushed the transmit button. "Two Four, this is Juliet Charlie, over."

At once Chloe's voice came back loud and clear. "Roger Juliet Charlie. Carry on, over."

"Juliet Charlie out." Jane knew that there was nothing to be gained by having a conversation. *Those bikies might know how to use the scan function and be able to hear us.*

She handed the radio back to Sgt Grey and relaxed slightly. *He is a Fourth Year and a sergeant. He can take command now,* she told herself.

Looking at the other three made her feel even better. They were the signals sergeant, Sgt Lynes, the medic sergeant, Sgt Jemma Small and the Q corporal, Cpl Brandt.

We should be alright now, she decided. She glanced at her watch and saw that it was a couple of minutes after 1400hrs. *I was right, about fifteen minutes. But it will take longer to go back.*

Sgt Lynes was both puzzled and angry. "What's going on? Why is Cummings using that radio?"

"Because CUO Roach and Sgt Lepson have gone to get help," Jane replied.

"Gone? But..." Sgt Lynes was obviously puzzled but did not pursue the topic. Sgt Grey cut in: "So what the hell is going on? Why have you stopped the exercise?'

As quickly and succinctly as she could Jane described what had happened. As she described the murder and shooting and how badly wounded Kim was, she noted looks of horror and almost disbelief on the faces of the four listening. But Cadet Leece backed her up and they appeared to accept that what she was telling them was the truth.

Sgt Grey frowned. "But what has all this got to do with us? These bikies won't harm us, surely?"

That was a question Jane had thought about. "I think they might take us hostage and even hurt us to get what they want," she replied.

"And what do they want?" Sgt Lynes demanded to know.

"I think they want to kill this Harley guy we have with us," she said.

For a few seconds Sgt Grey looked thoughtful and then he frowned. "But we can't put cadets at risk to save some stranger," he commented.

That was the nub of the matter. "You don't have to," Jane replied. "You can take yourselves off and go to camp or hide but I am not going to just let another human being be murdered. I want to sleep at night for the next ninety years without my conscience bothering me."

"But..."

"But we have already done this. We are committed," Jane continued. "And Chloe is determined."

"Well Chloe isn't in charge," Sgt Grey snapped.

"Oh yes she is!" Jane retorted. "And we will support her. Anyway, as I said, I can't make you help us. You choose. You can just make your way to a safe place, but we would like you to help us."

Sgt Grey looked torn and the others looked unhappy. Jane realised she had to win their support. "We are asking you to help. Sgt Grey, your little brother is with us. Sgt Small, we need your First Aid experience and stores and Sgt Lynes, you can call HQ on that RTF200 set; and four more people will make it easier to move the stretchers."

They were wavering she could see and wracked her brains to try to come up with more arguments. It was Cadet Leece who spoke next.

"Help us please! We need you. The more of us there is the safer everyone is and the easier it is."

"Oh alright," Sgt Grey muttered. He looked at the others in his group. "What do you blokes think?"

Sgt Small answered first. "I will go and help Kim," she said. She looked very anxious and Jane wondered if it was because she might have to face the first really serious casualty of her career.

"Sgt Lynes?"

Sgt Lynes shrugged. "Yeah. I will come and see what the go is and then I will decide," he said.

"Cpl Brandt?"

"I will go with Sgt Lynes," Brandt replied, lowering Jane's opinion of him considerably.

"So what do we do?" Sgt Grey queried.

"We walk back to join the platoon; and we use field craft. We don't want these bikies to see us," Jane answered. "If we hear them, we take cover."

Sensing that any more time spent talking might result in them changing their mind she turned and began climbing back up the slope. To her relief they picked up their gear and followed. As they did, she noted Sgt Lynes swing on an RTF200 set and she made the mental note to get him to try calling the CP once they were up on the ridge.

They did, but it was at once evident even to Jane that it was not working. Sgt Lynes listened and then held the hand set up for them to listen to. "The frequency is being jammed," he said.

"How could they keep doing that?" Jane queried.

"Just hold the pressel switch down and then tape it maybe," Sgt Lynes suggested.

"But... But which radio are they using?" Jane asked. And then it came to her and she answered her own question. "Capt Hamilton's in the safety vehicle."

Jane felt a bit downcast as she had been hoping to make contact with the officers.

Maybe CUO Roach and that turd Lepson have made it back by now, she thought as she resumed walking.

And she went fast, gripped by the urgent need to get Kim to medical help.

Chapter 22

NIGHTMARE

As Major Wickham watched 4 Platoon vanish down the Old Railway at 0900 he had experienced a niggling sense of worry.

I hope nothing goes wrong, he thought, telling himself it was a simple exercise. *All they have to do is walk two or three kilometres, then split into four patrols and watch that dirt road for a few hours and then come back,* he mused.

But the niggling concern would not go away, even though he immersed himself in unit administration and watching the First Year platoons doing their training. To help settle his gnawing concern he strolled over to the CP (A hutchie tied flat between four trees under which was the HQ box as a table and two cadets with a map board and several radios and clipboards). His watch told him it was 0940hrs.

"Any reports?" he queried.

Cpl Pretzel, the signals corporal, looked up and answered. "Yes sir. Hotel Two has just radioed in that they can see 4 Platoon on the Old Railway here." He pointed to the map.

Major Wickham studied the map. Hotel 2 was the Radio Relay Station and was marked on the correct hill.

I hope they are actually there, he thought ruefully, remembering other occasions when people had reported they were in a particular place but had actually been somewhere else. A glance at the map showed that 4 Platoon was only a little bit behind the time he had expected.

He was about to walk away when H2 called in another report. Cpl Pretzel wrote it down and logged it and then said, "Hotel Two reports that 4 Platoon have gone back out of sight and they think they have gone down into the creek bed."

"Good! That's what they should be doing, using the covered approaches, not strolling along the Old Railway," Major Wickham replied. "Have Hotel Three and Sierra One both reported."

Cpl Pretzel nodded. "Yes sir. Both have sent the codeword to say they are in position and ready."

"Good. Keep me informed." Major Wickham turned and went back to the folding table he was working at.

An hour later, at 1100hrs, Major Wickham again went to the CP. "Any reports from anyone?"

"No sir."

That was a bit of a worry. The exercise was planned to start at that time, but Sgt Grey's Control Group team were not to move until 1215, just to provide the cadets in the OPs with some character building waiting.

"Tell me when 4 Platoon says they are in position," he ordered.

His worry grew when there was still no codeword from 4 Platoon by 1140. *I hope nothing's gone wrong,* he thought picturing an injured cadet being carried up out of the dry creek to the Old railway. *I hope not!*

"Call them and ask when they think they will be in position," he instructed.

Cpl Pretzel tried, using the RTF200 with its 10-foot rod aerial. But there was no reply. Major Wickham frowned. "They are down in the gullies so there is probably a lot of screening. Call Hotel Two and ask them to relay."

Cpl Pretzel did and Major Wickham clearly heard them calling 4 Platoon. To his relief 4 Platoon replied and back came the message that they would be in position soon.

Good, Major Wickham thought.

He was now glad he had taken the effort to deploy the Radio Relay Station. "Now call Hotel Three and tell them not to move until 1245."

This was done and Major Wickham returned to his table. Nearby the First Year platoons were coming in from the morning's training and with them came the other OOCs who had been supervising. Capt Buchan dropped his webbing and then moved his pack into the shade to sit on.

"How goes the war?" he queried. "Are 4 Platoon doing their stuff?"

"Not yet. They are late," Major Wickham replied.

Capt Buchan gave a shrug and a cynical smile. "With Roach in command I'm not surprised," he said.

That nettled Major Wickham a bit. "You don't have to say that with such an I-told-you-so relish Mel! I had to give all the CUOs a command."

They settled to having lunch, Lt Cavendish, Lt Peters and Lt Barker joining them. But no message arrived to say that 4 Platoon was ready and Major Wickham began to fret.

What's the delay now? he wondered.

At 1205 he got up and went over to the CP. "Call 4 Platoon and ask what the delay is," he said. "Relay through Hotel Two if you have to."

Cpl Pretzel tried but got no response. So he called H2 and got them immediately. They also tried but also got no response. Major Wickham began to worry.

Something's gone wrong, he fretted. But what? Once again he pictured cadets falling over on the rocks or getting heat exhaustion. *It is certainly hot enough for that*, he thought as he wiped perspiration from his face. There was no breeze and the temperature was now in the high 20s. *At least we have water out there if they need it, and a safety vehicle.*

But when another 10 minutes had gone by and there was still no call Major Wickham swallowed the cold salmon he was chewing and again went to the CP.

"Call Capt Hamilton and ask him to investigate why 4 Platoon aren't answering," he said.

This was done and Captain Hamilton (CS Sierra 1) replied with a cheerful 'Wilco'. Major Wickham checked his watch and saw that it was now 1220. He went back to his lunch but found it tasteless and hard to swallow and the coffee he had brewed also tasted flat. His anxiety grew with every minute that no report came back.

Unable to relax he took his coffee and went to the CP again. "Anything?" he queried.

"No sir. We can get Hotel Two and Hotel Three but not Two Four."

"What about Sierra One?"

"We've tried sir but no answer"

"Get Hotel Two to relay to him," Major Wickham instructed. Now he was concerned. Cpl Pretzel sent the message and heard H2 trying to call S1 but after four attempts they radioed back that they could not contact him.

By this time Major Wickham's unease had communicated itself to the other officers and they joined him around the CP. "Problem?" Capt Buchan queried.

"We seem to have lost coms with Warwick and with 4 Platoon," Major Wickham replied. Next he took out his mobile phone and called Capt Hamilton. There was no answer.

Capt Buchan again queried the situation.

Major Wickham shook his head. "No answer. But then, mobile reception is very patchy down among all those hills, even with the mobile phone tower just here on the next hill," he commented. He then turned to Cpl Pretzel. "Tell Hotel Three to move and ask them to try to call 4 Platoon on their CBs. We need to get coms with them."

Cpl Pretzel did this and immediately got through. He listened and then looked up at Major Wickham. "They say they are ready to move. We…"

At that moment the CB radio hung on Cpl Pretzel's shirt began to crackle and speak. For this exercise the CP had two CBs in use, one on the Control Group channel and one on the unit's normal Company Net. The RTF200 set was only for the exercise as the First Year platoons had not been given them (The unit only had 5 and one of these was faulty). This call was on the Control Group CB channel.

The message was very faint and crackly. Major Wickham strained to hear but missed most of it.

"Who was that?" he queried.

"I think it was Two Four sir," Cpl Pretzel answered. "It sounded like a girl."

Major Wickham took his own CB and switched it to the Control Group channel. He had only just done this when there was another call. Again it was very faint and he only picked up a few words. "Two Four talking to Hotel Three I think," he said. That was good news in the sense that some sort of coms was being re-established but was a worry that the RTF200 set wasn't being used.

Probably faulty, he thought.

Years of trouble trying to communicate with the old radios made him very pessimistic about their reliability.

Several of the other OOCs also switched their radios to Channel 31 as the faint and garbled conversation continued. Major Wickham strained his ears.

"Did that just say 'hide'?" he asked as the call ended.

"I think so sir," Cpl Pretzel answered. He was also looking anxious and was obviously worried that he might somehow be in trouble for the breakdown in communications.

"You log all these messages Cpl Pretzel," Major Wickham said. Then the CB radio started talking again. Again, there was a lot of distortion and the signal was very faint but Major Wickham was sure he again heard the word 'hide'.

"Definitely 4 Platoon talking to Sgt Grey," he said.

"That sounds like Chloe," Lt Barker commented.

Major Wickham strained his ears to listen and then bit his lip. It did. *Why is Chloe calling on the radio?* he wondered. *Why not the signals corporal or CUO Roach, or even Sgt Lepson?*

But it was the next faint message that really got his mental alarm bells going. Quite distinctly he heard Chloe's voice say 'Hotel Two' and then after some faint and unreadable words the phrase 'Get the OC'.

Bloody hell! Something has gone wrong, Major Wickham thought.

He immediately turned to the officers. "Some sort of trouble. I will go and try to find out what it is. Lt Peters, you come with me. Mel, you look after the First Years. They can just go on with their fieldcraft training but keep them close to camp."

Capt Buchan bent to look at the map. "Where are you going?"

Major Wickham placed his finger on the map. "Along the dirt road beside the New Railway. That is what 4 Platoon is supposed to be watching and that is where Warwick is."

"Where was 4 Platoon last?" Capt Buchan queried.

"Here, where the dirt road crosses this creek. I will use my car. It should be OK on that road. Lt Peters, tell the CSM to grab his webbing and join us. Cpl Pretzel, call all stations and ask for a Sitrep," Major Wickham instructed.

A buzzing hum came from the CB radio. Cpl Pretzel frowned and looked at it but Capt Buchan shook his head. "That is a radio transmitting," he commented.

Major Wickham tried to call on his radio but it was quickly obvious that he wasn't getting through. The transmitting radio was cutting out everything. Faintly in the background he could hear voices.

"Someone has their 'Press to Talk' button pushed down," he muttered. "All stations, this is Sunray, stop transmitting, over."

It had no effect. Major Wickham bit his lip in concern. It was something that happened occasionally, usually when someone had the radio hooked to their webbing and the transmit button got accidentally pushed down. But that was usually intermittent and they could usually hear the cadets talking. But this was a continuous hum.

"Switch is stuck?" Lt Barker suggested.

Major Wickham bit his lip. "Maybe. Two Four this is Sunray, over." There was no response other than the constant transmission. After trying again Major Wickham said, "Try the army radio set Cpl Pretzel. Call Hotel Two."

But as soon as Cpl Pretzel finished calling that radio also began to hum. Capt Buchan raised an eyebrow. "That is transmitting too. This can't be an accident. Someone is playing silly games."

"I hope that's all it is," Major Wickham replied. He thought, but did not say, that if it was deliberate jamming they certainly had a problem. "I'll go and investigate. To the car Jenny."

Now feeling distinctly worried Major Wickham went and got his webbing and put it in the back of his station wagon. Quickly climbing into the driver's seat he fretted impatiently until both Lt Peters and CSM Glenn were seated. He at once started up and backed out. Driving as fast as was safe he drove the car to the front gate. CSM Glenn got out to open it but then had trouble with the mechanism. It was just an ordinary wire gate with a bar catch on a chain but the boy, being from the city and not a farm, was unfamiliar with such things. Major Wickham had to get out and show him. Then he had to drive through and get out to help refasten the gate. The last thing he wanted was trouble with the landowner if some of his cattle got out onto the highway.

Thus it took 7 minutes to go from the bivouac to the Flinders Highway. As he drove along the section of Old Highway which ran parallel to the New Highway outside the gate Major Wickham was surprised to see a man in bikie leathers seated on a motorcycle parked just near the access point. The man glanced at them curiously but then looked away.

Lt Peters also looked at the man. "Must be waiting for his mates," she commented.

"What do you mean?" Major Wickham asked.

"There was a whole gang of bikies go past earlier this morning. I think they were going to the hotel in Mingela," Lt Peters replied.

Major Wickham nodded. He remembered hearing the bikes. Carefully he drove out onto the Flinders Highway and turned right. As he did CSM Glenn spoke up: "He was a real bikie with colours."

"What do you mean?" Major Wickham asked as he accelerated the car.

"He was wearing the gang colours sir, the badge on the back of his leather jacket," CSM Glenn replied.

"I thought that was against the law?" Lt Peters commented.

"It is Miss," CSM Glenn assured her. "And they aren't supposed to go around in groups of three or more. Oh, here's another one."

They had driven around the first bend to the left on the way down the range and there on the left, at the point where the Highway passed under the powerline and began to curve back to the right, was another bikie sitting on his motorcycle. This time Major Wickham saw the colours on the back of the man's jacket as the bikie turned away to look at the hills. ATILLA'S AXEMEN it read.

"That's a dangerous place to stop on that curve," he commented.

By then he was driving at 100kph but a minute later, as the Highway began to curve back to the right again near the bottom he had to slow. Luckily there was no other traffic so he could do this safely. Carefully he turned the car off the bitumen and onto a dirt track on the left. There was another wire gate and he stopped for CSM Glenn to open it.

This worked faster and they were soon driving again, the gate shut behind them. The route took them left along a graded section of the Old Railway. As he drove along the dirt road Major Wickham looked up at the largest hill in front of him, his eyes searching for the cadets of the Radio Relay Station.

"I can't see Hotel Two," he said. "I hope they are up there."

But he had to look away and concentrate on his driving as the dirt road now turned off the Old Railway and up over a low but steep hill on the right. Then it wound down the other side. The New Railway came into view ahead along while a vista of much of the Haughton River Valley. The view opened out, revealing the valley bottom thick with trees and Mount Square Post standing up plainly in the middle of it.

Just before reaching the New Railway the dirt road went left and ran along parallel to it. The car went down across a small dry creek and then up over another low hill. As they crested the rise and began descending Major Wickham saw with relief that Captain Hamilton's Land Rover was parked at another dry creek just ahead. There were people there and that also caused Major Wickham some relief until he saw that only one was in army camouflage uniform. The others were three bikies and they all turned to look. Four motorcycles were parked on the low grassy flat on the right. The niggling sense of alarm returned to add to Major Wickham's already strong feeling of apprehension.

"What's going on here, I wonder?" he said. As he got closer Major Wickham noted that Captain Hamilton did not look happy and was shaking his head.

Obviously a problem, he thought. *I wonder what it is?*

He soon found out. As he braked the station wagon to a standstill two of the bikies walked over, their faces smiling a welcome. But then they swung sawn-off shotguns from behind their backs and thrust them in the windows. One of them, a big brute with a goatee beard, snarled.

"Get out of the car and put your hands up!"

Major Wickham stared at the twin muzzles that were only centimetres from his face and blanched. He was war veteran and knew only too well what damage such a weapon could do. Fear went coursing through him, mixed with disbelief and an awful sense of dread.

A glance showed dismay, grief and blood on Captain Hamilton's face and Major Wickham instantly understood why he was looking unhappy.

Warwick is a prisoner, he thought.

And so were he and the other two! It was obvious that any attempt to resist would be met by extreme violence, so he switched the motor off and climbed out of the car. The man with the goatee beard gestured with the gun.

"Hands up fatso!" he snarled.

The insult burned but did not hurt nearly as much as the realization that Lt Peters and CSM Glenn were also in the power of these men. Angry men, he could see, even desperate.

"What's going on? What's the meaning of this?" he retorted, outrage adding to his worry.

"We ask the questions Fatso so shut up or the girl gets hurt," Goatee replied.

Seeing the look in the man's eye Major Wickham's resolution to resist fled. *This guy is really dangerous,* he thought.

"What do you want?" he asked, managing with an effort to keep his voice under control.

"Some of your cadets have taken one of my men prisoner. We want him back and fast!" Goatee snarled.

Major Wickham was astonished. "My cadets?" he cried, glancing at

Capt Hamilton. As he did he noted bruising and more blood trickling down from a cut above his eye and from the left side of his lip.

Warwick's been really roughed up, he thought.

Goatee waved the gun at him. "What brings you here?" he queried.

"I couldn't get radio communication with my cadets. I came to see what the problem is."

"Has anyone told you?"

But Major Wickham did not want to give any information to these men. He looked at Capt Hamilton and the man with the goatee beard gestured to him. "This stubborn bugger hasn't answered any questions so you had better Fat Man, or else."

Major Wickham met Capt Hamilton's gaze and nodded in admiration. *Good old Warwick! I didn't think he would talk,* he told himself.

But now 'Goatee' made him almost instantly change his mind. "If you guys won't talk then I will hurt this girl, or the kid. So, have you called the cops or the ambulance?"

Major Wickham badly wanted to say that he had but decided the bluff wasn't worth it. "No. I have no idea what is going on," he replied.

Goatee looked puzzled. "So what is going on? Who's got my man?"

Major Wickham raised an eyebrow to Capt Hamilton and nodded. He baldy wanted to know the situation himself.

Capt Hamilton answered. "4 Platoon apparently. I don't know the details, but these guys claim they were attacked and shot at and that 4 Platoon have taken one of their gang with them." He gestured to the third bikie.

Major Wickham glanced at the man and amid his astonishment he noted with surprise that the man, a tall, mean looking character with his long hair in a ponytail, had an ugly wound on the side of his face. It had stopped bleeding but the bruising was really starting to show.

"Attacked you! Shot at you! What with? They haven't got any guns," he said.

The thin man scowled and pointed to his face. "A bitch of a girl smashed me in the face with a rock," he growled.

Major Wickham's mind instantly formed the name 'Chloe'. "But she didn't have a gun. What's this about them shooting at you?"

The man with the goatee now pointed to the left sleeve of his jacket and Major Wickham saw a long rent across it and what looked like dried blood. "That bitch took a gun off Harley and shot me. She could have killed me!"

Major Wickham's mind was in a whirl of speculation as he tried to imagine what had led to members of 4 Platoon (Chloe for sure!) fighting with a bikie gang. It was surreal and his mind struggled to accept it.

"If they did they must have had good reason. What happened?"

Goatee stepped right into his face. "Never mind that! Are you the boss man?"

Major Wickham nodded, but he had to swallow and struggle to keep the fear out of his face.

Goatee grabbed his shirt. "You just tell them to bring Harley here now," he snapped.

Already Major Wickham had made the deduction that something very bad had gone wrong but also that 4 Platoon must have had good reason to act as they did.

"And if I just call the police instead?" he suggested, reaching into his trouser pocket for his mobile phone.

The blow from behind threw him to the ground and stunned him. Before he could react, strong hands grabbed him and the phone was wrenched from his grasp. The thin man spoke next.

"Get his radio as well and the ones off these two. Take them off you two!" he ordered.

"OK Slasher," the third man said.

He bent and grabbed Major Wickham and hauled him up and then reefed the radio lanyard from around his neck. He then turned to Lt Peters and CSM Glenn.

"Take them radios off. You got a mobile phone bitch?"

Lt Peters had, and she meekly handed it over. Major Wickham stood unsteadily, his shocked brain reeling from the blow. He now had no illusions that the men meant serious business and his apprehension grew.

Goatee jerked a thumb at Capt Hamilton. "This idiot wouldn't co-operate but now we got a few hostages we got some leverage as they say. Now captain..."

"Major," the thin man called Slasher put in.

"Major. Whatever! Boss Man, will those kids do what you say?"

"They should," Major Wickham replied guardedly, unsure what the question implied and not wanting to commit himself.

Goatee thrust the radio at him. "Then you call them and tell them to come here, and fast."

"And if I don't?" Major Wickham asked, mustering some shreds of dignity.

"Then this here kid gets hurt and I give the lady officer to the boys for a bit of fun," Goatee replied.

The threat chilled Major Wickham and he knew he had to comply. Swallowing and spitting dust from his lips he took the radio. "Two Four, this is Sunray, over."

In reply all he got was the transmission sound. "I'm not getting through."

The one name Slasher gestured. "Muff, release the transmit button on that radio there."

Major Wickham saw the third bikie go to a CB radio that was lying on the Land Rover bonnet. The transmit button had been taped down with some black plastic tape.

Warwick's radio, Major Wickham thought. *We are being deliberately jammed!* he added with dismay.

As soon as the buzz stopped Major Wickham tried again. Instantly there was a reply, a girl's voice.

"Sunray this is Two Four, over."

Chloe for sure, Major Wickham thought.

"Two Four, put on your sunray, over."

"Sunray, the sunray for this Calls Sign is not here, over."

"Two Four, move the platoon to me now, over."

"Where is that Sunray? Over."

Major Wickham reached into his pocket and took out his map. "Grid Reference six three three, zero four two. I say again figures six three three, zero four two, over."

"Roger. We are on our way, over," Chloe replied.

"Keep me informed, Sunray out," Major Wickham said. He looked at Goatee. "Satisfied?"

Goatee scowled. "They better be quick!" he snarled. "Or there'll be tears."

Major Wickham swallowed and felt sick. *What on earth is going on?* he wondered.

Horrible sensations of dread began to well up making him nauseous.

Chapter 23

GEOGRAPHICALLY CONFUSED

B ut help wasn't on the way. Sgt Lepson and those with him were still geographically confused, even geographically embarrassed. When he realised they had been walking the wrong way, Sgt Lepson had sworn and cursed and thought that CUO Roach was a complete idiot.

Bloody fool! Sgt Lepson thought as he tried to focus his eyes on his map photocopy. "Where do you reckon we are?" he asked.

CUO Roach pointed to a spot in the next grid square to the one Sgt Lepson thought they were in. "Here," he said.

"You sure? That means we are near this powerline," Sgt Lepson replied, indicating the powerline that ran across the map.

CUO Roach lifted his head and looked north. "I can't see it," he muttered.

Sgt Lepson looked but could see no sign of any pylons or wires either so he then checked his own map. "You are looking north. The powerline is south of us," he said.

CUO Roach looked embarrassed. "You sure?"

Cpl Hankin snorted, derision clear in his voice. "You've got yer map the wrong way up Roachie," he said.

Sgt Lepson knew he should rebuke Cpl Hankin for calling the CUO by a nickname but he was too worried. Again the image of the murdered man flopping down flooded across his mind.

We have to get out of here! he told himself. He also looked around to check if his map was orientated.

CUO Roach looked pained. "You sure?" he queried.

Cpl Hankin curled his lip. "Get yer compass out and orientate the bloody thing or we will be wandering around these hills all bloody day,"

CUO Roach did and the group crouched while he placed the compass on the map and then began to rotate the compass. That really annoyed Sgt Lepson as the fear still gripped him.

"Don't turn the compass! Turn the map with the compass sitting on it!" he cried.

CUO Roach muttered but did as he was told and after several more minutes discussion they were all agreed that the map was orientated. Sgt Lepson stood and again looked for the powerline, this time scanning the hills to the south. But he could see no sign of it and that made him even more anxious.

"If we are where you say we are then it should be just here, running up this ridge," he commented.

During all of this Cadet Flegel had crouched, listening and watching and looking scared. Now he cried out in obvious anxiety. "So where are we then?"

"I don't know," CUO Roach admitted.

"Do a resection then!" Sgt Lepson snapped, fear sharpening his tongue.

"What on? We need three hills. Which one of these is one we can recognize?" CUO Roach retorted.

"You don't need three hills," Cpl Hankin replied. "Major Wickham said that often one is enough."

"So which one?"

Sgt Lepson looked out and saw the very obvious conical shape of Mount Square Post. "That one." he said. "It's on the map."

"You sure?" CUO Roach questioned.

Sgt Lepson pointed to it. CUO Roach still looked doubtful but finally agreed. He stood and took a compass bearing on the hill. "Twenty-four," he said at last.

"Can't be," Sgt Lepson said. "You mean two hundred and forty. The noughts aren't shown on the numbers."

"Isn't it two noughts that should be added?" Cpl Hankin queried.

They argued this for several minutes and then decided that it was actually two noughts. So using the magnetic bearing of 2400 mils they set out calculate the next step. "We have to turn it into a Grid Bearing," CUO Roach said.

"No, you convert it to a Magnetic Back Bearing," Cpl Hankin objected.

There was more argument before Sgt Lepson cut in. "Major said it didn't matter which one you do first. He makes us write those three headings one under the other, remember?"

They did and after more argument the headings MAG; GRID and

GBB were written onto three notebooks (Flegel just sat looking worried). There was then an argument about whether they had to subtract or add the magnetic variation to get a Gird Bearing. Sgt Lepson knew that there was a diagram they could draw to show them but he had not paid attention during that lesson, not believing that he would ever need any of the more obscure theory (Although he had not articulated it in those terms). Now his was angry, fear adding a raw edge to his temper.

"You are the CUO so you should know Roach!" he snarled.

CUO Roach looked defensive and then hurt. "And so should you! They teach this on Senior Leaders Course."

They did but Sgt Lepson was too upset to argue. "So which is it? Do we add or do we subtract."

"Grandma sucks," Cpl Hankin said.

"Major said not to use that rude reminder!" CUO Roach snapped.

"Major isn't here!" Cpl Hankin retorted. "But that's what you do in this part of the world."

Sgt Lepson thought so but was still confused and doubtful. "But if we do it wrong we get a double error," he said. "In Western Australia you have to do the opposite because the magnetic variation is west of north."

"We aren't in Western Australia; we are in eastern Australia," CUO Roach replied in a sarcastic tone that needled Sgt Lepson.

Hankin now cut in. "Are we? I thought we are in Queensland."

"We are, and Queensland is in the eastern half of Australia," CUO Roach pedantically explained.

Cpl Hankin looked a bit sheepish and then said, "So subtract."

Cadet Flegel shook his head. "Don't you add when you are converting from Magnetic to Grid?"

That led to more argument until CUO Roach remembered how to draw the little diagram. He drew a vertical line and printed GN at the top. Then he drew a line coming out at an angle from the bottom of the first line and wrote MN on it.

That jolted Sgt Lepson's memory and he said, "Now draw a third line out from the bottom and put 2400 on that."

This was done and he then got CUO Roach to shade in the arc between the MN and the 2400 lines. Cpl Hankin pointed to the angle between the GN and MN that was not shaded.

"We have to add that," he said.

They did. The magnetic variation on the map was 140 mils East and the result was 2540 mils. CUO Roach bit his lip and said: "Now we have to make it into this GBB thing."

"Grid Back Bearing," Sgt Lepson said.

There was then a short debate about how to do that until Cpl Hankin said, "Don't you add or subtract half a circle?"

"You do," CUO Roach agreed, trying to make it sound like he had known all along.

That only increased Sgt Lepson's anxiety and he looked fearfully in all directions. There was no sign of any bikies or other cadets so he turned his attention back to navigation. "So take half a circle from your Grid Bearing," he said.

CUO Roach looked at them. "How many mils in half a circle?"

"One hundred and eighty," Cpl Hankin replied.

CUO Roach started writing this but Sgt Lepson stopped him, exasperated. "That is degrees! There are one hundred and eighty degrees in half a circle. We want mils."

But he could not remember the number. Cadet Felgel provided it. "Three thousand two hundred," he said. "There are six thousand four hundred mils in a circle."

CUO Roach wrote the number underneath his grid bearing and then sucked his pencil. "Do I add it or take it away?" he asked.

Sgt Lepson knew that one. He had gotten it wrong on his Junior Leaders Course and the instructor had crucified him over it and made him do it so many times that it was now imprinted on his brain.

"If it is more than half a circle take it away. If it is less then add," he instructed.

CUO Roach added and came up with 5740. He then picked up the protractor and looked at the map, his hand hovering uncertainly.

"Where do I put the centre of the protractor if I don't know where we are?" he asked.

Sgt Lepson almost exploded. "If we knew where we were we wouldn't be wasting time doing this!" he cried.

Cpl Hankin pointed to the map. "On the hill you took the bearing on," he explained.

CUO Roach placed the protractor on the point indicated. Sgt Lepson watched and then snapped, "Make sure you get it exactly vertical!"

But to his dismay he saw that the 5700 mils reading on the protractor wasn't even on the map. It was off the NW edge.

That can't be right. What's going wrong? he wondered.

CUO Roach bit his lip and fiddled but then said, "That doesn't make sense. We haven't gone off the map. We are inside the railway lines."

Sgt Lepson took another fearful look around and then held out his hand. "Give me the compass and I will check the bearing."

CUO Roach looked resentful but untied the compass from his shirt buttonhole and handed it over. Sgt Lepson stood and held the compass so he could use the prism. Cpl Hankin also stood and took out his own compass. As Sgt Lepson squinted into the prism his eyes focused on the numbers inside the dial. Turning slowly right and then left he looked for the numbers 24 but could not find it. Then he noted the number 20°. Above it was another run of numbers and there was a 4 in that row.

He was still puzzling over it when Cpl Hankin said, "You dickhead Roachie! You have given us degrees and we have done everything else in mils."

Now the symbol for degrees seemed to leap out at Sgt Lepson and he felt annoyed. He also knew a corporal should not speak to an officer that way but he took no action.

Roach should be dealing with it, he rationalised.

"So we want forty one mils," he said.

"No," Cpl Hankin answered. "It is four hundred and twenty. The two zeros aren't marked remember."

There was some argument about the value of each gradation in the prismatic compass before this was agreed to. They then sat and began the calculations again. While they were doing this a rumble of noise made them look up and around. The very distinct throbbing of heavy diesel engines made Sgt Lepson look down the slope towards the New Railway. Into view from out of a deep cutting came two large diesel electric locomotives hauling a long train of ore wagons.

"A train!" Flegel cried.

Cpl Hankin jeered. "Well run down and stop it!" he retorted.

Sgt Lepson wished they could but he could see that the train was at least a kilometre away. As it vanished into a cutting they resumed their calculations. After a few minutes they came up with the answer 3760 mils. CUO Roach again placed the protractor on the map and then marked a point and ruled a line. It ran across the ridge to the west of the powerline.

"I told you we were north of the powerline," he said.

Flegel again cut in. "So why did we waste half an hour doing that? Why don't we just walk south?"

The questions were directed at CUO Roach and Sgt Lepson bridled at the disrespect in Flegel's voice, but he did glance at his watch. With a shock he noted that it was 1410hrs.

We have wasted more than half an hour, he thought.

That upset him even more as he knew they could have walked back to camp in that time. He bent and studied his map and then looked around. So did the others.

Flegel pointed down the ridge to the northwards. "There are cadets down there," he said.

Sgt Lepson looked and distinctly saw four or five tiny figures in camouflage uniforms move across the crest of a low rise and into a dip beyond. Then they suddenly vanished from sight.

Did they just go to ground? he thought. *Is that Grey's mob or our platoon?* The thought of the platoon sent a sharp stab of guilt through him.

Then a sound reached his ears that sent chills through him. *Motorcycles!* he thought. Then he glimpsed them, two tiny images briefly seen down on the dirt road near the New Railway.

"Bikies!" he gasped, pointing.

The bikies rode west along the dirt road. For a minute or so the group just stood and watched and then Cpl Hankin cried, "Let's get going! They might come this way."

He used his compass to find south and began walking. CUO Roach and Flegel at once followed. Sgt Lepson watched the bikes vanish into a small valley and then start to climb the next hill where the road and railway curved to the north. Then he turned and hurried after the others.

But his haste was his undoing. Within twenty paces he had stepped on a rock in the grass and it moved and threw him to the ground. In the process he twisted his ankle. Sharp stabs of pain lanced up his leg and he cried out and clutched at it. Fearing that he had done serious damage and might not be able to walk he looked anxiously around and was dismayed to see that the others were still hurrying away.

"Hey! Stop! Help me!" Sgt Lepson cried.

But they ignored him and he began to panic. Impelled by a surge of fear he rolled over and sat up then gingerly felt down his calf to the ankle. To his relief he found that his ankle was not broken. But it hurt and when he tried to get up stabbing darts of pain shot up his leg.

"Stop! Help me!" he cried.

This time both CUO Roach and Cpl Hankin did look back. With evident reluctance they came walking back. Flegel stopped but did not come back. CUO Roach looked down at Sgt Lepson. "What's wrong?"

"Twisted my ankle," Sgt Lepson cried.

Both of them knelt and looked at his ankle. There was a discussion on First Aid and Cpl Hankin suggested taking off the boot and strapping the ankle with the elastic bandages he had. Sgt Lepson knew that was wrong.

"You leave the boot on to control the swelling and to give the ankle support," he said. "Help me up."

Both of them knelt and looked at his ankle and then stood on either side and hoisted him to his feet. That hurt too but Sgt Lepson was now again gripped by a rising sense of anxiety and he gritted his teeth and tested his weight on the injured leg. To his relief he was able to bear the pain and started to limp forward.

They had only gone twenty paces when they came to the two-wheel ruts that ran up the ridge. Sgt Lepson noted them and felt relieved that he recognized some feature. With pain lancing up his leg at every step he shuffled and hobbled slowly along. CUO Roach soon let go and Cpl Hankin also eased his grip.

"You OK on yer own?" he asked.

Sgt Lepson was about to ask him to keep helping when the sound of an approaching motorcycle came to him. His heart almost stopped with fear and he glanced around.

A motorbike, and coming this way, he thought.

Panic began to build and he started hobbling quickly forwards, the pain half-forgotten in the wash of terror.

The others heard it too and CUO Roach looked down the ridge and cried, "It's coming this way. Run!"

And he did, leaving the others behind. Sgt Lepson knew he would never reach the next creek line in time. The ground was to almost flat and open and he decided that the others wouldn't either.

"Get down! Hide!" he shouted.

With that he threw himself face down behind a tiny scatter of football sized rocks, fearfully aware that he was only about thirty or forty paces from the vehicle track the bike was on.

The sound grew louder and louder and with each second Sgt Lepson's terror mounted. He cringed and began to gasp and found he could hardly see for lack of focus and perspiration. Salt from the sweat trickled into his eyes and he blinked furiously in an attempt to clear his vision. But he did not dare move to wipe his face.

Keep still! Heels down flat! he told himself, remembering all the fieldcraft lessons.

He was also physically aware of his bum pack and webbing and was sure it was sticking up and horribly visible. The pack's weight seemed to burn into his back.

And there it is! Into his peripheral vision came the motorcycle. And riding it was one of the bikies, black leathers, big boots and visored helmet and all. The man was swivelling his head from side to side obviously searching.

He must see me, Sgt Lepson thought, his mind racing to prepare arguments to plead for his life when caught.

And then the bike was directly behind him and still continuing up along the ridge. Sgt Lepson found it unbearable not to be able to see the man, so he risked moving his head and turned it to look.

To his enormous relief he saw the man continue on away from him. There was a brief, clear glimpse of the crossed sword and axe under the horned helmet logo on the back of the bikies leather jacket and then the man went from view over a low crest. He briefly re-appeared before vanishing again behind a small rise studded with rocks. The sound of his motorcycle echoed around the rocky hills.

For perhaps half a minute Sgt Lepson did not dare move, fearing it was just a ruse but then he heard scuffling noises and saw CUO Roach and Cpl Hankin getting to their feet and craning their necks to look for the bikie. The sound of the motorcycle's engine died away to a distant murmur and it became obvious that the man had continued on up the ridge. CUO Roach and Cpl Hankin began hurrying away.

The mongrels are leaving me! Sgt Lepson though in panic.

Driven by fear of being left behind he hoisted himself painfully to his feet and began to limp after the pair. Ahead of them he glimpsed Flegel running down into the next creek line. As he hobbled along Sgt Lepson kept glancing to his right, but the bikie had gone so far away that the sound of his bike died away completely.

But suddenly the motorcycle noise returned, louder and sounding as though it was coming closer. CUO Roach called, "Down! Get down Flegel!"

Flegel did and so did CUO Roach and Cpl Hankin, taking cover behind a clump of exposed rocks. As Sgt Lepson had no cover where he was he risked hobbling the remaining twenty paces to join them. CUO Roach saw him coming and gestured furiously. "Get down Lepson! Get down!"

Sgt Lepson heard the sound of the motorcycle get louder as he dropped behind the rocks. By then he was sweating and puffing and his heart hammered from the fear. Anxiously he looked around, trying to locate where the motorcycle was. But the sound had died down again although he could still hear it distinctly.

It sounds like it is going around in front of us, he thought.

But his questing eyes could see no sign of it. The others were watching and listening too and CUO Roach muttered, "It is in between us and camp."

That was bad news and Sgt Lepson felt his chest tighten as his anxiety level shot up again. He had a horrible trapped and hunted feeling and he just wanted it to be over. Trembling from worry and exertion he lay there, listening and fretting. The engine noise grew softer again and almost died away and then became louder and seemed to be more to his left.

Cpl Hankin thought so too and he pointed, "He's over there now," he said.

But they could not see the bike and remained lying there. Minutes ticked by and the sound of the bike died right away, only to swell louder and to come definitely from their left.

"That is east of us," Cpl Hankin muttered. "He must be riding right around us."

"Stay down," CUO Roach cautioned. "He might just come up another ridge."

So they lay there for at least 10 minutes, even after the engine noises had died right away to occasional murmurs.

"We need to be sure he is gone," CUO Roach explained.

Sgt Lepson began to relax but then heard more engine noises and his heart began to hammer in apprehension.

"That sounds like more of them coming from the right," he said.

They all listened as loud engine noises growled across their front in the distance.

"Motor bikes alright," CUO Roach commented.

That got Sgt Lepson's fears growing again. He remembered the groups of bikies he had seen going along the highway and his fears multiplied.

"The rest of the gang is coming to search for us," he cried, his voice almost cracking with emotion.

"Keep down!" CUO Roach snapped. So they lay and listened to the sounds pass to their left front and then die away.

"Going down the highway," Cpl Hankin suggested.

But they had no visual clues so they continued to lie there, sweating in the sun. Sgt Lepson found his imagination gripped by images of vengeful bikies riding around the ridges. Through his mind flitted terrifying images of the man being shot dead and then of bikies suddenly appearing and shooting him. So he hugged the dirt and trembled, hoping they wouldn't be found.

After another 10 minutes he heard another loud engine noise coming from his right front.

"More of them?" he suggested.

Cpl Hankin lifted his head to listen and then shook it. "That isn't a motorbike. That's just a big truck on the highway."

Sgt Lepson realised that most of the noises they could hear were just ordinary vehicles on the highway and he felt both foolish and embarrassed. CUO Roach cautiously stood up.

"Let's keep going but be ready to take cover," he said.

With some difficulty Sgt Lepson got to his feet. His sore ankle had now stiffened and really hurt when he tried to walk on it. But the others didn't offer to help or wait so he pushed himself to follow them as they continued on southwards. CUO Roach scuttled from one clump of rocks to the next, scouting as he went, his nervousness very obvious. Sgt Lepson just limped along behind. At each clump or rocks or bush they stopped and spent several minutes looking in all directions and listening before moving again.

Sgt Lepson was gripped by the feeling that they were moving in enemy territory and he shivered from time to time with dread. He found it very wearing on his nerves.

But at least we are making progress, he thought.

Better still the group were now moving down into a dip. At the bottom Flegel stopped and ducked down. CUO Roach and Cpl Hankin joined him and when Sgt Lepson at last limped down to join them he found them drinking from their water bottles. Seating himself with an effort he pulled out his own right water bottle and then found it empty. So he replaced it and took out his left.

As he did Flegel said, "Can I have some?"

"Use yer own," Cpl Hankin replied.

"I've drunk it all," Flegel replied in an aggrieved tone.

"Well you should have saved some," Cpl Hankin retorted before taking another big swig from his own water bottle.

Sgt Lepson wiped his lips and screwed the lid back on his water bottle. "This is the same creek we came up," he said.

"So?" CUO Roach queried.

"So we could go back down it to that Number One Mill place and then we would know where we were," Sgt Lepson suggested.

"And we could maybe get water," Cpl Hankin suggested.

CUO Roach shook his head. "No. We are going south back to camp. It isn't far. Come on."

Without waiting he stood up and began walking up the next slope, compass in hand. The other two followed and Sgt Lepson felt he had no choice but to go with them. So he hoisted himself to his feet, gingerly taking the weight on his sore ankle. Then he started limping after them. He realised it was no good asking them to help. Every step hurt but the pain was now more a dull, nagging ache so he gritted his teeth and grimly set himself to climb the long, gentle slope.

It was only a few hundred paces to the next crest and when he reached it he found CUO Roach and Cpl Hankin studying the map while Flegel lay in the grass looking hot and sulky. Cpl Hankin waved his hand around. "All these hills aren't marked on the map," he protested.

"That's because the contour interval is twenty metres and most of them are only ten metres high," CUO Roach explained.

Sgt Lepson had heard Major Wickham warn them of exactly that in the Ground Briefing at the start of the bivouac so he wasn't impressed. But the country did look forbidding. There seemed to be small rocky hills and ridges in every direction as far as the eye could see and he could no longer see back down to the wide valley.

Then his eyes focused on an object and his brain registered what he was looking at. *A power pylon,* he thought.

"There's the powerline, on that next rise," he called, pointing ahead. About two hundred metres in front was a line of steel girder pylons connected by the thin black lines of electricity transmission cables.

Nearly there! he thought with relief.

A check of the map showed that they were about a kilometre from the highway and only a few hundred more from the camp. There appeared to be only one more creek line to cross and he was looking down into that.

The group set off down the slope, picking their way around rocky areas and trying to avoid the small boulders that littered the area. Sgt Lepson began to fall behind but all he could do was try harder in an effort not to get left behind. Ahead of him he could see the top end of that creek line and for a moment he considered suggesting they detour around on the flatter high ground. But the other three were hurrying down to cross the small creek which ran diagonally across their front, so he kept going, puffing and grimacing from the pain and effort.

Suddenly Cadet Flegel went down. There was sharp cry of pain and then he sat up and began to sob loudly. CUO Roach turned and snarled, "Shut up Flegel! We don't want those bikies to hear us."

"I... I... I've hurt (sob)... my (sob)... knee," Flegel cried.

"Bloody idiot!" Cpl Hankin snarled, "You should have watched where you were walking."

By then Sgt Lepson was close. He hobbled over and found a large rock to sit down on. He knew as platoon sergeant he should organise the First Aid and evacuation but now he just wanted to get to camp.

"What did you do? What's wrong?" he snapped unsympathetically.

"Tripped on that rock and banged me knee," Flegel sobbed, indicating a large rock in the long grass.

"Bloody drongo!" Sgt Lepson snapped. "Pull the leg of your trouser up so we can check it."

Flegel began to do so. CUO Roach still stood twenty paces up the slope. "Is he alright?" he called.

"Just checking," Sgt Lepson replied.

"You look after him. We will go and get help," CUO Roach replied.

With that he turned and resumed walking. Cpl Hankin met Sgt Lepson's astonished gaze and then looked away and started to follow him. Fear immediately welled up in Sgt Lepson.

"Hey! Don't leave us! Give us a hand," he called.

"You'll be right. It isn't far," CUO Roach replied. He kept going. So did Cpl Hankin.

Panic began to build in St Lepson. *They are going to leave us behind!* he thought. Struggling to his feet he started hobbling after them.

Flegel looked at him in terrified surprise. "You gotta help me!" he cried. "You can't leave me."

Sgt Lepson closed his ears to Flegel's pleas and hobbled quickly after the other two. All he could think about was keeping those two figures in sight. Fear began to grab at him and knew he was sacred. Shame at doing the wrong thing also clouded his judgement. He came to an area studded with clumps of large rocks and small rocky knolls on one of which stood the nearest power pylon. CUO Roach and Cpl Hankin vanished from view around one of the rock piles and panic began to grip Sgt Lepson and he pushed himself even harder.

But his haste was his undoing. As he limped around the end of the rock pile he stepped on a rock which rolled away and down he went, hard. Half stunned but terrified of being left behind he struggled to get up. His anxious eyes scanned for the two and when they focused on them he was puzzled to note that they were standing stationary about 25 metres away, and they were clutching at each other. Mystified Sgt Lepson got to his hands and knees, ready to get up.

Then he saw CUO Roach and Cpl Hankin start running, but not back towards him. Instead they ran off to his right, scurrying around behind another big rock pile. At the same moment the sound of a motorcycle came to Sgt Lepson's ears and he understood their actions.

Bikies! Hide! he thought.

Throwing himself into a small dip at the top of a re-entrant on his left, Sgt Lepson lay and looked in all directions. Fear now so gripped him that he found he could not move. All he could do was stare frantically around and crouch low in the grass. His ears told him that the motorcycle was coming from somewhere off to their left-front, but he could not see it.

Then he was even more surprised to see both CUO Roach and Cpl Hankin look over their right shoulders and then jump in obvious fright. Sgt Lepson glanced in the direction they were looking and was horrified to see two armed bikies walking towards them. The men had obviously come from the west along the powerline and they looked hot and angry.

"Stand still and put your hands up!" shouted one of the bikies, levelling a shotgun at the pair.

CUO Roach and Cpl Hankin, both looking terrified, did as they were told. One of the bikies, a red-headed man with a sub machine gun, took out a mobile phone and began talking on it, having used the speed dial. Then he walked across in front of Sgt Lepson and stepped out beside the rock pile and waved his arms. The sound of the motorcycle engine changed, and the meaning registered on Sgt Lepson's fear-frozen brain.

That bikie is coming here! Then an even more appalling thought came to him. *That gutless bastard Roach will tell them I am somewhere here. Then they will start searching.* Panic surged through him and the boost of adrenalin got him moving. *I have to get away from here,* he thought.

Driven by a desperate urge to escape he turned and began crawling down the shallow dip as fast as he could go.

Chapter 24

BRUTALITY

Major Wickham swayed on his feet, his senses still reeling from the blow. The physical pain barely registered compared to the anguish and dread that was now filling him. He licked his lips and tasted both dirt and blood and wished he could get a drink. But instead he had to brace himself as Goatee glared at him.

"Who are these kids?" Goatee snarled, waving the muzzles of the double barrel shotgun in Major Wickham's face.

Major Wickham swallowed and cleared his throat. He did not like to admit it but he knew it was pure fear that was gripping him.

"They are a group called Number 4 Platoon."

"What are they doing here?" Goatee demanded.

Major Wickham explained the exercise. "Captain Hamilton is their Safety Vehicle," he explained.

Slasher curled his lip. "Bad luck for him! Wrong place! Wrong time!" he commented.

Capt Hamilton gestured with his head. "They killed a man," he said.

Major Wickham's eyes followed the gesture and he now noted the dried blood, buzzing flies, drag marks and the boots showing at the next bend down the little dry creek. His heart seemed to stop and then his stomach turned over.

Oh my God! It was much worse than he had thought.

The comment brought a stinging blow to Captain Hamilton's face from Slasher. "Shut up prick! Open your mouth again and you'll be next."

Capt Hamilton staggered back against the Land Rover and only then did Major Wickham realise that Capt Hamilton's hands were tied behind his back.

This is terrible! How can we get out of this? he wondered.

Goatee resumed the interrogation. "How many are there?"

Major Wickham turned to CSM Glenn. "CSM?"

"Twenty-one sir," CSM Glenn replied.

They can't kill them all, Major Wickham thought, but then felt sick at the idea of even one being hurt.

Goatee looked surprised. "I only saw five or six," he muttered.

Slasher suddenly held a big knife up in front of Major Wickham's face. "Who's the girl?"

Major Wickham did not want to answer. "Just a cadet," he said.

"Is she the boss?" Goatee queried.

"No. The platoon commander is a male cadet under-officer," Major Wickham replied.

"So why is she the one talking to us?"

"She might be the platoon signaller," Major Wickham answered.

Goatee glanced at Slasher. "Is that likely?" he asked.

Slasher shrugged. "Yeah, in the army they have a signaller in platoon headquarters, so the officer doesn't have to carry the radio."

This guy has been a soldier, Major Wickham thought while hoping they wouldn't realise that the CUO carried the CB radio himself. *But why doesn't CUO Roach answer?* he wondered.

Goatee nodded then said, "You said this platoon were to set up Observation Posts. What were they observing?"

Major Wickham didn't want to answer that either, so he just pressed his lips together and shook his head. The result was a stinging slap. Goatee glared at him.

"Answer shitface!" he snarled.

Major Wickham clenched his jaw and endured another blow. It was Slasher who stopped it. "Don't waste energy on him Brute. Hit the kid or the lady officer," he suggested.

At that Major Wickham relented. "There is a group of four cadets who have to walk along this road so they get seen," he said. Having placed Sgt Grey's patrol in jeopardy made him feel extraordinarily guilty and he reeled with nausea.

Slasher looked along the dirt road. "That's who that bitch was talking to when she told them to hide," he cried. "I told you they must be just along the road here somewhere."

"Yeah, but we didn't find them did we?" Goatee, alias Brute, replied.

"Nah! That bitch warned them," Slasher agreed. "Maybe Stinger will spot 'em?"

Who is Stinger? Major Wickham wondered.

The thought that there were more of the gang added to his sense of doom and defeat.

Brute looked impatient. "OK you two, tie those two up. Major Fatman, you just sit there and no trouble or they get really hurt. Muff, you guard them while we go and have another look."

This was done. Major Wickham sat beside the road while Lt Peters and CSM Glenn had their wrists tied roughly behind their backs. They and Capt Hamilton were then forced to sit down beside him. Muff took up position facing them with his shotgun levelled.

Slasher pointed behind them. "Stand behind them Muff. When you are guarding prisoners you stand behind them so they can't see you and can't get at you. And don't let 'em talk," he instructed. That confirmed Major Wickham's belief that Slasher had been a soldier.

Muff did as he was told and Brute and Slasher got on their motorcycles, started them up and went roaring off along the dirt road towards the west. Major Wickham slumped and tried to relax. He badly wanted to ask Captain Hamilton what he knew but the threat to the others held his tongue. So he sat there feeling ill and sick at heart while trying to come up with a plan to get the cadets out of this mess. It was hot and sweat trickled down his face and back. As he still held the radio he was able to wipe the perspiration away but the others just had to endure the annoying and painful situation as the salt stung their eyes.

The two motorcycles were only gone a few minutes. They came back down and were parked and Brute and Slasher strode over.

"No sign of 'em," Brute said to Muff. He then stood in front of Major Wickham. "Call them again and find out what they are doing, and no funny stuff or I start on the lady here."

Major Wickham lifted the CB radio. "Two Four, this is Sunray, Sitrep, over."

Brute watched and listened intently. "What's all this 'sunray' bullshit? Are you trying to use a secret code?" he queried.

It was Slasher who answered. "It's OK Brute. It is just standard army radio voice procedure. Sunray means the commander of that group. It's what's called a radio appointment title. It's OK. I'll know if they try anything funny," he explained.

Mollified Brute muttered and continued to listen. For a few seconds

Major Wickham feared he was not going to make contact but then Chloe's voice answered, faint and slightly distorted.

"Sunray, this is Two Four. We are on our way but it is very slow going carrying these stretchers down the hill, over."

"Stretchers?" Major Wickham cried, his heart suddenly seized by a clamp of anxiety.

"We have two seriously wounded Sunray, over," Chloe replied.

Seriously wounded! Oh my God! What the hell happened? Major Wickham thought.

He pressed the transmit button again. "Do you mean that someone has been shot, over?"

"Roger. Two. Call the ambulance, over," Chloe replied.

"Roger. Hurry up.. eeh!" The radio was wrenched from his grasp and he found the shotgun muzzle being driven hard into his right cheek.

"That's enough Major Fatboy," Brute growled. "Just get 'em here."

"You heard. They are on their way," Major Wickham replied. Now he felt utterly dismayed and physically ill. It was like his worst nightmare come true! "You must call the ambulance. If some of my cadets have been shot then you must! I insist!"

That earned him another punch. Brute leaned close. "We call the shots here Mister Major! I will call an ambulance when I think we need it. Anyway, I don't know about any of your cadets being shot. I thought it was only Harley."

"Who's Harley and how did he get.. aargh!" Major Wickham began to ask but was again hit. The blow was delivered by Slasher and almost knocked him senseless. He fell on his side and only with difficulty got to his hands and knees and then back to a sitting position.

Lt Peters screamed then cried, "Leave him alone, you brute!"

"Shut up Pussy Face or I'll do you here and now," Slasher warned. "Just sit and be quiet."

The threat chilled them all into silence. So they waited. And the minutes ticked by and the sun shone down with blazing intensity. They all sweated as there was no breeze down in the creek. Brute kept glancing at his watch and after twenty minutes he snarled

"It's nearly two O'clock! Where the hell are they? Call them again Major."

So Major Wickham did but this time there was no answer. He tried again but still no answer. Inside he felt a sinking sensation and his apprehension shot right up.

They are not coming, he decided. Fear of the possible consequences of their non-arrival began to flood his emotions.

"They aren't answering. Maybe they can't get radio transmission down in these gullies," he suggested. He was quite unable to keep his anxiety out of his voice.

"They had better arrive soon or the lady gets hurt," Brute warned.

Major Wickham felt his stomach churn. He could only shake his head and say, "Maybe they misunderstood and are heading for our camp."

"Where's that? Show me," Brute ordered, thrusting the now crumpled map in front of Major Wickham. Slasher stood close to watch. Major Wickham showed him and the two men moved away to discuss what to do next.

While they were doing this the sound of a motorbike came from up the hill. They all turned to look and Major Wickham clearly saw a motorbike come into view up on the bench cut of the Old Railway. That was at least half a kilometre away but in between was the long, gentle slope with no undergrowth and he was able to get a clear view under the tree canopies.

Slasher shaded his eyes. "That's Stinger," he commented as the motorcycle went out of sight to their left, heading towards the Flinders Highway.

The two men came back and Brute again held out the CB radio. "Call them again! Find out what the go is," he demanded.

So Major Wickham did. But there was no response and he felt even more anxious. *What on earth are 4 Platoon up to?* he fretted. *What is CUO Roach doing?*

But even as he thought this the name Chloe again flitted across his mind and he puzzled over why she was the one doing the talking.

What are CUO Roach and his corporals doing, Major Wickham thought.

Brute was furiously angry and began to rant and hit at him, but he was diverted by the sound of a motorcycle approaching. It was another bikie and he came to a stop nearby and switched off his bike. After taking off his helmet he gave the prisoners a curious glance then approached Brute.

"No sign of 'em Brute. I went right up that track to the railway on the other side of these hills and then out to a gate on the highway. Then I came along a vehicle track that put me on that old railway and I followed it to the highway near the bottom of the range. Then I came back here," the bikie explained

"Show us on this map Stinger," Brute said.

Stinger looked at the map. "Would have helped if I'd had this," he commented.

Slasher turned. "Some of these cadets should have a map. The major will have. Empty your pockets you lot," he ordered.

Major Wickham took out his map and handed it over but the others could not comply because their hands were tied. Major Wickham was ordered to search their map pockets and reluctantly knelt and did so.

As he did, he leaned close to Lt Peters and whispered, "Sorry Jenny. I'll try to find a way out of this mess."

"No talking you two!" Muff ordered.

Slasher took the maps and handed them to the others, keeping one himself. The gang went into a huddle over them and Major Wickham sat with his hopes going up and down as he tried to puzzle out what was going on and what 4 Platoon might be doing. Most of his thoughts were concentrated in trying to come up with a plan to get the cadets out of the situation but his thinking was coloured by anxiety over the possibility that one of the cadets had been shot.

This is a real mess, he thought miserably, picturing the paperwork, explanations and investigations that surely must follow. *If we survive!* he added with a wry smile.

Brute jabbed at a map with his forefinger. "This one's got red and blue marks on it. What do they mean?" he asked Slasher.

Slasher had just lit a cigarette, but he looked. "That red one shows an infantry section and that arrow is along this road. That will be the route they are to follow. And these little blue triangles will be where the OPs were supposed to be. See here? It says 4 Platoon RV."

"What's an RV?"

"Rendezvous. It's French and means a meeting place," Slasher explained. "It's just up this creek a couple of hundred metres."

"What's this blue squiggly thing?"

"Dunno," Slasher admitted.

Brute walked over and thrust the map in front of Major Wickham.

"What's this mean?"

Major Wickham pressed his lips together. Not only did he not want to place more cadets at risk, but he was hoping that somehow the Radio Relay Station might pass a message for help. But his resistance crumbled a few seconds later when Slasher strode over and jammed the lighted end of the cigarette on Lt Peters' cheek.

She screamed and jerked back but Slasher grabbed her and held her and then placed the glowing tip of the cigarette only a centimetre or so from her face.

"Don't be a silly old Major Fatman. Answer or the lady will look like she's had a bad attack of smallpox."

One glance at Lt Peters' terrified but still beautiful face and the blister that was already starkly evident was enough. Major Wickham felt sick at having been responsible.

"It's a radio relay station," he replied.

"Who is there?"

For a fraction of a second Major Wickham hesitated but Slasher moved the cigarette closer and Lt Peters whimpered. Seeing no honourable alternative Major Wickham muttered, "Two cadets with a radio."

Slasher sneered and thrust Lt Peters aside then kicked Major Wickham in the left thigh. "That wasn't so hard was it?" he said with a sneer.

Brute pointed to the map. "We gotta stop them reaching the highway. If they get contact with the cops we are in real trouble. We had better spread out and look."

Slasher shook his head and said, "We need more men Brute. The area's too big. We need people along the highway to stop them contacting truck drivers or anyone and we need to find this missing platoon."

Brute nodded. "You're right. I've placed Lance and Cokehead along it already, but we need more. I'll call for help. Just make sure you all stick to our story." With that he took out a mobile phone and punched in some numbers. But when he held it to his ear he got no response. "Bloody hell! No service! How can that be? There's a mobile phone tower up on top of the range," he snarled.

"Be all these hills," Slasher said. "Mobile phones are just little radios and they basically work on line-of-sight. If there are hills in the way they stop the signal. It's called screening."

"I don't need a lecture on any of your army shit!" Brute shouted.

"Yeah, but what are we gunna do?" Slasher answered, his temper plainly rising.

"I'll go and get more blokes. You go and look up the creek and Stinger, you ride around the place again and see if you can see 'em," Brute ordered.

"I reckon we should capture that radio relay station," Slasher objected. "That will make sure they have trouble calling anyone else. They've got an army radio set and so has the platoon we are after."

"Won't the jamming work?" Brute queried, gesturing to the Land Rover.

Major Wickham turned his head and saw that the 10-foot rod aerial of the RTF200 set Captain Hamilton had been using was protruding from the side window of the Land Rover canopy and that the handset was hooked on the window frame. Black plastic tape was wound around the handset, obviously holding the pressel switch in the transmit position.

Slasher shrugged. "Only as long as the batteries last," he answered. "But I'll bet they have one of these CB radios as well and from up on that hill they can probably get good coms with their base. We can't risk it."

"Where is it?" Brute asked while peering at the map.

Slasher pointed up the slope. "Up there, on that big hill. If it wasn't for the treetops, we'd be able to see them. Stinger and I will go and round them up and he can then do another ride around."

"Yeah, OK. And I'll go and get more guys," Brute agreed.

"Where will we meet up?" Slasher asked.

"Here?" Brute suggested.

Stinger shook his head. "At the gate up on top. It's right opposite the turn-off to Mingela, and if you put someone there they will block that platoon from that whole area."

"Right-o, the gate it is," Brute agreed.

Slasher held up the CB radio. "We could use these to communicate maybe."

Brute looked puzzled. "How? Aren't we jamming it?"

Slasher shook his head. "They are eighty channel CBs. We are only jamming one; their primary."

"Primary?"

"Yeah," Slasher replied. "It means the first or main one. They will have a secondary channel as well."

"And we aren't jamming that?" Brute asked, a frown crossing his already worried face.

Watching him Major Wickham felt some relief. *This guy is almost in a fluster. His plans have all come unstuck and he doesn't know what to do. He's out of his depth,* he decided.

From the look on Slasher's face he obviously thought so too. "No," he replied.

"So how do we find out what it is?" Brute asked.

"Just ask them," Slasher replied, his tone now almost sarcastic. He turned to CSM Glenn who was watching everything with anxious eyes. "What's your alternate frequency kid?"

CSM Glenn glanced at Major Wickham who nodded. *No point in trying to withhold that,* he thought.

He did not want one of the cadets hurt. CSM Glenn licked his lips and as Slasher took a pace towards him said, "Sixty four."

"Sixty four? It had better be kid," Brute snarled.

"Easy to check," Slasher said. "Get out your Field Message Notebook and open it at your exercise orders, kid," he ordered.

Brute looked mystified. As CSM Glenn held up his tied wrists to indicate he couldn't Brute said, "How do you know this?"

Slasher shrugged. "'Cause I spent six miserable years in the bloody army! And army does everything the same way, standard procedure stuff. So the cadets will be the same."

He walked over and quickly untied CSM Glenn's wrists. Then he stood over the CSM until he had fumbled his Field Message notebook out of his left map pocket. CSM Glenn flicked through the pages and held it up for Slasher.

Slasher took the notebook and scanned the page. "Here it is! I was right! Under the Command and Signals sub-heading." He leaned forward and gave CSM Glenn a clip over the ear. "Good work kid! You have done it all textbook style." Chuckling at his own cleverness he then read down, muttering to himself before saying aloud, "Alternate Frequency: Channel sixty-four. He wasn't making it up."

"But can these cadets change to any other channel?" Brute asked, still looking puzzled.

"Of course they bloody can! But they aren't likely to," Slasher snapped.

Muff now spoke. "But what if they do? How will we know?"

Slasher held up the CB radio. "We can use the 'scan' function to check," he said. So saying he pressed a button and watched the channel numbers change. No radio calls came from the radio and after a minute he shook his head. "Nobody talking on any other channel. Nah! They'll stick to orders and stay on those two."

Brute again frowned. "Could we use these ourselves rather than our phones, you know, in places like this where the phones don't work?"

Slasher hesitated and looked doubtful. "We could, but they might listen to us."

Brute again looked anxious. "Is that likely?"

Slasher shook his head. "Nah! I reckon they won't think of it and will just follow their orders. But we should all take one anyway and we can have it on scan and monitor for any calls," he said.

With that he moved to collect the CB radio from Lt Peters, giving her left breast a good fondle and then a sharp squeeze as he did. She cried out in surprise and pain and Slasher chuckled.

Major Wickham seethed with anger. "Leave her alone!" he protested.

Slasher sneered and deliberately gave her another painful fondle and then walked over and gave Major Wickham another whack. "Shut up you! If I want to play with pretty officer's titties I will. You object and I will do it twice as much. Now keep yer gob shut!" He then gave Major Wickham another hit on the head for his pains.

The radios were passed around and Slasher said, "We will use Channel 66."

The bikies looped the radios around their necks and Slasher showed them how to set the channel and where the scan button was. Brute pressed the switch and listened and then said, "OK, let's get moving."

"What do I do?" Muff queried.

"Guard this mob of course!" Brute snapped. He hurried over to his motorbike and pulled on his helmet. Slasher and Stinger did likewise and within a minute all three were riding back east along the dirt road. As they vanished over the crest Major Wickham glanced over his shoulder to see a very worried looking Muff watching them go.

Now, how can we take advantage of this? How can we escape? he wondered.

A few minutes later the sound of motorcycles sounded from up on the

Old Railway and Major Wickham saw two bikies, Slasher and Stinger he presumed, ride from left to right across his line of vision. They vanished around the curve of the hill on its western side. That sent his hopes down again.

They are going to capture the Radio Relay Station, he thought glumly. And there was nothing he could do to stop them!

The minutes began to drag slowly past. Major Wickham half expected 4 Platoon to appear at any moment, but also half hoped they wouldn't.

I hope they can get to safety, he thought.

A host of ideas on how to call for help flowed through his mind and he kept glancing at the others while trying to come up with a viable plan.

But nothing came to him and he noted with some unhappiness that the blister on Lt Peters' cheek was now puffy and cherry red. CSM Glenn was looking very unhappy and Captain Hamilton was obviously anxious and annoyed. Flies bothered them all but the others more because they could not use their hands to chase them away.

After twenty minutes Major Hamilton decided to take a risk. Turning his head he called out Muff. "Who's this Harley bloke?"

"He's our club president," Muff replied.

The word 'president' in conjunction with an outlaw motorcycle gang rang oddly in Major Wickham's mind but he decided to try for more information. "What's wrong with him? How did he come to be with the cadets?"

"We... er... he got shot by Peewee. They... they had an argument and then Peewee pulled a gun and shot him. But it... it didn't kill him, and he shot back and killed Peewee." At that he gestured towards where the body lay in the creek bed.

"Yeah, but how did he end up with the cadets?" Major Wickham persisted.

Muff obviously had to think. "Er... he ran up the creek there and then tripped. Slasher went to... to help him and they...the cadets I mean, started throwing stones at him. Then this blonde girl just came out of nowhere and hit Slasher in the face. She took his gun and that's when the shooting started again," he explained.

"The cadets shot at you?" Major Wickham cried in astonishment. He was certain from the description that the blonde girl in question was Chloe.

"Yeah. She... Hey! I said no talking! Shut up!" Muff cried.

Major Wickham closed his mouth, but his eyes met Captain Hamilton's. He mouthed the word 'Chloe' and Major Wickham gave a tiny nod.

Chloe alright, he decided. But why?

What possible combination of circumstances would lead her to hit a stranger in the face with a rock and then pick up his gun and shoot at people? And was the cadet group only Cpl Hankin's section or was it all of 4 Platoon? It was all very puzzling but also somehow reassuring. At least he had a better knowledge of the situation.

And this guy is lying. Half of what he said doesn't make sense, he decided.

At that moment the growl of motorcycles sounded and a few seconds later Brute rode down the slope followed by two bikies Major Wickham had never seen. The bikes were parked and Brute pointed to the creek.

"Peewee's body is over there."

The three of them walked over and stood looking down, muttering and talking angrily. Major Wickham only overheard a few words including 'Harley', 'shot in the back' and 'treacherous bastard!'.

Then Brute handed the pair a map and pointed to it. "I want this platoon of cadets found. Take this map and go up this creek here. They must have left tracks and they are carrying Harley on a stretcher so they should be easy to find."

"What do we do when we find 'em? Do we shoot 'em?" queried one, a tall man with red hair. He had a handgun and looked tough and his casual comment dismayed Major Wickham.

Brute shook his head. "Don't shoot unless they shoot at you. If they won't surrender then just keep 'em in sight and contact us," he explained.

"How do we do that?" the other man queried. "You said mobile phones don't work."

"They might up on top of the hills," Brute answered.

"And if they don't? We ain't got radios."

"One of you keep watching the cadets and the other one come and find us, either down here or at that top gate," Brute answered.

The man obviously wasn't happy about that, but he nodded and walked to his motorcycle and extracted a folded up shotgun from the saddle bags. It was full size shotgun and the sight of it filled Major

Wickham with horrified dismay. But then the red-headed man pulled a sub machine gun from his saddle bags and Major Wickham felt sick with apprehension all over again.

The second bikie screwed the barrels of his dismantled shotgun onto the wood before it was ready. Then he began to load it.

Brute became impatient. "Do that as you go! Get going!" he snapped.

The two still did not look happy but did as they were told. The redhead cocked his sub machine gun and his face took on a savage look of joy, but the other man just looked angry. As they vanished from view up the creek bed Major Wickham felt his hopes slide down again.

4 Platoon are in real trouble now, he thought.

Chapter 25

HUNTED

Jane paused at the crest of the next rise and anxiously scanned the country ahead. There was no sign of any bikies on the small sections of dirt road she could see but she was frightened of being seen by the men as the group crossed the bare slopes. Satisfied no-one was watching she hurried on across the rise and down into the re-entrant beyond. To her relief the others followed without any argument or straggling. They all looked anxious and she thought that was good.

I hope I convinced them of how serious this is, she told herself. She needed them convinced.

She went quickly up the next rise, almost running. Then she slowed to creep the last few metres to peek over. Still no sign of anyone. She waved the group to follow and set off at a fast walk across the wide ridge ahead of her. After about a hundred paces she came to the rough vehicle track which led up the ridge from the dirt road. There was almost no cover within 50 paces of this in any direction, so she just continued on across it, being careful not to step in the bare sand of the wheel ruts.

As she did the sound of motorcycles reached her ears and she felt her heart stop. Then her heart began to hammer as the fear flooded through her and the adrenalin was pumped into the bloodstream.

Oh no! Caught out in the open! she thought.

After glancing hastily around in the vain hope that there might be better cover, she shook her head and turned to face the group.

"Get down! Lie flat and don't move!" she called.

Suiting her own actions to the words she dropped onto the sandy, stony ground among the stubble of short dry grass and turned her head to watch. To her relief the others all obeyed at once and while they looked horribly visible to her she hoped their stillness might keep them hidden. Through her mind flashed the demonstration on 'Why things are seen' set up by Major Wickham when she was a First Year recruit. It had been in an old gravel scrape at a place called Macrossan, about 30 kilometres further west. At the time she had been astonished to find one of the NCOs in the demo squad lying in short grass in a tiny dip only about 15 paces in front of the squad of recruits and then even more surprised to be shown another who was lying 25 metres to their left in a tiny fold on completely bare earth.

Let's hope this works for us, she thought, half praying as she did.

Down on the dirt road a hundred metres to her left Jane glimpsed movement and the heads of two bikies appeared. The men were riding motorcycles and were heading west along the dirt road.

Going to search for Sgt Grey's patrol? she wondered.

To her great relief the two bikies went out of sight as they went down into the next dip. Jane lifted her head and screwed her neck around to keep watching, noting as she did that the other cadets in her group were all doing the same thing.

At least they will believe there are bikies now! she thought.

The two bikies re-appeared on the next slope and then vanished over the crest to go down out of sight into the creek line where she had meet Sgt Grey's patrol.

Now! she thought.

Jumping to her feet she waved and yelled, "Up! Run to the next dip but be ready to go down."

Jane began running, continually glancing back over her left shoulder as she did. Into her blurred and frantically focused vision came the two bikies. They were still riding their motorcycles along the dirt road and were still heading away from her. The dirt road went up a larger hill and she knew that she and the other cadets were taking a fearful risk by continuing to run out on such open ground.

If one of those bikies looks back they will see us at once, she thought.

But she also knew that if the two men stopped on top of that hill and looked back they would probably see them anyway if they had stayed where they were.

We need to get into a bit of dead ground, she reasoned.

There was a gentle dip ahead of her but it wasn't much cover. There were only a few spindly trees and a few rocks and small bushes scattered around the almost bare ground.

By then the two bikies were at the top of the hill and Jane knew her group had to take cover. Skidding to a stop she turned to face the cadets who were hurrying along behind her.

"Get down! Lie flat and don't move!" she called, gesturing furiously as she did.

Cadet Leece, Sgt Grey and Cpl Brandt did as they were told immediately but Sgt Lynes and Sgt Small did not. They kept running. Jane saw the two bikies bring their motorcycles to a stop and her chest tightened up with fear. "Get down!" she almost screamed.

"They will see you from that hill if you keep moving."

Acting partly to demonstrate and partly from self-preservation Jane dropped to the ground, facing back towards them. To her annoyance and dismay the two sergeants both stopped and looked back, Sgt Small looking urgently around in search of cover. Jane opened her mouth to call to them but the reality of the situation had obviously finally sunk in as both went down flat where they were.

Jane lay there panting, her eyes going out of focus from the exertion and anxiety. Her heart was hammering furiously and she had to blink and squint to counter the glare and trickles of sweat that further impaired her vision. She saw that they had been just in time. The two bikies now sat on their bikes looking in all directions, including towards where she and the others lay.

Sgt Lynes lifted his head to look behind. Jane shook her head and hissed, "Don't move! They are looking this way."

Sgt Lynes looked worried and lowered his head slowly. The others all lay still and Jane noted fear in their eyes. Several minutes ticked slowly by and Jane began to fret.

I hope they aren't going to stay there, she thought.

She was now worrying about what might be happening back at the platoon and the urge to get back there as quickly as possible gripped her.

The sound of motorbike engines revving carried to her and she noted the two bikies turn their bikes and start back down the hill towards them.

If they have seen us our goose is cooked! she thought.

But her mind also did some rapid calculations. "When I say go, get up and run fifteen paces and then take cover again," she called, confident that her voice would not be heard over the sound of the machines.

Tensing ready Jane watched the bikies ride back down the hill. As soon as they vanished into the creek line she sprang up.

"Go!" she cried.

Turning quickly around she sprinted for her life. The others also got to their feet and ran with her. As she ran Jane counted aloud, and at fourteen she sucked in a deep breath then cried, "Fifteen! Get down!"

Down they went. And it was just in time. The two bikies re-appeared briefly on the first rise and then went own out of sight into the small dip. But Jane shook her head at Sgt Grey who moved to get up.

"Not yet," she cautioned.

And she was right as the two bikies came into view a few seconds later down on their left. Because the cadets were now in the slight dip only the heads and upper bodies of the bikies were visible, but Jane glimpsed them come to a stop and then watched with dismay as their heads turned in her direction. The emotion changed to surging alarm when one of the men pointed up the ridge.

"They are coming this way. Stay still," she cautioned.

The motorcycle engines revved again and to her dismay Jane saw that she was half right. One of the bikies turned and began riding up the ridge, obviously following the rough vehicle track. The other bikie continued on back along the dirt road. But there was nothing to do but lie still in the short grass. So Jane did, her head turned to watch and her mouth dry with fear. Clenching her fists, she lay and prayed.

The first bikie's head appeared and then his upper body and finally his lower body. Only his boots and the lower half of the bike wheels remained hidden by the ground, so shallow was the dip they were lying in. The bikie rode slowly, his head swivelling from side to side so that he could scan the country. But he also had to focus on the rough going, and as he drew level with them, only 50 paces away, Jane began to hope.

The bikie went out of sight behind her and she had to carefully swing her head to look back over her right shoulder instead. Her heart kept thumping dramatically and she trembled with fear. Then she saw that the bikie was continuing on up the slope and every second took him further away.

He hasn't seen us, she reasoned.

Then she noted that she was shaking and feeling tight in the chest and lightheaded. Only then did she realise she was holding her breath.

Breathing slowly out she took several deep gulps of air and then shuddered. *That was close!* she thought.

Lifting her head carefully she saw that the bikie had gone from view among the rises and false crests and rock piles further up the ridge. The other bikie was nowhere to be seen and the sound of his motorbike had also faded off towards the creek where Capt Hamilton had been captured. For a few more seconds Jane hesitated, not wanting to leave what little cover they had but she knew they must take some risks.

I have to get back to Chloe, she told herself, mentally equating her friend with 4 Platoon.

After another cautious check Jane raised herself to her hands and knees to look in all directions. There was no sound of any motorcycle and no sign of any movement, so she stood up and signalled to the others to do the same.

"Let's go," she said.

Walking quickly, she hurried on down into the fold in the ground, still looking anxiously in all directions as she did. She was deeply conscious that the bikie who had ridden up the ridge might be able to see them from some vantage point further up but as she could not see any sign of him she decided they must keep taking the risk. So she kept moving. The others followed, also glancing fearfully around as they did.

Another five minutes of walking had them at the next crest line and again Jane approached it cautiously and then crept to the top. There was no sign of any bikies in any direction, but she could clearly see the rocky knoll where she had left Chloe and beyond that the big creek line and then the line of the Old Railway curving around the lower slopes of Railway Hill. There were tiny shapes on the top of that among the trees and rocks, but the distance was too far for Jane to see if they were the cadets from the Radio Relay Station or not.

Angling to the right Jane led the group over the lowest point in the skyline and down into the next small hollow. As she did, she glimpsed heads poking up from the grass at the bottom of the dip and realised it was 4 Platoon. Seeing them caused her a surge of relief mingled with exasperation that people were putting everyone at risk by poor fieldcraft.

As she hurried down the slope Jane saw movement on the knoll up to her left and she saw that it was Chloe waving to her. Chloe was a few metres back from the crest of the rocks and had been watching. Jane at once changed direction and led the group towards her. Two minutes later she stopped and crouched down beside her friend. Chloe just smiled and nodded, then looked at Sgt Small and pointed on down the slope.

"You'd better get down there and see what you can do," she said.

Sgt Small hesitated and for a moment Jane feared there would be a power struggle. But then Sgt Small just looked worried and nodded. She and Cpl Brandt turned and began making their way down the slope.

Chloe then turned to Jane. "Any problems?"

Jane shook her head. "No. We just had to take cover a couple of times from bikies."

Chloe nodded. "I saw that." She looked at Sgt Grey and Sgt Lynes. "I'm glad you are here. You can take command now," she said.

That was what Jane thought as well but now she saw flickers of concern and worry flit across the faces of the two sergeants and she experienced another sensation of doubt.

They don't look very keen, she thought.

Sgt Grey nodded but said nothing and Sgt Lynes just grunted, adding to Jane's concern. She turned and watched the two cadets making their way down to where the casualties lay in the bottom of the dip. "How are the wounded?" she asked.

Chloe again shook her head. "Don't know. I stayed up here," she replied.

"Any developments?"

Chloe nodded and looked grim. "Yes, and not good. The bikies have captured Major Wickham, Lt Peters and the CSM."

Jane felt her chest tighten up and her heart raced again. *Oh no!* she thought as despair welled up.

She had been pinning her hopes on getting word to the major and had not even considered that the bikies might do such a thing. "That might mean that Roach and Lepson made it back to camp and told them," she suggested.

Chloe looked doubtful. "Maybe," she muttered. "They certainly had time."

Sgt Grey now spoke. "What's going on? What are they doing down there?" he queried.

"Questioning them," Chloe answered. "Come and look."

She turned and began crawling back up to her observation point. Jane and the others followed.

"Keep off the skyline," Chloe hissed at Sgt Grey and Sgt Lynes.

Jane found a spot where she could see down to the creek where the dirt road crossed it and at once saw that her fears were confirmed. There were now two vehicles parked at the creek and quite a group of people. One in a camouflage uniform was being questioned by two bikies and even at that distance Jane could identify Major Wickham by his tubby build. Swallowing to ease her dry mouth she stared at the tableau, noting one of the bikies thrusting what looked like a CB radio at the major.

Chloe's CB radio suddenly crackled and Major Wickham's voice sounded loud and clear. "Two Four, this is Sunray, over."

Chloe lifted the radio and stared at it. Jane was tempted to tell her not to answer but Chloe obviously made a decision and pressed the transmit button.

"Sunray this is Two Four, over."

Major Wickham replied, relief evident in his tone. "Two Four, put on your sunray, over."

"Sunray, the sunray for this Call Sign is not here, over," Chloe answered.

"Two Four, move the platoon to me now, over."

"Where is that Sunray, over," Chloe answered, taking a pencil and notebook from her pocket as she did.

There was a short delay before Major Wickham answered. "Grid Reference six three three, zero four two. I say again figures six three three, zero four two, over."

"Roger. We are on our way, over," Chloe replied, noting the numerals.

"Keep me informed, Sunray out," Major Wickham said.

The radio went dead, and Jane clearly saw the big bikie with the goatee snatch it back off Major Wickham. Horrified at Chloe's answer she turned to look at her.

"You aren't going to do that surely?" she queried.

Chloe grinned and shook her head. "No fear!' she assured her.

Sgt Lynes frowned. "But you said that you were."

Chloe shook her head. "No, I didn't. I said we were on our way, and we will be too. We will go in the opposite direction."

Sgt Lynes shook his head. "But the major said to come to him," he said.

Chloe looked pained. "Yes, but he is acting under duress. Those mongrels are torturing Lt Peters and have hostages. They will be threatening them."

"But we have to obey orders," Sgt Lynes insisted.

Chloe shook her head. "Not when we know the orders are wrong," she replied.

"I say we go to the major," Sgt Lynes growled.

Again, Chloe shook her head and a stubborn look settled on her face. "No. You can go but we are not taking that man down there to be murdered. We are going to get to safety," she replied.

Sgt Lynes also looked stubborn. "It is an order! You are only a cadet. I am a sergeant and I am ordering you," he cried.

His attitude and loudness both annoyed Jane. She scowled at him and snapped, "Keep your voice down! We aren't going down there. Chloe is right. We have to keep this guy safe until we can hand him over to the police."

Sgt Lynes turned an angry glare on her. "You shut up Carson! You are just a cadet too." He then turned to Sgt Grey. "We have to do what the major said," he repeated.

Jane watched Sgt Grey's face and knew this was a moment of decision. Indecision showed plainly on Sgt Grey's face but then he swallowed and shook his head.

"I think we have to do what Chloe says. We can't risk anyone being hurt. We need to hide and get to safety."

Sgt Lynes curled his lip and sneered. "You are just a weakling Grey!" he cried. "We should obey orders."

Chloe interjected. "Well we aren't going to and you can't force us. Sgt Grey is right. The right thing to do is keep these wounded people safe and get to the police. Now let's get moving before they come looking for us."

Sgt Lynes glared angrily around. "You have to obey orders," he repeated.

But Chloe ignored him and began wriggling back off the skyline. Jane moved as well but then froze when Sgt Lynes grabbed at Chloe's sleeve and held her.

Sgt Lynes leaned down close to Chloe's face. "Do as you are told Cummings!" he snarled.

Chloe looked hard at him, then at her sleeve and then back up at him. "Let go of my sleeve. And stop making so much noise and placing others at risk. You can go if you want but don't tell them where we are or what we are doing."

For a few seconds Sgt Lynes kept his grip on Chloe's sleeve and he hissed at her to do what she was told. Her response was to stare defiantly back. Jane began to fear that Sgt Lynes would hit her or do something stupid and she tensed, ready to intervene.

A sudden roar of motorcycle engines down at the road made them all look around. Chloe glared at Sgt Lynes. "Get down!" she hissed.

To Jane's relief Sgt Lynes let go of Chloe's shirt and did so. Jane crawled back to where she could see down the slope towards the road and at once saw two bikies come riding up out of the creek line on their motorbikes. One was the big man with the goatee. Anxiously she watched the two as they rode west along the dirt road.

I wonder where they are off to? she thought.

She soon found out. The two bikies only went to the next ridge and then stopped at the junction with the vehicle track. For a minute or so the pair stood looking in all directions. Then they remounted their bikes and came riding back, to stop down at the creek. Jane watched as goatee again spoke to Major Wickham and handed him a radio.

Major Wickham's voice came through on the radio Chloe held. "Two Four, this is Sunray, Sitrep, over."

"Don't answer!" Sgt Lynes snapped.

Chloe lifted the radio but hesitated. Jane's attention was torn between the struggle of wills and the drama down in the creek. She saw that some sort of argument was going on.

Then Chloe shook her head. "We have to make them think we are co-operating," she said to Sgt Lynes. Pressing the transmit button she replied, "Sunray, this is Two Four. We are on our way, but it is very slow going carrying these stretchers down the hill, over."

"Stretchers?" Major Wickham answered and Jane's heart went out to him at the anguish evident in his tone.

"We have two seriously wounded Sunray, over," Chloe replied.

"Do you mean that someone has been shot, over?" Major Wickham asked.

"Roger. Two. Call the ambulance, over," Chloe replied.

"Roger. Hurry up... eeh!" Major Wickham said.

As he was cut off Jane glanced down the hill just in time to see the radio being wrenched from his grasp. To her horror she saw goatee ram a shotgun muzzle into his right cheek.

There were a few tense moments and then Jane's dismay was increased by seeing Major Wickham hit and knocked to the ground. Glancing sideways she saw that a sickly expression of horror was forming on Sgt Lynes' face.

She was tempted to tell him he could go down there if he liked but instead, she muttered, "We had better get moving."

Chloe nodded. "You are right. Let's go," she said.

Once again, she began crawling to the rear. Again, Sgt Lynes looked angry, but he said nothing and did not grab at her. Instead he unhooked his own CB radio.

As he lifted it to his mouth Jane shook her head. "Don't you do that!" she hissed.

Chloe turned and saw what he was going to do. Anger and determination showed on her face. "You talk on that and you will regret it," she muttered.

"Are you threatening me?" Sgt Lynes blustered.

"Yes," Chloe replied. "If you want to surrender then do so but don't give away any information about what we are doing. Now let's get out of here."

For a few tense seconds Jane thought that Sgt Lynes was going to defy Chloe. The pair glared at each other. But then he lowered the radio and shook his head. Jane let out a long sigh of relief and then took several deep breaths before sliding back down behind the rocks. Her webbing was lying there in the grass and she scooped it up and swung it on as Chloe started down the slope towards the platoon. She began walking down behind Chloe. Cadet Leece also retrieved his webbing and followed and Sgt Grey went with him. Sgt Lynes stood there angrily shaking his head and looking baffled.

At that moment the noise of a motorcycle engine echoed around the hills and Jane felt fear stab at her again. Anxiously she crouched down and looked around.

"Get down!" she cried.

Chapter 26

MORE PROBLEMS

Jane looked anxiously in all directions.

That sound isn't coming from down on the dirt road, she told herself.

But where was the motorbike? The noise seemed to echo around the hills making the direction of the source very hard to determine.

"Get down!" she repeated loudly.

The others did so. And just in time! Suddenly the noise clarified and Jane glimpsed movement directly in front of her up on the Old Railway across the creek. It was a bikie on a motorbike and he was riding from her right to her left.

That looks like the bloke who rode up the ridge past us, she thought. But she wasn't sure. All she could decide was that it was very hard to predict where a bikie might next appear from. *How many of them are there?* she wondered.

Chloe thought so too. As the bikie vanished from view around to the north side of Railway Hill she stuck her head up and muttered, "These bloody bikies seem to be everywhere."

"They do," Jane agreed.

"So how do we dodge them? I was planning to go across the creek and back along that Old Railway," she said.

Jane pointed up the hollow to their right. "We'll have to detour around in the low ground to keep this hill between us and the Old Railway," she suggested.

Chloe nodded. "That will do. Come on. Let's get the platoon moving." As she stood up she looked at Sgt Grey but to Jane's disappointment he just stared back and looked worried but said nothing.

The group made their way down to where the remainder of the platoon waited in the bottom of the gully. Jane did not really want to look at the casualties, but she forced herself to do so. What she saw appalled her. Kim was pale and sweating and in obvious terror of dying. The big man, Harley, was still unconscious and looked blue around the lips and very pale. The bandage around his head was half soaked with blood.

Sgt Small looked unhappy and sickly and kept gesturing with shrugs of her shoulders. "We have to get them to a hospital right away," she insisted.

"We will try," Chloe assured her. "Now corporals, get your stretcher parties ready to carry."

Jane watched and felt a real mix of emotions. She was aware she was still stunned and horrified and wanted it all to just end but she was also angry and determined. To add to her mental confusion was watching the power play in the group. She had been hoping one of the sergeants or corporals would step up and take charge and take the load of responsibility off her shoulders and off Chloe's but now saw that they were all looking to Chloe.

Weak bastards! she thought. *They don't deserve their rank.*

Chloe now redistributed the new patrol to help carry. "Sgt Grey, you take charge of Kim's stretcher and Sgt Lynes, you take charge of Harley's. Now, we are going to swap stretchers. So bring that Harley bloke's stretcher up here and put him beside Kim."

Jane approved of that. Harley was much too big for the improvised broomstick stretcher, so she helped transfer him to the proper army Litter Folding. Kim was first lifted off onto the grass and then lifted onto the improvised stretcher.

While they were doing this the radio crackled. It was Major Wickham calling again. This time Chloe listened and then bit her lip before shaking her head.

"No," she said. "I'm not going to answer. Now get on with it. Rod, you go Tail-end Charlie and Jane, you scout and navigate again."

Jane was happy with that. She studied the map and then pointed back up the hollow. The stretchers were lifted then the group set off, Chloe stepping in behind Jane. As before it was slow going, even with eight people on each stretcher and two spare carriers. The platoon struggled up the dip and slowly made their way around to the north side of the next small hill. That was a relief to Jane as they were now out of sight of anyone on either Railway Hill or the Old Railway around it but she was acutely aware that the rocky knoll they had been using as an OP was directly behind them.

If one of those bikies walks up to it they will spot us immediately, she reasoned.

But the extra people did make a difference and 10 minutes later the platoon was at the top end of the hollow and another decision on their route had to be taken. Chloe joined Jane at the crest and they studied the rocky ridges ahead and to their left.

"We could go west up this ridge," Chloe suggested.

Jane shook her head. "That's might be easier going but that is where that motorbike went. There is a vehicle track up it. I think we should go south and back to camp."

"OK kiddo. You lead," Chloe agreed.

At that moment the radio again broke into life, Major Wickham calling. He sounded quite anxious. Again, Chloe hesitated and then shook her head.

"No," she muttered. "Time to sow a bit of doubt and dissension in the minds of the enemy."

Jane took out a water bottle and while she unscrewed the cap looked back to check whether Sgt Lynes was using his radio. Noting that he wasn't she took a swig and then nodded. "That's what Major Wickham keeps telling us, in war you are fighting the mind of the enemy commander."

"So who is their commander?" Chloe asked.

"That big brute with the goatee beard," Jane answered.

Chloe nodded. "I think so too."

But Jane was troubled. "What if they hurt the major or Lt Peters when we don't answer?" she asked.

Chloe looked worried and then shook her head. "They might but giving in will cause people grief too. Better to defy them I think."

Jane still felt disturbed at taking such a risk but had to accept the logic. She was sure that if they gave in then Harley would die.

I don't want that on my conscience, she thought.

But nor did she want Kim's possible death on it either. "What about Kim?" she asked. "She might die if we don't get her to a doctor quickly."

Chloe nodded. "You are right but I think that is a risk we must take. We should get help within the hour. Surely Roach and Lepson have reached headquarters by now. It is nearly fifteen hundred."

Jane had doubts about that too but was still pinning half her hopes on it. "The gutless turds! I hope so," she replied. "But we need to move faster."

Chloe bit her lip and again nodded. "You are right. OK, let's get on."

She turned and raised her hand to signal but then paused and looked anxiously around. So did Jane. She had also heard the echoing sound of motorcycles. Quickly she crouched and looked in all directions. But the sound seemed to come from a distance and the noise level rose and fell and at times died quiet away. Jane felt herself gripped by dread and began to hyperventilate until she realised what she was doing. The worst thing for her was that she could not tell exactly where the noise was coming from. At times Jane thought the motorbikes were on the vehicle track on the ridge to her north and at other times she thought they might be on the Old Railway. But she saw no sign of them. Then the sounds died away, leaving Jane with the awful impression of lurking enemies on all sides.

For several minutes the girls stayed crouched under what little cover there was until Chloe at last shook her head.

"They've gone," she said. "We'd better move." So she stood and signalled for the sections to pick up the stretchers again.

Crossing that crest line took so long that Jane became very anxious. She was also a little puzzled over the direction to take as the map did not seem to match up to all of the rocky hills and knolls that dotted the ridges. But she decided that staying in the covered lines of advance was the best option so led the way around into another low dip that led down into a small re-entrant that in turn led into a much larger creek line that was almost a small valley.

It was only when they were well down it and Chloe called a halt to rest and change the people on the stretchers that Jane had some real doubts. She went back to Chloe and said, "I'm just going to scout down to the creek line there and see what the going is like."

"I'll come with you," Chloe said.

She signalled for the platoon to lie low and then took out the pistol and checked it. It was only then that Sgt Lynes saw it and he blanched. Jane had to smile as she was sure Chloe would have threatened him with it if she had been forced to.

The two girls carefully scouted down the small gully until they came to what was obviously the junction of two larger creeks. Jane crouched under cover and peered through the foliage. Doubts began to assail her.

"I think I have come too far to the left," she whispered. "I think that is the main creek we came down, that one there on the left."

Chloe crouched next to her and took out her map. "So this other creek here must be this one, and the two join here," she said, pointing.

Jane looked and felt a surge of dismay. *We've only come four or five hundred metres,* she thought.

She found that very disheartening, but she was careful not to add to Chloe's burden by saying anything so demoralizing. Instead she pointed and said, "So if we go down into the bigger creek and then turn right we will come to the Number One Bottom Mill."

Chloe nodded. "I think that's right. If we do that we can go back the way we came."

Jane was dubious. "Bit of a risk if the bikies are patrolling the Old Railway," she replied.

"Yeah, but it is the most direct route back to camp, or to the Flinders Highway," Chloe replied.

She was about to stand up when the thudding of boots and scuffling sounds on sand came to them from the main creek. The two girls looked at each other in alarm and then sank down behind the rock they had chosen for cover. Jane thought that the people coming might be cadets, but she also knew they could not risk being seen.

I hope nobody back in the platoon makes any noises, she thought anxiously.

To her later shame she found she was almost paralysed by the fear that swamped her whole being. All she could do was crouch there trembling while staring out through the thin screen of leaves.

Into view came two bikies. A glance told her that they were the 'real deal'. *Ridgie Digie bikies,* she thought, noting the hard faces, tattoos, leather jackets and studded belts.

Jane had never seen either man before. They were armed, one with a sub machine gun and the other with a shotgun and were plainly hunting for the platoon. As the men came to the creek junction ten metres away they stopped and one of them, a man with red hair, pointed at the sandy creek bed.

"They went this way," he said, pointing up the left-hand creek in front of the two girls.

As the men started walking again Jane froze, her heart hammering and mouth dry with fear.

If they look they will see us, her frightened mind cried.

And one of the men did look. He cast a quick glance at the side gully and for a moment Jane felt her whole being go stiff with terror. But then he looked back at the sandy creek bed and pointed up the bigger creek.

"Yep, they definitely went this way."

The two men hurried on and within a few seconds were lost to sight. Jane began to suck in gulps of air and found she was sweating. She shuddered and found she urgently needed to go to the toilet.

Chloe nudged her. "Now is our chance. If we move fast, we can slip across behind them while they are searching up that creek," she said.

Jane met her eyes and nodded, hoping that her friend had not noticed how scared she was. "I need a pee," she whispered.

Chloe grinned. "Then nip off up the main creek and do some scouting while I get the platoon. That should give you a few minutes."

Jane nodded and felt grateful. She found she was trembling and had to use her willpower to get herself to move. Chloe stood up and hurried back the other way. Jane was still so frightened that she had trouble focusing her vision and the thudding of her heart made it hard for her to hear. Carefully she eased her way out from behind the rock and peeked up the creek line the men had gone along. Hearing nothing and seeing no sign of them she hurried across, talking care not to step on soft sand as she did.

She reached the creek junction and was then certain it was the main creek. *There are our tracks from when we came down to start the exercise,* she noted.

After moving another few paces she was convinced. Knowing her exact location was comforting but also worrying. They were now back on the most obvious withdrawal route and that had not been what she wanted.

More of those bikies could come along at any moment, she fretted.

But she also urgently needed that pee and it put her in a real quandary. *I will really be caught with my pants down if those men come back now!* she thought.

But she either did that or wet herself so she decided that speed was the best option. Finding a small hollow behind some big rocks she hurriedly relieved herself. It was the most testing pee she had ever done and left her relieved but breathless with anxiety. Hastily she pulled up her trousers and did them up, then swung on her webbing again.

She was just in time as the sound of muttering voices and boots scuffing on rocks came to her. A frightened glance out of her cover showed her that it was Chloe and the first stretcher party, not more bikies. Shuddering with relief Jane stepped out and signalled it was safe. Chloe nodded and turned to help lift the stretcher down past the rocks and trees they had hid behind earlier. Then she directed the cadets to be very careful not to stand in the sand.

"We don't want any tracks," she explained.

Jane turned and began scouting southwards along the side of the main creek, taking care to keep close among the trees and rocks on the west bank. As she did she became aware that she could see the bench cut of the Old Railway up to her left.

If a bikie rides along that now he must see us, she told herself, her anxiety level shooting up again.

A glance at her watch told her it was already 15:20. She was amazed, remembering that it had been about 1200hrs when the action had begun.

The second stretcher party came into view and the cadets found it very difficult to stay on the rocks. At times they moved to the steeper slope of the hillside on their right but that left a few scuff marks and disturbed leaves and noting that Jane felt sure any half intelligent person would be able to track them. The feelings of risk and of being hunted so gripped her with dread that she found it hard to think straight or to function physically. Part of her wanted to just run and another part felt an intense desire to hide. But she managed to keep herself under control.

Chloe needs me and so do Kim and the others, she told herself.

So she kept doing her duty as scout to the best of her ability, moving carefully from tree to tree and making sure she stayed well ahead and under cover as much as possible.

And she found she was right. The bare, dung-splattered earth surrounding the No1 Bottom Mill came into view and then the windmill and drinking trough. A vehicle track led up on the left to the bench cut of the Old Railway and for a few moments she wondered whether that might not be the best route to take.

It will be much easier walking along the Old Railway, she thought.

But she also knew that the chances of meeting one of the bikies would be much higher. A study of her map decided her when she noted that the

Old Railway did a big semi-circle away before coming back to join the cattle pad they had come down that morning.

"So, straight ahead," she muttered.

But getting around the clearing under the trees was a problem. The main creek curved right and a small creek went off on the left up into the big curve of the Old Railway which Jane saw now went on a high embankment.

That creek ends just past the Old Railway, she thought as she studied the ground and compared it with her map.

And crossing the bare, trampled earth around the mill without leaving tracks would hard to do. The trail of boot prints from their earlier crossing were very plain; so clear that she could plainly see the actual tread marks in the dark soil and had no doubt anyone could determine the direction of travel from that.

If we cross that we will leave a track like an elephant, Jane thought.

So she decided that the best route was around the western side against the base of the hill with the main creek on their left. She directed Chloe and the first stretcher party to go that way. Then she moved on under the trees to check out the route up the hill.

This led her around to the junction with another creek. It was much smaller and went off to her right, Southwest she noted. For a minute Jane stopped to study her map, and while she was doing that she noted the cattle pad they had come down. It went up the slope from the clearing and seeing it gave her another boost of hope.

If we go up there we come to the Old Railway after a hundred metres or so and then we are only a kilometre or so from camp, she thought.

But again the fear of being caught on the Old Railway caused her to pause. Carefully she studied the ground and was dismayed to note that the main creek became very narrow and came down through a very steep-sided and rough little valley.

Carrying the stretchers up that creek is going to be bloody difficult, she thought.

So the Old Railway it had to be. That meant crossing the main creek but above the junction it was much narrower and had a rocky bottom so she felt confident they could obliterate their tracks.

She was just stepping across the creek bed when the sound of motorcycles starting up caused her heart rate to shoot right up. She jumped with fright and scuttled across to cover at the base of the spur that the cattle pad went up. Then she looked fearfully in the direction the sounds were coming from, her left.

She could not see the bikes but decided there were two or three. *They are up on the Old Railway,* she noted.

Glancing back she saw that consternation was gripping the first stretcher party. Cadets were struggling to put the stretcher down without dropping it and once they had they all scrambled for cover. Chloe came hurrying across, pistol in hand.

Jane was about to speak when the engine notes changed and began to move across from her left to her right. The noises became muffled and she understood that the bikes were passing through the deep cutting which ended at the point where the cattle pad came up to the Old Railway.

Have the bikies seen us? she worried.

Chloe crouched beside her, pistol ready, her eyes following the sound. But all they could see was the rock and tree studded grassy slope of the spur. No bikes came into sight and then the sound began to die away.

Chloe gestured. "They are going along the Old Railway," she said.

Jane nodded. "They are. I was going to lead us up to it because from the top here it is only half a kilometre or so of relatively flat ground to the Flinders Highway. But now I'm not sure if it is a good risk."

Chloe looked around, concentrating on the steep-sided re-entrant of the main creek and the side creek to the southwest.

"That looks a bit rough," she said. "I think you are right. I reckon we should try going up here."

"What if the bikies come back?"

Chloe shrugged. "We have to hide or try to slip past when they are away from here. There can't be that many of them and they can't cover everywhere."

Jane wasn't so sure. "There seem to be an awful lot."

Chloe shook her head. "No. We've only seen five or six. There can't be more than a dozen. I say go up."

"What if they've left someone at the top here to catch us?" Jane suggested, voicing one of her fears.

"Then we scout it first. Come on, you and I will do that while they bring the stretchers up. I will just tell Sgt Grey what we are doing," Chloe said.

She hurried back and spoke to Sgt Grey for a minute or so. Sgt Grey looked quite unhappy but nodded and Chloe came hurrying back. Gesturing up the cattle pad she whispered, "OK Kiddo, lead the way."

Jane was very aware that she was gripped by dread and knew that she did not want to go. But looking at Chloe she experienced the now familiar emotional mix of admiration and jealousy.

She is just so beautiful, and so brave! I can't let her know I'm scared, she thought.

So, after taking a deep breath and determined not to let her friend down she set off up the path.

Chapter 27

CHLOE MAKES AN ENEMY

As she went cautiously up the cattle pad Jane felt so scared and drained that she just wanted to stop and hide. But she forced herself to keep moving, being still driven by apprehension about Kim and the man Harley.

We must get them to a hospital, she told herself.

But she knew there were bikies somewhere up ahead and the fear of them was almost crippling. Her eyes kept flicking in all directions so as to detect them. And she found she was breathing so fast that she was almost hyperventilating and that didn't help. It caused her to feel light-headed and made her vision blurry and full of dancing black dots. With an effort of will power she calmed her breathing and kept herself moving.

The cattle pad led up the spine of the spur for a hundred metres or so through open savannah woodland. There was plenty of cover in the direction they were moving and a thick mass of tree canopies hid them from anyone out to their left on the Old Railway but she was anxiously aware that the rocks on the summit of the ridge provided excellent cover for any hostile watchers.

Higher up the ridge the pad led to the right of the large pile of boulders that clumped on the summit. At the point where the track went to the side of the ridge Jane was able to see clearly along the valley of the main creek and what she saw confirmed her earlier thoughts. The valley was now so deep and so steep-sided that she doubted if they could have carried the stretchers up it at all.

She paused and pointed this out to Chloe. Chloe looked and nodded then glanced back at the stretcher parties, the first of which was now about 50 metres behind and obviously struggling on the climb.

"I'll lead for a bit," she said, indicating her pistol.

Jane nodded but did not like the idea. She was appalled at the idea of Chloe having to use the gun, even though she recognized the possible necessity. Stepping aside she allowed Chloe to pass her on the narrow path and then followed her on up the hill.

As the two friends stealthily crept up the ridge Jane kept straining her ears for any sound of motorcycles. But, to her annoyance, she kept hearing cicadas and also the swashing thud of her own heartbeat. Her vision had now cleared and she anxiously scanned a rocky knoll that had come into view on their right front. It was on the other side of the main creek and to the right of it was a real jumble of rocky outcrops, knolls and small hollows.

As they neared the point where the cattle pad joined the Old Railway Jane spotted what her brain had told her must be there, the powerline. She waited until Chloe glanced back and then pointed. Chloe looked then nodded and smiled. "Not far now," she whispered.

Jane wasn't sure if Chloe meant to the Old Railway or to the camp but agreed with both ideas.

A kilometre to camp, she told herself, adding the comforting notion that she could walk that in ten or fifteen minutes if she chose to.

And there was the Old Railway! Jane saw Chloe stop among the last few boulders where she crouched under cover and looked to her left. Then she looked back and pointed to it. Jane moved up another ten paces and was able to see the Old Railway. It curved around from her left through the deep cutting and then ran smooth and level away from her under the powerlines and off between the rocky hill on the right and a bare slope on the left. The embankment where the Old Railway crossed the main creek was just visible at about the point where the powerline crossed it.

Jane was just starting to feel hopeful when Chloe suddenly gripped her wrist and squeezed it then slid down to crouch among the rocks and long grass at the point where the cattle pad made its way onto the Old Railway bench cut. Jane looked in the direction Chloe had indicated and her heart thudded and seemed to freeze. She could just see into the deep cutting on her left and moving through it towards her were three people, two cadets and a bikie!

Jane's eyes did an instant focus and her brain registered recognition as she focused on the bikie.

Slasher! she thought. *The man who tried to kill Harley.*

As her mind took this terrifying notion on board, she noted that he was armed and was pointing a gun at the two cadets who walked in front of him. One of the cadets was wheeling a motorbike.

Jane instantly crouched down and tried to calm her racing emotions and breathing. *Can we hide here?* she wondered anxiously.

Glancing around she thought they might but then the sound of voices back down the cattle pad came to her. They came from one of the stretcher parties.

Oh, be quiet you fools! she thought, desperation mounting.

Swallowing with apprehension she whispered to Chloe: "I'll go back and warn them."

Chloe glanced at her and shook her head. "Too late! Lie low," she hissed.

Jane hesitated and then realised Chloe was right. The group was only about twenty paces away and Slasher's voice came clearly to her. "Walk faster you pair! I ain't got all day," he snarled.

Jane had recognized the two cadets as Sergeant Harvey, the CQMS and Sgt Moyle, the signals sergeant.

The bikies have captured the Radio Relay Station, she thought.

That sent her hopes down a bit as she had still been vaguely wondering if they might have been able to get help. Now fear sent her lower in the short grass in an attempt to stay hidden so she was unable to see the approaching group.

But she could hear them and began to fervently hope that their voices would drown out any sound from the struggling stretcher parties. Fearful they would be heard she took the risk of crawling quickly back a few paces along the cattle pad on her hands and knees. By now her heart was hammering and she had to restrain an urge to just flee. She had seen that Slasher had a sawn-off shotgun and she was sure he would use it.

Harley is just there. That man will kill him. I must stop that happening, she thought.

Gripped by a growing sense of desperation she glanced around, judged she was hidden by the higher ground and got to her feet, then looked back down the track. She wanted very much to run but also knew that the sound of running boots carried a long way so she disciplined herself to stay still.

And there was the first stretcher party, about 50 paces back down the ridge. Jane began to frantically wave with one hand, gesturing them to get down, while using the forefinger of her other hand to indicate silence. Luckily Sgt Grey saw her and he shushed the others. They all looked and

Jane had the inspiration to give them a 'thumbs down', the silent field signal for enemy. Then she repeated the signal for silence and to take cover.

They did and she saw the group behind also go to ground. Jane then dithered for a few seconds. Her instincts were to run down the ridge to join the others but her loyalty to Chloe held her there.

Chloe might be seen, she thought. Anxiety over her friend's well-being got her to turn and take cover beside the cattle pad.

By this time Jane's senses were so heightened by the fear that she was acutely sensitive to all sounds and the sights she focused on. The dry mouth and trembling muscles were forgotten, although the bowels and bladder felt obvious. She was so aware that the bikie might appear at any moment that she moved into the grass with ultra-caution.

She had only just gone down when she noted Chloe crouched in the grass on the left of the track about a dozen paces away. Chloe looked at her and gave a tiny shake of the head. Jane took the hint, terror helping her to decide. She crouched even lower, heart hammering and ears prickling to detect any sounds.

And it was Slasher she heard. He was angry and now snarled, "You drop that bike over the edge kid and you will follow it, in pieces!"

She glanced up and saw the top half of Sgt Moyle. He was struggling to manoeuvre the motorcycle up on the Old Railway and had obviously had trouble turning it. The bike appeared to be half over the edge and when Sgt Moyle pulled it back it toppled on its side. The frightened sergeant gripped it and began to struggle to get it upright. But it was a big bike and obviously heavy.

Jane understood why Sgt Moyle was scared. She had heard one of the worst things a person could do to annoy a bikie was to damage his bike.

And there was Slasher! The bikie appeared beside Sgt Moyle and hit at him with the shotgun barrel. "Stupid little shit!" he shouted.

Sgt Moyle took the blow on his shoulder before he was able to react and as he staggered to hold the bike upright Slasher let go of the gun with one hand and used the other to grab the back of the bike. For a few moments it looked like the bike would tumble over the edge into the steep gully, but they held it and it slid to a stop half upright.

"Now get it back up you pair," Slasher snarled, again levelling the gun at them.

He stepped back and then looked around, causing Jane's heart to hammer with anxiety. She was terribly aware that she had only a thin screen of short grass hiding her and was sure her bum pack and webbing were poking up. Then Slasher moved a couple of paces to the top of the cattle pad and stood staring down at the ground.

Has he seen our boot tracks? Jane wondered. She did not think they had walked back that far. *He might be looking at the tracks the platoon made on the way out,* she thought.

But something had obviously attracted Slasher's attention and he now walked several paces along the track, eyes flicking down and then up as he did. In the process he moved to stand right next to where Chloe was crouching. Jane could just see parts of her through the spindly tufts of grass she was trying to hide behind.

Has he seen me? her terrified mind wondered.

Slasher stood and stared downhill towards her and frowned. He then took another pace. At that Jane decided he wasn't looking at her and she carefully turned her head slightly and glanced back over her shoulder.

Bloody Arthur! Jane saw Arthur's face for a fleeting second before it bobbed back down under cover. *The bloody fool!* she thought.

Slasher took another pace and hefted his shotgun across his front. "Hey you, the kid who just stuck his head up! Get up here or I'll shoot," he shouted.

Jane saw Slasher raise the butt of the shotgun to his shoulder as he aimed it down the hill. Her whole body began to tingle and her skin crawled in anticipation of being hit. She tensed ready to run even as her hopes went crashing.

We have been seen! Now we will have to surrender, she thought.

But then she saw Slasher turn his head as he detected movement close beside him.

It was Chloe. She had silently risen to her feet and now swung the gun in her hand. Slasher's eyes widened in recognition and he began to duck away. But he wasn't fast enough and the blow struck him on the side of the head. He went down instantly, and hard. Jane was now terrified that there might be a gun battle and she dithered, undecided whether to roll off down the steep slope or to throw rocks. With that in mind she picked up a convenient stone and sprang to her feet.

But Chloe was faster. She bent down and grabbed Slasher's right little finger and pulled it back hard until this hand opened and the shotgun fell out of it. She quickly snatched it up and reversed it, ready to use. Then she stepped back.

"Jane, help me!" Chloe cried.

Jane ran up to where Chloe stood over a groaning and writhing Slasher. Chloe held out the shotgun, barrel pointed up.

"Drop the rock Cave Girl and take this while I tie him up," she said.

Gingerly Jane did so, finding the sawn-off shotgun an unbalanced and fearsome thing. Carefully she held it so that the muzzles remained pointing skywards.

"Well done!" she cried.

Chloe nodded. "Had to. Did he see you?"

"No. That dickhead Arthur stuck his head up to look," Jane replied. She looked around, her mind racing with options. Nearby stood the two headquarters sergeants. They were holding Slasher's motorcycle which they had managed to get back upright and both were gaping at them. Jane noted that Sgt Moyle, who was the unit signals sergeant, was carrying an RTF200 radio as well as his webbing but that Sgt Harvey, the CQMS, only had her webbing.

Turning to Chloe, who had now swung her webbing off and was digging in it for nylon cord Jane said, "We need to get out of here fast, before any of his mates come along."

Chloe nodded. "We do. I have a plan."

Jane indicated the apparently unconscious but groaning Slasher. "Don't say it. He might be listening."

Chloe nodded and then quickly looked around. Sure that they were still safe she stood up with a roll of cord in her hands and hurried over to Jane.

Pointing down the hill and then west she whispered, "Run back and tell the platoon to go back down the hill and then up that other creek to the west, and make sure they don't leave any tracks. Then come back and help me."

Jane nodded and started running. Behind her she heard Chloe say to the two sergeants, "Sgt Harvey, come here and give me a hand, quickly!"

It took Jane less than thirty seconds to reach Sgt Grey's team. They were still lying in the grass looking anxious. She cast a withering glance at Arthur and then quickly passed on Chloe's instructions.

"Quickly! Go fast! We will catch you up," she cried.

Sgt Grey nodded and stood up, signalling the others up and getting them organised. By the time Jane had turned and started back up the track all of that group were on their feet and she could see some of the second stretcher party getting up and looking at them.

Jane had an idea what Chloe's plan might be and as she ran back up to where Slasher lay on the cattle pad her mind turned over a dozen options. She saw that Chloe had bound Slasher's wrists behind his back. She began undoing his belt.

Sgt Harvey stood there looking scared but puzzled. "What are you doing? Why don't we just run?" she queried.

Chloe looked up as she unbuckled the studded leather belt. "Because we have two casualties on stretchers," she replied.

"Casualties?" Sgt Harvey gasped.

"Yes. Does that radio work? Call HQ and get the police and ambulance," Chloe ordered.

A gawking Sgt Moyle indicated the motorcycle he was still struggling to keep upright. "What will I do with this?" he asked.

Sgt Harvey spoke. "Push it over the edge," she suggested.

But Chloe held up her hand. "No! That will really annoy these bikies and give us some long-term problems," she said.

Jane nodded. "That's right. Do things to their wives and girlfriends but don't do things to their bikes, not if you want to stay alive. Just hold it. Sgt Harvey, you use the radio."

Sgt Harvey nodded and did as she was told. But it was immediately apparent that the net was still being jammed.

"Try the alternate frequency," Jane suggested.

Sgt Harvey got Sgt Moyle to turn so she could adjust the tuning dials and then tried again. But there was no response. "Probably nobody listening on this frequency," she suggested.

"Keep trying," Jane ordered. She then turned back to see to her astonishment that Chloe had undone Slasher's trousers and was tugging them down. "Chloe! What are you doing?" she asked.

"Making sure this mongrel can't suddenly attack us or run," Chloe replied. She then reefed Slasher's pants down to his knees, exposing soiled underwear. Chloe studied him for a few seconds and then shook her head, her face a mask of distaste. "Ugly looking slug," she grunted.

Jane looked and silently agreed. Glancing up her eyes met Sgt Harvey's. She looked shocked and scared but nodded. Chloe then pointed. "OK Sgt Harvey, grab his other arm."

Sgt Harvey did. "Now lift him," Chloe ordered. The two girls lifted Slasher's upper body off the ground. "Now drag him," Chloe went on. "Jane, you scout ahead. Sgt Moyle, bring that motorbike."

Jane was now mystified as to what Chloe's plan might be but did as she was told. Quickly she walked south along the Old Railway, her eyes scanning ahead and ears tuned to detect any motorcycle sounds. To her dismay she heard engine noises but then realised that what she was hearing was a big truck on the Flinders Highway. That cheered her.

Not far now! Maybe half a kilometre, she told herself.

Within a minute she was standing on the embankment under the powerlines and she glanced back to check on the others. To her further mystification she saw Chloe hold up her hand to indicate stop and then point to her left.

She wants me to turn off Jane decided.

Glancing that way she saw that down on her left was a low grassy flat beside the main creek and on it were a couple of thorn trees.

The main creek goes straight back up to near camp, she thought, thinking this might be Chloe's plan but then worrying about who was going to take charge of the platoon to get them and the casualties to safety.

She waited there until the others joined them. Chloe and Sgt Harvey dragged Slasher along the Old Railway and down the bank, his boot heels scouring furrows in the sand. Chloe then pointed to their right. "Into that culvert," she instructed. "Sgt Moyle, bring the motorbike down."

Jane now looked and saw what she realised she should have known was there, a culvert under the Old Railway for the main creek to drain through. The culvert was nearly head-high and Chloe and Sgt Harvey hauled Slasher inside out of sight. At Chloe's command they lowered him to the floor of the concrete pipe. As they did something clicked in Jane's mind. "Chloe, he's got one of our radios!"

They all looked and Chloe reached down and grabbed the CB radio which was hung around Slasher's neck on a yellow lanyard. She turned it over and there in yellow paint was the number 26 and the unit name.

"Ours alright!" she said. "They must have taken it off the major."

"Give it to me," Jane said.

She hurried over and took the CB and hung it around her own neck while Chloe went through his pockets, extracting a mobile phone which she slid into her pocket.

As she did Slasher opened his eyes. He blinked several times and then began to squirm violently. "Let me go you bitches!" he shouted. Then he realised his pants had been pulled down and his anger grew so that he became even more violent.

"Shut up!" Chloe snapped, "Or I'll pull your underpants down and kick you in the nuts." She bent down and tried to shove a handkerchief into Slasher's mouth.

He flung his head rapidly from side to side to try to prevent this but then whacked it against the concrete pipe. "Ow! Ooh you bitch! You'll bloody pay for... mff... grf... gmmmf," he snarled.

Chloe got the gag in place and then gestured to Sgt Harvey. "You go back out and wait there," she said.

Sgt Harvey looked and then hesitated. Jane understood her anxiety. To get out of the culvert Sgt Harvey would have to step over Slasher's writhing form and she plainly viewed such an action with trepidation. Not so Chloe. She scrambled back, her boots thudding at Slasher's body and thighs. Slasher tried to trip her but failed. Sgt Harvey then scurried after Chloe.

Chloe turned to Sgt Moyle. "Just push that bike into the entrance to the culvert," she instructed, helping him to do so. Through all this Jane stood amazed and anxious.

Chloe has really made an enemy now! she thought.

She noted that Slasher had a huge 'egg' bruise growing on the right side of his temple where Chloe had struck him with the pistol. The left side of his face still showed the bruise from where she had struck him earlier. Seeing Slasher's bulging and hate-filled eyes she shivered.

Now what is her plan?

She now found out. As soon as Sgt Harvey re-joined them Chloe pointed south along the main creek and said, "We are going that way."

Jane glanced into the culvert and saw Slasher watching them. Hastily she put a finger to her lips and shook her head. "Chloe, that Slasher is watching."

Chloe cast a frightened look over her shoulder and then nodded.

Pointing again to the south she called, "Come away so that Flasher guy can't hear us."

They moved ten paces up the dry creek bed until they were out of sight of Slasher. Chloe then indicated for them to stop and she grinned. Jane realised that her looking frightened had all been an act.

It wasn't any act for me! she thought ruefully.

Chloe nodded. "Good! He thinks that is the way we are going."

"Aren't we?" Sgt Harvey queried, all the while casting frightened glances back towards the culvert.

Chloe shook her head. "I'd like you and Sgt Moyle to but we are going back to the platoon."

When Jane heard that she perversely felt relieved and her admiration for Chloe grew. She nodded and smiled at her.

Sgt Moyle pointed south towards the Flinders Highway. "The highway is just there and camp is just the other side of it," he said. "I can even hear vehicles."

Again Chloe nodded. "You are right, but the bikies are probably guarding the highway, so you will need to be very careful. Anyway, you two go that way and stop a car or truck and call for the ambulance and police or go back to camp and get the officers to do it. But make sure they know that the OC, Capt Hamilton and Lt Peters are hostages."

Sgt Harvey hesitated. "I would rather come with you. I think we should stay together."

Chloe shrugged and looked at Sgt Moyle. He just nodded. Jane wasn't sure if that was good idea. "It might be better if we split up," she said. "That makes it more likely someone will get to call the police and it also disperses the enemy effort."

Chloe agreed. "That's right. Major Wickham is always saying you should try to confuse the enemy. I really would like you two sergeants to go back to camp, or at least to the highway to call for help. We will bring the platoon to you."

"What about that mobile phone you took off that Slasher?" Jane asked.

Chloe nodded and pulled it out. "I tried it but it is locked. We need a password to get it to work."

"We could ask him," Sgt Harvey suggested.

Chloe made a face. "You ask him then. I'm not going back near him.

He will probably get free soon and he will be as mad as a cut snake. We need to move, and fast."

Jane could only agree with that. "Which way?" she queried.

Chloe pointed to their right up onto the embankment. "Back along the Old Railway but only after we have made some boot prints in the creek bed that point south."

With that she led the way down into the narrow sandy bed of the main creek and began walking quickly along it. Jane followed and then the two sergeants. They only went for about twenty paces before Chloe climbed out of the bed and turned right to climb the railway embankment near its far end. Jane followed and so did Sgt Harvey.

Chloe looked back. "Aren't you going to camp?" she queried.

Both sergeants looked unhappy at this but finally Sgt Harvey nodded and she and Sgt Moyle stepped back down into the creek and continued walking south. Chloe waved to them and climbed up onto the Old Railway and again turned right.

"Walk as quietly as you can so Flasher Man doesn't hear us," she whispered.

Jane understood that. *We have to walk back over the top of the culvert he is in,* she told herself.

And that was a scary thing to do. She found she was tip-toing and that her heart was hammering a rapid pitter-pat.

A minute later the two girls were back on the north side of the main creek and were hurrying along the Old Railway. Jane glanced back and was just able to detect the two sergeants who already looked to be halfway to the Flinders Highway. For a moment she wished she was with them but then she concentrated on the task. Very aware that bikies could appear from either in front of them or from behind at any moment she kept straining her ears and also looking in all directions.

As they hurried along Chloe pulled out her map and studied it. Suddenly she stopped and pointed up the slope to her right.

"This powerline goes across to the highway. It is just over there two hundred metres or so. Maybe we should go that way?"

Jane looked at the map and noted how the highway curved around so that it was east of where they stood. "We might be able to stop a car or truck and phone for help," she suggested.

"Good idea Jane. Let's have a quick look," Chloe said.

She at once turned and went scrambling up the overgrown vehicle track that Jane now saw ran under the powerline.

Chloe went up the slope at a speed that soon had Jane gasping in her wake. Jane began to feel anxious that they were moving rapidly away from the platoon but also believed that one phone call would be able to end it all. So she pushed herself to try to keep up.

A hundred paces up Jane reached the crest of the ridge. From there she was able to see the powerlines looping across a valley and up an even bigger hill a four or five hundred metres away. Better still part of the highway had come into view and was only another couple of hundred paces ahead. Even as she watched a car zipped into view going down the range. Her hopes shot right up.

By then Chloe was already halfway to the highway but as she crested a small rise she suddenly skidded to a stop and went into a crouch, then rose to peek over the grass. Shaking her head, she began hurrying back towards Jane. Instantly Jane felt her hopes plummet.

"What is it?" Jane asked, her disappointment biting sharply.

"A bikie sitting on his bike at that bend. He can see that whole stretch of highway," Chloe explained.

Jane swore in a most unladylike fashion and then nodded. "They must be watching the whole highway," she suggested.

"Well, not all of it but certainly the bits on the range," Chloe agreed. "We might have to do a bit more creeping and crawling to avoid them."

That was a worrying thought, but Jane could only nod and then turn back. Now it seemed even more important to be with the platoon. The two girls hurried side by side back up to the crest. Here they slowed to look into the valley where the Old Railway was. Jane was worried that Slasher might have gotten free but there was no sign of him.

Chloe was obviously also worried about him as she kept glancing to her left as they hurried down the overgrown track back to the Old Railway. As soon as they reached it the girls turned right and walked as fast as they could, both panting for breath and perspiring heavily.

To Jane the critical few seconds were as they reached the end of the deep cutting where the cattle pad to No1 Bottom Mill branched off. She became very tense as she approached it. But the girls reached that point without any problems. Chloe suddenly turned around and began walking backwards on the sand and dust of the cattle pad.

Jane had to smile. As a ploy she knew it would not fool a skilled tracker for a minute. *But these bikies are city hoodlums, not bushmen,* she told herself. So she copied Chloe's actions.

Once she was a dozen paces down the cattle pad Chloe turned around again and led the way back down. Jane followed, both girls almost running. It took them less than three minutes to reach the creek junction at the bottom and Jane was pleased to note that both stretcher parties were across the main creek and moving up the side creek she had indicated. Better still Rodney Leece was busy brushing out tracks.

What pleased her even more was the relief evident on the faces of the other cadets as they rejoined them.

Even the sergeants are glad we are back, Jane thought.

It did not improve her opinion of them but did make her determined to succeed.

Chloe went straight up the side creek to Harley's stretcher. "How is he?" she queried.

"Starting to come around," Sgt Grey replied. "But he still needs to get to a doctor fast."

Chloe nodded. "We will try." She then turned to Jane. "As soon as that Slasher saw Arthur, I knew we had to act. If he had caught Harley, he would have killed him."

Jane nodded. "That's what I thought too, but you took a terrible risk of him shooting you."

"So did you Bedrock Babe," Chloe replied with a wry grin. "You were planning to fight him with rocks."

"It worked the first time," Jane replied, feeling a bit defensive and foolish.

Chloe gave a low chuckle. "Yes. Now make sure that shotgun is on safe or is unloaded and go as scout again. I will follow. Go up this re-entrant on the left."

"Not this bigger creek on the right?" Jane asked.

Chloe shook her head. "We need to get to the highway as fast as we safely can. Lead on."

So Jane did. She had a drink, noting as she did that she had less than half a water bottle left. Then she made her way past the two stretcher parties and began scouting up the re-entrant. She saw that it as fairly short and quite steep and had a cattle pad running up it. To her it appeared to lead up behind the rocky knolls which were to the west of the Old Railway culvert where they had left Slasher.

And another problem at once reared its head, there were cattle in the re-entrant and when the cadets appeared these began hurrying up the cattle pad away from them.

Oh no! They will give us away, Jane thought.

But there was nothing for it but to push on. The urgent desire to get Kim and the wounded bikie to hospital over-rode her other worries. To her relief the cattle abruptly changed direction and scampered up over the low ridge line to their right.

Glancing behind Jane saw Chloe helping to carry Harley's stretcher. She was quietly encouraging the others and instructing cadets on when to change to have a rest.

I should be doing my share, Jane thought.

So she slowed and waited for the stretcher party to catch up. Chloe raised an eyebrow and Jane said, "I'll do that. You scout."

Chloe nodded and Jane handed her the shotgun and they changed places. As they did the radio she had taken off Slasher crackled. Brute's voice came through loud and clear. "Slasher, this is Brute. Where are you?" he said.

A mischievous grin formed on Chloe's face and she reached over and lifted the CB radio to her mouth. In her sweetest 'little girl' voice she said: "Sorry Brute, Slasher can't come to the phone. He's tied up right now."

Jane was shocked but also mentally applauded. There was a moment of silence and then Brute responded. "Who are you? Where's Slasher?"

Chloe smirked. "Bye, gotta go," she replied in her sweetest female voice.

Bloody Chloe! She's taunting him, Jane thought. She exchanged grins with Chloe but wasn't sure if that had been a good idea. *She's already made enough enemies,* she thought.

Brute called twice more but Chloe shook her head and did not respond. She handed the radio back to Jane. Jane listened and her mind raced.

If he can call as clear as that he isn't far away. He must be up on top of the range somewhere or there would be too much screening, she reasoned.

"His nickname's Brute," Chloe commented.

"The bikie boss? Yes, that suits him," Jane agreed.

They began moving up the re-entrant again but then Chloe stopped and looked back, her face wrinkled into a frown. "That is a truck I can hear isn't it?"

Jane listened and nodded. "Not a motorbike," she agreed. Then her mind clicked in another 'light bulb' moment she would remember for the rest of her life.

Trucks all have radios. We could call one of them for help.

She pointed at the CB radio hung around Chloe's neck. "Switch that to Channel 40 and see if we can contact a truck driver and get them to call the cops and ambulance," she said.

Chloe's sunburnt face broke into a huge smile. "You aren't just a pretty face are you Babe? Great idea!" She at once changed the channel and lifted the radio to her mouth. "Mayday! Mayday! Mayday! Help! Anyone help! Please help. Call the police and the ambulance. We have people shot by bikies and need help, over."

There was no response even though Jane could hear another truck out on the highway. Chloe shook her head slightly and lifted the radio again. "Mayday! Mayday! M…"

Suddenly the radio began to crackle. "Jamming," Sgt Grey commented. "The bikies are listening."

"On 'scan' probably," Sgt Lynes said. He looked haggard and scared.

"The bastards!" Chloe muttered. She tried again but it was at once obvious she wasn't transmitting. The radio now emitted the sound of people's voice. "Sssh! We can hear them," Jane gasped.

They all went silent and strained to listen. A distorted voice said: "Here, you keep jamming it. We gotta stop them calling the cops. The bloody smart bitch!"

Yes, I am, Jane thought, irritated that the man obviously thought it was Chloe's idea.

Brute's voice came through loud and clear. "Who is this bitch? What's her name?"

There was a tense pause and then Brute spoke again, less distinct this time. "Don't be a stubborn fool Tubby. If you won't talk I will get Slasher to pay some attention to this nice little girl here."

"He's threatening Major Wickham," Jane whispered, her stomach turning over in revulsion and horror at the threat.

Brute went on. "Do you know why he is called Slasher? No? Well I'll tell ya. He likes to have power over women, to dominate them; and he uses an old-fashioned razor to cut them up a bit when they don't co-operate. A few girls who gave him trouble used to be pretty but they aren't now. That's what he went to jail for so he's a bad bastard and you don't want these pretty little things to be his playthings do you?"

Jane swallowed in disgust and fear. A bitter sense of defeat tasted in her mouth. *We can't let Ma'am Peters get cut up. We will have to surrender,* she thought.

Then her emotions turned to dismay and more horror when she heard Major Wickham say: "Her name's Chloe."

There was a faint chuckle in Brute's voice when he answered. "Chloe eh? Well, no doubt Slasher will find ways to amuse himself with her when we catch her. Now call her and tell her to bring me Harley."

That appalled Jane even more. *Chloe has really made some enemies now,* she thought.

The others all looked at Chloe with a mixture of horror, fear and fascination in their expressions. Chloe went stony faced and pursed he lips. Jane shook her head.

Poor Chlo! She must be terrified.

Major Wickham now spoke on the radio, calling Chloe. Chloe listened and clenched her jaw and did not reply.

Sgt Lynes was both angry and amazed. "Answer him! You can save us!" he cried.

"And let a man be murdered?" Chloe replied.

"But they will cut up the girls or rape them," Sgt Lynes said.

Chloe sneered. "So you don't have to worry!" she retorted.

Sgt Lynes reached forward. "Give me that radio!"

Chloe shook her and stepped quickly away. "That won't save us. It might save you but it won't save me or Harley here."

Major Wickham called again. Again, Chloe gritted her teeth and did not reply. Jane felt sick with dread, but she agreed and said, "We should keep moving." But the others ignored her while the tense stand-off continued. Tears formed in the corners of Chloe's eyes.

Suddenly Brute's voice came clearly over the air. "Listen to me Chloe, you bring me Harley and we will all just go away. You will be fine," he radioed.

Chloe did not respond and Jane glanced around anxiously to check that none of the other NCOs with a radio was tempted to use it. She wasn't sure how she would stop them but she was determined to do so if she had to. Everyone was now staring at Chloe with a mixture of pity and awful fascination that made Jane think of stories she had heard about people watching a public hanging in the old days.

Brute repeated his offer. To Jane it sounded very false and she was sure Chloe did not believe the man. Then Brute changed his tone.

"Listen bitch, if you don't co-operate and bring me Harley quick smart then I will let Slasher start raping and cutting these girls and your pretty lady officer. You hear me?"

Still Chloe did not respond and Jane felt ill with apprehension. She was sure that Lt Peters and any other girl there would be absolutely terrified. Now she was completely torn over what to do and was then ashamed at being briefly tempted to trade a man's life for possible safety.

Brute became quite enraged. He shouted into the radio, "You stupid bitch! Don't you believe me? Just listen while we cut one of the girls."

Jane went cold with horror at this appalling threat and tensed herself ready to fight if need be. But this time Chloe answered.

"You hurt any of them and I will hunt you down," she said, "Even if it takes the rest of my life."

"Your life is going to be very short and you are going to die a horrible death if you don't do what I say," Brute shouted back. "Now bring me Harvey."

"No! Start running while you can," Chloe replied.

Jane was filled with admiration tinged by deep anxiety. But she was also pleased because Brute sounded almost beside himself with rage. He shouted more threats, but Chloe just gave a sour grin.

"That rattled the mongrel's cage," she muttered.

Sgt Lynes still looked angry and upset. "But what if that man does hurt some of the girls?"

"I don't think he will," Chloe replied. "Now let's keep moving."

"But he might!" Sgt Lynes cried. "We should hand this man over."

"You can piss off if you aren't going to help us," Chloe grated. "But don't tell them where we are or what we are doing."

"I'm a sergeant! You are only a cadet. Do what I say!" Sgt Lynes almost shouted.

"Shut up and keep you voice down!" Chloe snarled, stepping close to him. "Don't give away our position by making noise. This isn't Cadets! This is real and a man's life is at stake. Now co-operate or go!"

Jane was again ready to help her friend if Sgt Lynes lashed out but he just scowled and stepped back. Then he shook his head and muttered, plainly dominated by Chloe's fierce determination.

Chloe looked around. "Anyone else not want to help?"

There was silence and lowered eyes and head shakes. Chloe nodded and quietly said, "So pick up this stretcher again and let's get moving."

As they picked it up Jane saw with a shock that Harley had his eyes open but his gaze was fixed on Chloe until she moved away. Then he closed his eyes again. To Jane's relief the confrontation seemed to be over and the radio did not call again. But the jamming was resumed.

God I hope we aren't making a terrible mistake! she thought, imagining the bikies raping and mutilating.

The images made her shudder and she tried to force them out of her mind. But deep-down Jane knew that both she and Chloe were now in dreadful peril from the bikies.

They don't forgive or forget, she thought, her mouth dry with fear.

She was so upset that she felt dizzy and her heart hammered furiously. Chloe stepped over and grabbed her sleeve.

"You OK Jane?" she asked.

"Yes, why?" Jane queried, steadying herself with the stretcher.

"Because you just staggered," Chloe answered.

"Just upset," Jane replied. She looked her friend in the eyes and wanted to ask her if they were doing the right thing but the desire to support her friend held her tongue.

She doesn't need more argument now, she reasoned.

"Have a drink," Chloe suggested.

Jane nodded and took out her left water bottle and did so. In the process she drained it. "I'm out of water," she said. That was bad news.

Chloe nodded. "We probably all are, now let's get these people to safety," she said. With that she turned and headed up the re-entrant.

Jane replaced her water bottle in its holder and said, "OK, hands on!"

But Sgt Lynes had been watching Chloe, a sour look on his face. When she was about 25 metres away, he turned to the group. "I still think we should hand this guy over to the bikies."

Sgt Grey shook his head. "No. They can't hurt us all. There are too many of us."

Sgt Lynes gave a curt grunt and sneered. "They could! And they know they will get away with it. Nobody in their right mind is game to stand up in a court as a witness to anything bikies do."

Jane experienced another wave of chill and swallowed. *He's right,* she thought. But an even more chilling notion now hit her. *Chloe and I will never be safe. The gang will hunt us down.*

Fear of what that might imply and the horrible idea of having to watch her back for months or years to come hit her with such force that she trembled. Only the necessity of moving her arms and legs to lift the stretcher and to walk up the rocky hillside allowed her to keep her pride as it hid this from the others. But she was scared and knew it.

The fear gave sharpness to her tone. "If you don't agree then go away and hide! Go back north to some gully and wait a day or so until this is all over," she snapped. "And take anyone else with you who thinks you are right."

Sgt Lynes opened his mouth to answer but then shut it and scowled. The group continued on up the re-entrant. Jane noted that the powerlines were now in sight on the crest ahead of them. And carrying a big man like Harley over rough ground was much harder than Jane had expected.

This is a lot harder than doing little training exercises on nice flat ground, she thought ruefully. It was definitely an eight-person job.

A hundred metres up the gully the group came to a sweating standstill and the stretcher was lowered. Chloe had been watching and now came back and said, "My go. You go scout again Jane." She handed the shotgun to her and took her place. Jane was ashamed to admit she was thankful as carrying that heavy weight had been really testing. She set off up the re-entrant and the stretcher party followed.

A few minutes later she reached some piles of rocks at the top of the slope and noted that the powerlines were almost overhead. The country to the south appeared to be lots of little dips and hollows dotted with numerous piles of rock and large boulders. Beyond that the country looked as though it levelled out.

The Flinders Highway should be only about half a kilometre ahead, Jane reasoned. A quick study of her map showed her that this was right.

We are level with the culvert where we left Slasher and that is about two hundred metres to my left, she noted.

Carefully she moved to the top of the re-entrant. This became ever shallower and she came to a stop where she could just see over the top. What she saw caused her heart to start to hammer furiously. About 50 metres to her right front were CUO Roach and Cpl Hankin and they were standing with their hands up facing two armed bikies.

Jane at once signalled Chloe to come up and then crouched lower. She continued to watch and Chloe joined her and took a swift look.

"Bugger!" Chloe hissed. Then she glanced to her left front and gripped Jane's arm. Jane understood. The noise of a motorcycle was approaching from that direction. "We are cut off," she croaked, the fear making her mouth go dry.

At that moment the sound of someone crawling quickly towards them in the long grass came to Jane's ears.

That is someone heading this way, she thought. *And they are just at the top of this re-entrant.*

Fear of possible discovery churned with near despair at the possible failure of their efforts. She glanced down at the shotgun and clicked the safety catch off. Determined to keep the wounded safe she resolved to use it if need be.

Then the person making the rustling, scuffling sounds came into view and Jane could not restrain a gasp of astonishment.

Chapter 28

PANIC

Sgt Lepson was in the grip of panic. Vision blurred, heart hammering, breathing in rasping gulps he crawled quickly down the shallow dip, desperate to get away. Then he heard a person gasp and his heart seemed to stop and then turn over. His eyes registered the twin muzzles of a shotgun and he froze in terror.

Then his flustered, panicked vision took in that it was a cadet holding the shotgun, a girl cadet. And not just any girl cadet but Cadet Jane Carson. And crouched beside her was that damned Chloe!

Sgt Lepson came to a standstill while his mind absorbed the information and then he tried to get his muscles to do his bidding. He badly wanted his mouth to work but to his shame he began to stammer. Worse still he was driven by a compelling urge to get up and run.

"Carson! Cummings! What... Who... We must get out of here," he gabbled.

Jane made a wry face and pointed the shotgun away from him. "We can see that," she retorted in a sarcastic whisper.

That really annoyed Sgt Lepson and his anger helped calm him. "There are bikies there and they have captured CUO Roach and Cpl Hankin. We need to go the other way," he croaked.

Chloe nodded. "There's another one coming. Get down while I take a peek," she instructed. With that she eased herself up behind a bush next to a large clump of rocks. Then she slid back down again. "It is that bloke who rode around along the Old Railway earlier."

Jane nodded. "What's he doing?"

"He's joined the pair sticking up Roach and Hankin and now he looks like he is calling someone on his mobile phone," Chloe replied. She then bent close to Sgt Lepson. "Do they know you are with them?" she asked.

"Wh... Who?" Sgt Lepson stammered, now annoyed that Chloe had called the CUO and corporal by just their surnames and in a derogatory tone.

"Roach and Hankin of course!" Chloe snapped.

Sgt Lepson again bridled at the disrespect evident, but he nodded. "Yes," he muttered.

Chloe turned to Jane. "Then they will blab for sure. We need to go another way." She moved a couple of paces back down the dip and looked around. Then she again bent to face Sgt Lepson. "Where did those two bikies on foot come from?"

Sgt Lepson shook his head. He now just wanted to go but did not dare. "I don't know. I think they may have come from behind us."

"They followed you?" Chloe queried.

"I think so."

While they were talking Jane eased herself up to peep from cover. Carefully she studied the two men then turned her head.

"They are the two we just missed back at that creek junction the other side of the Number One Bottom Mill," she whispered.

Chloe nodded and chewed her lip. "Then they did follow you," she said. She again looked around and then moved to peek over the top as the sound of another motorcycle came to them.

Sgt Lepson badly wanted to look as well but could not muster the courage to raise himself. Instead he whispered, "Who is that?"

Jane answered. "It is their boss Brute, the guy with the goatee beard."

Chloe looked serious. "Now there will be trouble. He will torture Roach and Hankin if they don't talk and then he will get these guys looking for us. Our only hope is to double-bluff them. We will move over into the creek line they have already searched. We might just avoid being caught."

"Good idea," Jane nodded. "You go and get the platoon moving across that spur line where the cattle went and I will guard the rear."

Chloe shook her head and held out her hand. "No you won't kiddo. You are much too nice a person to use that gun. Give it to me and I will be the rearguard. Go on, get going! Lepson, you help carry a stretcher," she said.

Sgt Lepson was annoyed by the way she spoke to him and knew he should assert his authority. *Who is she to tell me what to do? She and Carson are only cadets. They don't even have one stripe,* he thought.

But all he could do was nod and start moving. The look in those two sets of hard female eyes seemed to make him shrivel inside. And he did want to get away. But he was also puzzled.

Stretchers? He wondered.

He soon found out. The two stretcher parties were about a hundred metres back down the re-entrant and the carriers were obviously struggling to get up the slope.

As he approached the stretcher party Cpl Callan turned and called to him, "Lepson, where have you been?"

Sgt Lepson was again annoyed but that emotion was overwhelmed by a sense of shame. For a few moments his dominant desire became to justify his actions, not wanting to admit, even to himself, that he been a coward.

"We went to get help," he replied as he stumbled across the rocky hillside, his sore ankle still causing him pain. As part of his excuse he deliberately exaggerated the limp.

"And did you get it?" Cpl Callan queried.

Sgt Lepson was very conscious that all the faces had turned to look at him. Licking his suddenly dry lips he shook his head. "No, we got delayed. I… I… sprained my ankle and now CUO Roach and Cpl Hankin have been captured."

Cpl Callan looked sceptical, but it was Cpl Lang who spoke next. "So where is Flegel?"

That really shook Sgt Lepson. *Flegel!* he thought.

Memories of leaving Flegel behind in a gully caused him another bout of shame. Embarrassed he shook his head. "He hurt his leg. We had to leave him behind," he explained, knowing that sounded very lame.

It must have sounded like a poor excuse to the others because Sgt Grey now cried, "Left him behind! Don't unit Standing Orders say that no-one is ever to be left on their own in the bush?"

Sgt Lepson blushed. "Yes, but this is different. We had to get help quickly," he muttered.

By then he had reached the first stretcher and saw that the wounded bikie lay on it. The sight of the dried blood and the man's sickly face caused Sgt Lepson another bout of fear, this time mixed with nausea.

To add annoyance and irritation to his emotional turmoil Jane now snapped, "Stop yakking and keep quiet! Those men are just back up there. Now, get these stretchers up and moving. Sgt Lepson, go with the front one. Come on you lot! Get them up and moving!"

They did. For a few seconds Sgt Lepson considered pleading his twisted ankle as an excuse for not helping but then shook his head. Realizing that if he was to retrieve any pride and authority from the situation he must do his best he took over at the back of the stretcher from Cadet Shepherd and started carrying.

Jane moved to the other side. "I'll take over Dipkins," she said. Then she glared at Cadet Arthur. "This is your fault Arthur, you bloody moron. If you hadn't stuck your stupid head up that bikie wouldn't have seen us. Now use both hands and lift!"

Arthur looked offended. "You can't talk to me like that!" he bleated.

"Shut up and carry!" Jane retorted. Then she looked around. "Don't try to go straight up the slope. Go to the right. Contour upwards."

So they did, angling up the side of the ridge, climbing slowly but actually approaching the crest quite fast as it angled downwards to their level. Sgt Lepson forgot his ankle in the effort of carrying until he stumbled over several stones in the grass. But all he did was wince and gasp and keep working.

After a couple of minutes they were close to the crest. Arthur cried out, "I need a break! Put it down."

Sgt Lepson opened his mouth to call out to stop but Jane beat him to it. "No! Don't stop!" she snapped. "Reserve people just grab the back and the back people shuffle forward to take over at the middle. Middle people go to the front and the front people can then let go and move to the back to become reserves," she ordered.

Sgt Lepson was again irritated but had to admit to himself that what she said made sense. So they changed positions on the move and struggled on up the slope. By then he was sweating and panting but with eight cadets on each stretcher and changing every 50 paces or so they made good time and soon reached the crestline. As they went over the crest Sgt Lepson looked ahead and noted that the ridge was quite wide and that the crest line was studded with small rocky outcrops and had a number of dips and hollows in it.

Jane obviously noted this as well as she looked back and then up the ridge to the left then pointed to their left front. "Into that dip over there and we will put the stretchers down and hide," she said.

Sgt Lepson didn't think that was a good idea. He thought they should just keep going. But rather than say that he said, "Aren't we going the wrong way?"

Jane nodded. "Yes. We are going westwards. But we have to hide if those blokes come searching," she answered. By then they were making their way into the small dip, a hollow about 15 paces wide by 25 paces long between three outcrops of rock.

"Halt! Prepare to lower. Lower!" she instructed.

They placed the stretcher down and as they did Sgt Lepson glanced at the wounded bikie lying on it and was alarmed to see that the man had his eyes open and was looking at him. The sight of the bloodied head, bulging muscles and tattoos sent a stab of fear through Sgt Lepson. Not wanting to speak to the man he looked away and noted that Chloe was hurrying diagonally across the slope towards them.

Jane now snapped: "Everyone get down except Cadet Leece and Cadet Sandilands. You two stay up as sentries behind those rocks. Chantelle, you look that way and Rod, you look north," she instructed.

The cadets nominated nodded and moved to do as they were told. All the others sat, knelt or lay down. Sgt Lepson crouched beside the stretcher and hoped no-one would question him about where he had been. He found he was gasping for breath and wiped sweaty palms on his trousers. To his added shame he knew he was terrified and his impulse was still to run, to get further away from the men. But the platoon also provided a sense of security.

They can't shoot us all, he reasoned.

Then the thought that he might not be noticed in the crowd and might be spared from any torture if they were caught crossed his mind. Shame at such a dishonourable idea caused him to flush again.

And he was then further annoyed. As Chloe arrived she gestured for them to get down. "Hide!" she hissed. "They are coming."

"How many?" Jane asked as she lay flat.

"Two for sure but our friend Slasher has also just turned up and he is hopping mad," Chloe replied.

"Slasher?" Sgt Grey queried.

"The bikie who had captured Sgt Harvey and Sgt Moyle," Chloe answered. "We took him prisoner and rescued them."

That was good news to Sgt Lepson. "Where are they now?" he asked.

"We sent them to get help," Chloe explained, pointing south.

That was even better news, but it irritated him that Chloe had told two sergeants what to do. "When was that? Where?" he asked.

Chloe gestured to the east. "Over on the Old Railway. They should be at the highway by now, if they haven't been caught again," she replied.

But she was not really paying attention. Instead she was looking at the wounded bikie. Sgt Lepson also looked at him and what he saw sent a shiver of fear through him. Harley was a big man with bulging muscles. His arms were heavily tattooed and even in his wounded state he looked mean and dangerous. The big knee length boots and dirty jeans and leather jacket with its badges all made up the very image of an outlaw motorcycle gang member. Just looking at the man made Sgt Lepson feel uneasy and he shuddered and just wanted to leave him and get going.

Chloe moved to crouch beside the bikie and whispered, "You are Harley are you?"

Harley nodded and winced. "Yes," he croaked. "What happened?"

"The guy with the goatee beard and Slasher shot you," Chloe replied.

"What about Peewee?" Harley asked, his right-hand gingerly exploring the side of his skull.

"They shot him. The guy with the goatee beard shot him in the back of the head," Chloe answered.

Sgt Lepson had searing flashbacks to the bullets cracking past and to the signaller being hit and he felt the fear flood in again. He opened his mouth to suggest they keep moving when Cadet Leece hissed, "Here they come!"

The fear hit Sgt Lepson again and with redoubled force. He found he was virtually paralysed and could only lie flat and stare, his breath coming in rasping gulps as his heart hammered. He looked anxiously around but could see nothing. To his annoyance he saw Chloe crawl up behind the rocks to peek out, the shotgun she held now ready for use. Sgt Lepson desperately wanted to get away or at least stay safe and he wanted to tell her to get under cover but found he could not speak.

It was humiliating and terrifying. His muscles just would not move and all he could do was lie there, desperately hoping. His hatred of Chloe grew and he ground his teeth, the hatred tempered by the humiliating knowledge that he was also depending on her to keep him safe.

The bitch! he thought.

Then he saw Chloe slip lower and pull Cadet Leece down as well. Both crouched and lay among the small rocks. Then the head of one of the bikies appeared on the skyline. Sgt Lepson felt his heart skip and seem to stop.

There they are! They must see us! his frightened mind reasoned.

But at that moment the man looked around and called, "Why don't we split up and one of us go down each creek?"

The voice of a second man carried to Sgt Lepson. "Because we can see into both creeks from up here on this spur line, that's why. Besides, we came across the top of that other creek on our left. That's when we spotted those cadets we just caught."

"We only missed one. He will be just hiding in the grass," the first bikie grumbled, his head bobbing along just in view as he came along the side of the ridge.

"It's the mob who have Harley that we are looking for," replied the second man. "There is a whole bunch of them and they are only kids so they should be easy to find."

By then the first bikie was almost past them and he briefly glanced back across the dip. Sgt Lepson held his breath but at that moment the man stumbled on a rock. He swore and then staggered a few paces before calling back, "Why did they take Harley anyway?"

"Beats me, but Brute wants to rescue him," the second man replied. The top of his head also came into view, level with the platoon.

"Wasn't Slasher mad?" the first man said with a laugh. By then he was past the dip but still making his away along the crest of the ridge.

The second man snickered. "He's ropeable! When he catches that bitch who hit him he will really teach her a few lessons,"

Sgt Lepson glanced at Chloe and saw her face go hard. *I'd like to teach her a few lessons too!* he thought bitterly.

By then the two men were past them and Sgt Lepson began to hope. To his dismay and shame he found that his whole body had started to tremble, and he fervently hoped nobody else had noticed. With an effort he brought the shaking down to a few tremors of shivering. He had to consciously ease his breathing and found his eyes going in and out of focus. Slowly his heart rate slowed down and his body began to return to normal.

To his annoyance Chloe now stood up and peeked over the rocks to watch the men. Then she turned and padded down into the dip.

"They are still going down the ridge," she whispered. "Everyone stay under cover," she added. Then she moved to crouch next to Harley. "Why did they shoot you and Peewee?" she queried.

Harley shrugged. His face looked drawn and ashen and he had obviously also been in the grip of fear as the men went by. He shook his head. "I think Brute wants to be boss," he replied.

"Brute?"

"The ugly prick with the goatee beard," Harley explained.

"Good name for the turd," Chloe said. "So they set up an ambush?"

"I guess so. They told us we were going there to collect a stash from a courier."

"Stash?"

"Drugs. You know, heroin, ice, that sort of shit," Harley explained.

Sgt Lepson listened to this with horror and was amazed at how easily Chloe could talk to the man. Personally, he felt terrified of even being near him.

I wish she'd shut up and just get us out of here, he thought.

To his astonishment Chloe now patted the man's shoulder. "Well, we've got you and if we can we will keep you alive," she said.

Harley gave a weak grin and reached up to grab her hand. "Thanks Babe. What's your name?"

"Chloe," Chloe answered, squeezing his hand and smiling. "Now you just relax. I want to see how our wounded girl is."

She got up and made her way back to where Kim lay on the broomstick stretcher. Sgt Lepson now realised she was doing his job and the niggle of embarrassment and annoyance got his stiff muscles to function. Grunting with pain he got up and hobbled over to where Chloe was now talking to Sgt Small and Kim.

Chloe took Kim's hand. "We will try to get you to the doctors as quick as we can Kim," she said.

As Sgt Lepson arrived Kim lifted her head. "Thanks," she croaked. "Oh Chloe, I'm sorry!"

"Why are you sorry Kim? It wasn't your fault you got shot," Chloe answered. "Now lie still petal so you don't open your wound."

"No!" Kim cried. "It isn't that. It was me! I was the one running around in the nuddy."

Chloe looked puzzled and then her face cleared and she nodded. "You mean back at the bivouac?"

"Yes. I did it to try to get you into trouble," Kim whispered.

Chloe shook her head. "You ran around naked pretending to be me?"

Kim nodded. "Yes. We.. I.. I put on a blonde wig the same style as your hair so people would think it was you. Oh, I'm sorry!"

"Blonde wig?" Chloe asked.

Kim again nodded. "It's in my pack back at camp," she said. "Oh, I'm sorry!"

At that Cpl Callan spoke, "There were two of you. Who was the other one?" he asked, glancing at Chantelle who was watching from the nearby rocks.

Kim shook hear head. "I don't dob on my mates," she croaked.

At that Chloe grinned and patted her shoulder. "Good for you kiddo!" she said. "In the nuddy eh? Did you enjoy it?"

Kim managed a sickly grin and even blushed amid her pallor but she did not reply. Chloe again patted her. "I'll bet you did. Now, stop talking. That's in the past and we need to get you to safety."

Kim obviously wanted to say more but Chloe shushed her and moved over to Sgt Lepson. "Where did you and Roach go when you left us?" she queried.

Sgt Lepson blushed and experienced a searing flush of shame and embarrassment. He shrugged and gestured around. "We... They... Roach got us lost," he answered, hotly aware that a sergeant should also be able to navigate.

Chloe gave him a scathing look of contempt which caused him another flush of shame tinged by anger and resentment. "So you did not get to contact the OC or the HQ?"

Sgt Lepson shook his head. "No. Now let's get moving. We need to get them to a hospital."

Chloe gave him another hard look. "I know we do but we also need to make sure we don't get caught. We will wait a few more minutes."

Sgt Lepson saw her glance at her watch and looked at his own. As he did he heard the roar of motorcycles come echoing up the gullies and his heart began to hammer again.

1640hrs he noted before thinking, *Those bikes sound like they are coming this way.* His rational mind told him that was impossible. *Nobody can ride a motorbike up these rocky ridges,* he told himself. But it certainly sounded like it and he tensed, ready to run.

Then he flushed with embarrassment as Jane pointed down the ridge. "Sounds like two bikes going back along the Old Railway," she said.

Chloe nodded. "They are certainly on the hunt for us now," she agreed.

Hearing that sent Sgt Lepson's fears churning again and he found he was trembling all over. With an effort he stopped this and then sat gulping in air.

I must get away! he thought.

Chapter 29

ANXIOUS HOURS

Major Wickham lay on the grass, his head throbbing from the blows he had received. But it was his emotional state that was worse. An intense feeling of apprehension gripped him, coupled to a deep feeling of having failed. His mind worked at a furious rate as he tried to come up with a plan to get everyone to safety.

How can we escape from here? he wondered while studying the guard, Muff, through half closed eyes.

CSM Glenn sat nearby, his hands gripped together. Major Wickham studied him and then felt a spark of hope.

They didn't retie the CSM's wrists!

But then he shook his head. The last thing he wanted was one of the cadets to try to do something heroic and then get hurt.

I mustn't encourage anything that might make things worse, he reluctantly decided.

But where were Chloe and 4 Platoon? *They have had plenty of time to get here,* he thought.

It was all very worrying and feeling impotent did nothing to ease his feelings. Wanting to know the time he slowly moved and rolled onto his side until he could see Capt Hamilton's watch.

1500hrs! How long can this go on for?

Ten more minutes dragged by and still 4 Platoon did not appear. The officers kept meeting each other's eyes, but each time Major Wickham shook his head to indicate not to speak and not to take any risks.

At 1515 the sound of approaching motorcycles reached Major Wickham's ears and he moved to watch the road to the east. A minute later two motorcycles appeared over the crest and came to a stop on the dirt road nearby.

The brute with the goatee and another bikie, Major Wickham noted. He studied the new arrival who dismounted and looked curiously around.

Brute strode over and kicked Major Wickham. "They ain't arrived yet Fatboy? They'd better! Give 'em another call on this radio."

He unlooked the CB and changed the channel then passed it to Major Wickham who called. There was no response.

"They might be in among the hills and unable to hear us," he suggested, handing the radio back.

Brute clicked the frequency back to Channel 66. "They better..." he began but at that moment the CB in his hand crackled into life. "Brute, this is Slasher, over."

"Brute here."

"We've captured the two cadets up on the hill. Where do you want 'em?"

Brute frowned and then said, "Take 'em to the gate on the highway up near the Mingela turn-off. I'll meet you there."

"Wilco, over," Slasher replied.

"Wilco?" Brute queried.

"Means I will do what you say; I will co-operate, over," Slasher replied.

"Never mind all that army shit! Just get on with it!" Brute snarled.

Major Wickham had listened to the exchange with a mixture of despair at the thought of two more cadets now being in the hands of the bikies and pleasure at seeing Brute baffled.

One of the cadets is Sgt Harvey, he thought with a mental groan. A teenage girl in the hands of these low mongrels!

The three bikies moved a few paces away but Major Wickham was just able to hear them. The new arrival asked what he was to do. Brute pointed towards the body in the creek behind them and said, "I need you to go to town and get a truck. We need to shift these two bikes and Peewee's body."

The new arrival frowned. "Why not just bury him here?"

"Because this whole place is going to be swarming with coppers tomorrow and we don't want to leave evidence. We will dispose of it in our usual spot," Brute answered angrily.

The bikie nicknamed 'Muff' gestured towards the prisoners. "What about them? What are we going to do with them?"

That sent a chill of terror through Major Wickham. *They might murder us to keep us silent,* he thought. But then he shook his head. *No. That wouldn't help because the cadets in 4 Platoon all saw things too. They can't commit mass murder just to get rid of inconvenient witnesses.*

The idea cheered him but the niggling doubt remained. He lay back and strained his ears to listen, pretending he was asleep. Brute went on, "I'll decide. But we gotta make sure they can't contact anyone until we've dealt with Harley. Now, Cokehead, first I want you and Muff to help me move these bikes and prisoners up to the highway. We are too out of the way here."

"How we gunna do that?" 'Cokehead' asked.

Brute pointed to the vehicles. "We put 'em in these and drive them up," he said.

"But what about our bikes?" Muff cried.

"Then you and Cokehead come back and get 'em. You do a shuttle," Brute explained. He then strode over and kicked Major Wickham hard in the side. "Get up Fatso! And you others!"

Major Wickham rolled over and got painfully to his feet, experiencing a moment of dizziness as he did. Through eyes that were now starting to puff up from the beating he saw Lt Peters struggle to her knees.

"I can't get up," she cried. "I need my hands untied."

Brute's answer was to grab her shirt and reef her to her feet. "There ya are Sweetie!" he snarled.

"What about my hands?"

"What about 'em?"

"If they stay tied too long with the blood flow cut off the hands will die and need to be amputated. I don't think we've done anything to deserve that and it will only add to your sentences when you are caught," Lt Peters replied.

Major Wickham felt a catch in his throat. *Oh Jenny! Don't antagonize them,* he thought, his admiration for her going up even though he appreciated the medical sense of her argument.

Brute hesitated but the word 'sentence' obviously struck a chord with Muff who cried, "Untie 'em Brute. We got guns and they can't run. Besides, we can cuff 'em."

Brute scowled but nodded. "Yeah, OK. Untie 'em. But if any of you people try to get away the lady here will get it. Then I'll hand her over to Slasher, understand?"

"Yes," Major Wickham replied, his mind crawling with anxiety over why 'Slasher' had such a nickname.

He acts like an animal. I wonder what he did?

Capt Hamilton was also untied and all four were moved to Major Wickham's car. Brute pointed to it. "This is your car?" he asked Major Wickham.

Major Wickham nodded. Brute pointed to the driver's seat. "Then you drive."

"But I'm not feeling very well," Major Wickham replied, aware that he was having trouble with blurred vision and that he felt nauseous.

Brute curled his lip. "So drive careful like or you'll feel even worse." He turned to CSM Glenn. "Now, kid, you get in the passenger seat."

Reluctantly Major Wickham took out his car keys and slid into the driver's seat. CSM Glenn moved to the other side. Lt Peters and Capt Hamilton were told to sit in the back seat and both Brute and Cokehead produced what looked like police handcuffs from the saddle bags of their bikes and secured the two OOCs to the door handles by them. Brute then moved into the back on the right. Here he took out and held up an automatic pistol.

"Now drive Fatboy, and no funny business," he instructed.

Major Wickham reluctantly did so, noting as he did that Cokehead had moved to his bike and Muff to the Land Rover. By now Major Wickham was in emotional turmoil. He did not want to leave that area as long as 4 Platoon was likely to appear, but equally he badly wanted to get up to the highway. It at least offered hope with its hundreds of passing vehicles.

All this took 10 minutes or so to organise before they set off. Major Wickham drove slowly and carefully, his eyes scanning Railway Hill and the bush for any sign of cadets as he did. A couple of minutes later the Flinders Highway came into view and the sight of several trucks driving past at once sent his hopes up.

Now how can I contact one of those truck drivers? he wondered.

But he couldn't. Brute and his gun made sure of that. They waited at the gate until the Land Rover and Cokehead on his bike joined them. Major Wickham began to turn left as he started off. Brute at once shouted, "Hey! Where do you think you are going?"

"There are double lines. I was going down to the bottom of the range to where it is safe to cross and do a U-turn," Major Wickham replied.

"Pigs arse! Just drive across and go up to the Mingela Turn-off," Brute snarled while waving the pistol at Major Wickham's face.

Reluctantly Major Wickham did as he was told, waiting for a gap in the traffic before accelerating across the double lines and turning right. Luckily there were two lanes going up the hill as a red sports car came racing around the corner as he did. A collision was narrowly avoided and the driver of the sports car set his horn blaring and scowled as he flashed by in the outside lane. Major Wickham was tempted to say, 'I told you so,' but the narrow escape gave him such a jolt he felt quite ill.

As the car was driven up the range, they passed the bikie sitting on his bike beside the road under the powerlines. Brute called out to him to arrest any cadets he saw, and Major Wickham felt even sicker. They drove on up the hill, being passed by a white 4WD as they did. Several cars and a truck went past in the opposite direction. For Major Wickham it was intensely frustrating to have all those people, probably with mobile phones, so close but unable to be contacted.

They started rounding the big curve to the right at the top of the range and the road narrowed back to one lane each way. As they did Brute swore and leaned forward.

"Where the hell is Lance?" he muttered. "He is supposed to be guarding this bit of road."

Major Wickham remembered seeing the man there when he had driven down the range and now experienced a spurt of malicious pleasure tinged with hope. But this was instantly dashed as they came to the long straight on top. There, about half a kilometre ahead, was a bikie on his bike and he was talking to two cadets on the side of the road.

Seeing that Brute grunted and then poked Major Wickham in the back with the gun. "Stop there so I can talk to 'em," he ordered.

Major Wickham did so but slowly and carefully as there was a car close up behind him by then and it was driven by an obviously impatient driver who accelerated past at the first opportunity. As Major Wickham braked to a standstill a truck going from the other direction came to a stop and the driver leaned out.

"What's going on?" he called to the bikie.

Lance waved his shotgun and smiled. "Just a training exercise. Nothing to worry about. Keep going," he shouted back.

The truck driver looked unconvinced but nodded and started driving again. Brute leaned out. "What's the go Lance?" he called.

"Caught these two trying to cross the highway," Lance replied.

Major Wickham experienced more waves of mixed emotions. Seeing the two cadets captured had sent his hopes down, but as he had driven to a stop near them he had recognized them.

That is Sgt Harvey and Sgt Moyle. They were the Radio Relay Station and that Slasher said they had been captured. So what has happened? How did they get away?

Brute obviously wanted to know as well but plainly did not know who the cadets were or where they had come from. He began to question them but was interrupted by a large semi-trailer coming to a shuddering stop behind them amid a volley of air brake releases because another big truck, a road train carrying cattle in three trailers and followed by a truck and three cars was coming the other way and he could not pull out to pass safely. The semi driver gave an impatient blast of his air horn.

Brute gestured to Lance and then pointed ahead. "Take 'em up to the turn-off up there so we are off this bloody road," he shouted.

Lance nodded and gestured the cadets aside. Major Wickham reluctantly accelerated after abandoning wild ideas of making a scene to get the truck drivers to call the police. The turn-off to Mingela was only a hundred metres ahead and he soon reached it and turned left to park where the coaches had stopped to unload the cadets on Friday night. The Land Rover and Cokehead on his motorcycle joined them. Brute pointed the gun at Major Wickham.

"Switch off and give me the keys and get out," he ordered.

Major Wickham reluctantly did as he was told. By now he was in a ferment of torment. There were vehicles rushing by along the highway every minute or so and he was unable to call for help.

And the remainder of the company are just over there, he thought, turning to stare into the bush in the faint hope that one of the cadets or officers might be visible.

Two minutes later Lance and the two cadet sergeants arrived. Brute pointed back along the road, "Lance, guard these kids but keep watch back to that other bend. Make sure no cadets cross this highway or come out to stop a truck or car!"

Lance nodded and moved to stand guard. Brute turned to Muff and Cokehead. "Go back in the Land Rover and bring my bike and then go back and get yours Muff. Then you go to town and get that truck Cokehead."

The two bikies climbed into the Land Rover and it did a U-turn and drove off. Brute turned to the two frightened but defiant cadets.

"OK you kids, who are you and where did you come from?"

Sgt Harvey answered, first giving their names. "We were a Radio Relay Station for a cadet exercise," she added.

"Radio Relay Station?" Brute queried, a tinge of alarm in his voice. "Were you the two captured by Slasher and Stinger up on a big hill?"

Sgt Harvey did not answer and looked scared and defiant, but Sgt Moyle gave a nod. Brute turned on him. "You were?"

"Y... yes," Sgt Moyle replied.

"So how come you are wandering around? What happened to Slasher and Stinger?" Brute snarled.

"We... We got set free," Sgt Moyle answered.

"Set free! Who by? What the bloody hell is going on? Tell me what happened!" Brute shouted.

Major Wickham had been enjoying Brute's obvious problem but also did not want one of the cadets hurt. When he saw Sgt Moyle press his lips together with the possible intention of defiance he called, "Tell him Sgt Moyle."

Sgt Moyle nodded. "Chlo... er... some other cadets came along and knocked out that man guarding us," he explained.

When he heard that stuttered 'Chlo' Major Wickham shook his head and glanced at Capt Hamilton who grinned. "Chloe," he whispered.

Brute was really angry now and Major Wickham could see he was scared. "So where is Slasher now?"

"Back there," Sgt Moyle replied, obviously not wanting to say too much.

"And what about Stinger, the big guy with short hair?" Brute queried.

"He rode off back down the Old Railway after we got to it," Sgt Moyle answered. "There was only the other man guarding us."

"And he's back there knocked out?" Brute asked.

Sgt Moyle nodded and glanced at Sgt Harvey who was wooden faced. Seeing this Major Wickham decided they were not telling the whole story. Brute took out his mobile phone and called but there was no answer. Then he picked up the CB radio hung around his neck and also called on that.

"Slasher, this is Brute. Where are you?" he said.

The radio crackled and a sweet-sounding girl's voice replied. "Sorry Brute, Slasher can't come to the phone. He's tied up right now."

Brute stared at the radio, shock evident on his face. This mottled with anger and he yelled into the radio. "Who are you? Where's Slasher?"

"Bye, gotta go," replied the sweet female voice.

Bloody Chloe! She's taunting him, Major Wickham thought. He exchanged a quick glance with Capt Hamilton who had to suppress a grin.

Brute called twice more but got no response. Major Wickham's mind was racing. *If she can call as clear as that she isn't far away. She must be up on top of the range somewhere or there would be too much screening,* he reasoned.

He turned to look northwards without making it obvious, but his questing eyes only took in more bush, the T-intersection, the fence and gate beyond it and another bikie sitting watching from near the overpass over the new railway.

Suddenly the CB radio hanging around Sgt Moyle's neck began to speak. It was Chloe again.

"Mayday! Mayday! Mayday! Help! Anyone help! Please help. Call the police and the ambulance. We have people shot by bikies and need help, over."

Brute stepped forward and snatched the radio up and stared at it. "It's on scan," he commented. Glaring at Sgt Moyle he shook the radio in his face. "This is on scan, why?"

Sgt Moyle went pale and swallowed. "B... B... Because I'm the signal sergeant and when we lost coms I tried the alternate and then put it on scan," he answered.

Brute swore and opened his mouth, but the radio suddenly began to call again. "Mayday! Mayday! M..."

Brute swore and squeezed the press to talk button and Lance, who had stepped closer looked and said, "She's calling on Channel 40. She's trying to get a truckie."

"The bitch!" Brute screamed. Reefing the radio from Sgt Moyle's neck, he passed it to Lance. "Here, you keep jamming it. Tape down that switch. We gotta stop them calling the cops. The bloody smart bitch!"

Major Wickham felt his admiration for Chloe going up another notch.

Brute turned to him. "Who is this bitch? What's her name?"

Major Wickham hesitated. Brute leaned closer and poked the muzzle of the pistol against Major Wickham's temple.

"Don't be a stubborn fool Tubby. If you won't talk, I will get Slasher to pay some attention to this nice little girl here."

He withdrew the pistol and stroked Sgt Harvey's face, causing her to flinch and pull away. Lance laughed and grabbed her and held her tight. Major Wickham felt his stomach turn over with dread and he swallowed to stop himself puking.

Brute went on. "Do you know why he is called Slasher? No? Well I'll tell ya. He likes to have power over women, to dominate them; and he uses an old-fashioned razor to cut them up a bit when they don't co-operate. A few girls who gave him trouble used to be pretty, but they aren't now. That's what he went to jail for so he's a bad bastard and you don't want these pretty little things to be his playthings do you?"

Major Wickham swallowed and shook his head, the terror in Sgt Harvey's eyes convincing him. Feeling a bitter sense of defeat and of being a Judas he said, "Her name's Chloe."

"Chloe eh? Well, no doubt Slasher will find ways to amuse himself with her when we catch her. Now call her and tell her to bring me Harvey."

Major Wickham was passed the radio and was told to call. He did but got no response. "Maybe they are on Channel 40 now?" he suggested.

So Lance stopped jamming that and Major Wickham tried that channel. There was still no response.

Brute snatched the radio back. "Listen to me Chloe, you bring me Harvey and we will all just go away. You will be fine," he radioed.

There was still no response and Brute repeated his offer. To Major Wickham it sounded very false and he was sure Chloe would not believe the man. Then Brute changed his tone.

"Listen bitch, if you don't co-operate and bring me Harvey quick smart then I will let Slasher start raping and cutting these girls and your pretty lady officer. You hear me?"

There was still no response but Major Wickham felt old and ill and could see that both Lt Peters and Sgt Harvey were looking sick and terrified. He was completely torn over what to do and was then ashamed to be temped to trade a man's life for the possible safety of the females.

Brute became quite enraged. He shouted into the radio, "You stupid bitch! Don't you believe me? Just listen while we cut one of the girls."

Major Wickham went cold with horror at this appalling threat and tensed himself ready to fight. But the radio suddenly answered. It was Chloe again. "You hurt any of them and I will hunt you down," she said, "Even if it takes the rest of my life."

"Your life is going to be very short and you are going to die a horrible death if you don't do what I say," Brute shouted. "Now bring me Harley."

"No! Start running while you can," Chloe replied.

Brute was almost beside himself with rage by this and he shouted more threats but there was no response. Major Wickham did not know what to feel, being torn by fear of the bikie's retribution and by admiration for Chloe and the belief that she had done the right thing. To his intense relief Brute made no move to harm either of the females.

At that moment a car turned off the highway and drove slowly past, the people in it staring at the group. For a second Major Wickham was tempted to jump out and stop it but Brute shook his head and gestured with the pistol he was hiding behind his back.

"Don't try anything stupid Tubby. You don't want to be responsible for innocent people getting hurt; and just keep in mind that nobody is game to stand up in a court as a witness to a bikie shooting."

Major Wickham experienced another wave of chill and swallowed. *He's right,* he thought. Over the years he had heard of several shootings in public by members of Outlaw Motorcycle Gangs. *And nobody saw anything!*

His mouth full of the bitter taste of defeat, he watched the car drive on. As it did, a motorbike came around the bend from the direction of Mingela. It passed the car and then came to a stop beside them. A big man in full leathers emblazoned with the gang's colours got off.

"What the hell's going on Brute?" he asked.

"Sorry Davo. I meant to get back to you," Brute answered. He passed the radio back to Lance and said, "Keep jamming and guard this lot," he instructed. Taking 'Davo' by the sleeve he led him away a few paces.

"What the hell's going on Brute?" Davo again demanded to know. Because the man spoke loudly in anger Major Wickham was just able to overhear and strained his ears to listen above the roar and rumble of the passing trucks on the highway.

Brute shrugged and said, "We still haven't found Harley."

"Yeah? So what's he done?" Davo queried.

"He shot Peewee and the courier and he's taken all the drugs and all of our money," Brute replied.

Davo looked shocked. "All of it? But what have these cadets got to do with it?"

"Harley took them hostage and to prove he meant business he shot one of them. We gotta find him man and get that money to the syndicate or we are going to have real trouble," Brute answered.

"We sound like we are in real trouble now!" Davo retorted. "So what are these cadet people here doing?"

"Helping us find Harley," Brute answered.

Davo looked around a, a puzzled expression on his face. "Yeah, but why have you got these cadet people bailed up?"

"So they don't contact the cops before we sort this out and clean it up," Brute replied.

Davo considered this and nodded. "But why are you guarding along the highway?" he asked.

"I'm worried that Harley might surrender to the police and go into one of those witness protection programs. He might turn Queen's Evidence to get off, and if he blabs we are all in really deep shit," Brute answered.

Davo looked shocked and worried. "Yeah... Yeah, that would be real bad. But... But I don't understand why Harley's done this," he said.

Brute shrugged. "I don't either, but we gotta catch him before the cops do. Now leave this to me and Slasher. You go back to town and make sure that the girls stay at the hotel and that they don't use their bloody mobile phones to tell all their friends on facebook that there is some sort of drama here."

Davo looked doubtful. "They are asking when we are going home," he said.

Brute looked worried and shook his head. "We ain't, not till we've got Harley. So take over the hotel so that they got somewhere to be. Make sure they get a feed and then come back here and guard this gate to make sure no cadets cross the highway."

Davo still looked doubtful but reluctantly got on his bike and rode away back towards the town. Major Wickham watched him go with mixed feelings. He was puzzled.

This Brute fellow is making that up. That isn't the same story he told the others. What the hell is going on?

Major Wickham glanced at his watch and noted it was now 1620hrs. As he did Brute walked back across to Lance. "Lance, guard these people. You kids put down that big radio and girlie, you give me that little one."

Sgt Harvey did as she was told and the CB radio was passed to Lance. "Channel 66 to talk to me," Brute instructed, showing him the channel select button. Lance nodded and slung the radio then changed the channel. "And keep that Channel 40 jammed," Brute added.

As he said this his mobile phone rang. Brute snatched it up and glanced at the screen before putting it to his ear. "Yeah Stinger, what ya got?"

"We've caught two more of these cadets. I think they are the leaders of this mob we are looking for," Stinger answered.

Major Wickham was just able to overhear this and his thoughts began racing.

The leaders of 4 Platoon? Why isn't CUO Roach with his troops?

"Is that bitch of a girl with them?" Brute asked.

"Nope. Just two boys. One of them says he is a thing called a cadet under-officer," came the reply.

"So where are the rest of them? Is Harley with them?" Brute demanded to know.

"Nope. No idea. And Mike and Julio haven't seen 'em either."

"I'll be right there. Where are you?"

"Under the powerlines next to a big pile of rocks. Come in the gate opposite the Mingela Turn-off and follow the vehicle track to the right. You'll see us," came the instructions.

Brute turned to Lance. "I'll go and see what Stinger's caught. Keep this lot sitting in the car and watch 'em. Don't let 'em speak to anyone in a car or to any other cadets. If more cadets arrive stick 'em up," he said.

He turned to Sgt Harvey and pointed the pistol at her face. "Now girlie, where is Slasher?"

Sgt Harvey blanched and could hardly speak. In a tremulous voice she replied, "In a culvert under the Old Railway, back where it goes under the powerlines."

"How did he get there? Is he tied up?" Brute snapped.

Sgt Harvey nodded and whispered, "Chloe…"

Brute swore and shouted angrily. "Bloody bitch! She'll get hers!" Then he hurried to his bike, leapt on and started it then accelerated away.

Major Wickham watched him go with a sinking heart. *He's caught Roach and Roach won't stand up to any sort of interrogation. If he knows where the rest of the platoon are they are in trouble,* he thought.

His fingers itched to get a radio to call Chloe to warn her.

It all depends on her now, he realised.

Chapter 30

DARK SOON

Jane lay in the grass, the afternoon sun blazing down on her. She had a headache and was feeling sick and exhausted. But what really gripped her was the fear, fear of being caught and then savagely raped and worse. She had heard that bikies were brutal people and she realised that she and Chloe could probably expect no mercy.

And even when we get the stretchers to the road and the police arrive it won't be over, she realised.

The awful knowledge that the police could not protect her at her home or at school during the weeks and months ahead came as a mind-numbing shock.

"We might to have to go into one of those witness protection programs like on TV," she muttered.

Then the even more dismaying thought that she might have to vanish, to change her name, home and identity to survive left her feeling drained and devastated.

I will lose all my friends and will have to leave Cadets, she thought.

Suddenly Cadets seemed very important to her, a rock to cling to in crisis. Images of Major Wickham's face floated across her mind, sometimes angry, sometimes stern, then laughing and then fatherly. Letting him down made her feel bad.

And she was thirsty!

So were others. Cadet Arthur grumbled, "I need more water. I'm thirsty!"

"Shut up Arthur!" Jane snapped. "We are all thirsty. If you hadn't stuck your head up we would probably be back at camp by now."

Arthur looked offended but when he noticed the looks of disapproval on the faces around him he looked away and stopped grumbling.

Sgt Lynes half got up to peek over the crest. "We should go," he said.

Chloe shook her head. "We will wait a bit longer."

"But it's sixteen forty. It's getting late," Sgt Lynes whined.

Jane made a wry face but did think they should take the risk and move. *We really need to get Kim to a doctor. She must be bleeding to death internally,* she reasoned.

It was another 10 minutes before Chloe rose and looked carefully in all directions before directing them to get up and move. Jane was glad to do that but found she now possessed a lot of stiff muscles she had not even known she owned. The same applied to most of the others and there were a lot of stifled groans and moans as they rose and picked up the stretchers.

They went straight over the ridge northwestwards into the next creek and down the slope as quickly as they could. It took only five minutes to reach the bottom, which was a narrow dry creek bed, mostly rocks. Chloe, who was leading, at once turned left and headed Southwest up the small valley.

Jane approved of that as it was again taking them towards the highway and possible help. But as she struggled along with the stretcher she found she was tiring quickly and stumbling a lot. Her mouth had gone dry and she realised she had stopped sweating. That rang a little alarm bell in her mind as she remembered the lessons on heat that the cadets were given several times a year.

When you stop sweating you are dehydrated and in danger of getting heat exhaustion or heat stroke, she thought.

A glance at the shirts and faces of those around her confirmed that most of them were not sweating either.

Dry shirts and dry red faces, she noted. *We had better get this over with pretty quickly or we will have some serious heat casualties to worry about as well.*

A glance at her watch showed her that it was 1712. The only good thing was that the sun had now gone down far enough for them to be mostly in shadow down in the creek bed. Thinking to warn Chloe of the possible trouble ahead, she looked up and was just in time to see Chloe spring back and aim the gun down at someone hidden in the bed of the creek.Jane's heart leapt in alarm, thinking they had been sprung by hidden bikies. But then she heard a quavering boy's voice cry out, "Don't shoot! It's me!"

Bloody Cadet Flegel! Jane thought, her relief fuelling anger.

Chloe obviously had the same reaction because, as the stretcher party closed up on her Jane heard her snap, "What are you doing here Flegel?"

"They... They left me behind!" Flegel cried, the sound of sobbing joining in.

"Who did?"

"CUO Roach and Sgt Lepson," Flegel cried.

"Why?"

"B... B... Because I sprained my ankle," Flegel sobbed.

The stretcher party had now reached them and Sgt Grey ordered the stretcher lowered. Chloe made a face and shook her head. "Why were you with them?"

Flegel looked scared and bit his lip before hanging his head. "I... I..."

"Just ran away!" Chloe snapped. "You should have stayed with your corporal."

Cpl Lang's group had just arrived and he overheard this. "That's right Flegel, you little toad! I didn't know what had happened to you. You stay with me next time," he snarled, his relief and anger both very obvious.

Flegel looked embarrassed and hurt. "But... But Sgt Lepson said to run, so I did," he cried.

Sgt Lepson gasped. "I did not, you lying little bastard!" he snarled.

Jane glanced across the stretcher at Sgt Lepson and saw him flush with embarrassment.

You gutless prick! she thought.

Aware that everyone was now looking at him Sgt Lepson blushed even more. "I... I... We... I had a twisted ankle as well. They left both of us," he blustered.

Cpl Callan curled his lip. "So you left Flegel and went after them," he said, as a flat statement.

That really stung Sgt Lepson and he almost choked as he stammered. "I... I... We had to get help!"

Jane curled her lip and she shook her head. Looking at Cpl Lang, she saw him look anxious. *That useless prick didn't even know his cadet was missing!* she thought.

Chloe also shook her head. "Never mind all that! We've got you back safe. Now, let's reorganise these stretcher parties. We need eight on Harley's stretcher all the time and people need a break."

To Jane's mild surprise not one of the four sergeants present objected when Chloe reallocated people to the two stretcher parties. They meekly obeyed and moved to the new positions. As they did Jane noticed

Chantelle take a drink and then hold her water bottle upside down over her mouth. Not even one drop came out.

"Chloe, we need water," Jane said quietly as Chloe came past.

Chloe nodded. "I know. I've been watching. We have a few with early heat exhaustion already. I feel pretty dry myself. We will wait here for a few minutes while I do another recce."

"I'll come with you," Jane offered.

"So will I," Cpl Callan said.

"Me too," Sgt Grey added.

Chloe shook her head. "Too many. Three will be fine. You stay and command the stretcher parties Sgt Grey."

Sgt Grey nodded and accepted this. Chloe turned and led Jane and Cpl Callan on up the shallow valley. Jane noted that it was now 1720hrs.

Be dark in half an hour, she thought, unsure if that was a good thing or not. On balance she decided it would be. *The bikies will have trouble seeing us in the dark,* she reasoned.

Five minutes of careful scouting had them 100 metres up the gully to where it narrowed under the powerlines. They passed under the powerline and continued on until the valley ended in a shallow dip. Once again there were a few clumps of rock to provide cover and they crawled up among them to get a better look.

Jane found herself looking south across a paddock dotted with a few large boulders and a scatter of small ironbarks. A hundred paces away stood a large black plastic water tank with a drinking trough and yards for cattle next to it. Two vehicle tracks met just beyond it and the single track went on south to a gate. Even as she studied the gate a large white semitrailer roared across her line of vision on the other side of it.

"The highway is just there on the other side of that gate," she said, her hopes soaring.

Cpl Callan took out his map, taking care to keep it low and hidden. "That is the junction where we got off the bus. Still four or five hundred metres," he said.

That was deflating to Jane. That was the 4th time they had been within half a kilometre of the highway that afternoon!

We can walk that in 10 minutes, even with the stretchers, she told herself.

But then her eye detected movement near the gate. She focused her tired and blurry vision and felt her heart turn over and her hopes plummet. There was a bikie sitting on his bike just outside the gate!

"No good," she muttered. "They are there."

Cpl Callan swore and Chloe shook her head when she had the bikie pointed out to her.

Chloe bent her head down to study Cpl Callan's map. "We might have to go more to the west, to the other side of the railway," she said.

"But that adds a lot of distance," Cpl Callan objected.

"Yes, but we can't cross this open ground without being seen," Chloe replied.

"What about in the dark?" Cpl Callan queried.

"It will still be very risky," Chloe said. "We will be better off detouring."

"But that takes us off the edge of the map!" Cpl Callan objected.

Chloe shook her head and looked exasperated. "I don't care if it's off the edge of the world. If that gets us to safety we go that way."

"But we won't know where to go," Cpl Callan said.

"West. That will take us to the road that goes from Mingela to Dotswood. And then south. That will take us to the Flinders Highway. We might even have to go to the township," Chloe replied.

Jane bit her lip and then agreed. "We had better move. It will be dark soon."

As she said this the radio hung around her neck began to crackle. A distorted voice sounded. "Mike, where are you and Julio?"

Chloe's eyes widened. "Brute!" she breathed, leaning closer to hear better.

Jane realised that the radio she was carrying was still on the channel chosen by the bikies. She also strained her ears to listen.

The answer was faint and distorted but she understood. "North of ... Num...crackle... Mill," the man answered.

"We are down where they shot. Pee... crackle... crackle.. We will meet... crackle, crackle.. at the rocks where crackle... crackle. You search up the next creek to the north of the one you... crackle. down."

"Got that. Where... crackle... you?'"

"Meet... crackle... at... gate at... Min.. crackle... turn-off."

Chloe glanced down at the map and then up, her face a mask of alarm. "I think that means they are going to come up this creek we are in!"

Jane thought so too. "We had better get out of it fast," she replied.

"Come on!" Chloe snapped.

She quickly crawled back down into the dip and got up. Then she hurried away. Jane followed, banging her left knee painfully a few times on rocks as she did. Hobbling and limping as she rubbed the knee she hurried after her. Cpl Callan came last. Now Jane's breath came in horrible, hot dry rasps as her chest tightened with apprehension. To make things harder she found herself half blinded by the last of the sunlight which came slanting in from her left front to half blind her.

It only took them five minutes of stumbling scramble to get back to where the others waited. By the time Jane arrived Chloe had stirred them into frantic activity.

"Hurry! Hurry! Hands on! Prepare to lift! Lift!" she ordered.

Harley's stretcher came up and with eight people carrying it and two spares ready to take over they set off diagonally up the slope to the west, Chloe directing their steps. Jane went to Kim's stretcher and helped with it by taking hold of the webbing straps under Kim's head.

It was a frantic, almost panicky scramble with frequent stumbles and trips on rocks hidden in the grass but they reached the crest of the next ridge in five minutes. Even Flegel limped along quickly, casting frightened glances over his shoulder. Chantelle saw this and summed up Jane's thoughts by snapping,

"I don't know what you are scared of Flegel. No-one's going to rape you!"

Flegel took on a look of injured dignity and Jane felt herself go queasy at the thought of the rape and possible sodomy she feared might be ahead of her.

It is really going to hurt, she thought, imagining her tender skin tissue being rubbed and torn till it bled. She remembered hearing stories of women being raped to death and she shuddered at the callous brutality of such an act. *Oh, please God, no!* she prayed.

The crest of the ridge was like the previous one, all studded with rocky outcrops and numerous dips and hollows. The creek line beyond it was in an even bigger valley with steeper sides. They were almost directly under the powerlines. Jane came to a gasping halt and stared ahead at the ridge to the north, the rocks on it starkly silhouetted by the setting sun.

She was about to comment when the heart-stopping vibration of motorcycle engines reached her ears. "Down!" she croaked, along with several others.

They lay down where they were, luckily in a small depression among rocks but still right on the crest. Jane felt very exposed and also very uncomfortable as the entire ridge felt like it was made of nothing but football-sized rocks.

Then her heart did skip a beat when her eyes detected movement on the next ridge to the north.

Motorbikes! she breathed to herself. *Two of them.*

The two bikes came up the ridge from her right and made their way along. Jane reasoned that they must be on the rough vehicle track she knew went up that way.

Brute and that other man. Or is it Slasher?

The idea of that man now sent a chill through her and she glanced across at where Chloe lay crouched behind some rocks. She was watching the men, an intense expression on her face.

Poor Chloe! She won't get any pity from those mongrels.

Heart in mouth Jane watched the two bikes until they disappeared among trees and rocks on a tree-covered knoll to her right front. But the motorcycle noises continued, now sounding off to her front, the volume rising and falling.

They are going up and down across this valley ahead of us, Jane thought.

Then the motorcycle noises moved left and sounded very close. Jane hunched lower and felt her skin start to crawl with fearful anticipation.

Have they seen us? she wondered, her mouth dry with anxiety.

She turned her head but could see no sign of the bikes because of a slight rise in the ground and the piles of rocks and scattered trees.

To her immense relief the motorcycle noises moved to directly behind her and then faded away. Chloe turned her head and grinned at her.

"They haven't seen us," she whispered. "They are going to the gate."

Jane could only nod, her mouth too dry to even croak. Others around her looked very relieved. Chloe rose to her hands and knees and looked around and then signalled to Sgt Grey. Jane took this to mean she wanted to talk so she also made her way over to where Chloe and Sgt Grey crouched in a small dip. Sgt Lepson and Sgt Lynes joined them.

Chloe pointed to the north. "It will be dark soon. I reckon we should stay here in one of these little depressions until it is."

"Why?" Sgt Lepson asked. "Why don't we move now?"

"Because we aren't really sure which creek these other two on foot are coming up," Chloe answered. "And I would like to do a recon of the best route while it is still daylight."

Jane went to speak but found her throat so dry she had to swallow. "We can get some water too," she suggested.

"Where from?" Sgt Grey asked.

Jane pointed back behind them. "There's a water trough just over there."

"Do you mean a cattle trough!" Sgt Lynes cried, disgust in his voice.

Jane nodded. "Yes. It will keep us alive."

Sgt Lynes wrinkled his nose. "It will make us sick. We can't do that!"

Chloe now spoke. "It doesn't matter if we get upset stomachs tomorrow. We will be safe by then."

"I forbid it!" Sgt Lynes snapped.

Jane shook her head and began to marshal her thoughts, but Chloe spoke first. "You can take a running jump! We have people here on the edge of collapse from heat exhaustion. If that becomes heat stroke they could die. We need water urgently."

Sgt Lynes opened his mouth to speak but Sgt Grey cut him off. "I agree with Chloe and Jane. We must have water. I think we should organise a water party to go to the trough as soon as it is dark."

"I agree," Chloe said. "But while it is still daylight, I want to check out the best place to cross this railway. Cpl Callan, you and Jane come with me."

Sgt Lynes looked angry but stopped arguing. Chloe turned to Sgt Grey, completely ignoring Sgt Lepson who crouched between them. "Sgt Grey, get everyone into this little hollow under the powerlines. That way we will be able to find you again in the dark. When we get back have every water bottle strung on toggle ropes ready to take."

Sgt Grey nodded and Chloe stood carefully up and looked around then gestured to Jane. She rose and moved with her, signalling to Cpl Callan who had been watching. Leaving the platoon to move a few metres into better cover the three slipped over the crest and began making their way diagonally westwards down into the next creek.

By this time Jane was feeling really exhausted. Her feet felt sore and her legs felt like they were made of lead and all her muscles seemed to ache and throb. She just wanted to lie down but there was no way she was going to let her friend down so she forced herself to move.

Within a couple of minutes the trio were down in the shadows of the creek line and they found a cattle pad that went the way they wanted and that made the going easier. Chloe led, the shotgun at the ready. Jane watched her seemingly effortless and graceful stride as she made her way along the valley bottom and could only shake her head in silent admiration.

Five more minutes' walk had them near the top of the valley at where it divided into two re-entrants. The right one was deeper and had more bushes along it, so Chloe took that. The ground on their right rose to a definite hill crowned with what looked like a real forest of trees. Then the re-entrant narrowed to a steep-sided gully with Chinese apple trees growing along it. These were so close together they formed a real thicket and in the gloom it was awkward to pick a safe path. Twice Jane got snagged and each time she let out a little cry of pain and swore.

Abruptly they came to the vehicle track, a grey ribbon of dust in the twilight. On the other side of that was a four-strand barbed wire fence and directly beyond that a steep drop that Jane recognized as a railway cutting. From where she stood the cutting was so deep she could not see the bottom. Careful not to leave tracks Chloe made her way across and signalled the others to follow.

Jane did so and found herself standing on the lip of an almost vertical drop of about ten metres. In the bottom were the two shiny rails of the main railway. The other side of the cutting was even higher, and Jane was dismayed.

"This is going to be a bit hard to get across," she whispered.

Leaning forward against the fence she looked to the right and saw that the cutting went on around a slight curve to the left, getting deeper as the ground rose to the hill on that side. Only as it went out of sight was there a hint that the ground was dropping again.

Then she looked to the left, her gaze following the steep-sided cutting until the railway passed under the highway a few hundred metres away. The railway cutting went on as far as she could see, slowly curving to the right.

There is no way we could get a stretcher across that! she thought with dismay.

Then she got another shock and she gasped. Standing on the concrete highway bridge over the railway cutting was another bikie! He was illuminated by the sunlight but had only become noticeable when he moved.

"Chloe! There's one of them on the bridge. Move back!" she croaked.

Chloe looked and at once stepped back out of sight. "I don't think he saw us. We are in shadow and down among bushes," Chloe muttered.

Cpl Callan swore softly. "But they are watching the railway to make sure we don't cross it," he added.

Chloe shook her head. "We couldn't get across here anyway, even without the stretchers. We will have to cross somewhere else."

"Where?" Cpl Callan queried glancing to his right.

Chloe pointed that way. "Around the bend. They can't possibly have enough men to watch all of the railway. Let's see if we can find a crossing. We just make sure that bastard back on the overpass doesn't see us."

She led the way northwards up the steep slope beside the vehicle track, glancing continually back to check they were not visible to the bikie. Jane followed and found going up that steep slope quite a challenge. There was a lot of deadfall, dry leaves and twigs and her boots kept slipping. She reached the top with her heart pounding and her breath coming in hot gasps.

On top, in among the trees, they were quite invisible from the overpass. Here they found a track junction and a quick examination of the wheel tracks showed that the motorbikes had been using the right-hand one. "That's the one that goes back down to where we were this morning," Chloe commented.

"Where those two motorbikes came up a few minutes ago," Cpl Callan agreed.

Chloe took the left track, again taking care to walk on the deadfall and not on the dusty wheel ruts. It took only a few minutes to discover that the vehicle track followed the fence beside the cutting. Here they were around the curve and out of sight of the overpass, but the cutting was at least 15 metres deep and real obstacle. Shaking her head at this Chloe continued on, the track going slowly downhill as it went Northwest.

At the bottom of the slope they found what they wanted. The vehicle track ended at another creek line and the cutting also ended. The creek went under the railway, but a glance revealed that it went through a culvert that was much too small to move stretchers through.

Another cutting began on the other side of the creek line, but Jane saw that it was possible to get across the railway at that point with only the barbed wire fences to cause any difficulty. Better still, on the other side she saw a dirt road that went up a bench cut on the side of the cutting opposite.

"That will do us," Chloe commented. "OK, let's see if we can get back before it gets completely dark."

Jane looked around and noticed that the last of the sun's rays were just touching the tops of the trees and that there was still a tinge of blue to the sky. But the evening gloom was gathering fast. Feeling considerably boosted she followed Chloe back up the hill. Three minutes' walk had them at the top of the forested hill and they quickly made their way down the steeper slope on the south side. At the bottom Jane expected Chloe to turn left but instead she continued on up the other side, this time following the vehicle track

"Chloe! Where are you going? We came this way," Jane hissed.

Chloe stopped and shook her head. "I am going to follow the powerlines back. It will be a lot easier than trying to get through all those thorn trees in the dark," she explained. "Mike, brush out our tracks," she added.

Cpl Callan had closed up and nodded his agreement, so they set off up the slope. The vehicle track did a sharp left turn in among the thicket of thorn trees and went up at an easier angle before turning sharp right.

They had just reached this bend which was in another dip which Jane realised was the top end of the gully they had not taken earlier when the sharp chink of stone on stone and then the sound of man swearing close below them on the left caused Jane's heart to flip in terror.

Bikies! her terrified mind cried.

The others had heard it too and the three of them stood frozen in the gloom, ears cocked. Then Chloe pointed to the left into the darker shadows in under the nearest thorn trees. Jane glanced to the right, noted that there was almost no cover there then nodded and moved left, very conscious of the sound of boots on rocks just down to her left. As she turned and made her way carefully into the shadows this meant the noises were directly in front of her. Once in under the tree she turned and faced back towards the road, putting the sounds behind her. By now her heart was thumping so hard there was a swashing sound in her ears that made it hard to hear but she distinctly heard a man cry out in pain.

"Ow! Bloody thorns!"

Then another male voice sounded nearby. "This is a complete mug's game. We aren't going to find these bloody cadets now."

"No," the first man agreed. "If we couldn't find them in daylight, we've got Buckley's in the dark."

"Not in all these bloody gullies," agreed the second man.

There was another oath and more stumbling footsteps. These were now behind Jane and she realised that the two men were in the deep gully they had come up. The footsteps stopped and then the first man spoke.

"Hey, this looks like a road."

The second man joined him, only ten or so metres to Jane's right rear. "It is. It must be the one the bikes went up a while ago," he agreed.

"Which way do we go?" the first bikie queried.

"Not sure. Left I think," the second man replied.

"I'll call Brute and ask," the first bikie commented.

Jane heard this without comprehending until she heard the radio around her neck suddenly start to crackle.

They are on the same channel! They will hear us! her terrified mind cried.

With desperately fumbling fingers she grabbed the on/off switch and twisted it just as the man began to call. The word 'Brute' came out loud and clear and the click of the switch being turned off sounded very loud to Jane and her heart seemed to stop. But it seemed that the men had not noticed. Jane glanced anxiously at Chloe who was crouched next to her in the gathering darkness. Her facial expression was just visible in the twilight and she shook her head and then nodded her approval.

"Brute," the man called, "We are on that vehicle track next to the railway at the top. Which way do we turn?"

"Crackle... Left. Hurry up you two. I want to tell you what to do next, over," came Brute's reply.

"Over! I'll give the bugger over!" muttered the first man, but not into the radio.

The sound of the two men's boots thudding on the road approached up the slope. Jane tensed and crouched ready to act. Beside her Chloe eased the shotgun forward ready to use.

Oh God, I hope Chloe doesn't have to shoot anyone, Jane thought.

The idea was so appalling she mentally cringed, aware that such an act would irrevocably alter Chloe's whole life for the worse.

And there were the two men, their shapes quite clear in the gloom! And they were not happy. "Oh! I'm buggered!" groaned the first man as he passed.

"Me too! I've had enough of stumbling up and down rocky bloody gullies, that's for sure."

"I wonder what Brute wants us to do now?" First Man said.

"Better not be more walking around these hills," Second Man replied.

"Ouch! Bloody tripped. Wish I had a torch," First Man said.

I'm glad you don't! Jane thought, her breath easing out as she relaxed.

The two men vanished from sight and the sounds of their voices and boots died away. Chloe crept out onto the track and beckoned the other two to follow. "Phew! That was close!" she whispered.

Cpl Callan grunted agreement. "If we'd gone back the way we came we would have run fair into them," he commented.

"You are right," Chloe agreed. "OK, let's get back to the platoon."

They set of up the slope but that worried Jane. "What if they are waiting up ahead?" she whispered.

Chloe shook her head. "That was no act to fool us. If they'd known we were there they would have grabbed us, or tried to. No. They are going to the gate."

So the three cadets continued carefully on the dirt road until the powerlines became visible overhead in the last of the light. Here Chloe paused and looked around, listening carefully. Then she shook her head and turned left to make her way across the stony ground under the powerline. In that fashion they found the platoon after only another five minutes of slow stumbling in the dark.

"Halt! Who's that?" came Cadet Leece's voice from the dark rocks to their left.

Jane sighed with relief. "It's us Rod," she answered.

Chapter 31

TERRIFYING MOMENTS

Sgt Lepson heard the recon group returning and sighed with relief. After they had gone, he had experienced a few bad moments fearing that the whole burden of responsibility might be thrust onto him. He now burned with shame at the cowardly way he had fled and he also burned with deep embarrassment at his inability to navigate. For the first time it struck him that his motivation had been wrong.

I was just after the glory and the power, he realised, hotly aware that he had done two 9-day promotion courses: a Junior Leaders Course and a Senior Leaders Course, both run by the army at Lavarack Barracks, but that he had not really bothered to learn the skills and techniques of navigation. On both courses, a year apart, he had scraped through with a bare pass. He was also ashamed at having left Flegel and of how he had panicked and scurried away when CUO Roach and Cpl Hankin had been captured. Bitter memories of his panic and fluster when he had run into Chloe and Jane added to his mental anguish.

Through his mind flitted images of the looks on the faces of Chloe and Jane and other cadets at various times since. Contempt was the word he decided fitted their expression and he burned again.

They despise me, he thought. *And they deserve to. I despise myself.*

For a while he sat in silent misery, aware of the whispers and reproachful looks from some of the cadets and of the sneers and curled lips of the other sergeants. Shame turned to resentment which morphed into anger.

All my own fault! he thought dejectedly.

But how could he possibly redeem himself? He knew that acting the injured cadet with the twisted ankle would not win him any sympathy. It came to him that it was respect he craved. *I don't want people just feeling sorry for me and looking down on me,* he thought.

But what to do?

And then he saw Cpl Lang drain his water bottle and the glimmering of a plan came to him.

I am the platoon sergeant. I can stop feeling sorry for myself and get off my arse and do that job, he reasoned.

He sensed that recovering some dignity and status might be a hard job, but he resolved to do it. So he stood up and undid his toggle rope from his basic pouch and went to Cpl Lang.

"Leece is your 2ic isn't he?"

"Yes."

"Get him to collect all your section's water bottles and thread them on his toggle rope," he ordered. Then he went to Sgt Lynes and gave the same instruction, now annoyed by the fact that the platoon had no lance corporals.

The major should have promoted them by now, he thought resentfully, aware that it was usually on the mid-year 'Senior' Field Exercise that this was done. So Cadets Warren and McDonald were chosen.

As he did this, he had to interrupt the other sergeants, Cpl Callan and Chloe and Jane who were deep in conversation.

"I am taking a water party to the water trough," he said. "So you blokes give me your water bottles."

There were surprised looks and then nods. The sergeants all handed over their water bottles. Sgt Lepson threaded these on his toggle rope and then tied the ends to make a loop which he slung over his shoulder.

"How do I find it?" he queried.

"I'll lead you there," Chloe offered.

Sgt Lepson would have preferred Cpl Callan to do that, but he could not bring himself to say so. Instead he grunted approval and then collected the other three cadets. A glance at his watch told him it was 1840hrs. While he considered this Chloe took Jane's water bottles and then Cpl Callan's.

Sgt Grey said, "Try to be quick. We want to start moving as soon as we can."

Chloe nodded. "You should follow us and move both stretchers to the edge of the vehicle track. That will save time."

"We will. Now get moving," Sgt Grey agreed.

That reminded Sgt Lepson that some of the water bottles were in the webbing comprising Kim's stretcher, so he went to it and crouched to take out the bottles. Both of Kim's had water in them and he shook them to see how much.

Chantelle pointed to Kim. "She hasn't had a drink for hours. Give her a drink before you go."

At once Cpl Reppington, the medic said no. "She has a stomach wound. You mustn't give people with stomach wounds a drink. It can kill them," she insisted.

"Oh bull!" Chantelle retorted, obviously ashamed that she hadn't thought of it earlier.

"It's true! You ask Sgt Small," Cpl Reppington insisted.

So Sgt Small was consulted and confirmed it. While they argued Sgt Lepson felt waves of dread and nausea as fear of dying swept through him. He stared at Kim with ghoulish fascination, wondering if he was actually watching a person die and then shivering at the possibility of being killed himself.

To end it he took the water bottle and said, "Come on water party."

Led by Chloe they stumbled west across the rocks, a setting half-moon providing a convenient navigation guide. It was slow going on the rough ground but took only five minutes to reach the vehicle track under the powerlines. Chloe at once turned left and began padding along beside the two-wheel ruts.

Sgt Lepson was confused. For some reason he had thought they would turn right and he hissed for her to stop.

"Are you going the right way?" he queried.

Chloe frowned and nodded. "We have to go south."

Sgt Lepson opened his mouth to ask how she knew she was going south but then he realised that the sounds of traffic on the highway were actually coming from the south and he bit back the question. But Chloe must have noted his indecision as she pointed up into the sky.

"There's the Southern Cross," she explained.

Sgt Lepson nodded and for the first time really understood how useful it was to know such things. "Lead on," he hissed to cover his confusion.

Chloe did, scouting and going very slowly and carefully in the dark. Sgt Lepson found the whole experience of possibly creeping towards a real enemy with guns un-nerving and he wished he hadn't been so rash as to volunteer for the task. In the starlight everything looked spooky and he found his heart was hammering fast and his mouth dry. At every step he feared to hear a warning shout or a shot and it took an effort of willpower for him to keep his legs moving forward.

Chloe annoyed him even more by doing everything right. Every ten paces she stopped and listened for ten seconds before moving again. Her skill impressed Sgt Lepson but also irritated him. He was deeply resentful that a girl and a mere cadet could be so good.

A few minutes later they came to the dark bulk of the water tank. Beyond it the steel rails of a cattle yard added a maze of confusing shadows. In the starlight the whole place looked eerie and sinister and Sgt Lepson found fear rise to almost paralyse him.

"Wait here," Chloe whispered. She padded off into the darkness. While she scouted the area, Sgt Lepson studied the layout. The water tank was about 4 metres high and as round and sat on the ground. It was on the right of the track and beyond it, on the southern side, was the actual water trough a few metres from it.

Chloe padded silently back and hissed, 'All clear!' then led them forward. "Stay this side. And be quiet. There's a bikie at the fence only a couple of hundred metres that way," she whispered.

The others all nodded and moved to line up along the water trough. Despite what Chloe had cautioned Sgt Lepson went around the far end, reasoning that there wasn't enough room.

The sooner these water bottles are filled and we are gone the better, he told himself.

But he was scared and found that he had trouble untying the rope as his fingers kept fumbling and he found he was trembling. Every few seconds he cast nervous glances into the night, particularly toward the highway where the headlights of passing cars and trucks flickered through the trees.

If only we could just walk down there and stop a vehicle, he thought.

After sliding off the ten water bottles he was carrying Sgt Lepson unscrewed the cap on one and stood to dip it into the water trough. To his surprise the water felt quite cold and it was very refreshing on the skin. With his other hand he splashed some on his sunburnt face and that was bliss. And his own thirst now came to dominate. As soon as the water bottle was full he lifted it to his lips. The water looked black and he suspected it was full of cow dung and dirt and his stomach turned over with revulsion. But he was also parched, and he suppressed his feelings and began to drink.

The water smelt and it tasted awful, gritty and stale but it was wet and cold and he really needed it so he gulped it down, all the while trying to ignore the idea of what he might be ingesting. The drink was such a relief that he had another, draining half the water bottle. Feeling better he refilled it and then placed it down beside the trough and then picked up another.

Minutes crept by. Sgt Lepson had another big drink and went on filling. He became aware of a cool breeze that set him shivering and he realised he was actually sick from lack of water, over-exertion and sunburn.

God I wish this was all over! he thought.

It was frustrating to think that the company bivouac was only a few minutes' walk the other side of the highway!

Opposite Sgt Lepson stood Chloe. She had drunk and refilled her own water bottles, Cpl Callan's and Jane's and now kept guard, mostly focusing on the south. Sgt Lepson was very aware of her presence, being both resentful and irritated by it. But he was also glad as he felt she knew what she was doing. Shaking his head with annoyance he began to fill another water bottle.

As he filled each one he added it to the line. To add to his annoyance Chloe kept telling the others to hurry up.

"Don't leave them on the ground McDonald," she hissed. "Take them off one end and thread them on the other end in case you have to move quickly."

As Sgt Lepson had all his empty ones in a row on the ground he blushed and hoped she wouldn't notice, resenting the fact that she was right and also that she was giving the orders that he should have been giving.

Pushy slut! I'll get even with her one day, he told himself.

As he knelt to thread the water bottles back onto the rope he glanced up at her as she took another drink. Even in the starlight he could see the swell of her breasts as her shirt strained taut when she tilted her head back and lifted her arm and he experienced a spurt of lust, mingled with frustrated anger.

But he was also so spooked by the situation that all his senses seemed heightened and his brain registered the flicker of reflected light which faintly showed on her shirt and in the glint of her eyes. It made him glance over his shoulder and what he saw made him freeze up with terror.

The headlights of what looked like three motorcycles had stopped at the gate!

Sgt Lepson stared in horror and tried to speak but his mouth seemed to be stuck open. Gasping with fear he pointed. But Chloe had seen them too and she lowered her water bottle and began screwing on the cap.

Turning to the others she pointed and hissed, "Motorbikes! At the gate! Quick! Grab your water bottles and go!"

Sgt Lepson's first impulse was to run but then Chloe grabbed at McDonald's sleeve. "Don't leave any water bottles. They might see them and will know we are close by," she said.

"But I haven't finished," Cadet McDonald protested.

"Go! Get all your water bottles and go!" Chloe hissed, pushing at his shoulder.

Cadet McDonald hastily screwed on the cap of the water bottle he had been filling and crouched to thread it onto the rope. Chloe crouched to help him.

As she did a motorbike roared into the paddock through the gateway. Only then did the fear hit Sgt Lepson so that he could move. He had also been going to just run but had accepted Chloe's instructions and he now crouched to grab at the rope holding the water bottles. But in his flustered state in the dark he could not find the end and only managed to knock over several of the bottles. Scrabbling in the dust and cow dung he found one end and then felt around for the other, knocking over two unfilled water bottles in the process. With panic now grabbing at his throat he snatched one up and threaded it onto the rope, then knelt to get the other.

In his haste he knocked it away and had to grope for it, his fingers encountering wet cow manure as he did. He found the empty water bottle and then looked frantically for the other end of the rope, hotly aware that the motorcycle was coming towards him. To his horror it approached so fast that the bouncing flicker of its headlight began to illuminate him. But the light also helped him find the end of the rope and he snatched it up and glanced fearfully around.

To his dismay he discovered that the other cadets had all gone, vanished into the shadows behind the water tank. And the first motorbike was rapidly approaching. One glance told Sgt Lepson that he had miscalculated, and that Chloe had been right.

I am on the wrong side of the water trough! he reasoned.

Worse still the motorcycle looked to be heading straight for him! Even in his panicked state Sgt Lepson understood that he was likely to be seen if he stood and tried to run away. There seemed to be only one option open to him, hide! And the only hiding place was under the water trough. So he took it, scurrying on hands and knees around the far end and then crouching behind it.

The water trough was about 5 metres long and stood on two concrete stumps. It was made of black painted steel and stood about twenty centimetres off the ground, not high enough to get right under but high enough for the lights to shine through and for people to see him. Sgt Lepson knelt there, shivering from terror as the motorbike came to a stop only metres away. Two more followed it and to his dismay they all stopped on the vehicle track close to the trough. For several seconds he was tempted to make a bolt for it but he managed to restrain the impulse.

I can't outrun a motorbike, and they might shoot, his frightened mind reasoned.

To his mingled relief and dismay the motorbikes switched off their lights and then their motors. The riders dismounted and Sgt Lepson crouched lower in case the riders came to the trough. Only then did he realise that he had one hand in a wet cow pat but the sticky sensation was so over-ridden by skull-gripping fear that he barely noticed.

And the bikies were coming to the trough! Sgt Lepson heard the thud of their boots in the dust and his heart almost stopped as terror clutched it. Crouching lower he slid as far under the curved bottom as he could until he realised he could see underneath. He was dimly aware that he was now lying in wet cow manure, but the proximity of the bikies drove all such trivial thoughts from his mind.

One of them spoke. "This is the drinking trough here," he said. A torch clicked on and its beam lit up the trough. Sgt Lepson cringed in fright and hunched even tighter against the cold, dirty steel.

"Ah yuk! You can drink it Brute!" answered another bikie who then chortled.

"Too right!" added a third. "I'll go back to the pub when I want a drink."

The torch beam swung to shine into the surrounding bush. Sgt Lepson began to tremble.

They will see our boot prints! his terrified mind decided.

He was now desperately aware that the bikies were only a few paces from him and he began considering what to say to surrender.

But they didn't and the torch was switched off. The one named Brute then said, "You ready to act Suzie?"

"Yeah," answered a female voice.

Act? Sgt Lepson thought, his heart hammering so hard he had difficulty hearing.

Suddenly the girl shouted at the top of her voice and then screamed. "No! No! Don't hurt me! Aaargh! Aaaaa! Aaaargh!"

The noise was so loud and unexpected that Sgt Lepson jerked up in terror, his head thumping hard against the bottom of the trough. Half stunned and gasping for breath he lay back flat and tried not to scream himself.

Brute grunted. "Again, and louder and sound more terrified," he ordered.

Again, the girl cried out and then screamed. The awful noise echoed off across the dark bush and Sgt Lepson shuddered with fear and clenched his fists and prayed. He had no idea what was going on, but it sounded dreadful and he could hardly contain his bowels.

Brute chuckled. "That's a bit better! Now louder, or I'll let Slasher have some fun so that you will really scream," he said.

"You're a prick Brute," the woman replied.

But she really screamed this time, a spine-chilling, high-pitched wail that echoed and made the heart hammer and the stomach churn. Sgt Lepson could only lie flat and swallow the bile that had risen to half choke him.

Brute chuckled again and the said, "That's better! Good girl Suzie. OK let's see if your play acting had any effect." His voice changed and he said, "4 Platoon. Chloe. Did you hear that? That was Slasher having some fun with one of your little girl cadets. Answer me, over."

Sgt Lepson was puzzled. *He is talking on the radio and that girl isn't one of our cadets,* he thought. Then it dawned on him what the 'act' might be. *They are trying to trick us.*

There was no reply on the radio so Brute repeated his message and then said, "OK Suz, give us a few more screams."

Suzie did, again sending Sgt Lepson's heart rate shooting up and making his hair stand on end and his skin crawl because it really did sound like she was suffering terrible pain. Brute got her to do it again and then he called on the radio.

"Chloe, that will be you if we catch you, but if you bring us Harley you will be safe, over."

There was silence and Sgt Lepson wondered if the cadets were listening and what they were thinking. When no answer came he frowned.

Maybe they are on a different channel? he wondered.

Brute must have thought the same as he muttered about channels and then made the same call twice more. Then he swore.

"The bitch either isn't listening or she is being really stubborn," he commented.

"Maybe they can't hear the screams properly," suggested the second bikie. "I mean we don't really know where they are."

"That's right," agreed the third bikie. "Why don't we go to those rocks where I caught those two this afternoon? They might be hiding just near there."

"Yeah, OK. We'll try that," answered Brute.

There was the thud of boots and then the sound of motorcycles being started. Sgt Lepson lay with his heart thudding with a mixture of fear and hope. He was able to peek under the trough and watch. As the headlights came on, he shielded his face with his sleeve and hat and lay flat, ignoring the wet squishy feeling, dust and prickles.

Luckily the headlights were facing side on, and when the bikes started moving they were swung away from him. He saw the first bike swing away and head off along the other vehicle track to the east and his hopes went even higher.

They haven't seen me! I might be safe, he thought.

The second and third motorcycles followed the first, their headlights lighting up the bush and rock piles. Within seconds the bikes were fifty metres away and then a hundred. The glow of their headlights vanished among the trees and rocks and Sgt Lepson let out a huge sigh of relief.

Now he allowed his urge to flee to take over. He crawled back out from under the trough and turned to run. But as he did he caught his right boot in the rope holding the water bottles and that sent him sprawling in the dust, and in another wet cow pat. Swearing softly and shocked by the fall he scrambled to his feet and then clawed at the rope around his ankle.

He was about to throw the rope away when some shred of sanity made him realise his reputation was involved.

It will look bad if I turn up without the water bottles, he told himself.

So he bent and untangled the rope and then hoisted it up. As he did he realised that his trousers were all wet. Puzzled he felt them.

That's not just cow shit. How did they get so wet?

For a few seconds wondered when he had splashed so much water on himself. And then he realised that he had pissed himself in fear when the girl had screamed. A hot wave of shame scoured through him.

How will I explain it to the others? he fretted.

But that potential embarrassment was nothing compared to being caught by the bikies! With that still his dominant motive he started walking towards the water tank.

I will just say it is water, and anyway, it is dark, he decided.

He reached the water tank and looked for the others but saw no sign of them. Then another shrill scream of agony split the still night air and he paused in his stride and nearly dived for cover again. However, his frightened and confused mind realised that the sound had come from some distance away and that it was only the bikie girl play acting again.

Hurrying on past the water tank he looked anxiously for the other cadets, but they were nowhere to be seen. "The cowardly mongrels have left me!" he muttered, anger adding to his emotional mix.

"Psst! Here we are," came Chloe's voice.

Sgt Lepson jumped with fright as a dark shadow moved among the rocks at his feet. Four others stood up. Swallowing to ease his throat Sgt Lepson gasped.

"Shit! You gave me a scare. You shouldn't have left me," he said.

"Pigs!" Chloe retorted. "Why should all of us get caught? I did warn you not to go around to the other side of the trough."

Sgt Lepson deeply resented that but could not find any sensible answer. "Did you hear what the bikies said?" he asked.

"No. What was that screaming?" Chloe asked.

"One of the bikie's molls play acting," Sgt Lepson answered. "She is pretending to be one of our cadets being tortured. Did you hear it on your radio?"

Chloe shook her head. "No. I turned it down while I was scouting." At that she reached up and turned the volume back up again. As she did another series of terrifying screams sounded in the distance. Then the radio crackled. It was Brute. "Chloe, answer me. That scream was one of your little girl cadets being tortured by Slasher. If you want to save her then bring us Harley, over."

Sgt Lepson listened to this and his unhappy mind clutched at straws. His mind cried for Chloe to agree.

Let them have him! he thought.

But somehow he could not make his lips and tongue form the words. Instead he stared at Chloe with fascination as she lifted the radio to her mouth.

What is she going to say? he wondered.

Chapter 32

ANGUISH

When Major Wickham watched Brute ride off and into the paddock north of the highway he was in near despair. A ghastly dread gripped him and his imagination conjured up worse. The greatest fear was that some of the cadets would be badly hurt or killed.

Or some more, I mean, he told himself as he remembered that at least one had been shot. *I wonder who?* he thought, listing the cadets in 4 Platoon in his mind.

Anguish over that person's possible fate and over the gang carrying out their threats against some of the girls added to his torment.

Minutes ticked slowly by and, to add to his frustration and dejection, cars and trucks kept passing both on the highway and on the Mingela Road. Over the long grass to the west he could just see the roofs of the houses and that added to his sense of infuriating impotence. So did the glimpse of a passing train as it went down into the big cutting just across the other side of the road.

Twisting his head around to study the situation Major Wickham noted that the man named Davo sat on his bike at the gate into the paddock to the north and that another bikie was standing on the concrete bridge that carried the highway over the railway cutting. Having driven the highway many times he knew that the cutting was very deep.

They are certainly trying to block 4 Platoon from the main road, he thought.

More minutes ticked by and Major Wickham checked his watch. *1640hrs. The other OOCs must be wondering what is going on,* he thought unhappily. But that also gave him a glimmer of hope. *They must have tried calling us and will know something has gone wrong. Maybe they will call the police?*

But then it occurred to him that the other Officers of Cadets might come out to investigate and be made prisoner as well.

This is unbelievable! A real nightmare, he thought.

A few minutes later the bikie guarding them, Lance, suddenly got up and looked behind. Major Wickham turned to look and saw two cadets walking through the gate followed by Brute and another bikie.

"CUO Roach and Cpl Hankin," he muttered to Capt Hamilton and Lt Peters.

To his relief Lance made no move to stop him speaking so Major Wickham took a risk and opened the car door.

At that Lance turned and aimed his gun. "Where are you going?" he snarled.

"Those are my cadets. I just wanted to find out what is going on," Major Wickham replied.

At that Lance nodded. "Don't we all!" he replied.

So the pair stood and waited until the two cadets and two bikies crossed the highway and walked across to them. As the group got closer to him Major Wickham saw that the other bikie was the one nicknamed 'Slasher' and that sent his emotions down another notch.

As the group got within ten metres Major Wickham called, "CUO Roach, what is going on?"

CUO Roach shrugged and looked miserable. Cpl Hankin just looked embarrassed. Their silence brought Major Wickham's emotions to an instant boil.

"Where is your platoon CUO Roach?"

"Don't know sir," CUO Roach mumbled.

By then Brute had wheeled his bike to a stop and stood it on its stand, as did Slasher. Brute moved quickly and slapped CUO Roach on the back of the head.

"Answer the major kid. Where's 4 Platoon?"

"Leave him alone!" Major Wickham snapped.

Brute turned to glare at him. "We give the orders mister. Now question the kid or I will really rough him up."

That set Major Wickham's emotions into turmoil as well, but he was now getting desperate for information. "You don't know? When did you last see them?" he asked.

CUO Roach gestured behind him and hung his head. "Back at the bottom of the range sir," he said.

"The bottom of the range? Do you mean down near the railway line where the shootings took place?"

"Yes sir."

Major Wickham stared in disbelief as possible reasons or scenarios flitted across his mind. He was vaguely aware that Capt Hamilton and Lt Peters were leaning out of the car beside him, still restrained by the handcuffs. The bikies did not object to this. It seemed by their expressions that they also badly wanted to know. Major Wickham went on: "Are you saying you left your platoon there?"

CUO Roach lifted his head and looked scared. "I went to get help sir," he said.

Major Wickham was flabbergasted and could not speak for a few seconds while the implications of what the CUO had said sank in. It was so far removed from his concept of duty and honour that it had not occurred to him.

"You left them? When? How soon after the shooting?"

CUO Roach shrugged and looked uncomfortable and then shook his head. "A... A few minutes sir. I'm not sure." He had trouble meeting Major Wickham's eyes and the whole image filled Major Wickham with more concern.

"You mean to tell me that you, the platoon commander, left your platoon out in the bush in a desperate life and death situation?"

CUO Roach hung his head. "I... er... I... yes sir," he mumbled.

"Why didn't you just radio for help?"

CUO Roach shrugged and looked miserable. "The radios wouldn't work sir."

"So why didn't you send some runners?"

This time CUO Roach blushed and Major Wickham guessed it had been fear that had spurred the actions. CUO Roach looked anxiously around and then shook his head.

"I was worried they might get lost sir," he said.

That astonished Major Wickham but also made him angry. "Are you saying that none of your corporals can navigate?"

"No sir."

At that Cpl Hankin looked offended. "Oh bull! It was you who got us lost!" he cried.

At that another worrying idea came into Major Wickham's head. He glanced at his watch and then said, "The shootings were nearly five hours ago. You can walk from there to here in thirty minutes. What took you so long?"

CUO Roach looked around, his face a mask of misery and doubt. Finally, he hung his head and mumbled: "We got lost sir."

Major Wickham was dumbfounded. He was also very disappointed and angry, mostly with himself for appointing the CUO to command 4 Platoon.

"So Sgt Lepson is in command?"

CUO Roach glanced up and shook his head. His facial expression indicated doubt and Major Wickham experienced another mental shock. He braced himself for more bad news. CUO Roach licked his lips and said, "No sir, possibly."

"Why only possibly?" Major Wickham cried, unable to keep the astonishment out of his tone.

"Because he was with me and Cpl Hankin just before we got captured," CUO Roach explained, gesturing behind him again.

"So where is he now?"

"I don't know sir," the now obviously miserable CUO Roach muttered. Tears began to form in the corners of his eyes and Major Wickham felt both anger and contempt.

"So you left the platoon without any senior leaders?" Major Wickham snapped.

"Yes sir."

"So who is in command now? Which one of the corporals did you leave in charge?"

CUO Roach again shook his head and then hung it. "None sir."

"So who is in command?"

"Don't know sir," CUO Roach mumbled.

Chloe, Major Wickham thought.

Brute now spoke. "That bitch Chloe," he said.

"Chloe!" CUO Roach said in surprise.

Major Wickham nodded. "Apparently. Now what happened? Describe the incident to me."

CUO Roach glanced around licked his lips and shook his head. "I... I didn't see much sir," he cried.

At that Slasher jabbed him hard in the ribs with a pistol. "Talk kid! Tell your OC what he needs to know."

CUO Roach glanced at Slasher, fear in every line of his face. "I... We... I didn't see much. I just knew there was shooting and then this big bikie ran up the creek and got shot near us. We took cover and that's when I decided we must get help."

Major Wickham was dismayed. "Was one of your cadets shot?" he asked.

CUO Roach nodded. "Kim sir… er... Cadet Keeler sir," he replied.

"What sort of wound?" Major Wickham queried, now sick at heart with apprehension.

To his added dismay CUO Roach shook his head. "I… I'm not sure sir. In... In the body I think," he said. Shaking his head, he looked so upset that he was unable to speak for a few seconds. "I only knew that the signaller wasn't badly hurt."

"Signaller?" Major Wickham cried.

"Travis. A bullet knocked him down, but he got up and said something about being hit in the head," CUO Roach explained. By now he was almost incoherent.

Major Wickham glanced at Capt Hamilton and the two exchanged worried frowns. "So you left the platoon?" he said to CUO Roach.

"Er... Yes sir. They... she... wouldn't do what I said. They wouldn't obey orders," CUO Roach cried.

"They?"

"Chloe and her mate Jane," CUO Roach answered, anger now showing.

Major Wickham pursed his lips. *This just keeps getting worse!* he thought.

"So what were they doing?"

"Bossing people around and giving orders," CUO Roach cried, anger and resentment now very evident in his expression and tone.

At least somebody was! Major Wickham thought.

"So what happened?"

"I... We... came to get help. They wouldn't obey orders," CUO Roach explained in an aggrieved tone.

"So you just left?" Major Wickham snapped. He was both horrified and angry. "We will talk about this later CUO Roach," he said.

Brute now intervened. "You kids sit over there near the fence. You officers get back in the car, except you major. You use this radio to call that Chloe again and tell her to bring me Harley."

Major Wickham did as he was told. He took the CB radio and called but there was no response. After waiting a few seconds, he tried again. Still no reply. That got him worried but at that moment the Land Rover driven by Muff returned. Brute went to it.

"Where's Cokehead?" he asked.

"Gone to town to get a truck like you said," Muff replied. He then gestured behind him. "What about Julio and Mike's bikes? Do we go and get them too?"

Brute shook his head. "Nah. They can get 'em later. I wonder where they are?"

He came and snatched the radio back from Major Wickham and began calling. There was no response from the two bikies. Brute glanced at the channel and then swore and clicked it to another one.

"Mike, Julio, where are you?"

There was no answer and Major Wickham felt a tiny spurt of glee. It gave him some pleasure to see the bikies having trouble.

Brute tried again and then swore and called, "Come on Slasher. You and me will do another ride around to see if we can find this mob. Lance, you go back to the bend where the highway goes down the hill and guard that. Muff, you stay here and guard this lot," he instructed.

The bikies did as they were told. Muff took out a full-size shotgun and sat on the bonnet of the Land Rover.

"You all sit against the fence where I can see ya," he ordered.

Feeling sick at heart and thoroughly depressed Major Wickham did as he was told. Capt Hamilton waved his arms. "We are still handcuffed here," he explained.

"Stay there then," Muff replied, so Capt Hamilton and Lt Peters remained in the car while the five cadets sat along the barbed wire fence in the long grass. CUO Roach moved to sit as far from the major as he could. Major Wickham noted this and shook his head.

Bloody weakling! he thought.

Muff would not let them talk so all they could do was sit in silence. Major Wickham brooded and tried hard to come up with a plan to end the situation. He watched Brute and Slasher talk to Davo for a few minutes before riding off down the highway. Minutes ticked slowly by and Major Wickham noted that it was now 1730.

Be dark soon, he thought. That both depressed him as it meant that Kim was still without medical treatment but also gave him hope. *If they haven't found 4 Platoon by then they won't,* he decided. And darkness could be used to advantage.

By then he had a splitting headache and from time to time he felt nauseous and dizzy. *From being hit in the head,* he deduced. *And from not drinking enough.*

That gave him another idea and he tried it, partly to test Muff's reaction. "Hey Muff, we are all dehydrating. We need a drink."

"Too bad!" Muff retorted.

Major Wickham persisted. "There are water bottles in the car and a full jerry can of water. Be sensible. You don't want one of these cadets collapsing from heat stroke. That will only make it worse for you."

Muff looked sulky but then nodded. He looked at CSM Glenn. "Hey you! You get the water and give everybody a drink."

CSM Glenn did as he was told. It took 10 minutes and meant sharing water bottles but, in the circumstances, Major Wickham did not care. He was just thankful to get a drink.

And then there was another complication. Major Wickham saw Muff suddenly sit up and stare. Glancing along the road Major Wickham saw that Capt Buchan was walking towards them.

Oh bugger! he thought. *I was hoping that Mel or Ashley would have called the police by now.*

As Capt Buchan got closer and saw them seated in a line in the long grass a quizzical expression formed on his face. But it did not stay there long.

Muff suddenly lifted the shotgun into view and snarled, "You join these others sitting here fella. And no nonsense or I'll blast ya."

Capt Buchan stopped, astonishment on his face. Then he looked at Major Wickham. Major Wickham could only shake his head and say, "Do as he says Mel. These guys mean business."

Capt Buchan moved and sat on the end of the line beside Major Wickham. He gave him a questioning look and said, "What's going on?"

Muff immediately waved his shotgun in a threatening manner. "No talking!" he warned.

This just keeps getting worse, Major Wickham brooded.

He now felt so ill he wanted to lie down. He knew it was from the heat and sun and not drinking enough and the beatings as well as the situation.

Maybe I'm getting too old for this, he thought.

Muff's CB radio began to crackle. Luckily, he was close enough for Major Wickham to overhear. Brute's distorted voice sounded: "Mike, where are you and Julio?"

The answer was faint and broken but could be understood. "North of… Num… crackle… Mill," the man answered.

"We are down where they shot. Pee… crackle… crackle… We will meet… crackle, crackle… at the rocks where crackle… crackle. You search up the next creek to the north of the one you… crackle. down."

"Got that. Where…. crackle… you?'"

"Meet… crackle… at… gate at… Min… crackle… turn-off."

It wasn't much but it still cheered Major Wickham up. *They still haven't found 4 Platoon. It will be dark soon and they have a good chance then,* he thought.

And they still hadn't a few minutes later when Brute and Slasher appeared at the gate across the road. Again, they spoke briefly to Davo who obviously wasn't happy and took some convincing. Then the pair rode across and stopped. Brute dismounted and stared at Capt Buchan.

"Who's this?' he cried.

Muff shrugged. "Didn't ask him. Another one of the cadet officers."

Brute strode over and stood over Capt Buchan. "Who are you?"

Capt Buchan told him and Brute nodded. Slasher joined him, his face now one great bruise.

"What are you doing here?" he asked.

"I came to find out what is going on since we couldn't get the radios to work," Capt Buchan replied.

"Who is we? Where did you come from?" Brute asked.

Capt Buchan pointed towards where the company was bivouacked. "The Officers of Cadets. We have a company of cadets camped just over there."

"What have you been doing?"

"A field exercise with the First Years but we have been getting worried," Capt Buchan answered.

"Have you called the police?" Brute queried.

Capt Buchan glanced at Major Wickham. He made a face and nodded. "Tell him Mel," he said.

Capt Buchan shook his head. "No."

"Have you got a mobile phone?"

"We all have," Capt Buchan answered.

"Get it Slasher, and his radio," Brute ordered.

Slasher did so, and as he stepped back he pointed into the bush to the south. "What we gunna do about the rest of 'em Brute? They will call the cops when it gets dark if this lot aren't back."

A worried look crossed Brute's face and he nodded. "Yeah. We gotta stop that."

"Yeah, but how?" Muff queried.

Slasher answered. "Take 'em all hostage. That will shut them up and give us a bit more leverage."

"Are you crazy man!" Muff cried. "We got enough trouble coming from the cops and the syndicate without doing something mad like that."

Brute looked very anxious. "Muff's right Slasher. Nobody's gunna take much notice of a bikie gang having a bit of a shootout but if we kidnap a bunch of kids it will be real headline stuff."

Slasher snorted and shook his head. "We already have Brute." he gestured to indicate the prisoners sitting along the fence. "It won't make it any worse. We gotta stop the cops interfering until we got Harley. If we don't, we are for the chop anyway so the cops are the least of our worries."

Brute still looked worried but nodded. "Yeah. Yeah, I think you are right." he muttered.

Major Wickham felt his stomach turn over. *Oh no! They can't mean it!* he thought.

But Brute had made a decision. "Yeah, we will make 'em all hostages," he said.

"How are we gunna do that?" Muff cried.

Slasher sneered. "Easy. We use their Chain of Command. The major here will just tell 'em all to come in and sit in a bunch and we guard 'em," he explained.

Major Wickham shook his head. "And if I don't?"

Slasher gave an evil grin. "Then I start to enjoy myself with these girls!" With that he leered at Lt Peters and Sgt Harvey, causing both to blanch and look terrified.

Major Wickham could only give in. Nodding he muttered, "Yes."

"Good!" Slasher said. "Now, how far away is this camp?"

Major Wickham pointed. "A few minutes' walk. About three hundred metres," he explained.

Slasher nodded. "Good! Now here's what we do. You two officers get in that car and Muff will drive it. Brute, you follow them and I will walk with these kids. Where's the gate into the paddock?"

Major Wickham explained and reluctantly he and Capt Buchan got up and climbed into the station wagon. As he squeezed in among the others Major Wickham felt both sick and desperate.

This is a real nightmare, he thought. But he could not think of any way out of it.

Muff was given the car keys by Brute and he got in and started up. He then did a U-turn, almost colliding with a car that he didn't see because the setting sun was now slanting in directly into his eyes. The car was then driven back to the T junction at the highway and turned right. A minute later it was turned off at the point where Lance sat on his bike. He gave them a quizzical look and Muff stopped to explain. When he heard that all of the cadets were to be taken hostage the look changed to a worried frown.

"Brute's gone mad!" he cried.

Muff nodded. "Maybe, but if we don't get Harley quick we are dead."

With that he drove in off the highway a few metres and at Major Wickham's direction turned right onto the overgrown Old Highway and along it for a hundred metres back to the gate into the paddock. Capt Buchan got out to open this and they drove through and waited till Brute had followed.

As Major Wickham slowed to a stop Brute called loudly, "Leave the bloody gate open."

"What about cattle getting out onto the highway?" Capt Buchan queried.

"Stuff the cattle!" Brute shouted angrily. "Get in!"

So Capt Buchan did and they drove on along the Old Highway. Major Wickham stared through the front windscreen, very conscious that the last rays of the setting sun were shining on the treetops. His mind was racing, trying to come up with a solution to the problem. But he could not think of any practical plan.

As they arrived at where the other vehicles were parked Major Wickham saw Lt Barker and Lt Cavendish come out of the CP. They walked towards the side of the Old Highway and stood waiting. Major Wickham urgently wished he could warn them.

If only one of them can get away so they can use their mobile phones to call the police, he thought.

But it was not to be. Brute had obviously thought about that, and as he dismounted he pointed a pistol at them. "Keep your mouths shut and hand over your phones," he ordered.

Mouths wide with astonishment and disbelief the two OOCs looked at the car and all Major Wickham could do was call and tell them to do as they were told. Reluctantly they did. Brute then looked around and hesitated. Not so Slasher who came walking down from the low rise across the Old Highway with the five cadets who were already prisoners.

"Sit 'em in a bunch Brute," he said.

Major Wickham and the others were told by Slasher to sit on the gentle slope on the other side of the Old Highway opposite the vehicles. He then told Muff to unlock the handcuffs so that Capt Hamilton and Lt Peters could join them. They were then handcuffed together by one handcuff and then Lt Cavendish was handcuffed to Lt Peters.

Slasher studied Lt Barker and said, "We need to watch this one. Handcuff him and tie his legs," he said to Muff.

This was done to a very angry Lt Barker. Brute stood looking worried. "What about all the others?" he queried.

"I'll get 'em and bring 'em here," Slasher answered. He went over to WO2 Glenn. "Hey kid, are you the CSM?"

"Yes sir," CSM Glenn answered.

"So come with me and get all these cadets to move here. And no funny stuff or the girls suffer, got it?"

"Yes sir."

CSM Glenn and Slasher move off to where groups of cadets could be seen moving around among hutchies. Major Wickham slumped down and lay back to rest his spinning head. By this time he was certain he was suffering at least mild concussion from the blows to the head.

What can I do? he fretted. *How can I end this without anyone getting hurt?*

While he lay there the platoons began arriving, the cadets being told by CSM Glenn to sit in their sections. They were all puzzled and talking until Brute shouted at them: "Shut up you kids!"

That shocked most of them and the noise ended as though cut off with a knife. In the ensuing silence CSM Glenn called on the platoon sergeants to report. While they did the cadets studied the armed bikies, their faces showing a mixture of curiosity and concern.

When Brute had shouted Major Wickham had sat up, knowing that he must convince the cadets of the seriousness of the situation.

I don't want another cadet shot because of heroics or a misunderstanding, he thought.

It was a sickening responsibility and made him appreciate how unwilling collaborators in conquered countries might feel.

With an effort that set his sore head spinning Major Wickham struggled to his feet. He saw that the sun had now dipped behind the tree line and darkness was rapidly setting in. Walking to the front of the company he waited until CSM Glenn had called them to attention and handed over. Brute went to speak but Slasher stopped him and nodded at Major Wickham.

"These men," Major Wickham said, indicating the bikies, "Are members of an Outlaw Motorcycle gang called 'Attila's Axemen'. They are looking for their gang president and are engaged in some sort of gang feud or power struggle. In the process there have been people shot, including at least one of our cadets."

That got their attention and there was a ripple of murmuring until Major Wickham called for silence and went on. The cadets listened in absolute silence.

"I want to impress on you the seriousness of the situation. These men are deadly serious. You will do what they say without question and without any back answering. They have warned that if there is any trouble, if anyone tries to escape or tries to contact the police or truck drivers they will torture and rape some of our girls."

There were gasps of disbelief and horror at this and Brute stepped forward. "You'd better believe it," he snarled. "We mean business. Do what we say and nobody will get hurt. But if you give trouble there will be misery and tears. Got it?"

The cadets replied with a collective 'Sir!" as they did when spoken to by an officer. By then Major Wickham found that he was getting dizzy and he staggered and moved to lie down. Capt Hamilton grabbed him and helped him to sit. It was almost dark by then and Major Wickham could see that the cadets weren't sure what to do or what to believe. They began talking animatedly among themselves.

Brute again shouted at them to be quiet and silence descended. In it Major Wickham heard Brute say to his cronies, "What the hell do we do now? How do we control this mob?"

Slasher answered. "We sit 'em here under guard. Put the headlights of a vehicle on 'em. Then we roster a couple of us to keep watch."

"What? For how long?" Muff queried.

"All bloody night if we have to!" Slasher snapped. "Now you go back and get that Land Rover and bring it in, then get your bike."

Muttering and swearing Muff did as he was told, vanishing into the gloom behind the company. The talking and whispering among the cadets again grew in volume and Brute growled at them, but then Slasher said, "Let 'em talk Brute. We will go nuts trying to keep a hundred kids quiet. We just need to watch these adults and a few selected hostages."

"OK. You pick 'em," Brute agreed.

Slasher took a torch off a cadet and shone it on the company. A tense silence fell. Slasher shone the beam around and then pointed it at the prettiest girl he could see, Cadet Heidi Hope.

"You come and sit with the officers, sweetie," he said, with an evil chuckle.

A very anxious looking Heidi did as she was told, almost scurrying down to sit beside Capt Buchan. Slasher then fixed the beam of his torch on her section commander, busty young Cpl Rebecca Beatson. "And you."

Soon he had four girls in the group and he walked around looking down at others. His torch lit up 1 Section which had five girls in it. He gave an evil chuckle and told them to get up. As they went to move their corporal, Duncan Forster, stood up.

"Stay there girls. Take me instead," he said.

Major Wickham opened his mouth to warn Cpl Forster, but he was too late. Slasher's response was violent and instantaneous. A smashing blow to the groin with his knee caused Cpl Forster to double up. He fell to the ground writhing in agony. Slasher waved his pistol at the company and shouted,

"Don't be stupid kids! We mean business. Just do as we say and you will be alright."

There was shocked silence and for the first time a real frisson of fear shivered through the company. From then on the bikies had no trouble. Ten girls were seated separate. By then Muff had returned and the lights of the Land Rover were directed on the company from the left, lighting them all up. Muff was told to stand guard and Brute drew Slasher aside.

"Well that's done. But what do we do now?"

Which was exactly what Major Wickham was thinking.

Chapter 33

DESPERATELY HARD

When Jane heard the girl start screaming her heart missed a beat and then leapt into her mouth. It was such a frightening sound that her skin came out in goose bumps and the hair on the back of her neck stood on end.

"Oh my God! What's that?" she muttered.

The others heard it too and all sat up and stared into the darkness. Then the screams began again and everyone began to mutter exclamations. Muttering broke out and there was a general stirring among the platoon.

"Who's that? Have they caught Chloe?" Sgt Grey said, a distinct quaver in his voice.

Oh my God! I hope not, Jane thought.

She stood up and strained her ears to listen. But the screams were coming from the direction of the water trough and her anxiety for her friend quite choked her up. And then there was a third shriek, so spine-chilling that Jane bit her lip and put her hands up to her ears.

Then she shook her head. *That's not Chloe,* she decided. But it certainly sounded like a girl in mortal agony. *Oh my God! What are those beasts doing to that poor girl?* she wondered, picturing Sgt Harvey or one of the girls in the other platoons being tortured.

Suddenly the CB Radio she had slung around her neck crackled into life and Brute's voice sounded loud and clear. "4 Platoon. Chloe. Did you hear that? That was Slasher having some fun with one of your little girl cadets. Answer me, over."

Jane got such a fright she jumped. *Oh, that is loud,* she thought. *If those men are close they might hear it.*

Flustered, sick at heart and scared she fumbled at the volume switch and turned it down, too far as it turned out as she hardly heard the next message, which was a repeat of the previous one.

He want's Chloe, so that means she is safe, Jane decided. *But what to do? Should I answer it?*

Several others who also had radios and had heard the message also wondered. Sgt Lynes moved next to her. "Do you think we should answer that?" he asked.

Jane bit her lip and shook her head. "No," she croaked.

"But they are hurting one of our girls," Sgt Grey whispered.

"Yes, but we have a patrol out and I don't think we should do anything yet," Jane answered.

She felt terribly torn, fearing that silence could lead to more agony for the poor girl but, at the same time, not wanting to make the wrong decision.

I will wait till Chloe gets back, she decided.

But Sgt Lynes was very agitated. "We have to answer. We must save the poor girl," he cried.

"Sssh! Keep your voice down!" Jane hissed. "I think those people are only over near the water trough and they could hear us."

"But we must do something!" Sgt Lynes replied, his voice an emotional sob. "We must save her."

That annoyed Jane. "The only way we can do that is hand over this Harley fellow and I am not doing that, not without Chloe's agreement," she snapped back.

"Stuff Chloe! She's not the boss! We outrank her," Sgt Lynes replied angrily.

Jane could see that he was highly agitated and becoming very emotional. So were some of the others. She was afraid that one of them would defy her and use their radio. But none did.

Chantelle crept over beside her. "Who is it do you know?" she whispered.

Jane shook her head. "Not Chloe. Must be one of the headquarters girls. Sssh! Motorbikes! Down!"

Motorbike engines had spluttered and roared into life over near the water trough. Then headlights came on, three of them, almost pointing directly at them. The cadets went flat and Jane felt her heart hammering with anxiety, worrying that the bikies had heard them. But then the motorbikes started moving and turned away, roaring off along the dirt vehicle track that led east towards the Old Railway.

Jane watched them until the glow of their headlights was lost among the rock piles and trees to the east. To her puzzlement she heard the engines stop and decided the bikies had just moved to another location.

"I don't think they know where we are and they are going to try another spot," she suggested.

Suddenly the still night air was again rent by shrieks of agony. They were so horrible that they sent Jane's heart rate shooting up and her skin crawled in fear and empathy. It really did sound like the girl was suffering terrible pain. Then there was silence for a minute or so during which the cadets all fidgeted. This time when the radio crackled into life Jane was ready and had turned the volume up slightly. It was Brute again.

"Chloe, that will be you if we catch you, but if you bring us Harley you will be safe, over."

Again, Sgt Lynes and Sgt Grey began arguing that they answer. Sgt Small joined them and listened. But still Jane was adamant.

"We wait for Chloe," she insisted.

"But she might not ever come back. They might be lost!" Sgt Lynes cried.

"You might get lost, but Chloe won't!" Jane retorted. "Anyway... Here she comes."

Even as she started speaking, she heard the scuffle and thud of boots on rocks and then Cadet Leece call a soft challenge. A few moments later the water party made their way out of the darkness.

Chloe was leading and she came straight over to the group. "Have any of you answered the radio?" she asked.

"No," Jane replied. She was going to add that they wanted to but Chloe spoke again.

"Good! Because it is not real. So don't."

"What do you mean not real!" Sgt Lynes protested. "We heard it."

Chloe nodded. "We all did. But it is just an act. It isn't one of our cadets doing the screaming. It is one of the bikie's girlfriends and she is just acting," she explained.

"She didn't sound like she was acting," muttered Sgt Lynes.

Chloe gave a grim chuckle. "She was acting hard because that Brute mongrel was there threatening to let Slasher have her if she didn't. I'd bloody well act like that under those circumstances! No. It is just a ruse to bluff us into giving up Harley."

"You mean it's a trick?" Sgt Grey queried.

"Yes."

"I don't believe you!" Sgt Lynes cried.

"Then ask Sgt Lepson. He was right next to them under the water trough when they did their performance," Chloe said.

Sgt Lepson now stepped forward. "That's right. There aren't any cadets there, just four bikies, or three and one of their girls."

There was silence while they all considered this. Then Chloe turned to Sgt Lepson. "OK Sgt Lepson, get that water distributed and we will organise ourselves to get moving."

As she said this the radio crackled into life again. It was Brute calling 4 Platoon and Chloe again and he was obviously getting angry. Jane saw Chloe bite her lip and really felt for the emotional burden she must be bearing. Chloe then took a deep breath and lifted the radio. Jane went to stop her.

"Chloe, are you sure?" she gasped.

Chloe nodded. The others seemed to be holding their breaths. "Brute, this is Chloe, over." she said.

"About bloody time!" Brute snapped. "Now, you understand the deal? You bring us Harley and we will leave you alone. You will all be safe. And we will then call an ambulance for your injured girl."

"You call the ambulance first, over," Chloe replied.

"No! We get Harley and then you get help," Brute replied.

"OK, but we aren't sure where we are. We've been lost for hours because all our leaders ran away," Chloe answered.

"Just walk south," Brute answered.

"Which way is that? No one here has a compass," Chloe replied, winking at Jane as she did.

Jane grinned at that. *Good old Chloe! She has a plan!* she thought.

Chloe had. When Brute said, "Light a fire and we will come to you," she replied, "It will need to be big. We are in a big deep gully and can't move the stretchers in the dark. The hills are all rough and rocky, over."

"OK, light a fire and we will come," Brute agreed.

"It will take 10 minutes or so to collect firewood," Chloe cautioned. "Give us a few minutes."

"OK, but no funny business or the deal is off and your hide is personally on the line," Brute snapped back.

Hearing that sent chills of apprehension through Jane and she wasn't sure that she believed the agreement anyway.

I think that bastard will want revenge on Chloe afterwards, she thought. Then she added the name Slasher to the list of bikies who would have it in for Chloe. *This won't be over when they get Harley.*

But in her heart she was deeply disappointed. She had really approved of Chloe trying to save Harley's life but now it seemed she had given in. The idea filled her mouth with bitterness and she opened it to argue with Chloe not to surrender.

But Chloe beat her to it. She emitted a mischievous chuckle of the sort Jane knew only too well. "Good! That's got them bluffed for a quarter of an hour or so," she said. "Now, let's get out of here."

Sgt Lynes scowled at her in the moonlight. "What do you mean? Aren't you going to give him Harley?"

"Not on your Nelly!" Chloe replied. "I am not going to be party to cold blooded murder. We are going the other way, and fast."

"But... but..." Sgt Lynes spluttered. "But you agreed!"

"I lied," Chloe answered calmly. "All's fair in love and war. Now, I want two fit male volunteers."

"What for?" Sgt Grey asked.

"As decoys. To light a fire in the biggest, deepest gully to the north," Chloe answered.

Jane was struck with admiration. "What a good idea!" she muttered.

Sgt Grey thought so too. "I'll go. I'm still good for a while," he said.

Cpl Callan pushed forward. "Me too. I can run a few kilometres."

"Where do you want us to go?" Sgt Grey asked.

Chloe pulled out her map and her pocket torch and knelt down to shield the beam when she switched it on. With her finger she pointed to the gully to the north of the vehicle track. "Here, if you can make it in about a quarter of an hour. I will use the radio to stall the bikies till you get a fire going."

Sgt Grey nodded, his eyes alight with excitement. "I know exactly where that is. That's where Jane found us when we were hiding. That's a good spot. It will really bugger them about if they go blundering around there in the dark."

Cpl Callan agreed. "Where do we go afterwards?" he asked.

"I don't want you to stay there. Just get a big fire going and then bug out," Chloe said. Her finger traced a line along the New Railway. "You could possibly withdraw along the railway here. I don't mean along the actual line. I mean cross over and walk through the bush and just use the railway as a navigation guide. That way you could get to the highway down past the bottom of the range. They can't be watching all of that. You can stop a car or truck and go to get help."

"Or we could go to one of those cattle station homesteads down in the Haughton Valley," suggested Cpl Callan.

"Yes," agreed Chloe. "Or you can just hide in the gullies and come in tomorrow in daylight when this is all over."

"Do you want us to radio when we have the fire going?" Sgt Grey asked.

Chloe looked thoughtful then nodded. "Yes. But just do two lots of clicks with the pressel switch. Just click, click, click twice."

"OK. Give us our water bottles and let's get going," Sgt Grey said.

"Go along the vehicle track here," Chloe added. "Cpl Callan, you saw the track junction up on the next hill? Turn right there."

Cpl Callan grunted agreement, took his water bottles and stood up. Sgt Grey joined him and the two walked the few paces to the vehicle track. A few seconds later they were gone, padding rapidly down the track to the right.

Chloe now moved to the first stretcher. "How are you Harley?" she whispered.

"Pretty crook Babe," Harley croaked back. "I am having trouble moving my neck and I've got a splitting headache."

So have I! thought Jane as she moved to crouch beside them.

"Do you think that bullet in your back is a stomach wound?" she asked.

Harley shook his head and then groaned and winced. "Nope. I reckon it is lodged in the kidneys or something."

Chloe knelt and felt along his side, pressing until Harley flinched. "Ow! Take it easy Babe!" he gasped.

Chloe grunted. "It is probably just lodged in fat," she commented.

"Hey!" Harley cried in mock indignation. "That's muscle girlie!"

"Give big boy a drink Jane. I don't think it will kill him but dehydration might. I'll just check on Kim," Chloe said.

She ghosted off to the next stretcher and Jane took out her water bottle and offered it to Harley, helping him to sit half up as she did. As she did she wrinkled her nose as she found the smell and feel of the big man repulsive, his odours a mingled mix of stale sweat and tobacco.

Harley gulped greedily at the water and then sighed. "Thanks kiddo. What's your name?"

"Jane."

"Are you Chloe's friend?"

Jane nodded. "Yes. Now drink some more and lie down. We need to be moving."

Harley did and then wiped his lips as he handed the bottle back. "I heard you arguing not to give me up," Harley whispered. "I owe you for that. Thanks."

He lay back down and Jane did a quick count to check that there were eight people around the stretcher.

"Hands on! Prepare to lift! Lift!" she ordered.

They did, Jane taking the front right corner. Harley's sheer weight made her stagger and she realised that it was going to take a real effort to carry him to safety.

"Start walking," she said, thinking that the traditional 'Quick March!' was not the best idea on the rocks in the dark.

The group began stumbling along. Behind them came several cadets and then the second stretcher with Chloe giving the orders. And it was hard going. Not only was Harley a big, bulky burden but the numerous rocks kept tripping them up in the dark. As soon as they came to the vehicle track Jane turned right and they went downhill. That presented a whole new set of problems as they had to try to hold the front end higher than the back. Jane's muscles quickly drained and then became hot and started to tremble.

In the starlight Jane could just make out the vehicle track but the individual stones were hard to see. And the potholes and ruts were almost as awkward to traverse safely as the rocks in the grass. There were frequent stumbles by the cadets and lots of muttering and gasping. Several times cadets tripped or slipped and lost their grip but because they had eight on the stretcher it wasn't dropped.

After about 25 more paces she ordered them to lower the stretcher and beckoned a new cadet to relieve Sgt Small who was audibly gasping. Then they picked up the stretcher and continued. It took three such lifts to reach the bend where they had hidden from the two men and another to reach the dip where the top end of the gully met the track and the railway cutting.

Being there made Jane feel very uneasy. *We will really be trapped if any of those bikies come along now,* she thought.

On their left was the fence and railway cutting and on their right the thicket of thorn bushes. Ahead was the steep slope up to the forested knoll and getting up that was desperately hard. Jane stayed with the stretcher until they were at the top. It took 10 minutes to go a hundred paces and required four stops to rest and change bearers. To avoid the slipping on the loose gravel and dust and to try to hide their tracks she had them walk in the bush beside the track.

By the time they put the stretcher down near the track junction on the crest Jane was trembling and sweating. She found she was puffing and felt light-headed.

"Drink!" she croaked.

They did and Jane found the musty, dirty water still tasted great. Greedily she gulped half a bottle, draining what was left after Harley had drunk some more. While they did the second stretcher party struggled noisily up the steep slope, stirring up dust and making what seemed like a lot of noise, gasping, groaning, panting and swearing.

I hope the sound doesn't travel to the bikie on the rail overpass, Jane fretted.

As she thought this the radio came to life again. It was Brute. "Hey Chloe, where's this bloody fire?" he called.

Chloe answered at once. "Give us time! We are still collecting wood. It's hard to find in the dark and the cadets are scared they might pick up a snake instead," she replied.

"You've had fifteen minutes. Get it going in the next five or there will trouble," Brute snarled.

"Ten. Be fair! We are doing our best. It is hard going," Chloe answered.

"Ten then."

"By 2120," Chloe answered.

"Eh? What did you say?"

"By 2120 hours," Chloe said again. Jane had to smile.

Chloe is annoying the prick while acting innocent, she thought.

"Don't give me that army twenty-four-hour time crap! What time is that?" Brute snarled back.

Chloe grinned. "Nine twenty. When Mickey's little hand is between the..."

"Don't get smart bitch! Just get that fire going!" Brute growled.

At that moment the radio sounded with two lots of rapid clicks. *Grey and Callan have the fire going,* Jane thought. *Oh well done!*

Brute heard it too. "What's that?" he queried.

"Just me playing with the switch. I'm nervous. I'm scared of you," Chloe answered.

"You need to be!" Brute replied.

Jane shuddered. *I am too,* she told herself.

Chloe shook her head. "I am. Now hurry up and get here. We want to get Kim to hospital."

"OK Chloe. We will move as soon as we see the fire," Brute answered.

Chloe put the radio down and gestured up the slope. "Quick! Get up the hill and over the top. The bikies might come this way if they see the glow."

Jane hadn't thought of that but now realised that the bikie's most likely route would be along this vehicle track. Something close to panic grabbed her and she immediately bent to pick up the stretcher.

"Quick! Hands on! Lift!" she cried, her voice quavering with alarm.

In something of a fluster they lifted and began to move. As they went over the highest point Jane glanced out to her right front and felt her heart skip a beat. A kilometre or so away she could see a glow lighting up the hills. The closer ridge was starkly silhouetted but the bigger hills beyond were plain to see.

That's our fire, she thought. *The bikies must see that if they are at the powerline.*

They obviously did because the sound of motorcycles starting in the distance came to her. Again, her heart hammered faster and her mouth went dry with panic as the second stretcher was still at least 50 paces back down the other slope.

We are past the junction but Chloe's group isn't, she thought with growing alarm.

Chloe had obviously heard the bikes as well because she began urging her group to go faster. One of the cadets, Little Grey Jane thought, cried out he needed a rest, but Chloe snarled at him.

"Keep going! If they catch us people will die! Help us McDonald!"

Jane wanted to leave her stretcher and hurry back but instead kept her group moving. They shuffled and stumbled on down the other slope in a cloud of dust, cadets tripping, muttering and swearing as they did. And the bikes were coming their way! Jane saw the flicker of headlights back on the other rise and her heart went into her mouth.

Will we make it in time? she worried.

As the bikes went down into the dip towards the railway cutting Chloe's group came up over the crest and past the track junction.

This is going to be close! Jane thought as she glanced back and saw them silhouetted against the rapidly increasing glow.

And then another horrible thought crossed her mind, what if the bikes missed the turn and came on along the track they were on?

"Get off the track! Go right!" she cried.

Pulling the stretcher that way she stumbled into the bush beside the track and then, as the trees above her were lit up by the flicker of the headlights, she ordered the group to put the stretcher down and to lie down. Hastily they did so, and Jane scuttled behind the nearest tree and looked back. She was just in time to see Chloe's group also leave the road, all of them silhouetted by the headlights. Worse still they had stirred up quite a cloud of dust.

Jane was appalled. *Even if the bikies don't see our boot prints they must see all that dust,* she thought.

Chloe's group vanished into the trees and long grass just as the first motorbike bounced into view at the crest. Its headlights lit up everything and Jane cringed down as low as she could, aware that all of Chloe's group lay just beside the track and to her were obvious as dark lumps and bumps among the trees. And the headlight beam really showed up the dust!

The bike skidded to a stop and then it was turned side on, the beam of its headlight sweeping over them, and particularly over Chloe's group.

He's seen us! Jane thought and she tensed ready for action.

Through her mind flashed various options such as the group scattering in all direction so that the cadets at least would be safe, but she knew that Chloe had the guns and was likely to use them. Her heart went into her mouth with dread.

But the motorbike suddenly accelerated and went back up slope a few metres and went off along the side-track that led eastwards down the long ridge. Jane shook her head in disbelief.

He didn't see us! she thought.

Now dust billowed over them and she knew that the second motorbike would not notice either dust or boot prints at all. To her immense relief she saw the second motorcycle turn right and go eastwards down the ridge. The third followed.

Missed us! her mind cried.

Jane lay there for a minute or so until she was sure there were no more motorbikes. Then she stood up. "Come on! Grab this stretcher and let's get out of here!" she croaked, her mouth dry and filled with grit. Others began coughing but she quickly hissed them to silence and got the stretcher up and moving. Chloe's group did likewise. Then it was a hundred metres down a long, rough slope to the bottom of the hill.

This took 10 minutes and four lifts and Jane found it really exhausting. Finally, she had to give up and relinquish her place to Cadet Leece. Croaking and shaking from the overexertion she led the way to where the vehicle track ended at the steep little drain.

"Stop! Prepare to lower! Lower!" she gasped.

The stretcher was put down and Sgt Lynes looked around. "Where do we go now?" he croaked.

Jane pointed. "Through this fence and across the railway line," she replied. But for the moment she was shaking too much to move further and knew they all needed a rest. A few flopped down in the long grass and a couple took out their water bottles and began drinking. Jane did likewise, noting that Chloe's group had now caught up.

As Chloe's stretcher was lowered to the dirt track nearby a curious rumble and flicker of light came to Jane's attention. She tensed.

Is that the bikies coming back? she worried.

But then the deeper rumble made her shiver with anxiety and she looked around. Beside her she saw a flicker of twin lines of silver, and she realised that it was light reflecting on the tops of the railway lines. For a moment she puzzled over how the bikies could have got onto the railway line and how they could ride along it and then the truth burst into her mind like a door being kicked open.

"A train!" she gasped.

Chloe had just flopped down but now she sprang to her feet. "Stop it! We must get help! Stop the train!"

Chapter 34

EXHAUSTION

Sgt Lepson was feeling utterly drained. He stood behind the second stretcher gasping and trembling. His heart was hammering both from fear of the bikies finding them and from over-exertion. In his right-hand was the shotgun Chloe had just passed him.

"At 'Action'," she had said as she did so.

For a few moments that had left Sgt Lepson confused and puzzled. He knew that the word implied a very specific degree of weapon readiness, but the meaning eluded him for a few seconds. Then he remembered and with it came a sharp stab of emotions, admiration that Chloe could remember such a thing at a time like this, and resentment that she, a mere cadet, could know such things better than him, a Third Year.

He had heard someone, people, cry out the word 'train' but only now did the flickering lights and shiny reflections off polished steel penetrate his mind. He blinked and shook his head then looked. It was a train. It was coming from the north and its headlight was lighting up the whole cutting. Only the fact that the cadets stood back a bit from the line and were in the shadows cast by the next deep cutting prevented them from being brightly illuminated as well.

The rumbling thunder of big diesel engines filled the air and the ground seemed to shudder. Sgt Lepson saw Chloe dash to the fence and throw herself underneath. But her haste led to her webbing getting hooked. Squirming frantically on her back she reached up to rip the barbs free, helped by Jane who hurried over and reached down to grasp the offending strand. Chloe rolled clear into the long grass beside the railway, but Sgt Lepson could see she was too late. By then the front of the first locomotive (*Two huge diesel electrics coupled together pulling the train,* he noted) was passing her.

Chloe sprang to her feet and scrambled out beside the tracks, dancing up and down and waving her arms frantically. Sgt Lepson thought he saw the white blur of the driver's face but wasn't sure. But it made no difference. The beat of the locomotive's engine did not change and the train went lumbering past, wagon after wagon, steel wheels grinding and squeaking on the steel rails and the couplings groaning and clanking as the engines strained to pull all that weight uphill. There were dozens of wagons on the train, all ore wagons Sgt Lepson noted, and it seemed to take forever to pass.

Chloe stood out beside the track, shaking her head, her arms now by her side. Then she turned and made her way back to the fence as the end of the train went rattling and shuddering by. "Too late!" she said to Jane.

"They couldn't have stopped anyway," Sgt Lynes said. "Trains take a long distance to pull up. They are too heavy for their brakes to work straight away."

"I don't know if the driver saw me or not," Chloe said. She was obviously disappointed.

Nobody could add to that. Jane said, "Never mind. Good try Chlo! Let's get through this fence and across the track."

Cadet MacDonald then said, "But what if another train comes along?"

Sgt Lynes snorted and shook his head. "Don't be ridiculous! It's a single-track railway and the next train won't be for hours."

Sgt Lepson did not care. He now urgently wanted to on the other side of that railway and safe. The noise of the train rapidly died away and he glimpsed the red tail-lights vanish from view around the bend. That reminded him that the bikies had a guard on the railway overpass just around that bend.

"Sssh! Less noise," he hissed. "Remember the bikies have a guard just along the line."

They began the difficult process of getting the first stretcher over the top stand of the barbed wire fence. Chloe now took control and gave rapid instructions. Acting on these webbing was taken off and seven more cadets crawled under. Their webbing was passed across and Chloe ordered them to put it on. Then the stretcher was hoisted to shoulder height and the front end passed over to the waiting cadets. Harley was apparently asleep or unconscious and that helped as he just lay there while the cadets lifted and pushed. Several others held down the top strand. As soon as a cadet could no longer hold the back end they rushed to get under the fence. During this struggle there was a lot of puffing and grunting and several yelps of pain as people got caught on barbs but at last the stretcher was on the other side.

Chloe told them to keep going across the railway and then came over to the fence.

"Can I have the gun again Sgt Lepson?" she said.

Sgt Lepson just handed it to her and then realised he should have asserted his authority and kept the weapon. He then blushed some more and became angry when she reproved him.

"It is loaded sergeant. Please don't hand a gun to anyone barrel first."

Bitch! Sgt Lepson thought.

But, to his shame, he knew she was right and that what he had done was a very dangerous thing. That made him both embarrassed and angry and he began to quietly snap at the team trying to pass Kim's stretcher over the fence. She was also asleep or unconscious.

Or maybe even dead, he thought, chills of terror gripping the back of his head at the thought.

Chloe padded off across the railway and went up the sloping roadway on the other side, her figure just visible in the starlight against the background of dark bush. The first stretcher team began crossing the railway and the sound of their boots crunching on the gravel of the stone ballast sounded very loud in the still night air. Only the occasional passing vehicle on the now distant highway broke the silence of the night.

Sgt Lepson crawled under the fence, ignoring the unit policy and going on his front. He had also been too tired to take his webbing off and push it under. Within seconds he regretted this as his webbing became caught and he had to wriggle and struggle to try to get free.

Cpl Lang came over and helped, adding to his annoyance by saying, "On your back Sarge."

That kept Sgt Lepson in a bad mood and after he had stood up he did not help to get the stretcher across the fence on the other side. This took nearly five minutes by the time cadets took off their webbing, pushed it under the bottom strand or passed it to a mate, crawled under the barbed wire themselves, then put their webbing back on before standing to help grab the stretcher. .

Then Flegel tripped on the steel rails and fell, making a real metallic 'ting!' as some part of his equipment struck the metal.

"Bloody fool!" Sgt Lepson hissed. "Be quiet."

"But I've hurt myself!" Flegel wailed.

"Sssh! Shut up or I'll shut you up!" Sgt Lepson retorted. He looked anxiously around to check that no bikies were close.

At that moment the radios began to softly crackle and the whole group froze to listen. The stretchers were lowered without orders and everyone strained to try to make out what was being said.

Sgt Lepson moved closer to Cpl Lang and heard: "Crackle… are you?… crackle."

"They are at the fire," Jane whispered.

"Now the fun will begin!" Cadet Warren chuckled.

Fun! Sgt Lepson thought. *Now the bikies will be even more angry!* Fear of those men coursed through him, making him shiver uncontrollably.

There were several more radio calls and then Sgt Lepson distinctly heard the word 'Bitch!'.

Yes she is, he thought, but conceded she was a clever bitch. *What will the bikies do now?* he worried.

Chloe came padding quietly back down the ramp to join them. In the starlight Sgt Lepson saw that she was grinning.

"They have discovered we aren't there," she said. "So let's keep moving."

The radio kept crackling, Brute trying to contact Chloe, but she ignored it. "They have no idea where we have gone," she replied to Sgt Lynes comment.

"But what if they now take it out on our girls?" Sgt Lynes argued.

Chloe shrugged. "That's a risk we have to take. But I don't think they will. They will have enough legal problems tomorrow without adding to them by doing things like that."

I hope she's right! Sgt Lepson thought. Then he bent to take his turn carrying Kim's stretcher.

The platoon struggled on up the sloping roadway to the top of the cutting. In the starlight the drop on the left looked a long way and Sgt Lepson was surprised and anxious. At the top they rested for a few minutes and Sgt Lepson straightened up stiffly and looked around. The sound of distant vehicle engines attracted his attention and he looked, noting the glow of headlights.

That is a truck on the highway, he decided, estimating it was about half a kilometre away.

The radio crackled some more, each time sending his heart into his mouth and making his stomach churn. It was obvious from the tone that the bikie boss was very angry and he made some horrible threats to Chloe, or at least that was what Sgt Lepson thought as the transmissions were very broken and weak.

All those hills getting in the way, he decided. *But Chloe is done for!* That idea filled him with both satisfaction and dread.

At the top there was another fence to get through and this took about 10 minutes. Sgt Lepson was astonished to note that it was 2120hrs, more than an hour since they had started moving.

It has taken us half an hour just to cross the railway! he thought. He found it very demoralising to work so hard and to achieve so little. *We have only moved a few hundred metres!* he thought gloomily.

But they were at least in another paddock and among dark bush. And from the crest of a gentle rise he got glimpses of headlights on the highway and, in the distance, the lights of Mingela township.

There's the town! We can go there, he thought.

But Chloe started them moving right, northwards, and away from the town. Sgt Lepson was annoyed. "Here Kane, take this stretcher," he snapped. When a sulky Cadet Kane had done so Sgt Lepson hurried up to the front, stumbling on dead logs and small spiky bushes as he did. To Chloe he hissed: "Hey! We are going the wrong way!"

Chloe stopped and looked back. "We can't go there direct. They have a man standing on the railway overpass. He will be able to see along the highway for a kilometre or more. We have to detour way out to the west."

Sgt Lepson opened his mouth to argue but realised it would make him look stupid. "Alright, but we will have a rest first."

To his relief Chloe did not argue with this and most of the cadets sighed with relief and sat down. A few lay full length, but not for long, as there were ants and lots of prickles. Sgt Lepson realised he was perspiring despite the coolness of the night air and then noted that his tongue felt dry and furry. He took out his left water bottle and had a big drink. Others did likewise. It was then that LCpl Travis, the signaller, said, "I'm out of water. Can anyone give me some?"

That annoyed Sgt Lepson. "You can't have drunk two water bottles in an hour!" he snapped.

"I haven't!" Travis replied in an aggrieved tone. "I was only given one back and it was only half full."

That jolted Sgt Lepson and his mind raced. *I took Travis's water bottles. Did I leave one behind when the bikies arrived?* he wondered. A sudden surge of guilt added to his already jangled emotions. But then he shook his head. *Even if I did it doesn't matter. We will be at the town soon.*

To silence Travis he handed him his right water bottle. The signaller had a big drink and then paused to take a breath before putting the bottle to his mouth again.

"Hey! Don't drink it all!" Sgt Lepson cried in irritation.

Travis took another gulp then lowered the bottle and wiped his mouth before handing it back. "Well, you lost mine!" he grumbled.

Sgt Lepson flushed with anger and embarrassment, hoping that the others had not paid attention to the exchange. Before placing that water bottle back he had another drink and then did up the cap and clipped the bottle back into his webbing. As he stood there he realised he was swaying and he quickly sat down. Blinking to unglue blurry eyes he also realised he had a very bad headache.

I am dehydrated, he thought.

Further analysis of his physical state made him very conscious that he was exhausted. His muscles felt drained and his feet were sore and he felt weak all over. The others were suffering as well, resting for nearly fifteen minutes before Chloe roused them.

She motioned them to get up. "Come on! Kim needs to be in hospital."

"Is she still alive?" Sgt Lynes asked.

Chantelle answered that. "Yes, but her breathing is very shallow and her pulse is weak. She feels all cold and clammy. I'm scared she is going into shock and bleeding internally."

Sgt Lepson shuddered and forced himself to get up. In the process he got several prickles in his left-hand. With his eyes watering at the pain he swore softly. Scratching and plucking at them he looked around, noting the lights of a passing road train, the side of each trailer marked by a row of tiny red lights.

If only we could just go to the highway and stop a truck, he thought.

Feeling frustrated, sore and annoyed he urged the others to their feet. The stretchers were picked up and the platoon started moving again.

For about 50 metres the route was across the crest of a very gentle rise from where the lights of the town and the highway were quite visible. But then they went down into a dip and across the heads of several small gullies. This was hard going and caused Chloe to turn left and go back up onto the rim of the depression. In that area there was short grass and only a scattering of large trees in the depression and no sign of the vehicle track that had come up the ramp.

Overgrown? Sgt Lepson decided.

They stumbled across a couple of concrete slabs and then encountered some rusty corrugated iron sheeting among the spiky little bushes.

When the iron sheets were stepped on the noise was so loud they all stopped and listened. Sgt Lepson suffered the experience of his heart hammering so loudly he had difficulty hearing. When nothing happened they backed off and went more carefully, their eyes straining in the starlight to see such objects in the long grass and bushes. After about a hundred metres they came out of the trees into what might have been termed an open paddock except that it was badly overgrown with weeds, mostly a waist high tangle to prickly bushes. These grew so close together that it took a real effort to thread a route between them. Sometimes this was not possible and they had to trample and force a path. It was hard going and soon everyone was sweating and panting again.

Sgt Lepson took his turn on the stretcher and found it very wearing. *I'm buggered! I don't know how much more of this I can take,* he thought.

After another five minutes effort sheer fatigue brought them all to a stop and there was another 10-minute rest, the cadets sitting or lying in among the bushes. Sgt Lepson estimated that they were now further from the highway and the lights of the township were on their left rear.

Where is this dumb bitch taking us? he wondered.

Cpl Lang stood up and looked. "I think those bikies are back over there," he said.

Sgt Lepson was gripped by near panic but he mastered this and stood up to look. He was concerned to see that back from where he thought they had come he was getting a few glimpses of headlights flickering through the trees. To confirm this he heard snatches of sound that indicated motorcycle engines.

"I think you are right," he agreed.

"They are on the other side of the railway, aren't they?" Cadet Warren commented.

"Yes," Cpl Lang answered.

Hearing that helped calm Sgt Lepson. He had become so tense he found he was trembling. When he realised this he was glad it was so dark.

The noises and lights died away but then the radio called again. It was Brute. "Chloe, answer me you bitch. Talk!"

Chloe shook her head and pursed her lips. Sgt Lepson was tempted to take Cpl Lang's radio and call, just to end it all. But he lacked the courage, and to his shame knew it, so did nothing. Brute called again twice more, obviously closer.

Then he snarled, "OK Chloe, your choice. We are going back to your camp and will take it out on some of your cadet girls. Your fault slut!"

Chloe looked grim in the starlight but again shook her head. The radio went silent and they heard distant motorbikes, the sound dying away and then being drowned by the rumble of a big truck heading for Charters Towers.

2200hrs came up and Chloe stood up. "Move!" she croaked.

Sgt Lepson felt so tired and worn out it took him a real effort to get to his feet. He just wanted to lie there and hide but knew he had to appear to be making an effort. So he moved to the front of Kim's stretcher and took hold.

"Hands on! Grab hold MacDonald! Prepare to lift! Lift!"

They got it up and began shuffling and stumbling across the overgrown paddock. It took them 10 minutes and four rests to go a hundred metres. Very slowly they approached a thicket of small trees. Closer acquaintance revealed that the trees were all stunted and gnarled and growing close together. It was very difficult to even bend to get under the low branches which poked at faces and eyes. Chloe quickly gave up the attempt and detoured to the right, moving into the shadows of larger trees where there was at least fewer prickly bushes.

The route led them over the gentle crest and they lost sight of the lights of the town. Sgt Lepson became anxious about this and the next time they halted he handed over his place on the stretcher and moved up to the front to confront Chloe.

"Where are we going?" he queried angrily.

"Detouring around this patch of scrub," Chloe replied, indicating the dark mass of small trees on their left.

"How do you know where you are going?" Sgt Lepson demanded to know. "You aren't using a compass."

Chloe pointed up. "By the stars. There's Venus," she said.

Sgt Lepson now saw the star for the first time and realised it was both very bright and very obvious. That rankled, but he also noted that Venus was now down among the treetops to his left, and he said, "It is about to set."

Chloe pointed upwards. "That's alright. There's Orion," she said.

That upset Sgt Lepson as well. He was now both exhausted and scared and was filled by an urge to be somewhere safe.

"Do you know where we are?" he snapped.

"More or less," Chloe replied.

"Show me on the map," Sgt Lepson snarled. He put his hand to his head to ease the throbbing ache that made it hard to think.

"I can't! We have gone off the edge of the map," Chloe retorted, also sounding angry. "But the Dotswood Road is over there to our left somewhere and beyond that are an airfield and a rodeo ground."

"How do you know that?" Sgt Lepson queried, quite astonished by her local knowledge and calm assurance.

"Because I have been to the rodeo twice," Chloe answered in a matter of fact tone.

"What were you doing there?" Sgt Lepson asked before realising it was an irrelevant question.

"Singing and dancing; not riding the buckjumpers or bull wrestling," Chloe replied, her voice taking on a sarcastic tone.

At that Cadet Dipkins sniggered. "I thought you'd like wrestling with the bulls," he muttered.

"Shut up Dipkins or you'll never get to be a bull," Chloe snapped. "Now let's keep moving."

They struggled on for another couple of hundred metres, the effort taking more than 10 minutes and leaving them all puffing and feeling drained.

"I can't go on!" sobbed Chantelle. She sank to the ground and began sobbing.

"OK, rest!" Chloe said.

They lowered the stretcher and all sat down, perspiring and puffing. It was now very quiet and just starting to get cold. Sgt Lepson wanted to keep going in his mind but his body was now so exhausted that he was thankful for the break. Trembling in his legs and arms he lay back and sighed with relief. Others did likewise. Feeling uncomfortable he squirmed until he was more comfortable, the webbing making that difficult.

It was bad dream and he woke gasping, trying to run, trying to escape the dark thing that was pursuing him. For a minute or so Sgt Lepson lay staring at the stars, wondering where he was. Then he noted he was shivering from the cold and realization burst on him.

I went to sleep, he thought. Glancing beside him he saw another cadet huddled against the stretcher, obviously asleep as well. Then he realised that they all were. *We've all gone to sleep! We must get up and moving. We must get away from here!* he thought, a rising panic attack clutching at his throat.

Sitting up with an effort that drew a stifled groan from him he looked around and saw only a huddled mass of dim shapes in the long grass. A glance at his watch showed him it was just after 0400hrs.

4 O'clock! We've been asleep for hours! he thought with dismay.

Alarmed and frightened he began shaking the cadet next to him. It was Cpl Lang. Once he was stirring Sgt Lepson got to his feet and painfully hobbled along kicking and shaking people and urging them up. It gave him a little spurt of satisfaction to be the one to rouse Chloe.

The slut isn't as good as she thinks she is! he thought.

Chloe sat up and glanced at her watch then gave a gasp of alarm. "Oh my God! We've gone to sleep! We have to move fast. We must get out of here before daylight," she cried.

She shook Jane awake. "Wake up Janie! Wake up! We have been asleep. Sorry. It is my fault," she said as Jane opened her eyes and sat up.

"I'm freezing!" Jane muttered, her teeth audibly chattering.

"Get up and warm up babe. Oh, this is my fault! I shouldn't have gone to sleep!" Chloe replied.

As soon as Jane was standing up Chloe continued along waking others. But it took nearly 10 minutes to get everyone awake and up and the stretchers moving. Some of the cadets were shaking with cold and Sgt Lepson thought they might be on the edge of hyperthermia, so he had them start running on the spot or jumping up and down to get their circulation going. He found it almost a relief to start moving again.

The platoon started shuffling and stumbling onwards through the dark bush, with lots of muffled groans and curses as sore and stiff muscles were put back to work. Sgt Lepson found himself aching in what seemed like every muscle and joint in his body and he had a splitting headache. His whole body trembled from time to time. But he was able to make himself walk and even urged others to try harder.

A big log blocked their path so they detoured around it to the right and then paused for another short rest. By then they had gone another hundred metres and all were awake and warming up.

As they put the stretcher down after a hundred metres the radio crackled again, louder and clearer this time. It was a bikie.

"Brute, this is Slasher, over."

Brute answered at once. "What ya want Slasher?"

"I'm at that water trough and I've just found an army water bottle. The little bastards have been here. There are tracks all over the place."

Oh no! They've found our tracks, Sgt Lepson thought, the panic rising to choke him. Then he blushed with shame as he realised it was probably his fault. *That might be Travis's water bottle.*

But he could not remember if he had dropped it or not. To add to his emotional turmoil shameful and humiliating memories of scrabbling in the cow dung with terror and panic mentally flustering him paralysed him for several seconds.

Brute radioed back: "We will be there in a couple of minutes Slasher. Wait for us."

Oh no! Here they come! How can we get away? Sgt Lepson thought.

In the darkness he stood there trembling and close to collapse as a fresh panic attack assailed him. So exhausted did he feel, both physically and emotionally, that he did not think he could even run away.

Oh help! he mentally wailed.

Chapter 35

UTTER DISTRESS

By sundown Major Wickham was in a state of deep distress. He was both physically and emotionally battered and was feeling utterly exhausted. But he sensed that the real crisis was not on them yet and he gritted his teeth and used his willpower to summon up the strength to keep functioning.

The first hope was that there was only one bikie guarding them. Muff stood beside the Land Rover. He was hard to see because he was behind the headlights and hidden by their glare, but Major Wickham began speculating on how he could be over-powered and disarmed. Regretfully he concluded that the risk was far too high.

And soon after another bikie with a leather-clad female as his pillion passenger arrived. The bike was parked and the new arrivals eyed the prisoners with amazement and obvious anxiety. The pair spoke at length to Muff, obviously wanting to know what was going on.

"Brute sent us," the man said. "And he and Slasher have taken Suzie with them."

"Guard this lot," Muff said, "While I go and get my bike."

That seemed to offer another chance but again Major Wickham had to caution the others not to try anything. The man was at least ten paces away and also had a shotgun.

We couldn't possibly reach him before he fired, he thought.

Having seen the effects of gunfire as a young soldier on active service he had no illusions about how deadly such a weapon could be.

But the two newcomers made no attempt to stop their prisoners talking. Major Wickham tested this by whispering to the other OOCs and when the bikies said nothing he explained as much as he could to the others.

Lt Cavendish was mystified. "So what can we do?" she asked.

Major Wickham shrugged. "Nothing at the moment, and I don't want any of you to try anything until I give the word. We do not want a shotgun discharged into a bunch of cadets."

That was a sobering thought and they all fell silent for a while. The cadets also began to talk but when their volume rose rapidly the bikie growled at them to be quiet and the noise subsided. Into the ensuing silence came the sound of engines, vehicles on the highway and a motorcycle approaching. It was Muff returning with his bike. He parked it ready to leave and then joined the other two.

The bikie with the girl called, "What's goin' on Muff? What's Brute up to?"

"He's got a plan to catch them cadets. He's carrying it out now," Muff replied, grinning as he did.

That was bad news to Major Wickham and he lay back and brooded while considering possible courses of action. The bikies began to talk quietly, only occasionally being loud enough for him to overhear anything and none of it was useful. The main thing he could deduce was that they were very worried people and that something had gone badly wrong.

Then, into the relative silence, came a sound that made Major Wickham sit up in alarm. The others heard it too and all sat up and stared into the darkness.

"What was that?" Lt Peters gasped.

"Sssh!" Major Wickham replied.

Then the sound came again and there was no doubt. It was a girl screaming in pain. All the cadets fell silent to listen. The sound was coming from some distance away to the north.

Over in the paddock the other side of the road, Major Wickham decided.

The girl started screaming again and his heart missed a beat and then leapt into his mouth. It was such a penetrating sound that his skin came out in goose bumps and the hair on the back of his neck stood on end.

"Oh my God! Who is that?" he muttered.

But he was puzzled as well as horrified. *I don't remember the bikies taking any of the girls away. Have they captured 4 Platoon?* he wondered.

Then the screams began again and everyone began to murmur exclamations. Muttering broke out and there was a general stirring among the cadets.

"Who's that screaming? Have they caught Chloe?" CUO Roach said, a distinct quaver in his voice.

Oh my God! I hope not, Major Wickham thought.

The thought of the brutes defiling her made him mentally wince. Anxiously he strained his ears to listen. There was another scream of agony and he became quite choked up with emotion. And then there was a third shriek, so spine-chilling that he bit his lip and experienced the urge to put his hands up to his ears.

What eased his fears was realizing that the three bikies were quietly chuckling. *That's odd,* he thought. *Something's not right here.* But what? It certainly sounded like a girl in mortal agony. *Oh my God! What are those beasts doing to that poor girl?* he wondered, picturing Chloe or one of the girls in 4 Platoon being tortured.

Suddenly the CB Radio Muff had slung around his neck crackled into life and Brute's voice sounded loud and clear. "4 Platoon. Chloe. Did you hear that? That was Slasher having some fun with one of your little girl cadets. Answer me, over."

Flustered, sick at heart and scared for the cadets, Major Wickham strained his ears to listen as Brute called again. Then he frowned and his puzzlement deepened.

He want's Chloe, so that means she is safe, he decided. *But who is being tortured and what can I do? Should I tell Chloe to surrender?*

The other officers had also heard the message. Capt Hamilton leaned over and whispered. "They haven't caught 4 Platoon at all. This is all a bit odd I think."

Lt Cavendish frowned. "Why is he calling Chloe?" she asked.

Lt Peters answered. "Because Chloe is in command of 4 Platoon."

Lt Cavendish sniffed to show her opinion of Chloe but then said, "Do you think we should tell her to give these men what they want?"

Major Wickham shook his head. "No," he croaked. There was no way he wanted to be party to the murder of a human being.

"But they are hurting one of our girls," Lt Cavendish whispered.

"Maybe, but they haven't caught Chloe so they haven't got their president either. I don't think we should do anything yet," he answered.

But he felt torn, fearing that silence could lead to more agony for the poor girl but, at the same time, not wanting to make the wrong decision.

I will wait till Chloe answers, he decided.

A glance at his watch told him it was 1950hrs. Thankfully the screaming stopped and instead he heard the faint sound of motorbikes in the distance.

What are those bikies doing? he wondered.

A few minutes later the still night air was again rent by shrieks of agony. This time they were further away, so distant that they could hardly heard them, but they were so horrible that they sent Major Wickham's heart rate shooting up and his skin crawled in fear and empathy. It really did sound like the girl was suffering terrible pain. Then there was silence for a minute or so during which the officers all held their breath and the cadets fidgeted.

The radio crackled into life again and Muff turned the volume up slightly. It was Brute again.

"Chloe, that will be you if we catch you, but if you bring us Harley you will be safe, over."

Capt Hamilton smiled. "They haven't got her at all. This is some sort of a ruse to trick them I reckon," he suggested.

"So who is the girl being tortured?" Lt Cavendish queried.

Capt Hamilton shrugged. "None of the girls from here, and if they haven't got Chloe I reckon they haven't got any girls from 4 Platoon either. I reckon it is one of their girlfriends play acting."

"Oh, I hope you are right!" Lt Cavendish cried. She looked desperately upset.

So do I! Major Wickham thought, adding a fervent prayer to end the situation.

"She didn't sound like she was acting," muttered Capt Buchan.

Capt Hamilton gave a grim chuckle. "If I was Slasher's girlfriend and he told me to act, I would put on an Oscar winning performance!" he commented.

With which Major Wickham could only agree. The image of Slasher mutilating one of the girls caused him to shudder and once again he considered surrendering.

The OOCs quietly discussed this but Major Wickham was adamant. "We cannot allow a threat like that to result in murder," he insisted.

"But the men might not harm this Harley. He's their president after all," Lt Cavendish replied.

"They've tried to murder him once," Major Wickham answered.

Capt Hamilton nodded. "They shot a guy named Peewee in the same ambush. I saw his body. They mean it alright. That Brute guy wants to be the president. He won't let Harley live if he gets his hands on him."

"But they might hurt more cadets!" Lt Peters wailed. She was so upset she was almost distraught.

As she said this the radio crackled into life again. It was Brute calling 4 Platoon and Chloe again and he was obviously getting angry. Major Wickham bit his lip and really felt for the emotional burden she must be bearing. He was so pent up he clenched his fists, digging his nails into his palms until it hurt.

I should be taking responsibility, he told himself. But would Chloe obey? *What will she do?* he wondered.

He got an answer a moment later. The radio hummed and Chloe spoke: "Brute, this is Chloe, over."

"About bloody time!" Brute snapped. "Now, you understand the deal? You bring us Harley and we will leave you alone. You will all be safe. And we will then call an ambulance for your injured girl."

"You call the ambulance first, over," Chloe replied.

"No! We get Harley and then you get help," Brute replied.

"OK, but we aren't sure where we are. We've been lost for hours because all our leaders ran away," Chloe answered.

On hearing that Major Wickham and the other officers all turned to look at CUO Roach. He hung his head in shame.

Brute answered Chloe. "Just walk south," he said.

"Which way is that? No one here has a compass," Chloe replied.

Major Wickham's initial reaction was annoyance at the insinuation that nobody in 4 Platoon could navigate.

The corporals have compasses, he thought.

Then he shook his head and felt relieved that Chloe was back in contact. Most of all he was struck by the calm and confident way Chloe was speaking.

She's got real ability that girl, he decided. So, despite his anguish, he grinned. *Good! Chloe has a plan!* he thought.

Brute said, "Light a fire and we will come to you."

Chloe replied, "It will need to be big. We are in a big deep gully and can't move the stretchers in the dark. The hills are all rough and rocky, over."

"OK, light a fire and we will come," Brute agreed.

"It will take 10 minutes or so to collect firewood," Chloe cautioned. "Give us a few minutes."

"OK, but no funny business or the deal is off and your hide is personally on the line," Brute snapped back.

Hearing that sent chills of apprehension through Major Wickham and he wasn't sure that he believed the agreement anyway.

I think that mongrel Brute will want revenge on Chloe afterwards, he thought. Then he added Slasher's name to the list of bikies who would have it in for Chloe. *This won't be over when they get Harley.*

But in his heart he was disappointed. He had really approved of Chloe trying to save Harley's life but now it seemed she had given in. The idea filled his mouth with bitterness, but he felt powerless to influence the situation. And he was annoyed that Chloe had said they could not navigate.

All those bloody lessons on navigation by the sun and the stars we have taught! he thought resentfully. His fingers itched with the desire to get a radio and call her and tell her not to surrender.

The radio fell silent and the group waited. Lt Cavendish became quite restless. "It's getting cold sir. Do you think these bikies will allow the cadets to get their sleeping bags and pullovers?"

"I don't know. I will ask," Major Wickham replied. He realised he was quite chilled himself. He called Muff who listened and then shook his head. "They'll be right," he said.

"Don't be ridiculous!" Lt Cavendish snapped. "They are children. Do you want to be responsible for harming them?"

"If you give us Harley, they will be right as rain," Muff replied.

"You won't get much sympathy from a jury if one of these children dies from hyperthermia," Lt Cavendish retorted.

Muff sneered but then reluctantly agreed to the idea. He insisted they go in small groups guarded by the other bikie who he called Terry.

It took nearly half an hour for this to be done and the last members of 3 Platoon were still coming back under Terry's guard when the radio came to life again. It was Brute.

"Hey Chloe, where's this bloody fire?" he called.

Chloe answered at once. "Give us time! We are still collecting wood. It's hard to find in the dark and the cadets are scared they might pick up a snake instead," she replied.

"You've had fifteen minutes. Get it going in the next five or there will trouble," Brute snarled.

"Ten. Be fair! We are doing our best. It is hard going," Chloe answered.

"Ten then."

"By 2120," Chloe answered.

"Eh? What did you say?"

"By 2120 hours," Chloe said again.

Major Wickham had been listening to the exchange, almost holding his breath with apprehension but now he relaxed and smiled.

Chloe is annoying him while acting innocent, he decided.

Brute clearly wasn't amused. "Don't give me that army twenty-four-hour time crap! What time is that?" he snarled back.

Chloe's reply caused Capt Hamilton to grin. She said: "Nine twenty. When Mickey's little hand is between the..."

"Don't get smart bitch! Just get that fire going!" Brute growled.

At that Muff chortled and said to Terry and the girl: "That bitch is winding Brute up. Boy is she gunna get it when Brute and Slasher get their hands on her!"

Major Wickham shuddered at the images that conjured up and he prayed for her to be safe. At that moment the radio sounded with two lots of distinct clicks.

What was that? Major Wickham wondered.

Brute was obviously puzzled too. "What's that?" he queried.

Chloe answered: "Just me playing with the switch. I'm nervous. I'm scared of you."

"You need to be!" Brute replied.

Major Wickham shuddered. *I am,* he told himself. But he was also sure Chloe was up to something and he did not know if that was good news or potentially bad. *If she really annoys these guys, they could go off the rails completely and do something really violent,* he fretted.

Chloe spoke again. "I am. Now hurry up and get here. We want to get Kim to hospital."

"OK Chloe. We will move as soon as we see the fire," Brute answered.

The radio went silent, leaving Major Wickham torn by hope and near despair. The situation certainly wasn't resolved.

And we've got a girl out there with a bullet in her and that Harley guy needs a doctor too, he thought, misery clouding his already battered emotions.

And not knowing was also adding to his emotional turmoil. The officers sat there and quietly debated what they should do, what they could do, and what Chloe might be doing.

Lt Cavendish was the most emotional. "Why is Chloe making these decisions? She is just a cadet. Why don't the sergeants with her take command?" she asked.

Major Wickham went to answer but Lt Barker beat him too it. "Because she is the only one out there with any balls!" he said.

"Oh! That's not true, and there's no need to be vulgar," Lt Cavendish replied huffily. "What about Sgt Lepson?"

"My case rests," Lt Barker replied. And Major Wickham could only agree.

The platoon commander ran away and so did the platoon sergeant.

"Chloe is obviously stronger willed and clearer headed than the corporals," he commented

"I still think she is a bad influence and should be thrown out," Lt Cavendish muttered.

That ended the conversation for a while and they sat in silence until Lt Cavendish called to Muff saying that she needed to go to the toilet.

"Do it there dearie! The boys won't mind," he retorted.

"Don't be a low animal! Are you a pervert?" Lt Cavendish snapped back.

Major Wickham took a sharp breath, fearing a strong reaction but to his relief and surprise the girl with the bikies said, "She's right Muff. Don't be so crude."

"Get stuffed Angela!" Muff retorted.

Angela wasn't cowed. "You can be a real deviate at times!" she snapped back. "Let the girls have some privacy. Anyway, I need to go too."

"So you take 'em," Muff replied angrily. "And don't let any escape or it'll be Slasher for you."

The girls were all called out, including the ten who sat with the officers. When they were all standing in a group with Lt Cavendish and Lt Peters they were warned that if any of them tried to get away they might get shot and that the other girls would suffer. They were then led away into the darkness towards the gate. While they were gone Major Wickham told the boys to turn around and go a few paces and relieve themselves. They did so and he and the male officers faced the other way and did likewise. By the time the girls and female OOCs returned they were all seated again, closely watched by a very suspicious Muff. Lt Peters sat down and Major Wickham hoped that she would not be handcuffed again but Muff remembered and made sure it was done.

Silence settled, with many of the cadets getting into their sleeping bags and lying down. The OOCs sat in line and talked quietly and Major Wickham fretted. He could hear trucks out on the highway and he heard a train come up out of the cutting and go west through Mingela. Knowing that help was potentially so close he found very galling.

If only we could contact a truck driver. They all have mobile phones and radios, he thought.

Time began to drag and Major Wickham noted that it was now 2115hrs. *What are 4 Platoon doing? Are they lighting this fire?* he wondered.

At that moment the radios began to softly crackle and he froze to listen. Terry moved closer to Muff who turned his radio up. Brute called: "Crackle… are you?... crackle."

"Are the bikies at the fire?" Capt Buchan whispered, straining to hear.

"Not sure," Major Wickham replied, the tension and anxiety eating up his insides.

But although there were several more radio calls he could not understand them. But then he distinctly heard the word 'Bitch!' and his stomach churned with concern.

What has Chloe done? he thought. It was obvious from the angry tone that she had done something that had upset Brute and that added to his concern. *What will the bikies do now?* he worried.

The radio kept crackling, Brute trying to contact Chloe, but she did not answer. That got the OOCs worried.

"What has Chloe done?" Lt Cavendish queried.

"Don't know," Major Wickham replied. "But it has upset them."

"She's nothing but trouble that girl! I hope they don't take it out on our girls?" she snapped.

Major Wickham shrugged. "That's a risk we have to take. But I don't think they will. They will have enough legal problems tomorrow without adding to them by doing things like that."

More minutes ticked by. Another check of the time showed it to be 2145hrs. Not knowing was the worst. Major Wickham was wracked by doubt and anxiety and now felt quite ill.

The radio crackled some more, each time sending his heart into his mouth and making his stomach churn. It was obvious from the tone that the bikie boss was very angry and he made some horrible threats to Chloe, or at least that was what Major Wickham thought as the transmissions were very broken and weak.

All those hills getting in the way, he decided. *But Chloe is in real trouble. These men will want their revenge!* That idea filled him with dread and he quietly prayed for her. By now he was sagging from exhaustion and mental anguish. *It is all like a never-ending nightmare!*

Just before 2200hrs the radio called again. This time they were loud and clear and Major Wickham deduced the bikies were back on top of the range somewhere.

"Close now," he muttered.

Capt Buchan nodded. "Possibly in that paddock on the other side of the highway?" he commented.

The radio called again. It was Brute. "Chloe, answer me you bitch. Talk!"

There was no answer and Major Wickham shook his head with concern. He was sorely tempted to ask for Muff's radio so he could call and end it all. But not knowing Chloe's plan he decided not to interfere.

She obviously has a plan and it is working, he thought.

Brute called again twice more, obviously closer. Then he snarled, "OK Chloe, your choice. We are going back to your camp now and will take it out on some of your cadet girls. Your fault slut!"

Major Wickham clenched his teeth together. A glance showed the other OOCs looking grim in the starlight. The radio went silent and they heard distant motorbikes, the sound dying away and then being drowned by the rumble of a big truck heading for Charters Towers.

Then headlights appeared along the Old Highway near the gate and Major Wickham's apprehension level shot up. "Here they come!" he muttered. He was filled with dread over what might happen next.

And he was right to be afraid. The three motorcycles were parked on the other side of the Land Rover and three bikies and another leather-clad girl strode into the light. It was Brute with his cronies Slasher and Stinger. Brute strode straight over to Major Wickham who stood up to face him. Brute thrust his CB radio at him.

"Call that bitch and tell her to surrender, or else!" he snarled.

This guy is desperate, Major Wickham thought. *He is liable to snap at any moment.* Sick at heart he decided he had to try to end it, if only to save the cadets. *I must get Kim to hospital, even if it costs Harley his life,* he decided.

He took the radio and called: "Two Four, this is Sunray, over."

There was no answer. He tried again and then, his desperation mounting, dropped the army radio procedure.

"Chloe, this is Major Wickham. Talk to me, over."

She didn't. Brute snapped at him to try harder and waved an automatic pistol under his nose. Major Wickham did try. Then he shook his head. "She's not answering."

"Then I'll start on you lot!" Brute shouted.

"I'll try another channel," Major Wickham said, now desperate to avert a tragedy.

With shaking hands he changed the channel and tried again. Twice more he called. Still no answer! He found he was trembling and that he had begun to perspire with anxiety. In desperation he tried another channel and still got no response. Shrugging with defeat he faced Brute.

Brute snarled with rage and snatched the radio from him then turned and before Major Wickham realised his peril, he punched. Major Wickham took the blow full in the face and fell backwards to the ground. Brute began kicking him, his frustration boiling over.

"Bastards!" he shouted. "Slasher, cut one of the girls up."

Oh no! Major Wickham thought, his mind reeling on the edge of unconsciousness.

The other OOCs scrambled to their feet, except Lt Barker who had his ankles bound. Capt Hamilton growled "Don't!"

But it was Angela who eased the situation. "Hey! Take it easy Brute! Don't you do anything yet Slasher. We are in enough trouble as it is."

Through eyes that were half closed Major Wickham saw Slasher hesitate and sneer at the girl. But he stopped and then Terry said, "What the hell's goin' on Brute? What happened out there?"

Brute swore foully, causing shocked gasps from the cadets, some of whom were also standing. Then he shook his head, frustration and anger evident in every line of his body.

"That bitch! She got a fire going alright but when we got there they weren't there."

Stinger nodded. "They were hiding and when we left the bikes to go up this bloody rocky gully a couple of them ran out and pushed our bikes over. Bastards damaged mine but luckily Angela was there and she saw them and called out. So they ran away before they could really do some damage."

"Where'd they go?" Muff asked.

"They ran off down the gully and under the railway line," Slasher replied.

"Under the railway?"

"Yeah, through one of those big culverts," Slasher added.

Muff looked puzzled. "Where was this?"

"Down past where we... where... where Peewee got shot," Slasher answered.

Muff looked alarmed. "Does that mean they are now on the other side of that railway right down at the bottom of the range?" he cried.

Major Wickham visualized the map and felt his hopes surge.

Brute answered. "Yeah, it looks like it."

Muff was obviously appalled. "But... but... but how will we stop them getting somewhere to call the cops? Are there houses down that way?"

It was obvious to Major Wickham that the bikies did not know the local area by the pause before Slasher nodded. "Must be a couple. I remember seeing some turn-offs."

"What will we do?" Muff cried, anxiety making his voice quaver.

For a few seconds Brute looked baffled and scared. Then he shrugged, "We need to send people to watch the houses," he suggested.

"And patrol the highway at the bottom of the range," Slasher added.

"Yeah, but who? There's only a dozen of us," Muff said.

Brute again shook his head. His indecision added to the sense of tension. "Us I guess, until daylight anyway. Then we have a chance of finding them."

Slasher nodded. "Yeah. But it would be better if we were a long way away by sun-up. This Chloe is the key to this. If we can get her to cooperate, we can finish this quickly."

Brute nodded and moved a couple of paces and fronted the standing OOCs. "This Chloe, tell me about here. She is some sort of leader eh?"

There was no reply and Major Wickham rolled over to see the four OOCs standing defiantly. Brute at once punched Lt Peters in the stomach.

"Talk you fools or Slasher will start on her!" he screamed.

Lt Peters crumpled up and was only held up by the handcuffs. Major Wickham was appalled as were most of the cadets who were watching with fear and horror on their faces.

It won't harm Chloe any more if they know, he thought.

"Stop hitting her! Help me up," he croaked.

Capt Buchan helped him to struggle to his feet. For a few seconds he stood swaying and then he became so dizzy that he sat down again and then lay back.

"Sorry. I can't. You tell them Mel," he gasped.

He was appalled at how sick he felt and desperately wanted to be able to take control of the situation.

Capt Buchan let go of him and then checked on Lt Peters who also sat, groaning in pain. Facing Brute grim-faced, he said, "I'll tell you but it won't do you any good. Now leave the women alone."

Brute sneered at him but then nodded. "Don't tell me what to do! Just talk. Now answer the question. Is this Chloe a leader?"

Capt Buchan gave a nod. "She's a leader alright, but not by rank. She's only a cadet."

Slasher stepped closer. "You mean like a private in the army?"

"Yes. Cadet is the lowest rank," Capt Buchan agreed.

"So how come she is calling the shots?" Brute snapped.

Capt Buchan shrugged. "Obviously she is the strongest personality out there."

"How old is she?" Slasher asked.

"Too young for you! She's only fourteen," Capt Buchan replied.

"Fourteen!" Brute cried.

He was plainly annoyed at learning this. That gave Major Wickham some satisfaction.

That must be hurting his pride and his standing with his gang, he thought. *To be beaten by a fourteen year old girl!*

It gave him some hope that the resulting anger might cause Brute to make some poor decisions.

Brute's anger became palpable. "She is dead! If she doesn't give up then she is going to die a horrible death. You can have her Slasher."

"Is she pretty?" Slasher asked, his face lighting up with a leering grin that made Major Wickham shudder to see.

"Very," Capt Buchan replied.

Slasher gave an evil chuckle. "She won't be when I finish with her," he said.

Major Wickham was so appalled at that he almost threw up. By now he was in utter distress and was wondering what he could do. He was blinking to clear his blurred vision when he noticed the headlights of a vehicle coming towards them along the Old Highway.

The others saw it too, and Brute muttered, "Who the hell is this?"

The bikies spread out, using the cadets and the Land Rover as cover. The vehicle, a truck of some sort, came to a stop about 25 metres away and its headlights and motor were switched off. Doors opened and in the reflected light Major Wickham saw that the driver was another bikie. His hopes fell. Then his distress increased when the bikie dragged two people from the other side at gun point and shoved them roughly forward. They were cadets.

Sgt Grey and Cpl Callan, he recognized.

Both cadets looked scared but defiant. The bikie with them gestured at them with his pistol. "Found these two down on the highway near that truck parking bay," the bikie commented. Major Wickham now recognized the man.

Cokehead. He was sent to get a truck to remove the bikes and bodies. Damn!

Brute nodded. "Good! Why didn't ya ring me?"

"I tried but mobiles don't work down in that valley," Cokehead said.

"What happened?" Brute queried.

"I'd picked up the bikes and Peewee and had just come out onto the highway and was heading down the range when these two stepped out and waved me down," Cokehead explained. "So I twigged what they was up to and just stuck 'em up and here we are."

"Good!" Brute growled.

Damn! Major Wickham thought. *The boys thought they were doing the right thing by flagging down a vehicle, but they've got the wrong one!* His disappointment was so sharp he sobbed. *Of all the bad luck! Only one truck driven by a bikie and they have to choose it!*

Slasher strode over to confront Sgt Grey. "Are you the kids who lit the fire?"

Sgt Grey looked very scared and all he could do was nod. Before anyone realised what he was going to do, he punched Sgt Grey in the face, knocking him to the ground.

"You little bastard! You damaged my bike and scratched the chrome on the petrol tank!" He began to kick at him.

Major Wickham tried to roll onto his front to get to his feet but had only managed to get to his hands and knees before the four OOCs who could stand all moved forward.

"Leave him alone!" Capt Hamilton shouted. From on the ground Lt Barker yelled angrily.

But it was Stinger who dragged Slasher back. "Fair go mate! You'll kill him," he cried.

"Bastards damaged our bikes!" Slasher snarled.

Baring his teeth he gave one more kick at the now prostrate Sgt Grey before stepping away.

Many others had been crying out as well and it took a minute or so before things settled. Brute then faced Cpl Callan.

"Were you with that Chloe?"

Cpl Callan nodded and croaked, "Yes."

"Is that Harley with you?"

"Yes."

"Where are they?"

Cpl Callan glanced around, obviously not wanting to answer but Brute grabbed his shirt front. "Answer me kid or you'll get worse. I'll have Slasher cut yer nuts off."

Major Wickham had now risen unsteadily to his feet and was leaning on Capt Buchan for support.

"Tell him Cpl Callan," he croaked.

Cpl Callan licked his lips and nodded. "I... I don't really know. We were sent to light the fire and they went another way. I think she said she was taking the platoon across the railway."

"Bugger!" Brute snarled.

"Shit! How will we ever catch them now?" Muff cried. "What are we gunna do now Brute?"

Terry spoke first. "I reckon we should clear out now. This place will be crawling with cops by daylight."

Brute swung to face him, dismay and anger on his face. "No! We must catch Harley and recover the loot."

"How?"

"Like I said, we send people to the houses and we ride up and down the highway. You and Muff stay here and guard this lot. And make sure those bloody officers are chained up so they can't do anything."

Terry was obviously amazed. "You mean we stay awake all night guarding this lot! Pig's bum! You'd better make some arrangement for us to get some sleep."

Brute scowled at him and snapped, "Do as you're told!"

Muff now joined in. "Fair go Brute! You wanna be the boss then you do the planning and make this work for us. Don't abuse us or shout orders or we might not vote you in as president."

Brute glared at him and for a moment looked like he would explode with anger. But then Slasher stepped in. "The boys are right Brute. Let's get organised. You go and set things up for the night while Stinger and I do another ride around."

Brute cast an angry glance at Muff but then calmed down and nodded. "OK. Let's get going. We gotta stop that Chloe calling the police before we get Harley."

Major Wickham watched the argument with satisfaction. *That's right Brute; if you want to be the boss you've got to have a plan that works and you've got to look after your people.*

Having suffered many times in his life from unhappy subordinates he knew this with sour certainty. As he watched the bikies getting organised another thought came to him.

That Slasher is the real brains of the organisation. Brute's tenure as boss might be fairly short.

A few minutes later Brute, Slasher, Stinger & Suzie rode off to search. Cokehead turned the truck and drove it away. Muff and Terry sat the four OOCs down and discussed how to chain them up without a chain. Terry shook his head.

"They are handcuffed together. Just tie their feet as well. Get some rope."

They did this and the cadets were all settled in a tight group again, the headlights of the Land Rover still lighting up the place. During all of this Major Wickham lay on the ground beside Lt Barker and hoped the gang would not remember he wasn't handcuffed. They didn't. All they did was tie his boots together with nylon cord.

Good! he thought, the glimmerings of a plan forming in his mind.

Lt Cavendish then annoyed them by asking for sleeping bags for the officers. Muff refused but Angela insisted.

"It's getting bloody cool! They can share a couple and you and me can have any others," she said.

So Lt Cavendish was set free and taken to collect the sleeping bags. One was spread over Major Wickham who was feeling very sick by then and he murmured a grateful thanks. By now he was in a state of emotional exhaustion, wrung out by utter distress.

What should I do? he wondered, agonizing over the options.

Presently he drifted into a deep sleep, from which he half surfaced from time to time as nightmares tormented him and his battered body reacted. Twitching and writhing he moaned a few times but then snuggled gratefully into the warmth of the sleeping bag thrown over him and went back to sleep.

At some stage he was again roused from his slumbers by the bikies talking. Still only half awake and staring though eyes that were gummed and blurry he noted that the bikies were changing over the vehicle that was shining its headlights on them. Apparently, the Land Rover had run out of fuel and it was that change in noise that had roused him. They now went to Capt Buchan's Station Wagon and started it up then switched on its headlights. After moving it a few metres so that the headlights illuminated the cadets the bikies sat in a huddle muttering.

They don't sound very happy, Major Wickham thought.

But his mind was so fogged as to feel like he was drugged and he had trouble thinking straight. All he managed to do was turn his head to note that all of the cadets appeared to be asleep and so did the line of OOCs beside him.

At that moment Muff's radio crackled again. Major Wickham had just been drifting into sleep but now jerked awake. It was Slasher.

"Brute, this is Slasher, over."

Brute answered at once, loud and clear and obviously not far away.

"What ya want Slasher?"

"I'm at that water trough and I've just found an army water bottle. The little bastards have been here. There are tracks all over the place."

Oh no! They've found 4 Platoon's tracks, Major Wickham thought, the dismay and apprehension rising to choke him.

Brute radioed back: "We will be there in a couple of minutes Slasher. Wait for us."

Oh no! Can they get away? Major Wickham thought.

In the darkness he lay there trembling and close to collapse as an attack of utter distress assailed him.

"I must do something!" he muttered.

Chapter 36

CORNERED!

When that radio message came Jane was very near the end of her strength and she knew it. Despite the sleep her whole body seemed battered and drained of energy and her hands were sore and blistered. She licked dry, cracked lips and held her sunburnt head as it throbbed from a headache worse than any she could ever remember.

So when she heard Slasher's call about finding the water bottle she was dismayed and her spirits dropped. Knowing that she would have to force herself to make an effort to keep going caused her to groan with near despair.

I just want it to end! she thought.

Chloe came and crouched next to her. "They are onto us Janie Babe," she murmured.

"I know," Jane croaked. Wincing at the pain of her muscles that had gone stiff she made herself sit up. "We'd better get going."

Chloe nodded. "We need to get across the next road, the one to Dotswood, before they work out they can cut us off," she said. "Oh, I wish I hadn't gone to sleep!"

Jane reached out and patted her. "Not your fault. We were all exhausted and I went to sleep too," she replied.

Chloe nodded. "Thanks. Come on, let's move. We might still do it."

"But they are only a kilometre or so behind," Jane replied, her eyes searching the dark bush off to the east for any sign of headlights. "They can catch us in 10 minutes on foot."

This time Chloe shook her head. "No. It will take longer than that, and anyway, I don't think they'll be very keen to track us far in the dark. They know we've got guns."

Jane shuddered with apprehension. *I wouldn't want to be trying to track people in the bush at night if they had guns,* she thought. But her fears made her very anxious.

"But their boss might make them," she argued.

Chloe snorted. "Huh! These aren't soldiers who are hunting us. They are only bikies. They are gangsters who are in it for money or power. They won't be very keen to sacrifice themselves for that," she said.

That made sense to Jane, who by then had risen painfully to her feet. "You are right," she replied. "That Slasher mongrel might but not the others." She nudged a sleeping form with her boot. "OK you lot, on your feet!"

With many groans and grumbles; the tired cadets got up. Chloe went along the line quietly urging them to their feet, with a nudge of her boot at Flegel who was making no move to get up. "Get up Flegel. We are moving," she hissed.

"I can't! I'm tired," Flegel replied in a sulky tone. "And I've got a sprained ankle."

Chloe stood over him. "Fine. You can stay here and we will pick you up in the morning, that is if the bikies don't find you first," she said.

That got him moving and Jane had to smile, wincing when her already cracked lips split the scab again. To ease it she took out a water bottle and had a quick gulp before taking her place at Harley's stretcher. A quick check revealed that he was shivering but asleep.

As they lifted him the distant vibration of motors came to Jane's ears and her heart skipped a few beats. Looking to the east she caught a few glimpses of flickering headlights.

There they are, on that hill where the track junction is, she reasoned. Her anxiety level went right up and she had to fight down the urge to just drop the stretcher and run. *They are on the other side of the railway,* she reasoned. *They surely won't try to follow us through this bush on motorbikes?*

Even though her rational mind told Jane that two fences and the railway and other obstacles would make it all but impossible for people to chase them through the bush in the dark fear still gripped her. Impelled by this she got the group moving. Kim's stretcher, under the command of Sgt Lynes, followed. Chloe led, navigating by the stars. It took them a real effort to get moving, with many groans and complaints about sore muscles and sore hands and feet. Jane silently agreed but kept her misery to herself. Her feet felt like they were on fire and it seemed to her that her boots were made of lead. And her palms were blistered and rubbed raw, causing her sharp stabs of pain.

Gritting her teeth Jane pushed herself to keep going, encouraging the others who were obviously also suffering as well. For several minutes they walked and stumbled through the dark bush. All the while she kept glancing behind, fearing to see the glimmer of headlights. But she saw no more and there was no sound of motorcycles, just the occasional noise of a vehicle on the now distant highway.

To her dismay they came to a gully. It was only washout a metre deep and a metre wide but in the dark it was an awkward obstacle to negotiate and they stopped to rest while they considered it. Jane looked around in the starlight and saw that the head of the gully was a series of small washouts in among the thicket of stunted trees on their left while to the right it became deeper and wider, a true gully. Reluctantly they made the crossing, people having to slide in and then hold the stretcher up while others passed it across. Some just scrambled around to take their places at the front.

The soil appeared to be crumbly black soil and the ground around was mostly bare but, as Jane discovered to her painful cost, some of the patches of growth were actually 'bull heads', those hard, little pea-sized burs with two really sharp prongs sticking out in any direction. When one drove its thorns into the palm of her hand as she climbed out of the gully she gasped and had to stifle a cry of pain. The pain was so intense that her eyes watered and she was momentarily unable to help with the stretcher. Muttering and swearing she plucked the offending thorn out and then warned others before stepping in to grab the middle of the stretcher again.

Through all of this she felt impelled by the urgency of the situation. *We must get out of this paddock and across that next road before the bikies work out where we are,* she thought.

But then they encountered another gully, almost identical to the previous one. This also stook several minutes and much effort and muscle wrenching strain to get across. By the time they had made it they were all perspiring despite the cold and Jane found she was sobbing with exhaustion and unhappiness.

And there was another gully. For a moment Chloe considered turning left to detour around the washouts at the head of it but a glance that way showed that the thicket of small twisted trees was so dense at that point that moving through it would be a real challenge. So they crossed this gully as well and then hurried on as fast as they could.

Chloe seemed to be everywhere, encouraging, helping and guiding.

Jane was once again struck by that familiar mixture of admiration and jealousy.

Where does she find the energy? she wondered.

And now she was driving them with her tongue, urging speed when all they wanted to do was flop down exhausted.

"Hurry! Keep going!" Chloe cried. "We must get across the Dotswood Road before the bikies find us."

"Where is this fucken road?" snarled Cadet Kane.

"Over on our left," Chloe replied, "And there's no need to swear in the presence of ladies thank you!"

"Ladies!" muttered Cadet Kane, but he was careful to keep his voice down so that Chloe didn't hear him. "How do you know its there?" he challenged.

"The bottom end of it is on your map," Chloe answered. "But I noted it last year when we did that CPX that was set here."

Jane's memory flashed back to July the previous year when those cadets who were interested had spent a weekend at Heatley doing a Command Post Exercise. This was run as a giant war game by Major Wickham. Five classrooms in a row had been used. At each end were the CPs of the Friendly commander and the OPFOR HQ. In between were three 'battle' rooms. In each battle room was a different part of the battlefield. In each room were two identical maps made up of photocopied 1:5,000 scale A4 map enlargements. A screen of hutchies hung from ropes separated the maps of the two 'sides'. The Friendlies were on one side and the Opposing Forces on the other so they could not see each other's deployment and game moves.

Small balsa tokens with military symbols on them were used to mark the deployment of both sides, the tokens being moved when the adjudicator (One of the officers) said they could move. There was a simple set of war game rules and each game move equated to 15 minutes of game time. In reality each move took over half an hour as all three rooms had to be adjudicated to stay at the same game time. After all had finished moving the adjudicator would then place on the other side's map the tokens for any enemy they had encountered or discovered. If there was action then dice were used to determine the outcomes. The real aim was to generate lots of map reading and many radio and telephone messages.

Jane had quite enjoyed the activity and had been amazed at how little grasp most of the CUOs and NCOs had of what armies actually did. But she had been in the next map room which covered the Flinders Highway to Macrossan. Chloe had been in the Mingela Battle Room and had obviously noted the layout of the area.

She's a clever girl, Jane conceded.

Then she noted that Chloe had no hat, her blonde hair almost glowing in the starlight. "Chloe, where's your hat?" she queried.

Chloe patted her hair and shrugged. "Lost it in those trees I think," she replied. "Come on, keep moving. Let's get across that road."

But first they had to get around the end of the thicket. Twice the stretchers were put down for a few minutes rest but Chloe refused to let them stay long. Even as the sweat chilled on their trembling bodies she urged them on. Jane began to despair, fearful that she would black out from sheer exhaustion. Gritting her teeth to ignore the pain from her blistered hands and now cramping muscles she made herself keep going. She even managed to utter words of encouragement to those around her. These had, in her exhausted mind, just become a struggling, gasping mass.

She was aware that a few had fallen behind but she did not have the mental energy to worry about them. She was just dimly aware that Sgt Lepson was with them, harrying them and urging them on. A glance showed that he was even helping a limping Flegel while carrying some other cadet's webbing. Jane was surprised.

Maybe he isn't completely useless after all? she thought.

And they were going left. Jane's almost fuddled brain noted the stars changing position and saw black clumps of vegetation still on her left but none straight ahead. Chloe came hurrying back.

"Nearly there," she hissed. "The fence is only a hundred paces. Keep going!"

They did but it was difficult as they were now crossing a grassy area studded with clumps of the prickly bush and also patches of some sort of vine. This caught at their ankles and made it hard to move and several cadets tripped. Twice Jane had to suddenly catch at the stretcher as the person next to her went down. Each time there was a sharp wrench at her already over strained muscles and she began to sob with effort.

And then her eyes detected a flickering light and she saw a glow growing down to her left. Even as she wondered if it was a motorbike a single bright light came clearly into view around a bend. "Down!" she croaked.

They almost dropped the stretcher and fell into the long grass. Jane's morale went down as fast as her body.

Too late! she thought, despair flooding through her as she noted that it was single headlight and therefore probably on a motorcycle.

It was. The motorbike roared up the Dotstwood Road and went racing past, its headlight lighting up the bush on both sides of the road and along the road clearing. As the motorbike went past Jane lifted her head and saw with a sense of bitter defeat that the darkly silhouetted figure riding the bike was most definitely a bikie. She also noted that the Dotswood Road was bitumen. She had imagined it to be a gravel road.

The motorbike vanished around a bend about a kilometre to their right. Sgt Lynes at once stood up.

"Quick! Let's get across the road while we can," he cried.

But, to Jane's surprise, Chloe stopped him. "No! Wait till we see what the bikies are doing," she cautioned.

"But now's our chance," Sgt Lynes cried.

Chloe shook her head. "Not necessarily. It will take quite a while to get across and if he comes back while we are doing that we will be sprung. Let's see if there are any more or if he comes back."

Sgt Lynes wasn't happy but Jane agreed with Chloe. *It took us half an hour to get across that railway line,* she thought, remembering the struggle it had been to pass the stretchers over each fence.

So they lay in the grass and waited. Jane was glad of the break. Her muscles were now quivering and cramps began to assail her upper arm muscles with stabbing darts of pure agony. She knew she was near the end of her endurance.

And it was as well that they did because a few minutes later another motorcycle came from the left. This one went much slower and from time to time it stopped and directed its headlight into the bush. That sent more stabs of fear through Jane and she hissed at the others to get under cover properly. With her own heart hammering with near panic and breath rasping in hot gasps in her dry throat she squirmed in against a prickly bush, only later wondering if there might be a snake curled in it ready to strike at her face.

But there was the bike and the man on it presented far more of a threat than any snake. Cringing and trembling Jane lay flat, holding her breath and praying while the beam swung back and forth over their heads.

They have worked out we are in this paddock alright, she decided. *Not that that would have been hard. We must have left a trail like a herd of elephants up that road and under the fences,* she told herself.

In the illumination Jane could clearly see some of the other cadets as they cowered in what little cover there was. She saw Chantelle's eyes wide with terror. She was biting her knuckles and visibly shaking. So was Dipkins. Not so Chloe. She lay flat, the shotgun held ready to use. The sight of her friend ready to fight sent a shiver of apprehension through Jane.

That bikie will regret it if he does see us, she thought. But her fear was for the probable legal and emotional consequences for her friend. *Oh, I hope she doesn't have to shoot!*

She didn't. The headlight swung away and the motorbike roared on up the road for another fifty metres before repeating the search procedure. Jane let out huge sigh of relief and lifted her head to look. The motorbike slowly worked its way north to the distant bend. Jane moved to her hands and knees to see over the long grass better and saw Chloe crawling forward to the fence. This was covered by a matt of creeper or a vine of some sort and there were a few bushy little trees growing right beside the fence at that point. Chloe stood up behind a bush and leaned out to look both ways along the road.

The second motorbike went out of sight around the corner and Chloe gestured to them to get up. Jane groaned and struggled to her feet and began urging the others to do likewise. But suddenly Chloe signalled and hissed, "Down!"

Jane looked around in alarm and saw that a headlight was coming in their direction around the bend to her right: either the same motorbike coming back or the first one. Muttering with frustration and near despair she dropped behind cover again. The motorbike came slowly down the road, weaving and stopping to direct its headlight beam into the paddocks on both sides of the road as it did. It took five minutes to reach them and another five minutes to pass out of sight around the bend to their left.

As she watched it going way from them Jane realised she could see down a very long, gentle slope to where the lights of a road train were visible moving along the highway.

And there is Mingela, she thought, noting the glimmer of a dozen lights a couple of kilometres away on the next long rise. Suddenly she was overwhelmed by emotion.

Those lights seemed to beckon like the beacons to a promised land where there was peace and plenty and they weren't being hunted by terrible men bent on murder!

Sobbing with pent up emotion Jane knelt and shuddered. Chloe came and knelt with her and reached out to enfold her in her arms.

"Sssh! It will be alright Janie. We will be out of this soon," she murmured.

Jane felt immediately comforted and quickly picked up. "I'm alright," she whispered. "I'm just a bit run down."

The two friends stood and watched the motorbike go out of sight. Jane then looked the other way and began to hope they could cross safely. But still Chloe held up her hand.

"No. Let's wait another couple of minutes," she said, as much to Sgt Lynes who was looking impatient as to Jane.

And she was right. Around the bend from their left came the motorbike that had just ridden down to the highway. On the way back north, it again kept stopping and shining its headlight into the bush on both sides. Once again, the cadets hid until it was past but no sooner had it gone than the second bike appeared from their right and came south doing the same thing.

"Bloody hell!" muttered Sgt Lynes. "Surely they aren't going to do that all bloody night."

"They might," Chloe said. "Or at least until they run out of petrol."

Jane agreed. "I think they are getting pretty desperate, but they really mean to catch and kill this Harley guy." She glanced at her watch to check how much of 'all night' might be left. To her surprise she saw that it was 0445hrs.

Where did all that time go? she wondered.

"Only half an hour or so to daylight," she added.

"Then the fat will be in the fire," Chloe muttered. "If we can't get across this road soon we might have to pull back to a hideout in the bush somewhere."

But they were unable to move. The two patrolling motorcycles came past so often and lit up the bush so much Jane decided they would now have great difficulty moving away unseen. Chloe agreed so they lay there waiting. As the cold began to seep back into her Jane trembled and knew she was very scared.

We are cornered! she thought. *How can we get out of this?*

Chapter 37

DESPERATION AT DAWN

Sgt Lepson lay shivering in the long grass.

We are trapped! he thought, the fear rising to clutch at his throat again.

He watched one of the motorcycles patrol slowly by, its headlight slashing through the darkness, and felt even more scared. He had overheard Chloe and Jane talking and agreed that they should withdraw to a safer place while they could.

But not while those two bikes come past so often.

During a lull between bikes Sgt Lepson stood up and went over to urge the others to get under cover. Chloe agreed and they all moved to cluster around the stretchers. These were picked up and they began to move but they had only gone ten paces back away from the fence before one of the motorbikes headed in their direction again.

"Down!" ordered Chloe. They all took cover and Sgt Lepson lay between two prickly bushes and shivered. He noted that Chloe was hatless and a part of his mind wanted to rebuke her for not wearing it. But somehow that didn't seem important enough to comment on.

Jane briefly lifted her head. "I don't think they know exactly where we are," she commented.

"No," Chloe agreed. "But they must think we are in this paddock."

After the bike had slowly gone past Jane stood up against a tree and watched it. "I think one of them is also riding back and forth along the highway," she said.

"That would make sense," Chloe agreed. "If it was me I'd have someone patrolling from the railway overpass to that truck stop and toilet further along the highway."

Sgt Lepson heard this with astonishment. *How does she know all this?* he wondered. But then he remembered stopping at the facility on a drive to Charters Towers with his parents. *When we went to that auction of old furniture and cups and plates and things.*

Another shudder ran through him but when it stopped he realised the person beside him was also shivering violently. With something of a shock he saw that it was Kim on her stretcher. He got up to crouch over her and looked but could not bring himself to touch her.

"Kim is very cold," he muttered.

"At least she's still alive," Cpl Lang replied from her other side.

"Yeah, but I think she's got hyperthermia," Sgt Lepson said. That idea filled him with anxiety as he knew hyperthermia could kill her.

Chloe heard him and came back to bend down and feel Kim's face and hands.

"You are right. She'll die if we don't get her warm," she said.

With that she took off her webbing and lay down so that she could put her arms and legs around the wounded girl.

"Chantelle, help me! Warm Kim up," she ordered.

A reluctant but anxious Chantelle got up to look and then did the same as Chloe. A reluctant Cpl Lang moved out of her way. The two girls half covered Kim and Sgt Lepson saw Chloe hug herself against her. For a few brief seconds his male mind speculated on what it might feel like to have Chloe press herself against him. He was at first astonished at the strength of his lust in that desperate circumstance but then he shuddered.

It will never happen! he thought bitterly but a savage surge of desire for Chloe churned in him, to be mingled with jealous hatred.

One of the motorbikes came slowly past from the south and the cadets all lay flat under cover until it had. Chloe and Chantelle stayed hugging Kim and it must have helped because the shivering became less violent and then came and went in short spasms.

At least she's still alive! Sgt Lepson thought, dread of dying making his teeth chatter briefly.

With a shock Sgt Lepson realised this and he flushed with shame. *People will think I am cold,* he hoped, lifting his head to look around.

To his dismay he found he could see better and he noted that the first grey hint of dawn was now showing through the trees to the east. A glance at his watch showed it to be 0515. He knew that 'First Light' was about 0520 at that time of the year and he did not know whether to be relieved or scared.

The same motorcycle came back again and this time there was enough light for Sgt Lepson to see details of the rider. The bikie wore no helmet so his head was plain to see. He looked to be one of the men he had seen the day before.

Is he is the guy who captured CUO Roach? he wondered.

Five minutes later the same man rode slowly back northwards on his motorcycle. As he went past his head swivelled from side to side as he scanned the bush. Sgt Lepson lay low behind his bush and held his breath. Only when the man had gone from sight and sound around the bend to the north did he lift his head.

Jane was also watching the bikie. "There's only one now. I wonder where the other one went?" she queried.

No-one answered that. Sgt Lepson again suggested they start moving but Chloe shook her head. "Too late. We will be seen. We will just have to hide here." she said.

"But what if they find us?" Cpl Lang cried.

Chloe held up the shotgun which she had placed beside her. "Then it will be bloody," she said grimly.

That was very sobering and Sgt Lepson mentally quailed at the idea. Jane lifted her head to look around. "I think we should split up now. We have the stretchers next to the road where the ambulance can reach them easily. What we now need to do is call them."

Chloe nodded. "Good thinking Janie. What do you suggest?"

"That a couple stay here to look after the casualties. I will. The others should all split into groups and go in different directions. If they are seen they should all scatter and hide. One group can get across the road and go west to the rodeo ground or that truck stop and another group can go south and across the highway to try to get to a phone in the town or stop a car. And a group can go north. There are homesteads up this road and they must have phones."

"Good thinking," Chloe agreed. "I'll stay with you. I am not letting the gang get Harley without a fight."

That was even more frightening to Sgt Lepson and he determined to be one of those going north.

That way I don't even have to risk crossing this road, he reasoned.

As he looked around, he saw with something of a shock that the wounded bikie was awake and was looking at Chloe.

The wounded bikie lifted his head. "Good for you Chloe," he muttered. "But you don't have to risk yourself for me."

Chloe turned to look at him. "Oh, you're awake! How do you feel?"

"Bloody cold, and bloody sore," Harley replied amid a few moans.

Jane looked at him and said, "We can also... Hey! Here comes a vehicle!"

Sgt Lepson had heard it but as there hadn't been a vehicle along that road all night it took a moment for the meaning of the sound to register. He lifted his head and saw that the noise was a vehicle coming south along the Dotswood Road. His hopes surged.

Jane got to her knees. "We must stop it!" she cried. Before anyone could speak she had unclipped her webbing and dropped it and started running towards the fence. Chloe got half off Kim and called, "Jane! Jane! Take care! It might be them!"

Jane nodded but kept running, her hat blowing off as she did. In ten more paces she was at the fence and threw herself down to roll under it. Sgt Lepson heard cloth tear and then saw the glow of the vehicle's headlights. It was a small truck of some kind.

Will she be in time? he fretted.

A moment later he saw Jane on her feet on the other side of the fence, her body lit up by the headlights and her arms waving frantically. There were a few moments of fear as Sgt Lepson wondered if the vehicle would stop but then he heard the squeal of brakes and the headlights slowed. Chloe sprang up and went running towards the fence, snatching up the shotgun as she went. That sight sent Sgt Lepson's heart rate hammering again.

By the time Chloe had scrambled under the fence Jane was standing beside the cab of the stationary truck talking to the driver. It was an old, open-backed truck, the tray littered with tools. The driver looked like an old farmer.

Certainly not a bikie, Sgt Lepson thought, his initial fears subsiding. But that did not stop him looking anxiously along the road in both directions.

As Chloe stood up Jane came scurrying around the front of the truck to the passenger door. As she opened it Chloe grabbed at her sleeve.

"Jane, what are you doing?"

"Going to phone the police and the ambulance," Jane replied.

"Where? Don't go to the town. I think the bikies are there."

Jane shook her head. "We won't. This nice man is going to Charters Towers but there is a farmhouse a couple of kilometres along the highway and we will stop there to use their phone. You get back under cover."

"Take care!" Chloe cried, letting go of her sleeve. The two girls then embraced.

Bloody lemons! Sgt Lepson thought.

He was now leaning on the fence and straining to hear their conversation. Jane climbed in and the farmer engaged the gears to set the truck in motion. Jane waved and Chloe returned it then turned and began walking back towards the fence. Her slow pace irritated Sgt Lepson.

"Hurry up and get under cover!" he snapped at her. "One of those bikies might come along."

Chloe ignored him and stopped at the fence to watch the truck. Sgt Lepson did not have the courage to order her to take cover so instead looked again in both directions. There was no sign of any motorcycles, so he stayed standing and leaned out to watch as the truck went around the bend. But it didn't go out of sight as it was higher than the grass and fences and he was able to watch as it continued on towards the crossroads at the Flinders Highway. It was now just light enough to see.

From where he stood Sgt Lepson could see traffic going in both directions along the highway. The truck's brake lights came on and it came to a stop at the intersection. As it did Chloe let out a gasp and put her hand to her mouth. "Oh no! That is a bikie!" she cried.

Even though the distance was about a kilometre Sgt Lepson saw a person who looked like a bikie come out from behind the long grass at the junction and step up onto the step beside the driver. The truck stayed stopped and the driver's door was opened and the old man climbed out, his hands in the air.

"He's caught them!" Sgt Lepson gasped, his fears welling up again.

Chloe bit her lip and stared hard at the distant scene. "Oh no! I wondered where that second bikie had gone to. If only they had been able to just keep driving!"

They were joined at the fence by Sgt Small and Sgt Lynes. Sgt Lepson felt sick despair as the defeat hit him. "They will know we are here now!" he cried.

Chloe gave him a withering look of contempt. "It will take a lot to make Jane talk!" she snapped angrily back.

Down at the highway junction the bikie motioned the driver to get back into the cab. As he did the bikie climbed up onto the tray behind him. The truck then began moving again but, to Chloe's evident dismay and distress, it didn't turn right and go along the highway. Instead it crossed and continued on along the side road towards the township.

"Oh no!" she muttered. "They've got Jane."

"And they will torture her if she doesn't talk," Sgt Lynes said.

Sgt Small looked pale and ill. "And it means she won't be able to phone the ambulance."

Chloe bit her lip and looked agitated. "Oh! We must do something!"

At that moment Sgt Lepson heard the dreaded sound of a motorcycle behind him. He turned and looked that way. The machine was not yet in sight but on the still morning air he could clearly hear it coming.

"That other bikie is coming back!" he cried. "Get under cover!"

As he moved to crouch behind the bushes and vines Chloe cried, "I'm going to capture him! Who's got a long rope?"

"Don't be stupid!" Sgt Lynes replied as he crouched down. "What are you going to do with a rope?"

"Tie it across the road like they do in the movies," Chloe replied. She was now almost dancing with excitement.

Sgt Lepson was appalled. He remembered seeing several movies where motorcycle riders had been decapitated by wires strung across the road. "You could kill him!" he cried. "Don't do it!"

"You don't need to!" Sgt Small added.

Chloe shook her head. "Yes, I do. He might have a phone, and even if he doesn't he will make a hostage," she replied. She now crouched in the long grass and began groping at something beside the fence.

Sgt Lepson accepted her logic but was still dismayed and afraid. But she ignored his orders to stop and hide. Instead she went into a crouch, the shotgun held in her right-hand and a length of dead wood about three metres long in her left.

"Don't!" Sgt Lepson cried as the motorcycle roared into view.

Chloe just ignored him and crouched with her head just above the grass and bushes. Then, as the motorcycle came within about 50 paces, she sprang up and ran out onto the road. She put down the stick and held her arms wide. Sgt Lepson could only stare in horror and fear. He saw the face of the bikie change from puzzlement to alarm and for a moment he slowed the machine. But then he must have changed his mind as the engine roared and the bike began to accelerate and change direction to avoid her.

Chloe went to aim the shotgun but then changed her mind and bobbed down to place it on the road. In its place she scooped up the length of rotten wood and, as the bikie went to pass her on her left, she flung it at him.

A look of alarm crossed the bikie's face and he put one arm up to shield himself. At the same time he must have jerked the handlebars because the bike suddenly slewed sharply and a moment later it crashed sideways, the driver being flung hard onto the rough bitumen. For an awful few seconds bike and rider went sliding along, the bike half on top of the rider. Sgt Lepson could only stare in horror.

Bike and rider slithered to a grinding stop ten metres further on and before the rider could extricate himself from the machine Chloe had snatched up the shotgun and run over to shove the barrels in his face.

"Don't move!" she snarled.

The bikie was so stunned and shocked that he only nodded and then cried, "No! I won't! Don't shoot! Ah! Argh! I have to! The bike's on me leg and it's hot."

"Then crawl out and lie still," Chloe commanded, stepping back a couple of paces but keeping the gun levelled on the man.

"I can't! The bike's too heavy," the bikie cried. "Ah! Oh! Help me!"

Chloe turned her head. "Sgt Lepson! Sgt Lynes! Help lift the bike."

Sgt Lepson had been so stunned by the speed of events that it took a second call from Chloe to get him moving. But he understood the problem and quickly crawled under the fence and made his way across to where the man was writhing in pain. Sgt Lynes joined him and between them they lifted the heavy bike.

A classic Harley Davidson, Sgt Lepson noted.

The man still lay there groaning. He was plainly hurt as his left wrist was bent at a funny angle and he was clutching his left leg.

"Me leg's busted! Ah! Ow!" he cried.

Chloe ignored this and went closer to reach down and extract an automatic pistol from the back of the man's waistband. She then stepped clear and motioned towards the fence.

"Sgt Lepson, move the bike off the road. Sgt Lynes, get him across to the other side of the fence and under cover."

Sgt Lynes objected. "But he's hurt! He's got a broken wrist."

"I can see that!" Chloe retorted. "But he's also got dangerous mates and we need to get him out of sight. Now move him! Get moving buster!" she snarled at the bikie, while making threatening gestures at him.

The man looked scared and nodded and despite his obvious pain he got to his feet with Sgt Lynes helping. But then he couldn't walk.

"Done me knee!" he wailed.

"Hop then!" Chloe snarled.

The bikie took one look at her angry, determined face and did as he was told. With some difficulty he was gotten under the fence and seated against a post. By then Sgt Lepson had wheeled the bike off the bitumen. He parked it against the fence, being loath to lay such a magnificent machine in the long grass. Chloe didn't like that and told him to hide it but he shook his head.

"If I lie it down the hot exhaust could start a grass fire," he objected.

Chloe gave a reluctant nod of assent and then crawled under the fence herself. She then moved to face the injured bikie.

"What's your name?" she queried.

The bikie stared back at her defiantly, and as Sgt Lepson crawled back under the fence he had the malicious pleasure of wondering how Chloe might make him talk.

But she didn't need to. Harley took over, calling out from his stretcher a few paces away.

"His name's Lance. What's goin' on Lance?"

Lance stared at Harley in obvious surprise and shock. "Bloody hell! Harley! You are alive!"

"No thanks to some bastards I could name!" Harley snarled. He then tried to sit up but grimaced in pain and lay back. He gestured to the cadets around him. "Pick this stretcher up you kids and carry me over there."

The cadets looked scared and several glanced at Chloe who nodded. There were only four there and they had trouble lifting the big man, so Sgt Lepson and Sgt Lynes moved to help while Sgt Small went to get her First Aid kit.

While they did this Chloe faced Lance. "You got a mobile phone?" she asked.

Lance nodded and reached into his jacket with his right-hand. All the while he kept his eyes on the shotgun Chloe kept unwaveringly aimed at him. "Careful with that gun girlie. It's not a normal shotgun."

"Just give me the phone!" Chloe snapped. Lance at once did so and Chloe moved a few paces away. After switching the phone on and studying the screen briefly she began using it.

While he helped carry Harley closer to Lance Sgt Lepson heard her start to speak.

"Police please. Hello, police? This is a desperate emergency involving armed bikies. Who am I? I'm Chloe Cummings and I'm an army cadet. We urgently need armed police and at least three ambulances. There have been people shot. Where? Near Mingela."

There were more questions by the operator which Chloe answered and then she said, "We are not in the town. No, we are not at a house. There is no street number. We are in the bush. We are on the Dotswood, Mingela Road one kilometre north of the Flinders Highway turn-off. Yes. One kilometre north on the Dotswood Road. Hurry! We have two with serious gunshot wounds and a third with broken bones."

The operator obviously wasn't convinced as there were more questions. Exasperated Chloe snapped: "This isn't a hoax! Hurry! It is really urgent. And we have a hostage situation. One of our girls, Jane Carson, has been taken prisoner by the bikies. Hurry or they will torture her!"

As Chloe talked Sgt Lepson began to relax. *Finally! We have made contact with the police. Everything will be alright now.*

Chloe re-joined the group, pocketing the mobile phone as she did. "Ok, the police and ambulance are on their way," she said.

"Thank God!" Sgt Small cried. "Now all we have to do is hide until they get here."

Chloe stood and looked down, her face grim. "No. I have to save Jane," she replied.

Sgt Lepson was amazed. "How can you do that!" he said. His astonishment made him sneer.

"I'm not sure yet," Chloe answered. "But I aim to try. Harley, question this bloke so we get a better idea of what's going on."

Harley, now half sitting up, nodded. "OK Chloe Babe. Yeah Lance, what's goin' on man?"

"I was gunn ask you that," Lance replied. "Brute said that you murdered Peewee and that you'd done a runner with the drugs and the money and that we were now in bad shit because of ya."

Harley snorted with anger and then winced as pain lanced through his head. He pressed his fingers to his temple for a few seconds then snorted again.

"Oh pigs! Brute and Slasher and Muff ambushed Peewee and me. They shot us both in the back," he cried. By rolling half on his side he indicated the wound and also the one in his leg. "I tried to run but they got me twice more."

Harley winced again and then gestured to the cadets. "That's when these cadets saved me. Chloe here bashed Slasher and took his gun. If she hadn't, I would be dead. Thanks Chloe, you are a gem."

Chloe gave a coy smile which annoyed Sgt Lepson. She looked so much the innocent little girl that it made him angry.

Deceitful bitch! he thought.

"Yeah!" said Lance with a malicious grin. "She hit him again later and he's real wild about that. His whole face is black and blue and he's really got it in for her."

Hearing that caused Sgt Lepson to feel a mixture of fear and ghoulish anticipation.

I'm glad he doesn't have it in for me! he thought.

It took another five minutes for Harley to explain to Lance his version of the story. Lance looked both puzzled and annoyed. From time to time he flinched with pain.

"Well Brute and Slasher are tellin' a different story," he said.

"They would!" Harley said, snorting derisively again.

Chloe now spoke. "Harley is telling the truth. We saw it all. We were hiding in a dry creek and saw him, and Peewee get ambushed. I saw Brute walk over and shoot Peewee in the back of the head to finish him off."

Lance looked very thoughtful and nodded. "Oh yeah, and all these kids saw that?"

"Not all but half a dozen of us did," Chloe agreed. "Brute is a murdering liar."

"Brute want's ya dead Harley, that's for sure," Lance commented.

"He just wants to be the boss without having to put it to the vote," Harley retorted.

"Like as not," Lance agreed.

"So what's goin' on?" Harley queried. "What are all the others doin' and what do they think?'

Lance pointed down the road. "Half of 'em are in Mingela with most of the girls. And they ain't happy. Slasher is down the road there at the highway and Al is ridin' up and down the highway. I think Cory is still at that railway overpass and he's gettin' pretty pissed off because he's been there since yesterday afternoon. I think Stinger's patrollin' the dirt track the other side to the railway."

Chloe knelt to face him. "Do they know we are in this paddock?"

Lance nodded. "We ain't sure but we found yer tracks where ya crossed the railway and so Brute reckoned ya must be somewhere here. Slasher agrees and we was gunna bring everyone and come looking for yer when the sun gets up."

They all glanced around at that and Sgt Lepson noted that the first pink flush of dawn was showing on the few clouds and that the first weak rays of sunlight were hitting the treetops.

Which will be soon! he thought, the fear coursing through him again. *And they will know exactly where we are because that bloody Jane will tell them!*

All he could think of to ease his mounting feeling of desperation was to hope the police would arrive soon. But how long would it take them to get there? He estimated that it would be half an hour or more.

"We need to move away and hide," he suggested.

To his shame Harley flicked him a glance filled with contempt and then looked at the others. "How many in the town Lance?"

"When I left there were Davo, Mike and Julio and six of the girls. They all stayed at the pub an' the lady who owns it ain't happy, but we made sure she couldn't phone the cops."

Harley frowned. "Where's Brute?"

"He comes and goes on his bike," Lance answered.

Chloe now knelt closer. "What about the cadets? Are any of your people at the cadet camp?"

"I don't know anything about any cadet camp," Lance said. "Brute didn't say but maybe that's where Muff and Terry and Angela are?"

Chloe bit her lip and then said, "The man down at the highway just captured my friend. Where do you reckon they will take her?"

"To Brute at the hotel probably," Lance answered.

Harley frowned and groaned then asked. "What sort of mood are the boys in? How many will support Brute do ya reckon?"

Lance thought hard for a few moments then shook his head. "Not many. Only Slasher and Stinger and Muff I reckon. Most of us don't like Brute at all and we are sick of the way Slasher bosses us around. Most of us want a new Sergeant at Arms as well. I can tell ya they aren't happy with what's been goin' on. They reckon they've been lied to, or at least not told the whole story."

"They have been!" Harley cried. He tried to get up but pain obviously hit him as he gasped and groaned and lay back down again. "I need to speak to them."

"Be good if ya could," Lance agreed.

Chloe nodded. "You could save Jane," she agreed.

"I could," Harley agreed. "But I need a bike if I'm goin' to town. Help me up you lot." Again, he went to rise and managed to get to a sitting position.

Chloe helped him but Sgt Small objected. "You are wounded. You shouldn't try to get up."

Harley gave her a hard look. "I gotta girlie. I got me own life to save and I'd like to ter save young Jane too. I owe her."

Chloe supported him but then shook her head. "Wait till we check if Lance's bike still works. You can't walk all the way to town."

Lance held up his broken arm and held his left knee. "I can't walk either," he grumbled.

Sgt Lepson suddenly saw an opportunity to redeem himself. "I know about motorbikes," he said. "My brother's got one and I ride it sometimes."

Chloe turned to him. "Then check if Lance's bike is still a goer," she said.

Harley winced then grinned at Chloe. "You look like a bit of a goer," he murmured.

Chloe lowered her eyelashes and gave him a sultry look. "I can be, if I like the man," she whispered back.

Sgt Lepson was both disgusted and aroused.

She's flirting with him! he thought in amazement. *Oh the cheap slut!*

Chloe smiled at Harley and then held out the automatic pistol she had taken off Lance. "You'll need a gun. Here's Lance's automatic. It's a nine-millimetre Beretta. Probably has a nine-shot magazine." She glanced at Lance and raised a questioning eyebrow.

Lance nodded and Sgt Lepson, who was by then crawling back under the fence was both alarmed and annoyed.

She's giving that bikie boss a gun! He can just hold us up or shoot us now. And then another little niggle of irritation hit him. *How does she know all this stuff anyway? She's only a dumb blonde bitch!*

After standing and doing a careful check for bikies in both directions, it only took Sgt Lepson a minute or so to determine that the motorcycle was damaged. He leaned back over the fence and shook his head.

"No go! The fuel line is busted right off and there looks to be a cylinder head bashed right out of shape, not to mention a few dints and scratches."

He then had the satisfaction of seeing Lance glare at Chloe. "That'll cost ya, bitch!" he snapped.

To Sgt Lepson's surprise it was Harley who answered. "No it won't Lance. I'll pay for the repairs. I owe her my life and you'll treat her with respect or you'll have me to answer to."

Lance nodded and looked scared and Sgt Lepson was annoyed. *Bloody Chloe! Now she's got this bikie boss hooked around her little finger!*

Harley frowned and went on. "Well we gotta do something. I need to speak to the boys and I want to save Janie. So we need to flag down another truck or something."

Another idea then came to Sgt Lepson. "If that was Slasher down there at the highway junction there might be a bike there."

"Why do you say that?" Harley asked.

"Because the bikie.. er... the man there left his bike there when he went off on the truck with Jane and the farmer," Sgt Lepson replied.

"Good idea. Can you go and get it?"

Sgt Lepson hadn't thought of that and was almost stunned by the suggestion. He had not intended to place himself at risk but looking at the expectant faces he could not think of any way out of offering.

If I don't they will think I am a coward, he thought, fear and shame adding to his misery.

"Yes, OK. But what if there are no keys?"

"Just wheel it back here. We'll soon get it going," Harley answered.

Chloe nodded. "I'll come with you to cover you," she said. "We will go down through the bush. Come back inside the fence."

Sgt Lepson was glad to do that as that put him at least in some cover. Chloe slid the Glock pistol out of her webbing and held it out to Sgt Lynes. "Here Sgt Lynes. It is loaded but not at action."

"But... But!" spluttered a plainly scared Sgt Lynes.

"You don't have to use it," Chloe said. "Just bluff."

"That's right," agreed Harley. "If there's any real shooting to do I'll do it."

Chloe knelt and had a big drink then slid the water bottle back into her webbing, which she left lying on the ground.

"Leave your webbing Sgt Lepson, we need to go fast. Jane is in trouble." Picking up the shotgun she hurried off.

Sgt Lepson did so. A minute later he found himself hurrying through the bush behind Chloe. As they left the group his fear continued to grow until he had to use all his willpower to force his legs to keep moving. But he managed it.

Chloe led the way through the thicket of small trees, detouring away from the fence and walking quickly. The distance was about a kilometre and took them about 15 minutes. By the time they were down near the highway the sunlight was striking across through the trees. Only during the last few hundred metres was there almost no cover. They came out in a field of waist-high weeds and prickly bushes. The only thing offering any cover was a small electricity substation inside a chain wire enclosure and it was right down near the highway.

There was only one incident on the way but it stopped Sgt Lepson's heart for a few beats and sent icy chills of terror into his skull. For a few seconds it froze him so that he could not move. Chloe suddenly sprang back with a cry of alarm and something big moved rapidly in front of her. Only as the paralysing fear coursed through him did Sgt Lepson's frightened brain work out that the large dark object that was bounding off to his left was not a bikie.

"Bloody emu!" Chloe cried with a chuckle. She lowered the shotgun and shook her head. "Startled the crap out of me," she added.

Sgt Lepson had to swallow to speak and then tried to act as though he hadn't been scared at all. "Don't emus usually go around in pairs?" he said.

"Might be a female. They go alone," Chloe replied. She resumed her hurrying walk. By now they were clearly visible to anyone on the highway who might be looking, and Sgt Lepson could plainly see a truck and a car racing past in opposite directions.

If I can see them they should be able to see us, he reasoned. *And we must be visible to anyone in the town who looks,* he added, fearfully aware that he could plainly see the buildings on the next rise a kilometre away.

"Should we crawl" he called.

Chloe shook her head. "Take too long. Jane is in trouble and I don't want to waste half an hour," she replied.

Only for the last 50 paces did she slow down and only at the fence near the junction did she stop and go to ground. Sgt Lepson joined her in the weeds. At that moment a car raced past towards Charters Towers.

"We could flag down a car," he suggested.

"I have already rung the cops. We just need the bike," Chloe said.

It was there, parked over against the fence on the other side of the junction. To reach it they had to crawl under the fence and then walk across fifty metres of short grass and bitumen. Sgt Lepson felt very exposed and kept glancing anxiously along the highway and towards the town.

But no-one appeared and they reached the bike without any more problems. And as he had feared there was no key. As soon as Sgt Lepson told her this Chloe bit her lip and glanced anxiously towards the town.

"So you wheel the bike back to the platoon. Go as fast as you can," she instructed.

"What are you going to do?" Sgt Lepson queried, as he had expected her to come with him and to help push.

Chloe sighed and her whole body seemed to slump. Then she slid the shotgun into a saddle bag on the bike. "I'm going to talk to the bikies," she said.

"But... But!" Sgt Lepson gabbled. He was flabbergasted. "But they could hurt you!" He meant torture and kill but could not bring himself to say it.

Chloe nodded and looked grim. "Maybe, but I reckon if the gang know the truth they won't," she said. Then she shrugged again. "Anyway, I reckon I don't have many choices. If they come looking for me for revenge after this I am dead."

Sgt Lepson was appalled. "But! But the police can protect you!"

Chloe snorted. "Oh crap! They can't guard me day and night for years to come! And I'm not going to live in fear, looking over my shoulder all the time and fretting about when they might hit me. I am going to settle it once and for all right now. So get going and maybe Harley can help."

"But!"

"But nothing! Push that bike as fast as you can. And tell Harley I won't let them know where you are," Chloe snapped. Then she gave a wry smile. "Or I'll try not to," she said in a tone full of bitter regret. With that Chloe turned and hurried across the momentarily empty highway.

As she did Sgt Lepson saw tears streaming down her face and he was appalled and gripped by dread and admiration. He knew it was the sort of life and death decision he could never make. For a few seconds he watched her, his mind trying to dredge up arguments to persuade her not got go. But then he was gripped by urgent desperation.

Maybe if I hurry that Harley can save her? he thought.

So he pushed himself as he had never done before, almost running as he wheeled the big bike, another classic 'Harley Davidson', up the long, uphill slope. He pushed until his hammering, apprehension-filled heart felt like it was going to burst. His breath began to come in rasping sobs and tears began to run down his cheeks as well.

From time to time he glanced back and each time he saw with anguish that lonely figure getting smaller and closer to the town as Chloe walked up the long, open road towards her fate.

Chapter 38

RAW COURAGE

Despite wanting desperately to do something Major Wickham could not think of any plan to escape. The bikies still sat watching and the car headlights made any movement obvious.

Oh, what can I do? he thought as the emotional anguish tore at him.

Agonizing minutes dragged by but there were no more radio messages and the sound of motorbikes faded. Only the noise of an occasional vehicle passing along the highway disturbed the night.

Around midnight Major Wickham again drifted into an exhausted, fitful sleep. More pains and nightmares assailed him and he woke trembling and distressed. His head ached and he felt so sick he wanted to throw up. After taking a drink of water he lay back and looked around but again decided he could not move as Terry was watching his every move. Regretfully he lay back and closed his eyes, his brain turning over ideas.

Again the cessation of a running motor brought him back to semi-consciousness. Blinking and wincing at the pains that speared through his skull he looked up and saw that it was still dark. The sky was a million stars with not a cloud to be seen. It was cool but not too cold. A glance revealed that the Station Wagon's engine had stopped. The headlights were still shining but were looking decidedly dim.

Out of fuel? Major Wickham wondered.

For a few more moments he lay there thinking he must do his duty but feeling too ill and battered to want to move.

Then a peculiar crunching noise sparked his interest and he did make the effort to lift his head and look around. In the dim light he saw that Terry and his girlfriend were lying huddled together and apparently sound asleep and that there was no sign of Muff. Then the meaning of the unusual noise became apparent.

That is a motorbike being wheeled away along the Old Highway, he thought.

Carefully rolling onto his side Major Wickham shielded his eyes from the dying glow of the vehicle's headlights and tried to peer into the darkness. But the sound faded into the distance before he could see anything.

Is that Muff doing a bunk? he wondered. Again he looked in all directions but there was no sign of the other bikie.

Down the road near the gate a motorbike engine roared into life and then a headlight came on, pointing away from him. Major Wickham sat up and glimpsed a person ride a motorcycle out the gate and down onto the highway.

Definitely Muff going somewhere, he decided. But was he just joining the search or running away?

He shifted his gaze to the sleeping pair. *If they are the guards they aren't doing a very good job,* he decided.

His anxiety level shot up and he again looked in all directions. By then the car headlights had died away to two dim red glows so starlight dominated. Then it came to him.

This is our chance!

For a few seconds he was too excited and anxious to move. Lying back he did a quick appreciation and then made a simple plan. But putting it into action took real courage and as he knew that it could spark deadly consequences.

Do it! he told himself. *You must take control of this situation.*

Sucking in a deep breath to steady his now racing pulse Major Wickham resolved to move. Very quietly he slid the sleeping bag off and rolled over. After a pause to listen and look he sat up, then waited a few moments to see if there was any reaction from the bikies. There was none. The sleeping pair slept on and no other voice called from the surrounding darkness.

Except it wasn't very dark anymore. With a shock Major Wickham realised that it was getting light. In the dim greyness he looked at his watch and saw that it was 0535hrs.

After First Light, he thought. That knowledge spurred him to move faster. *It will be daylight soon and those bikies might come back.*

Very carefully he moved to his hands and knees, sore and stiff muscles sending little stabs of pain through him. Carefully he flexed them, not wanting stiff muscles to slow him or a cramp to hit him if he had to fight. While he did this, he saw that Lt Barker had his eyes open and was watching him. Not wanting him to speak or move Major Wickham put his forefinger to his lips and shook his head. Lt Barker nodded and lay there watching. Next Major Wickham moved to untie his ankles, but the effort of bending sent such sharp stabs of pain through him that he had to stop and stifle the gasps they caused. But he persevered and soon had the bindings undone.

They weren't very well tied, he thought. *They should have paid more attention in the knots lessons!*

Now free to move Major Wickham raised himself to his feet, stifling a groan as he did. A wave of dizziness swept over him and he braced himself for a few moments until it passed.

Heart in mouth he began 'Ghost Walking' across towards the two sleeping bikies. It was very hard to move silently on the Old Highway as the gritty surface crunched under his boots and he had to move with all the skill he had acquired in nearly half a century of service. The whole time he kept his gaze focused on Terry and he tensed himself ready for instant and violent action. He was resolved to do whatever it took to disarm the bikies and free the cadets. Nagging continually at the back of his mind was the knowledge that Kim's life might be at stake.

Major Wickham got within five paces of the sleeping pair without rousing them. For a few seconds he paused to study the layout. Across the road lay the great huddled mass of sleeping cadets but there was no sign of any other bikie. Then his questing eyes detected what he was looking for, the guard's shotgun. It was leaning against the car beside him.

For a moment Major Wickham paused to stiffen his resolve and to ensure his muscles were working. His heart hammered hard and he nerved himself to move. The final spur was hearing what sounded like a motorcycle travelling east along the highway towards the gate. Fearing that it might be Muff or one of the others returning he knew he had to act now.

Instead of creeping the last five paces Major Wickham strode quickly over, his eyes on the sleeping man's head and his hand reaching for the gun. The crunching sound obviously penetrated Terry's sleeping brain as he began to move. By the time his sleep fuddled head emerged from the sleeping bag Major Wickham had snatched up the gun and taken two steps backwards. He had resolved to use the gun butt on the man's head if forced to but now saw that such a violent option wasn't needed. A quick glance revealed that the gun was a simple double barrel sporting gun and that the safety catch was on. Swinging the butt up under his right arm he aimed the gun from the hip and clicked off the safety catch.

Terry's sleep-gummed eyes opened and then opened even wider in surprise and shock. "Hey!" he gasped. He moved to sit up, blinking to clear his vision as he did.

"Don't move!" Major Wickham growled. "If you try to get out of that sleeping bag I will blast you. Be sure of that."

Terry nodded and fear clouded his face as the reality of what had happened sank in. "Wha?... Where?...Where's Muff?" he croaked as he looked anxiously around.

"Gone," Major Wickham replied. "Done a runner I think. You are all on your own. Now, take note that I have been a soldier for thirty years and I know how to use this gun and I will use it if you do the wrong thing. Do you understand?"

Terry nodded and swallowed, his gaze focusing on the twin barrels pointing at his face. Beside him his girlfriend began to stir.

Major Wickham took another step back and then glanced over his shoulder. To his relief he saw that both Capt Buchan and Capt Hamilton were also awake and watching.

Now the next part of my plan, he thought.

"Take out the key to the handcuffs and throw it to me," he ordered.

Terry shook his head. "I ain't got it. Muff has."

The girl stuck a tousled head out of the sleeping bag. "What's goin' on?" she queried.

Then she saw Major Wickham and the gun and she gasped and clutched the sleeping bag up to her chin.

"Don't do anything silly," Major Wickham warned her.

For a few moments he felt stumped as he had been counting on the handcuff keys. He looked around and saw that CSM Glenn was watching and that some of the cadets were stirring and raising their heads.

"CSM, get the axe from the bonnet of the Land Rover and take it to Capt Hamilton," Major Wickham ordered.

Turning back to the two bikies he gestured with the gun. "Take your hands out of the sleeping bags and put them where I can see them."

Reluctantly the pair did as they were told. The girl's surprise was now giving way to anger. "Where the hell's Muff?" she cried.

Terry shrugged. "Dunno. Done a flit I think."

"Gutless turd!" the girl shrieked. Glaring at Major Wickham she rubbed her eyes and patted her hair down then said, "Let us go!"

"No. The police will want to speak to you," Major Wickham replied.

"You will regret it if you don't!" the girls snarled.

Major Wickham gave a grim smile. "I think you are in no position to make threats. You are in so much legal trouble you should be busy trying to think up what you are going to tell your lawyers." Through his mind flitted the words 'phone your lawyers' and that gave him another idea. "Get out your mobile phones and pass them here."

"Haven't got one," Terry muttered. Major Wickham looked at the girl.

"No!" the girl answered.

For a few seconds Major Wickham hesitated but then his resolve was stiffened by the urgent need to call for help. Seeing that most of the cadets were now sitting watching he did some quick thinking, weighing the risks, both legal and actual. For a moment he considered getting the biggest, strongest boys to get the phone but then he shook his head.

Better to have females deal with a female, he decided. *That might limit the legal consequences.*

He called, "CUO Summers, Sgt Clarke, Sgt Whalley, get the mobile phone off this girl."

The girl, Angela, struggled to get out of the sleeping bag but the three girls ran to her and held her down. For a couple of minutes there was a real tussle, with clawing hands and swearing from Angela. But at the end of it the three girls had her held down and CUO Summers extracted a mobile phone from Angela's pocket and passed it over.

By then Capt Hamilton had untied all the OOC's legs and had used the axe to snap the chain between Capt Buchan and Lt Barker, the chain backed onto a log to give the blow strength. He passed the axe to Capt Buchan who got Lt Cavendish and Capt Hamilton to position their handcuff chain. One sharp blow and that was also severed.

Capt Hamilton came over. "I'll take the gun boss. You use the phone," he said.

Major Wickham handed over the gun and took the mobile phone. To his annoyance he found it had a security lock. Looking at the girl he said, "What's the security code, the password?"

Angela glared defiantly back and would not speak. Major Wickham stared at her in disbelief. Anger flared and he shouted, "You don't understand, do you? One of our girls has been shot by you people and she urgently needs a doctor. If I can't phone the ambulance she will die and that will be your doing."

At that Angela looked sulky but still defiant. Major Wickham was exasperated. "Do you want someone's death on your conscience?" he queried. Shaking his head, he went on: "I am sure the judge will take a dim view of it if you let a girl die by being defiant. If you co-operate it might make things easier for you when you go to court."

By then Terry was looking pasty faced with anxiety. "He's right Angie Babe," he said. "Tell him."

That got through to her. Still pouting with a sour look on her face, she told Major Wickham the PIN and he tapped it in and unlocked the phone. Quickly he tapped in the 000 to call the emergency services. As the phone rang, he glanced at his watch, noting with surprise that it was 0605.

The operator answered and he quickly asked for the police. After what seemed like a long wait, but was in reality only seconds, he was connected.

"This is Major Wickham, Officer Commanding One Thirty Army Cadet Unit. We urgently need the police and an ambulance at a place called Mingela."

The police operator answered at once. "We know about this incident sir. We have just received a call from a girl named Chloe who claims to be a cadet."

Bloody Chloe! he thought. *Thank God!*

"She is. Is our girl who was shot still alive?" he asked.

"Yes. And so is the man who was shot. The ambulances are on the way," the operator replied.

"You need to send armed police. There are at least a dozen armed bikies here. Attila's Axemen is the gang's name. They are armed and dangerous."

"We know that sir. We understand that one of your girls has been taken hostage by them," the operator replied.

"The whole company was but we are free now. We have two bikies in custody," Major Wickham replied.

"That is good sir. But does that include a girl named Jane Carson?"

Oh no! Major Wickham thought. *Not more trouble!*

Shaking with emotion he replied, "No. Jane is with Number 4 Platoon and they are not with us. I don't know where they are."

The operator answered at once, "The girl named Chloe gave us this information saying that Jane Carson was taken hostage about fifteen minutes ago."

Major Wickham was aghast. "Do they know where she is?" he asked.

"Apparently she has been taken to this place named Mingela by a bikie," the operator informed him.

This gets worse and worse! Major Wickham thought, his emotions again churning. "Did Chloe say where she was?"

"Yes. She is beside the Dotswood Road one kilometre north of the Flinders Highway junction," came the answer.

That was such good news that Major Wickham shuddered with relief. *Oh well done 4 Platoon! Well done Chloe!* he thought. Then he realised that the police operator was asking him where he was.

"We are beside the Mingela turn-off at the Flinders Highway. We have seventy cadets and six adults and also two bikies as prisoners," Major Wickham explained.

He then answered a few more questions before ending the call and turning to face the officers. They were now free and stood expectantly. They had been listening and were full of questions. Major Wickham held up his hand to quieten them and then told them what he knew.

"Chloe's just rung the police," he said.

Half a dozen people muttered Chloe's name and more questions were called. Major Wickham told them what he knew then began to give rapid orders.

"Tie these two up and guard them Lt Barker. Capt Hamilton, check the vehicles. CSM get the company seated in section lines and then get the platoon sergeants to mark their roll books. Platoon commanders, once the roll has been called take your platoons to their platoon areas and get all water bottles filled and make sure everyone has spare food in their webbing. Be ready to withdraw on foot through the bush to Number One Top Mill if ordered. Move!"

CUO Lewis put his hand up. "What about hutchies sir?" he asked.

What a stupid bloody question! Major Wickham thought.

"Just leave the gear! We must first make sure our people are safe. Things don't matter! We can come back and get them later. Now move!"

Not going to be 'Best CUO' if his judgement is that poor! he fumed.

Lt Barker called the same three girls to tie the prisoner's hand and foot while he stood guard. As he did, he called, "Boss, what do we do if any of the other bikies come back?"

That was the real conundrum, but Major Wickham was determined to keep the cadets safe. "We arrest them, and if they try to use guns then we adults fight while the cadets take cover," he answered.

Lt Barker held up the shotgun and gave a savage grin. "We will do that," he agreed.

Capt Buchan turned from watching the cadets moving into their section lines. "Are we going to withdraw to Number One Top Mill?"

Major Wickham shook his head. "Not yet. I want us close to the road so the police and ambulances can find us easily. Just be ready to do it."

"Why? What are you going to do?" Capt Buchan asked.

Major Wickham now made another hard decision. "I am going to leave you in charge while I go to the town," he said.

Capt Buchan looked aghast. "To Mingela? Why?" he queried.

"To try to persuade the bikies to let Jane go," Major Wickham answered.

There were a few seconds of silence while they all considered that and then Capt Buchan shook his head.

"Don't do it! Leave it to the police."

Major Wickham also shook his head. He was now absolutely determined. For the last 18 hours he had been feeling he had let the cadets down and not done his best and he was driven by a strong urge to atone for that.

"It is my responsibility. I have to go."

Lt Barker held up the shotgun. "We will both go and I will use this to persuade them."

"No. No guns," Major Wickham answered. He did not want to spark a violent confrontation. "I think they will see sense when they learn that the police have been called. Anyway, I am going. Do any of the vehicles work?"

Capt Hamilton nodded his head. "The Land Rover and Mel's Station Wagon are both out of fuel, but your car should be OK."

Major Wickham shook his head. "No, that Muff character has my car keys. I'll walk," he answered.

Lt Peters stepped forward. "You shouldn't go on your own! I will come with you."

"No. We don't want to give them more hostages."

But Lt Peters stood her ground and set her jaw. "I am coming. One of our girls is a hostage and she might need a female OOC when we free her."

That made sense so Major Wickham relented. "Alright. But you walk two hundred metres behind and stay under cover to watch what .. what happens." He was going to say 'what they do to me' as he was gripped by dread that he might just be shot or tortured.

Lt Cavendish thought so too as she cried, "Don't go sir! They might shoot you!"

"They might," Major Wickham replied. "But I have to go."

With that he looked at the now seated company who were listening to every word. To his surprise he noted that several of the girls were crying and he quickly looked away.

I am too emotional already! he told himself.

His eyes met Capt Buchan's. "Here, you take this mobile phone. CSM, get those rolls marked!" he snapped.

Gritting his teeth and mentally preparing himself to die he turned and began walking along the Old Highway towards Mingela.

Chapter 39

CONFRONTATION

Jane was gripped by anxiety as the truck slowed and came to a stop at the Flinders Highway junction. She had been hoping that they could just keep driving but there was a truck coming from the right so they had to pull up. As they did a man stepped out from behind the corner of the fence and held up his hand to stop. Instantly her heart skipped and began to hammer as her eyes took in that he was a bikie in full leathers, and he had a sawn–off shotgun! The bikie stepped up and shoved the gun into the old farmer's face. Then he saw Jane and his eyes lit up.

Skull-crawling, stomach-churning terror gripped her and she almost fainted with sheer funk. Somehow, she stayed conscious but her muscles felt almost paralysed. Images of Slasher flashed across her brain.

They've got me! Oh my God! she thought, dread of what might come next adding to her fear.

The bikie dragged the old farmer out. "Where did you pick her up?" he snarled.

The old farmer pointed and said, "Back up the road a bit."

"Were there any other cadets with her?"

Jane held her breath and her mind suddenly clicked into gear and began to race.

What story can I tell? How can I delay the bikies just going straight to where Chloe and the others are? she wondered.

To her surprise and relief the old farmer shook his head. "Didn't see any. Now take that damned gun outa my face and let me go."

The bikie now levelled the gun at Jane, her fear turning her stomach and bowels to water. "Where are the others girlie?" he asked.

Jane shook her head. "I don't know! I got separated in the night and I've been wandering around lost," Jane replied.

The Old Farmer intervened. "Hey! Stop pointing guns at people and let us go or I'll have the police onto you."

"Shut up pop! Just get in and drive me to town," the bikie ordered.

Reluctantly the Old Farmer climbed back in. He put the truck into gear and started driving, glancing in his rear vision mirror at the bikie who had jumped up on the tray. "Sorry Missie," he croaked.

"Thanks for not saying where my friends are?" Jane replied.

"What's going on? Who are these people?" he asked.

Jane began describing what had happened. She was in the middle of this when there was banging on the roof of the cab.

"Shut up and stop talking!" the bikie shouted.

Reluctantly they lapsed into silence, aware that the bikie could see them through the back window. The truck was driven across the highway and up the kilometre of bare hillside to where the scattered buildings of the town straggled on the either side of the railway line. After passing two houses on the left the truck bumped across the railway level crossing and was turned left into the tiny main street. On the left along the railway were a line of small trees. Between the trees and the buildings on the other side of the wide street were an expanse of bare earth, the bitumen road and more bare sand. On the right were four derelict old shops and then the old hotel. This was a low, single story structure a hundred years old with a front veranda held up by posts. Parked in front were a row of shiny motorcycles.

No-one was in sight. The bikie directed them to park on the open area on the left opposite the hotel and as soon as the vehicle came to a halt he jumped down and jerked the driver's door open.

"Get out and don't try anything stupid," he snarled while aiming the gun at them again.

Trembling with shock and fear Jane did as she was told. For a few seconds she was hidden from the bikie by the body of the truck but her rational mind told her it would be suicidal to try to run. A glance showed her a fence between her and the railway and the row of bushes and small trees growing along it gave almost no cover. With an effort of willpower, she forced her trembling muscles to function and made herself walk around the front of the truck and towards the hotel.

As she did a bikie appeared at one of the open doors along the back of the veranda. "What ya got there Al?" he called.

"Caught Old Farmer Jones here giving this girl cadet a lift Mike," Al replied. "Is Brute there?"

"Nope. I think he's off hunting them cadets," Mike replied. "Davo's here though."

"I'd better call Brute then. Ya got a phone? Mine's gone flat," Al said.

He ushered the two prisoners across the wide road to the front steps. Here he pointed. "You two stand here," he ordered. Taking the phone off the bikie named Mike he said, "Thanks Mike. Keep an eye on 'em." He then dialled a number.

As Al started talking two female bikies appeared at the door. "You coming to have yer breakfast Mike? Oh, hello! What we got here?"

Al shrugged. "Caught this old guy giving the girl a lift."

"Is she one of them?" asked a hard-faced woman of about thirty.

"Yeah, but she claims she doesn't know where the others are," Al explained. He then resumed his phone conversation.

The hard-faced female bikie gave Jane a look that caused her stomach to churn. "Slasher'll soon find your tongue," she commented.

As they spoke someone inside called out, wanting to know what was going on and there was some shouted conversation and then more people, all bikies or female bikies, appeared at the door and peered out. A couple were eating what looked like hamburgers.

Or bacon and egg rolls, Jane decided, the waft of frying food adding to the confusion of her senses and emotions.

Her stomach growled with a mixture of fear and hunger and she told herself she just wanted to faint.

More people crowded out onto the veranda and Jane and the Old Farmer were left standing on the sandy parking space in front of the hotel. Feeling terrified and utterly miserable she looked along the road to the east, towards where she knew the company were bivouacked. But there was no help in sight and she was left feeling even more dejected. The only other thing her mind noted was the tinge of pink on the undersides of some clouds away off to the east.

The sun will be up soon. Oh please God, get this over with quickly! she prayed.

Al half turned to look at Jane then said into the phone, "Nah! She's got dark hair."

Brute was hoping he'd caught Chloe, Jane reasoned. It made her fearful of what might happen to Chloe if the bikies did catch her.

Al called to her. "What's yer name girlie?"

For a moment Jane considered withholding the information but then decided that might lead to real pain so she answered, "Jane."

This was passed on to Brute and the phone conversation continued. After another minute Al ended the phone conversation and handed the phone back to Mike. "Brute said to tie 'em up and keep 'em here until he and Slasher get here," he said.

That led to some heated discussion. One of the bikies went to find some rope but others began to question what was being done. "What the hell's going on? Where's Harley? Why have you cadets taken him?" queried a big woman with a bosom so large it strained at the leather jacket she wore.

Jane took that as her cue. "Harley got shot by Brute who was going to…"

"Shut up Bitch!" screamed Al, shaking his clenched fist in her face. "Wait till Brute and Slasher get here before you start tellin' stories."

The big woman scowled. "But I wanta know!"

Al turned on her, "Shut it Trudi! We wait for Brute an' Slasher."

Trudi tried arguing with the man but he was so angry that Jane did not dare speak again. Others joined in. One bikie muttered, "This is all gunna end in tears." and another commented that it was certainly a lot of bad shit. "We should be getting out of here while we can," added a third.

Jane took that as her cue. "That's right. The police have been called and they are on their way. You will be in real trouble then."

That led to more argument and she could see that her words had hit home. But Al shook his head. "If you have phoned the police when did you do that, and where? I don't believe ya. If you have why are you going to town with this old codger?"

Mike walked over to where the Old farmer was being tied to the end post of the veranda. "Hey mister, where were you taking this girl?" he asked.

The Old Farmer didn't want to talk but a couple of threats and some jabs in the ribs loosened his tongue. "To a farmhouse down the road," he answered.

"To call the cops?"

The Old Farmer nodded and looked miserable. Jane felt very unhappy at having gotten the old man into such a situation. Al finished tying the Old Farmer to the post and then gestured to Jane.

"Stand with your back against that post girlie!" he ordered, pointing to the next post.

Jane did as she was told so that she stood facing the street and railway. But that led to another argument among the bikies and their women.

"This is crazy!" cried one woman. "This is gunna land us in deep shit. We shouldn't be doing this."

"Brute said to," was Al's response.

Another bikie, a big man in a long sleeved, pale blue shirt under his leather vest shook his head. "Brute ain't the boss yet."

"Maybe not Davo, but he probably soon will be," retorted Al.

He then quickly tied Jane's wrists behind the post. That hurt, as did the way her arms were pulled back behind her back. But she found it a relief to lean against the post as her legs were shaking so much she had trouble standing.

"Can I have a drink please," she croaked.

That led to another argument until one of the women (There were six, Jane counted) snapped, "Don't be idiots! We will be in enough trouble without adding to it by that sort of rot. Give the girl a drink!"

So a glass of water was brought by the woman with the big bosom, Trudi, and she held it while Jane greedily gulped it down, heedless of the trickles down her chin and chest.

"Thanks," Jane muttered.

The woman gave her a sympathetic look and went back inside. The bikies began to argue amongst themselves again and a few drifted back inside to finish their breakfast. Jane's stomach grumbled and she felt weak from lack of food.

Do I dare ask for some, she wondered.

After spending a few minutes summoning her courage she did but Al vetoed that. "She will talk better on an empty stomach," he asserted.

Jane sagged with exhaustion and allowed her legs to buckle. Slowly she slid down the post until she was sitting on the edge of the veranda. That was a relief and she sighed and tried to calm herself. More minutes ticked by. The bikies began to get impatient.

"Where the hell is Brute?" the one in the blue shirt, Davo, muttered.

"He and Slasher were following the cadet's tracks in the bush somewhere," answered Al. "Hang on, this might be them now."

Jane heard an approaching motorcycle and her heart rate instantly shot right up again. Craning her head forward she was able to see along the road to the right. To her partial relief she saw that it was a single motorcycle coming along the access road from the junction where the cadets had debussed.

The bikie parked his bike at the far end of the row of bikes and strolled over, taking his helmet off as he did. With a sigh of relief Jane saw that it was neither Brute nor Slasher. The bikie looked at the group and then at the two prisoners.

"What's the go? Who are these pair?" he asked.

His name was Cory and the situation was explained. Cory looked hard at Jane and then shrugged and asked, "Any chance of breakfast?"

He was directed inside and his arrival sparked another bout of debate and discussion about what to do from the people in there. This quickly became a heated argument and that cheered Jane a bit.

These people are not happy and they don't understand what's going on either, she thought.

But she could see no escape and after a few minutes she slumped down again and closed her eyes. These felt so hot and gritty that it was very little relief, but she found she was so frightened and tense that she was simply collapsing from nervous exhaustion.

At least ten more minutes dragged by. Bikies came and went from inside and the arguments continued. Jane leaned back and opened her eyes and saw that the first bars of sunlight were striking the treetops across the other side of the highway. For a while she brooded over what might be happening back at the platoon. What bothered her was not knowing if her capture had been witnessed or not.

If they didn't see us get caught, they will be relaxing thinking I have called the cops, she thought.

She glanced at the Old Farmer and he met her eyes and made a wry grimace. Jane shook her head and felt distressed.

"Sorry," she croaked.

"That's OK girlie," the Old Farmer replied.

"Shut up!" snarled Al, waving his fist at them.

They did and more minutes dragged by. One of the female bikies queried having the prisoners tied up where passing cars might see them, but she was told to mind her own business and shouted down. It was very obvious to Jane that the bikie gang were not a happy band and were not united.

They are wondering what is going on too, she decided.

"Quarter past six! Where the hell are Brute and Slasher?" muttered Davo.

As though in answer the sound of motorcycles came from off to the east again and Jane saw two bikes come into view around the bend near where the company was bivouacked. Her heart rate again shot up and she felt her chest tighten in apprehension.

Oh, I hope it isn't Brute or Slasher, she thought.

But it was. The pair parked their bikes at the far end of the row and placed their helmets on them. Grim-faced and angry they came striding towards her. Jane noted that Slasher's face was badly bruised and he had two really black eyes. She felt her heart skip several beats and her stomach turned over with dread. She nerved herself to face whatever she might have to endure. As the two bikies came to a halt in front of her the people inside began to crowd out onto the veranda.

"What have we got?" Brute snarled.

Al explained again what had happened. Brute leaned close to Jane's face. "So where are the others girlie?" he snarled.

"I don't know," Jane whispered. She was so frightened she had trouble making her constricted dry throat function.

"Why were you on your own?" Brute insisted.

"I got lost during the night. I went to sleep in the grass and the others got up and kept walking and didn't wake me. When I woke up I didn't know which way they had gone," Jane lied.

To add to her act she decided to pretend to be even more upset and cry. And then she wasn't acting at all. Real tears of distress streamed down her face and she sobbed and sniffled until Brute snarled at her.

"Get on with it or I'll give yer somethin' ter cry about!" he snapped.

Jane sniffled and stifled her sobs. "So I walked around and came to the road. Then I saw this truck driving past and flagged it down. This nice man gave me a lift."

Slasher suddenly leaned closer. "You! You're the bitch who threw sand in my eyes the first time!" he cried angrily.

I did too! Jane thought, getting a tiny spurt of malicious satisfaction by seeing the scabs of dried blood and the black, dark blue and greeny-yellow bruises on his battered face.

Something of this must have registered in her eyes as his face went even darker. Before Jane could react, Slasher grabbed her shirt front and hauled her roughly to her feet. Slamming her back against the post he shouted in her face.

"Tell us the truth kid! Where are the others?"

"I don't know," Jane insisted, even though she was so frightened she was on the edge of fainting. Her legs felt so weak she just wanted to slide back down.

Slasher reached behind his back and into view flashed the blade of a wicked looking stainless-steel hunting knife. It was held in front of her face and she quailed and whimpered with fear.

"Tell me!" he snarled.

"I... I don't know," Jane repeated, her trembling now so violent she had trouble staying on her feet.

"I'll make you talk," Slasher warned, placing the blade of the knife flat on Jane's cheek below her left eye. The metal was cold and as the terror flooded through her she almost vomited with fear.

At that some of the female bikies cried out and began to object but Slasher just ignored them. He gave a leering grin. Then he turned the blade and placed the point just below her eye. It pricked the skin and the grin became positively evil. Jane gasped and did not dare move, terrified of losing her eye. She felt the cold metal on her skin and fear flooded through her so forcefully she almost blacked out

Slasher lifted the point so that it was right in front of her eye. "Now talk sweetie or I cut ya," he snarled.

At that the big woman pushed forward between Jane and Slasher and grabbed his arm.

"Stop that!" she shouted. "She's only a girl. Don't you dare carry out any of your vile threats."

Slasher reacted angrily, wrenching his arm free and waving the knife in the woman's face. "Stay outa this Trudi! I am going to get the truth outa this little bitch. She owes me," he snarled.

But Trudi stood her ground, fists on hips. Two other women came and stood either side of her, standing between Slasher and Jane. Trudi shook her head.

"You ain't gunna cut her up! She's just a kid. How could you even think of mutilating a young girl, you animal!"

"I'll cut you up Trudi, now get outa my way!" Slasher shouted.

But still Trudi blocked his moves and the hard-faced one also closed in. "Stop your disgusting nonsense Slasher! We are in enough trouble already without you harming a little girl," she shouted.

"She don't look so little to me," Slasher retorted. "Now get outa my way Hot Throttle!"

But Hot Throttle didn't. She shook her head and said, "You are deviate Slasher! Leave her alone. She's only a kid."

She was joined by a fourth person: Davo. "Back off Slasher. Let her talk and don't do anything stupid that's gunna get us into even more trouble with the law."

So did some of the others, including a tall bikie female who called, "We gotta find Harley and settle things with him."

Slasher nodded vigorously. "You chicks stay outa this!" he shouted angrily. He looked so furious that Jane quailed before his rage and feared he would just shove the women aside and slash her.

Trudi shouted back. "We need to find Harley!" she screamed.

"And we need to find out what the hell is going on," Hot Throttle added.

Jane saw an opening but knew it could spark an attack by Slasher, so she hesitated for a moment. The intervention of the women had given her a pulse of hope, but she was scared. The memory of that point of the knife on her cheek right under the left eye caused her to shudder in fear. But every fibre of her body was now cringing in anticipation of being cut and the ghastly horror of it swamped her senses.

Slasher glared at the women, but he lowered the knife. "Ok," he said to the women. Then he looked at Jane. "Now tell us the truth little girl," he whispered in a silky, threatening tone.

That voice sent shivers through Jane, but it was the evident enjoyment the man was getting that really chilled her. The sheer awfulness of being mutilated and slashed made her tremble and she tried to brace herself to endure.

I mustn't let Chloe and the others down, she told herself.

"I don't know where they are!" Jane sobbed. She knew her resistance was nearing an end and the thought of being mutilated was more than she could bear.

"You are lying!" Slasher shouted, waving the knife. Tell the truth or I will slice you up!"

It was Hot Throttle who came to her aid. "Stop it! For God's sake

Slasher! We will be in enough legal trouble over abducting children without adding sexual assault charges to it. Leave her alone you bloody pervert!"

Slasher scowled at her but Brute nodded and reached forward to pull Slasher back. "Hot Throttle's right Slasher. Let's question this old guy."

Reluctantly Slasher put the knife away, giving Jane a scowling leer as he did. Sneering he stepped back and studied her lasciviously before following Brute across to where the obviously appalled Old Farmer was watching. Jane slumped against the post but found her eyes drawn to the drama beside her, even as the relief flooded through her at her temporary reprieve.

Brute faced the Old Farmer. "Where are the other cadets Old Man?" he snarled.

The Old Farmer, who had watched with horror as Jane was being interrogated now stood straight up and pressed his lips together. When he did not answer Brute shouted at him, "Talk Dumb Bum!"

Still the Old Farmer remained defiantly silent. Brute suddenly lost his temper and lashed out, punching the Old Farmer in the face. Jane saw his head bounce back against the post he was lashed to and he went instantly limp.

Slasher strode over and grabbed the Old Farmer and tried to pull him upright. But he just slumped down again. "You've knocked him out Brute," he commented.

Brute swore but the bikie girl with the hard face stepped across. "You bloody idiots! You might have killed him."

That was a sickening thought and sent a wave of concern through the group. Two of the female bikies moved to check the unconscious Old Farmer and they were joined by a male bikie and by a lady who pushed through from inside the hotel.

"Oh poor Old Mister Pugh!" she cried. "What have you done?"

Brute looked worried but then shook his head. "Untie the silly old bastard and take him inside," he snarled. The group began to do that.

"Time we got out of here!" cried the bikie who had arrived a few minutes before.

Brute turned on the man. "Like hell! Hey, what are you doin' here Cory? You are supposed to be watching that railway overpass. Who's doing that now?"

Cory became all defensive. "I came to have some bloody breakfast. I bin standin' there all bloody afternoon and all bloody night! Anyway, who are you to give the orders? You ain't the boss, not yet."

"That's right," Davo agreed.

Brute scowled at him. "Maybe we should put it to the vote?" he suggested.

Davo shook his head. "Not until Harley's here," he said firmly.

Brute scowled again and turned back to shake a fist in Cory's face. "If those cadets get away you'll be sorry," he threatened.

"I still reckon we should be leaving," Davo added.

Slasher and Brute both shook their heads. "No!" shouted Brute. "We gotta get that money to the right people and find out what Harley's up to." With that he walked over to Jane again. "Where are they girl? Where's Harley?"

Jane had recovered a bit and managed to summon the courage to defy him. Shaking her head she pressed her lips tightly together.

That enraged Brute and he slapped her hard. Then Slasher stepped closer and elbowed Brute aside. "I'll make her talk Brute," he said, his knife coming out again and his leering eyes feasting on Jane's bosom.

Jane felt extraordinarily vulnerable, wincingly conscious of just how soft and delicate her body was. She saw the knife blade come up, glinting in the early morning sun and she sobbed and tried to pull away. The point of the blade was placed on her left breast.

"Now tell us everything," Slasher whispered, plainly enjoying himself.

Trudi again pushed in. "Stop it Slasher!" she shouted but Slasher just pushed her away and Brute blocked the other women.

When Jane did not answer Slasher again waved the knife in front of her face and snarled, "Talk you little slut or I'll rape ya!"

"Stop that!" shouted a voice.

Major Wickham! Jane thought, her terrified mind sorting through the myriad of emotions and fears that were swirling through her mind. She jerked back and looked to her right.

It was. Major Wickham stood a few paces away in the middle of the main street. He had obviously walked along it from the bivouac. But Jane realised that she was only recognizing him by his stance, build and voice as his whole face was a mass of black and purple bruises.

Oh my God! Major's been bashed! she thought.

Major Wickham placed his fists on his hips and called again, "Leave her alone! Now get out of here. The police have been called and will be here soon."

Oh thank God! Jane thought. *Saved!*

Chapter 40

HIGH NOON AT DAYBREAK

Major Wickham stood in the main street outside the hotel and stared at the scene in horror. He had seen Slasher wave the knife point near Jane's face and felt a spurt of rage mixed with fear. Appalled at the thought of a girl's beauty being mutilated he shouted again for the bikies to stop.

He had been crawling under the fence beside the access road when Brute and Slasher had ridden past but they had not heard his shouts to stop. Fearful of what they might do to Jane when they got to the township, he had pushed his tired and battered body as fast as he could. And his worst fears had looked to be happening as he had hurried past the first house on the edge of town.

All the way on that leaden walk he had been wracking his brains for the right combination of words to persuade the bikies to end the situation but he now found himself so upset and angry he forgot most of his carefully reasoned arguments.

Bracing himself and gathering his thoughts to try to find the compelling words he licked his dry lips. Through eyes made blurry by thirst and the beatings he confronted the people.

Seven bikies and five females, he counted.

Three of the males were standing in front of the hotel facing Jane: Slasher and Brute and the man named Davo. Next to them was a tall, hard-faced female bikie. Two other bikie females stood beside Jane The others stood clustered on the veranda behind her.

At his words they all spun round to stare at him, some surprised and others deeply worried. In an attempt to retain the initiative Major Wickham called out again.

"We have phoned the police. They will be here any minute now. If I was you I would get going while I could. Now let her go and clear out."

The words obviously had an impact as several bikies looked even more worried and a couple moved as though they were going to do what he said. But Brute swung to face him from 20 paces away and scowled.

"No! Nobody leaves till we have Harley!" he shouted. From behind his back he pulled an automatic pistol which he aimed at Major Wickham.

Major Wickham braced himself. For the whole of that long walk he had been preparing himself for this but even so he felt the flood of mortal terror which weakened his muscles and his resolve. But he had faced death before and was very determined. Licking lips that had suddenly gone dry he studied Brute. He noted that the gun was held by a shaking hand.

This guy is really frightened. He is desperate, he thought.

That bothered him as he wondered what possible argument might persuade him to give up or go without any further violence.

Brute steadied himself. "Shut up and put your hands up Fat man!" he shouted. "We aren't going until we have Harley. Where is he?"

With a deliberate effort of willpower Major Wickham ignored the order to put up his hands. "I don't know," he lied. "I have been your prisoner until a few minutes ago."

That shook Brute. "What? How? How did you get away?" he cried.

"Your man Muff vanished in the night and Terry and his girlfriend Angela went to sleep so we disarmed them and took his gun," Major Wickham answered. "So we have Terry and his girlfriend prisoner and we are now armed."

"Let them go!" Brute shouted.

Major Wickham shook his head. His eyes shifted to Jane who stared at him with hope. "Let Jane go and we will let your people go," he countered.

Brute looked anxious and chewed his lip. But it was Slasher who spoke. He stepped out and waved his knife, the blade glinting in the morning sun.

"No way! We have to get Harley. Don't trade Brute. Terry's just a useless prick and they are welcome to that slut Angela."

This comment drew hisses and gasps from the gang, particularly from the female members.

This gang isn't united, Major Wickham thought. *If I can come up with the right argument they might disintegrate.* But his priority was to save Jane and he glanced at her again.

"The police will get you anyway," he said. "So save yourselves from more prison time by stopping. Let Jane go."

Once again Brute looked as though he might agree but Slasher made several furious slashing motions with his knife.

"No! No chance! We either get Harley or we are done for Brute. Don't give in," he screamed.

This guy is on the edge! Major Wickham thought fearfully.

He could see that Brute was also under great stress. His face had gone white and he was perspiring and trembling. Not wanting to push the men into extreme actions Major Wickham shook his head.

"Save yourselves," he said in a pleading tone.

But that sparked Slasher to act. He turned and grabbed Jane and thrust the knife point against her throat. "No! You tell us where Harley is or she gets sliced up."

Major Wickham was appalled. He shook his head but stood his ground. *What can I say? How can I persuade them?* he fretted.

"I told you, I don't know where 4 Platoon or Harley are. I only know what you do from overhearing bits on your radios. For God's sake, she's just a young girl. Don't hurt her," he pleaded.

Brute looked over his right shoulder. "Mike, Al, grab this bastard and tie him to that post. I got another idea," he ordered.

Major Wickham let out a loud sigh and slumped in defeat. He had hoped that reason might prevail but now accepted that it wouldn't. He made no attempt to resist the two bikies who came and hustled him over against the veranda post next along from Jane. She began to squirm and cry out but was slapped by Slasher.

"Shut up slut or you'll get it!" he threatened.

A rope was found and Major Wickham had his hands roughly tied around the post behind his back. Slasher then stepped over and waved the knife under his nose.

"Now Major Fatman, how will it be if I just rape young Janie while you watch?" he hissed in a silky tone that made Major Wickham's flesh crawl.

Through his mind raced all the options but then he decided that he must take a calculated risk and hope the police would arrive before the bikies could act. He opened his mouth to speak but Jane beat him to it.

"Rape me as much as you like but I won't tell!" she cried.

"You will if I cut yer tits off!" Slasher snarled.

That threat drew more gasps and hisses from the gang and several of the female bikies cried out in protest. One with huge breasts which strained at her leather jacket stepped forward. "You will not! Don't you dare!" she screamed.

Slasher waved the knife in her face. "Shut up Trudi! You watch out or you'll get yours!" he snarled.

But then the tall, hard-faced woman screamed at him and other women joined in, all telling him to leave Jane alone. Slasher looked angry and made slicing motions with his blade.

"You molls stay out of this or I'll cut you too!" he added.

There was a tense moment of silence and Major Wickham found he was holding his breath and clenching his bound fists. Then a crafty look crossed Slasher's face and he gave an evil grin.

"Nah! I got a better idea!" he said with a chuckle. He turned and walked over to Major Wickham, who cringed in fear as Slasher approached.

Slasher placed the knife point against Major Wickham's large stomach. "If Janie Babe won't talk I will cut your nuts off major. And then I will slice you open up this big, fat gut."

To emphasize his point he stabbed the knife in suddenly. The point penetrated Major Wickham's shirt and then his skin and he felt a stab of agony as well as a flood of pure terror. He braced himself to die. Involuntarily he gasped and then clenched his teeth together in defiance.

Jane also gasped and then cried out. "Stop! I'll tell you," she said, her voice cracking with desperation.

*****

Jane had been watching with horror, misery flooding her very soul and now she resolve to act. She gritted her teeth.

I must save the major, she resolved.

And a plan had come to her. "I think I know where 4 Platoon has gone," she cried.

Slasher took his knife away from the major's stomach and turned to face her. Jane noted blood staining the major's shirt front and she blanched.

That Slasher is a maniac, she thought, faltering in her resolve. But having started she realised she must go on.

Slasher waved the knife at her. "So tell us Janie Babe," he demanded.

For a moment Jane could not speak as her throat was so dry and choked up with emotion. With an effort she swallowed and then nodded.

"I... We... Last night when it got dark, we split up. We were still down near where you shot Harley," she lied. She was making her story up as she went and the effort brought her out in beads of perspiration. Licking her upper lip, she continued: "We split into four groups. You caught some of them, I think."

She saw Brute nod and that encouraged her to keep going. *I must include enough of the facts to make it plausible,* she told herself.

"Anyway, my group came up a big gully to the powerline. We saw you people at the gate on the highway so we hid until it got dark. Then we made our way to a cattle trough to get some water as we had cadets starting to get sick with heat exhaustion. We had a drink and refilled our water bottles. That's when you started torturing that poor girl."

Once again she saw Brute nod and Slasher did as well. The two men exchanged quick glances. Jane licked her lips and went on.

"We crossed the railway in the dark. That took hours because there is this huge cutting and it seemed to go on for ever. Anyway, we did get across and it was midnight by then. We had a rest and we all fell asleep. When I woke up I found that the others had gone. I was so scared! For a while I just sat there hoping that they might come back, but they didn't. So when it started to get light I started walking and that's when I came to the road."

"Which way did the rest of your group go?" Brute queried.

"They were going to make for this town here but when we saw you riding up and down along the highway it was decided to go north to look for a station homestead or farm," Jane explained.

"Why didn't you go north to try to catch them up?" Slasher asked.

"Because I don't have a compass and it was dark," Jane answered.

She was starting to feel a bit more confident and her mind raced to make up more believable tales. Her fervent desire was to send the bikies in the opposite direction to her friend. She was also hoping that she could talk long enough to give the police time to arrive.

Slasher looked troubled. "So where are the main group, I mean Harley and this Chloe?"

"They went the other way," Jane answered. "It was too hard to carry the stretchers up over those hills so they took them downhill."

"Downhill! Which way is that?" Brute queried, his face clouded with worry.

"Across the railway down at the bottom of the range," Jane replied. She gestured to the east with her head.

Slasher looked aghast. "Were those two who lit the fire last night with them?"

Jane nodded. "They were and, as I understand the plan, they were to be left to act as decoys while the main group got away," she said. She saw worried looks on the men's face and that cheered her and encouraged her to keep talking.

Brute looked appalled. "That means they might be anywhere down there in all that bush!" he cried.

Slasher nodded. "Making for a homestead to call the cops," he added.

Brute reached into his pocket to pull out his now very crumpled and torn map. Opening it he studied it with almost feverish intensity. "Where is the nearest homestead?" he queried.

Slasher moved to join him and they both studied the map. Brute broke into a sweat and then shook his head. "I can't see one marked." He turned to Jane. "Where is the nearest homestead? Tell me!" he shrieked.

Jane opened her mouth to answer but Major Wickham beat her to it. "It is the Maidavale Station homestead. It's on this side of the highway down at the bottom of the range," he said.

"Here it is!" Brute cried, his forefinger jabbing at the map. "Maidavale."

Slasher looked and frowned. "But she just said they were the other side of the railway. Is there a homestead there as well?"

Jane didn't know and shrugged. Again Major Wickham answered. "Yes, 'Square Post' it's called. The homestead turnoff is a few hundred metres this side of the Haughton River Bridge. It's not on that map."

Brute swore. "Christ! What will we do? How will we catch Harley there?"

Slasher also swore. Then he bit his lip and waved his knife around. "We obviously send people to both places and if that cadet platoon turns up we go there and get Harley."

Brute nodded and looked at his gang. "Who wants to go?" he said.

But before any could answer Davo pointed along the street to Jane's left. "Look!" he cried.

Jane also looked and then gasped. A mixture of anxiety and relief flooded through her.

Walking towards them in the middle of the main street about 50 paces away was Chloe. She had no hat on and had obviously just walked into view across the railway level crossing at the west side of the town. Her approach had not been noticed because of the drama at the hotel.

Jane stared at Chloe and was filled with a mixture of worry and admiration. The morning sun shone full on her and she appeared to glow with a golden aura. Her blonde hair shimmered. But to Jane's concern Chloe was not carrying a weapon and was quite alone.

Why is she here? What does she think she is doing? she worried.

Seeing that she was at last observed Chloe came to a halt and stood with hands on hips. "Let Jane go!" she shouted.

Brute stepped a couple of paces towards her. "Who are you?" he bellowed.

"Chloe," Chloe replied. From among the assembled gang there were gasps of surprise mingled with the name 'Chloe'. It was apparent to Jane that Chloe was now a person the bikies both feared and respected.

Slasher swore and glared at Chloe. "She's the bitch who hit me!" he snarled.

Twice! Jane thought, relishing the memory even among her fear. She watched anxiously as Slasher's hands clenched and unclenched and saw that the knife was held low. *He's itching to use that,* she thought.

"What do you want?" Brute queried.

"I want you to let Jane go," Chloe answered calmly.

"Where's Harley?" Brute replied.

"He's safe, and he's alive, even though you shot him in the back three times," Chloe retorted. "Now let Jane go and start running because we have called the cops and they are on their way."

Brute swore and ground his teeth in fury. He raised his pistol and aimed it. To Jane's dismay Chloe did not move.

Brute shouted angrily, "I should just kill you bitch!"

Chloe curled her lip. "Not from that range you won't. You're not that good a shot. You didn't get me last time and I got you. So watch out!"

Bang!

Jane screamed and so did several others as Brute's pistol cracked. She saw the puff of smoke at the muzzle and then the gun and hand jerk upwards. Filled with concern for her friend Jane looked towards Chloe and saw to her amazement that Chloe was still standing and was still curling her lip in contempt.

"I told you so!" she retorted in a jeering tone. Then she pointed at Brute. "You people don't want to trust this guy. He is a liar and a coward. We saw him and Slasher shoot Peewee and Harley in the back yesterday and I'll bet he hasn't been telling you the truth. He just wants to be the boss and wants Harley dead."

"Lies!" Brute screamed and he levelled the pistol again. To Jane's horror Chloe again stood defiant. At that moment Davo called loudly. "Stop it Brute! Don't shoot! I'm the Vice President and I'm giving an order."

To Jane's intense relief Brute held his fire but she was filled with apprehension as she could see his face working with fear and rage and his whole body was shaking.

Chloe is taking a terrible risk, she thought. *She is so brave, and such a good friend!*

That notion was reinforced when Chloe called, "Let Jane and the major go. You can have me as a hostage instead."

"Good idea! Come here," Brute answered, lowering his gun.

"Not till you let Jane and the major go."

Brute scowled and thought hard and then turned. "Untie the major," he ordered. He turned back to face Chloe. "We will let Jane go when you come here."

Chloe nodded and stood while Major Wickham was untied. Then she started walking towards them. Jane was horrified.

"Chloe! Chloe don't! Stay away! Don't trust them! They will have both of us then." she cried.

At that Slasher whirled around and placed his knife point near her face. "Shut up you!"

Jane was so scared she closed her mouth, but her whole being now agitated from extreme anxiety.

"I don't trust them," Chloe called back, her face filled with contempt as she looked at Brute.

Slasher turned and called to Brute. "Shoot her Brute!" he called.

But Davo put out a hand to restrain Brute. "Wait a minute! We want to hear what she has to say," he said.

Slasher was furious. He mouthed obscenities and appeared to dance with rage. "Brute! Don't trust her either. She's got a gun. Watch out she doesn't pull it out when she gets close. She winged you last time. She might plug you this time."

Brute nodded and a look of indecision crossed his face. "Yeah, you're right. Stop there Chloe and get rid of yer gun," he ordered.

"I haven't got it. Harley has it," Chloe replied.

"Show me! Turn around and pull up yer shirt," Brute ordered.

Chloe did so. As she exposed her bare midriff Slasher called, "Make her take that shirt off Brute. She might be hiding a weapon under it."

There was a snigger from Cory and he cried, "Looks like she's hiding a coupl'a big weapons under it!"

"Shut up Cory!" snapped Trudi.

But Brute agreed and called to Chloe to take off her top. Chloe shrugged and then stood there about 30 paces away and slowly unbuttoned her shirt and shrugged it off. Under it she wore a bikini top and once again Jane was struck by just how shapely and attractive Chloe was. That usual mixture of envy and admiration filled her.

The sight drew leering looks and lewd comments from the bikies, but Chloe wasn't in the mood. "Let Jane go," she called. "And start running. Don't you trust Brute you people. He's a liar."

"You're the liar!" Brute shouted back.

Chloe gave a grunt of derision. "We can produce a whole platoon of witnesses, so it's not even your word against mine!" she retorted. "Now let Jane go and I will be your hostage."

Brute swore and looked furiously around and Jane was appalled by the change in him. His face went from red to white and he began muttering to himself.

"It's not true!" he cried at the gang. "Harley took the drugs and kept the money and shot at us when we turned up."

Chloe jeered and waved her shirt towards him. "We saw you shoot Peewee in the back of the head after he'd been gunned down by you. And you took the money and the drugs. I saw you put them in the saddle bag of your motorbike."

"Lies!" Brute screamed.

Davo stepped up beside him. "Easy to check. Al, go and look in Brute's saddlebags," he ordered.

At that Brute roared with rage and flung up the gun.

Bang!

Missed! Jane noted, even as she screamed for Chloe to run.

Brute tore free of Davo's restraining hand and began to run towards her. His gun came up.

This time Chloe moved. With surprising speed and dexterity she threw herself sideways as Brute fired.

Bang! Bang!

Again he missed and Chloe kept rolling and ended on her feet. Then she fled. Jane was appalled.

Oh, how can she possibly escape! she thought, noting that there was almost nowhere for Chloe to hide or take cover.

In all directions there were about 25 metres of open ground and the direct line of escape was directly away along the main street.

But Chloe was game and she could run. And as she ran she jinked. Twice more Brute fired but each shot went wide. Then Brute began chasing her, firing as he ran. Jane even saw a spurt of sand flung up well to one side of Chloe. But it seemed like Chloe was done for. The distance to any sort of cover was just too far. Jane let out a wail of despair.

At that moment a motorcycle ridden by a large bikie came roaring across the railway level crossing 50 metres in front of Chloe and Jane felt her despair deepen.

Oh no! She is trapped, she thought. But then she noted that the bikie had a bandage around his head.

"Harley!" she gasped.

It was. Harley swung the bike left onto the main street and headed straight for Chloe. Chloe saw him and skidded to a stop then sprang sideways. This probably saved her life as Brute stopped and fired again, but missed.

Harley gunned the motorcycle to close the range and then suddenly braked and slewed it sideways to come to a skidding standstill only ten metres from an astonished Brute, who stood gaping at him.

"Here I am you treacherous bastard!" Harley shouted. "Now try to kill me!"

With that he reached behind his back and when his hand reappeared it had a pistol in it. Brute's eyes goggled and he gasped and then raised his own gun.

Bang! Blam!

Both guns went off at almost the same moment. To her horror Jane saw Harley jerk back and then bike and man toppled sideways away from her. Harley went sprawling on the bitumen. But Brute had also been hit and he just dropped where he was.

For a few seconds nobody moved as the reality of what they had seen sank in. Then Trudi let out a cry of 'Harley!' and ran to where he lay. So did Chloe.

But Slasher also moved. "Bitch!" he shouted, running along the street towards Chloe, the knife glittering in his right-hand.

Jane was appalled. Chloe was looking towards Harley and had not seen this.

"Chloe! Chloe, watch out!" she screamed.

Desperate to save her friend she jerked and strained at the rope binding her wrists. Chloe heard her and looked around. But by then Slasher had covered half the distance. To Jane's dismay Chloe turned to face him instead of running away.

"Oh, Chloe run!" she screamed.

But Chloe didn't. Instead she began wrapping her shirt around her left forearm and then started dancing sideways. Slasher charged straight at her but she leapt sideways and avoided his first stabbing lunge. He swore and slashed at her several times but she danced quickly on the tips of her toes and managed to avoid these as well.

At that moment Jane was distracted by someone grabbing at her from behind and then by hands wrenching at the bindings behind her. A glance showed it to be the hard-faced woman: Hot Throttle. Hot Throttle leaned forward and hissed at her. "Get going girl. Run! Get out of here!"

Jane felt the rope pulled off her wrists and she almost fell. But her eyes were again riveted on the fight 50 paces along the street. Her horrified gaze noted that Chloe still had not run away and was still trying to avoid Slasher's lunges and swipes. Slasher appeared to be beside himself with rage and was screaming obscenities and shouting that Chloe owed him and was going to get it.

Jane saw the knife blade glitter in the sunlight as it swept around and she gasped with horror. But again Chloe managed to avoid the slicing blow and this time her own left arm shot out and she flung her shirt out so that it tangled around Slasher's knife and wrist.

Slasher bellowed with rage and wrenched the shirt hard to try to pull it from Chloe's grasp. She managed to keep a grip but was pulled off balance as he did. Jane saw that Chloe had tried to use the opportunity to kick Slasher in the nuts but the sudden jerk spoiled her attempt, her boot connecting with his thigh instead. That drew another bellow and more obscenities. But to Jane's horror she saw Chloe go sprawling on the sand beside the bitumen.

I must help her, Jane thought. She began racing towards her, heart in mouth at the worry she might be too late.

Slasher sprang across and lunged down at Chloe. In the nick of time Chloe rolled aside and managed to avoid the blow. Jane heard the blade strike the bitumen and Slasher swore loudly again. He untangled the shirt from his knife and dragged at the shirt but Chloe, still lying on her back, let it go. Slasher staggered back a couple of paces before jumping forward to attack again. Chloe met the assault with her boots, suddenly hunching and then lashing out with both boots. Jane thought her target was again Slasher's nuts but instead one of Chloe's boots connected with Slasher's lower left leg and he went reeling back, his blow striking down to snag in the cloth of Chloe's lower right trouser leg.

Slasher wrenched the knife free and this time he grabbed at Chloe's flailing right leg and held her tight as she squirmed violently.

I'm going to be too late! Jane thought.

And she nearly was too late. Through eyes misted with desperate anxiety she saw Slasher's arm go up preparatory to striking and at that she screamed and then ran full tilt into his back. The impact flung Slasher forward and down onto the bitumen, Jane landing in a tumble of arms and legs on top of him. To her horror and disgust she felt his sweaty flesh and smelt his foul odour and almost paralysing fear flooded through her.

Get away! Roll away! her terrified mind screamed.

With a convulsive jerk she broke free of the hand that clutched at her and rolled away. She ended up on the bitumen beside Brute. Jane's eyes noted the hole in the front of his forehead and the big pool of blood spreading from under his skull onto the roadway and she knew instantly that he was dead. But dead bodies were the least of her worries. Slasher was scrambling to his feet close beside her!

Gasping for breath Jane sprang to her feet and turned to face him. To her surprise she saw that his eyes were not on her. They were focused on the road near his feet. Then she understood. When she had cannoned into him he had dropped his knife. To her horror she saw that he was reaching down for it, and so was Chloe, who lay sprawled on the bitumen beside him! Jane saw his clawing hand close over it a fraction of a second before Chloe could reach it. Chloe's grasping fingers just failed to get to the knife in time. Slasher cried out in triumph and reached down to grab Chloe's hair while hefting the knife to a blade downwards striking position.

"Take this you bitch!" he screamed.

Jane screamed too, knowing she would be too late even as she sprang towards Slasher in a desperate attempt to spoil the strike.

Bang! Bang!

Right in front of Jane's eyes she saw Slasher jerk backwards and his upraised arm stayed up. Then his fingers twitched open in a spasm of jerky movements and the knife fell from them. His right-hand come down to his chest and Jane saw a look of astonishment on his face. Then a light seem to go out in his eyes and he suddenly crumpled face downwards on the road.

For a few moments Jane could not work out who had fired the shots but then she glanced to her left and saw that Harley was lying on the road and was holding a smoking pistol. He lay on his side, propped up by one elbow and his left leg appeared to be still under the motorbike.

"Got the mongrel!" he muttered. Then he groaned and lay back down. "Get this bloody bike off me!" he called.

He's alive! Jane thought.

She had believed him dead. But then her focus went back to Chloe and she knelt to hold her. "You OK Babe?" she queried.

Chloe nodded and rolled onto her hands and knees. "Yeah. Thanks Janie Babe. You saved my life. Now help me up please."

Jane did and then the two girls embraced. For a quite a few seconds Jane just stood there hugging her friend and trembling with reaction. Only as she began to calm a little did her eyes take in the curious picture of bikies and their girlfriends either moving toward them or hurrying away. She noted several bikies running towards motorbikes or leaping astride them and riding quickly away.

People seemed to be moving hurriedly in all directions including, she noted, Major Wickham who was now free and hurrying towards them.

Chloe shuddered and Jane hugged and patted her. "You were magnificent Chlo Babe," she murmured.

"Thanks," Chloe muttered. But then she stiffened and let her go. "Harley!" she cried.

Jane turned to look as Chloe hurried to where the bikie woman with the big breasts and a couple of other bikies were lifting the motorcycle off Harley. As she followed Chloe Jane saw her and the woman both kneel on either side of Harley. Chloe leaned over with concern all over her face.

"Where did he hit you Harley?" she asked.

Harley shook his head. "He didn't. My wounded leg just gave way and I fell over," he muttered. Then his eyes roved across Chloe's almost bare front and he grinned and shook his head in wonder. "Geez Chloe, you're a nice looking girl!"

At that Trudi gave him a playful slap and leaned over him as well. "Hey! I'm your woman remember!" she cried.

"Sorry!" Harley muttered, but he grinned and murmured, "And I love ya Trudi."

"Then don't say rude things to young girls!" Trudi snapped, relief giving an edge to her tongue. She then turned to Chloe and shook her head. "Sorry luv. Bikies aren't very politically correct. Hope he didn't offend you."

Chloe grinned. "His manners need improving but his eyesight's good," she quipped, glancing down at herself as she did.

Harley grinned. "How old are ya Chlo Babe?" he queried.

"Only fourteen," Chloe answered.

Trudi hit at Harley's chest. "Hey! Stop flirting! She's too young for you!" she cried. Trudi turned and gave Chloe what Jane interpreted as a warning: 'keep-your-claws-off-him, he's-mine' look and then smiled.

"I'm Trudi. Thanks for saving him," she said.

"I'm Chloe," Chloe replied. "That's OK. He looks worth saving, even though he's so ugly."

"Hey!" Harley cried in mock hurt.

Trudi and Chloe both giggled, the release of tension making their laughter brittle and a little hysterical. At that moment the tension was broken by Al crying loudly, "Hey! That's my bloody bike you've crashed Harley!"

Jane barely heard him. What took her attention was Major Wickham leaning forward to drape Chloe's shirt over her back.

Then movement along the street towards the railway level crossing caught her eye and she sucked her breath in and then sobbed with relief. Two police cars had skidded to a stop and armed police in black uniforms and wearing helmets and webbing were spilling out to aim weapons at them.

"Now we really are saved," she muttered.

Chapter 41

CONSEQUENCES

When Major Wickham saw Chloe standing alone in the middle of the road and enveloped by a golden aura he had goggled with disbelief and dismay. Her subsequent words and offers had filled him with admiration and respect.

She is risking her life to save her friend! he had thought in wonder.

But he was also almost overwhelmed with apprehension, fearing the bikie's would take revenge. And when they tried to he was even more dismayed.

When Chloe just stood and took Brute's fire he was sick with worry but also filled with admiration for her courage. He knew it was an image that he would remember for the rest of his life. By then he had been untied and he urgently wanted to move to try to take sort of control of a situation that looked to him to be rapidly spiralling downwards. To his intense frustration he found he couldn't. Cramps and a bout of dizziness caused him to keep holding the post while the shooting took place. When Harley had appeared and he and Brute had exchanged shots Major Wickham was so surprised and shocked that he did not know whether to cheer or cry out with concern.

But his heart went into his mouth when Slasher went for Chloe with the knife. To his even greater dismay Major Wickham saw Jane run to join in. Tormented by his weak legs and cramps he had stumbled and staggered towards them, desperately hoping to prevent a tragedy but well aware that he would not fare well in a knife fight with a clearly enraged Slasher. When Jane knocked Slasher down he had cheered but still been 30 paces away. He was still too far off to help when Harley ended the fight with the fatal shots.

Through eyes blurred by fatigue, overexertion and emotion Major Wickham saw Jane help Chloe to her feet and he sighed with relief that she had not been cut. Watching Jane and Chloe embrace slowed him to a hobble but his gaze could not helping flick to Chloe's splendid body as she turned to go to Harley. Ashamed of himself and conscious of his duty he scooped up her shirt from the bitumen and hurried over to drape it over Chloe's bare back.

He was just in time to overhear the exchange between Chloe, Harley and Trudi and that also surprised, and annoyed him.

Bloody Chloe! he thought. *She is flirting! Bloody hell, she is magnificent!*

Hotly conscious of his relief and attraction to her he looked away and found himself staring at Jane. To his relief she also looked uninjured and she even managed a weak grin. He was about to speak when he heard vehicles behind him and then a loudspeaker boomed out: "Armed police! Put your hands up and lie on the road!"

Glancing over his shoulder Major Wickham saw the police cars and black-uniformed officers with guns. He experienced such a rush of relief he almost collapsed. He turned and began walking towards them. But a policeman shouted at him to lie down and he understood that they needed to get control of the situation. Knowing that co-operation was the best path to a quick resolution he did as he was told and then looked around and called on Chloe and Jane to do likewise.

They did and armed police began hurrying forward to search for weapons and to find out what was going on. Seeing Major Wickham's uniform a police Inspector gestured to him to get up. That took some doing as his sore muscles and joints almost refused to work. Groaning and feeling almost at the end of his tether he managed to get to his feet.

"Are you Major Wickham?" the Inspector queried.

Major Wickham told him he was and explained the outline of the situation. The police Inspector looked around at the litter of bodies, bikes and prisoners and shook his head.

"Like the gunfight at the OK Corral!" he muttered.

"It was!" Major Wickham assured him, shuddering at the sight of the bodies and blood. That got him worried about the girls being traumatized by such sights but both Chloe and Jane seemed to be taking them in their stride.

The Inspector pointed to Chloe and Jane who lay nearby. "Are these two cadets?"

"Yes," Major Wickham croaked. "Never mind us, there is a girl who's been shot. You must get her to the hospital."

"Being done now," the Inspector replied, pointing to his right across the railway.

Major Wickham looked that way, peering through the gaps between the bushes along the railway to note a helicopter coming down to land off to the north. He had heard the rotor noise but had been so overwhelmed by events that its real meaning had not registered.

Jane looked up and pointed towards the hotel. "There's an injured man in there who needs a doctor too," she said. "He is an old farmer who gave me a lift and got caught and beaten up."

The Inspector nodded and quickly directed two officers to investigate. Jane was told to stand up and was asked who she was. After a few questions she was told to sit in the shade and then Chloe was told to get up. As she did the front of the shirt gaped apart and Major Wickham saw the police officer's eyes goggle as they stared at her bosom. He opened his mouth to tell her to pull the shirt closed but was beaten to it by Jane.

Chloe nodded but instead of doing that she turned her back on them and swung the shirt right off and then slid her arms through the sleeves and put it on properly, granting them all an eyeful of shapely female as she did. The sight caused Major Wickham another wash of shame at his own interest and he quickly looked away.

The Police Inspector shook his head. "Hello Chloe," he said as she turned around, still buttoning the shirt up.

"Hello sir," Chloe replied, looking quite sheepish at the greeting.

The Inspector smiled. "I hear you have been a hero," he said.

Chloe shrugged and glanced anxiously at Major Wickham. "I did my best sir," she answered.

"It makes a change to congratulate you," the Inspector commented.

"Thank you Inspector Waters," Chloe replied, casting another anxious and embarrassed glance at Major Wickham. He frowned and felt another niggle of emotion. It was not good that Chloe was known to the police.

And obviously for getting up to mischief!

Major Wickham was then surprised to find Capt Hamilton, Lt Barker, Lt Cavendish and Lt Peters hurrying to join him. "What are you lot doing here?" he queried. "You should be looking after the cadets."

Capt Hamilton answered. "Mel is doing that. There was no way we were going to let you face the bikies on your own. We reckoned they wouldn't shoot us all. I just wish we'd been a bit quicker catching up."

"Did you see what happened?" Major Wickham asked, his whole being suffusing with a warm glow of affection for them.

Capt Hamilton nodded. "We did. But we couldn't hear a lot of what people were saying."

Major Wickham shook his head. "You took a terrible risk!"

"So did you!" Lt Barker replied. "Anyway, we reckoned they wouldn't shoot us all."

Major Wickham was almost overwhelmed by the display of loyalty and potential sacrifice the staff had displayed. He nodded and gripped Capt Hamilton's hand.

"Thanks!" he cried with emotion.

His emotions were then further tested when Lt Cavendish flung her arms around him and held him tight.

"Oh! I was so scared when they tied you up!" she cried.

Lt Cavendish began to fuss over Major Wickham until he sent her and Lt Peters to look after the two girls. She did that with obvious reluctance and it then dawned on Major Wickham that perhaps she had a soft spot for him.

Bloody hell! he thought. *I don't need more attractive females complicating my life!*

By then the living and uninjured bikies were being stood up, searched and herded over near a derelict shop further along the street. Jane stood up and turned on Chloe, anger in her voice.

"Chloe, why didn't you try to run away from that Slasher mongrel?" she asked.

Chloe shrugged and gave a foolish grin. "I thought I had a chance," she replied. "I do Judo and Medieval Martial Arts," she added.

"He nearly killed you!" Jane snapped.

"But I nearly had him," Chloe replied.

"He nearly stabbed you to death twice," Jane cried angrily. Tears began to trickle down her cheeks.

"And you saved me! Thanks Janie Babe. That was very brave," Chloe said.

She held out her arms and the two girls embraced. That left Major Wickham standing there wondering what he was going to do with them.

This is going to be world news! he thought with dismay, conjuring up images on TV and then the subsequent explanations he would have to make to the army headquarters and to parents. *Bloody hell! What do I do with this pair?*

He stared at the two girls in silent wonder and admiration, amazed at what they had done. And while he watched he was struck by the differences between them. It suddenly dawned on him that while Chloe seemed to be the centre of attention and was getting all the praise in fact Jane was worthy of the same.

Jane is just as brave and she's a real leader under stress, he decided. *She has a cool head in a crisis and a good brain and is more sensible than Chloe.*

The two girls separated and Chloe looked down and then gasped. "Jane, you've been cut!" she cried.

Major Wickham looked and saw a trickle of blood on Jane's neck. Concern had him calling to the police and within minutes an ambulance pulled up. Jane kept insisting she was alright.

"It's nothing much, just a little nick," she insisted.

"Just get over to that ambulance!" Major Wickham cried.

"Make sure they don't leave my webbing in the bush," Jane said as she turned.

That comment confirmed everything Major Wickham had just been thinking. *Cool head alright! Now what do we do with her and Chloe?*

And then there was another little incident that gave him even more food for thought. Another ambulance had pulled up nearby while they were talking and two paramedics had placed Harley on a stretcher. As they started wheeling it towards the ambulance Chloe, who had walked over to it with her arm around Jane's shoulders, went over to the stretcher. A policeman tried to stop her, worried that there might be an incident but Trudi, who was walking beside Harley, asked if they could speak. Jane joined the group and Major Wickham walked closer to listen.

Harley took Chloe's hand. "You saved my life Babe, several times. I owe you," he said.

Chloe squeezed his hand and pointed with her left-hand at Jane. "And Jane! She is the brains of the organisation. I'm just the pretty face."

"You are that!" Harley affirmed with fervent admiration. "Yeah Jane, you saved my life by not letting those other weaklings hand me over to Brute. You could have walked away and been safe but you stuck by me. I won't forget that. So, if either of you girls is ever in trouble and you need help you just call and I'll come a runnin'; and not just me. You can count on Attila's Axemen anytime."

"Thanks Harley," Chloe replied. "Gee, it's lucky you only got shot in the head and the leg."

"Why is that?" Harley asked.

"Because there will be no brain damage," Chloe answered teasingly.

"Hey!" Harley cried.

Trudi trilled with laughter. "Didn't he get shot in the bum as well?" she asked.

Harley looked all indignant. "No! In the hip," he replied.

"Oh well, that was close to where his real brain is," Trudi said to Chloe. The two girls shrieked with giggles and Major Wickham frowned at the innuendo. Harley snorted but then Chloe suddenly bent over and kissed him. "Take care, and get well soon," she said.

"See ya in jail in then," Harley replied.

As the medics lifted his stretcher into the ambulance Major Wickham saw that all three girls were weeping.

Yes, I suppose he might go to jail, he thought.

But there and then he decided to plead that in both cases when he shot Brute and Slasher Harley had acted to save the lives of Chloe and Jane.

"And I'm glad he did," he muttered.

The round-up and clean-up continued. More police cars and ambulances arrived and another helicopter. That reminded Major Wickham to ask about Kim and he was very relieved to learn that she was still alive and airborne on her way to the Townsville Hospital. That also cheered the two girls and they broke into more sobs.

The Inspector pointed to an ambulance. "You can go in that one Major," he said.

"Not yet," Major Wickham replied, even though his head was throbbing and his thoughts spinning. "I need to make sure of things here first. No disrespect to you Inspector but I'd like to speak to my 2ic about the cadet unit and also to speak to the other members of my Number 4 Platoon. These two girls can go in it."

"Oh sir! We don't need that," Chloe cried indignantly. "We aren't hurt, just a bit worn out. We want to come with you."

Major Wickham wasn't sure if that was a good idea but agreed. He asked if a police vehicle could drive them to the unit. The Inspector agreed to this and one was placed at their disposal. But before they got into it he asked for a mobile phone and called the army headquarters in Townsville to prepare them for the media storm he was sure was about to burst.

And he was right. The first TV News helicopter came clattering over as they were driven to the company bivouac area. There Major Wickham found everything under control with the cadets packing up and police present dealing with the prisoners. Capt Buchan assured him they had already phoned for coaches to take them home and Major Wickham told the cadet platoon commanders and CSM what he knew. Quite confident that the officers could take care of things he told Capt Hamilton, Lt Barker and Lt Peters to stay with the company and for Lt Cavendish to come with him. He then asked to be driven to 4 Platoon.

He found the platoon seated beside the Dotswood Road and while he spoke to them, praising their efforts, he noted both Chloe and Jane crawl under the fence to retrieve their webbing from the long grass. Jane even picked up her hat from the bushes and put it on.

They are good, he mused.

As the details of the saga emerged Major Wickham was even more struck with admiration for what Chloe and Jane had done.

They are certainly strong characters and strong leaders, he decided. Then he noted Sgt Lepson sitting among the ranks and he pursed his lips. *Much better than the senior ranks they had with them,* he added.

Taking Lt Cavendish a little aside he gestured towards the two girls and said, "What are we going to do with that pair?"

Lt Cavendish looked at them and a sour smile formed on her lips, almost a grimace.

"Well, I still think they are a pair of trollops and real troublemakers and if it was up to me I'd chuck them out. But I suppose, in the circumstances, we will have to go down the other road and give them medals and promote them."

And that, ultimately, is what was done. The bravery medals took a year or so to work their way through the bureaucratic system but at the dismissal parade that afternoon at Heatley, in front of hundreds of anxious and amazed family members and a scrum of media representatives, plus the colonel and staff officers from Lavarack Barracks, he called them both out and handed them lance corporal's stripes.

"It's not much," he said as he shook hands with them. "But you have saved many lives and done a magnificent job. Well done. And Chloe, where's your hat?"

Chloe's face dimpled into a mischievous grin and she shook her head. "Lost it during the night sir. Sorry."

Major Wickham had to smile. "I think, in the circumstances, it won't be 'member to pay'," he said. "But you must take more care of uniform items."

"Oh sir!" Chloe whispered. "You know how hard it is for me to keep any sort of clothing on."

"Chloe!" Major Wickham muttered, simultaneously thrilled and shocked.

God, I hope the media don't get to learn about her behaviours!

But they did and Chloe and Jane both became celebrities. To Jane's annoyance the media focused more on Chloe than on her. But despite this the girls remained firm friends and also, despite some disapproval from some officers at the headquarters level, they were allowed to stay in cadets.

In due course both Chloe and Jane were awarded Bravery Medals, as was Major Wickham. But that was in the future and Chloe and Jane were in trouble again long before then. And there were more rumours to trouble Major Wickham. One was that Chloe had been visiting the bikie's clubhouse and doing naked dances and other things with them. Knowing that Chloe's mother was an 'exotic dancer', Major Wickham was not surprised but he was a little saddened.

And what of the others?

CUO Roach left the unit immediately and soon after that so did Sgt Lepson. Both Kim and Chantelle were disciplined and had to wait another year to prove themselves before being allowed a chance at promotion. Chloe and Jane were both selected to attend the Junior Leaders Course to qualify for promotion to corporal at the end of the year.

But will Chloe even make it through her corporals course? Will she be able to control her uninhibited impulses and stay out of mischief? Remember she has many enemies and there are officers who want her discharged from Cadets. Will she be able to rise to the challenges ahead?

Enjoy more C.R. Cummings stories

The Air Cadets

The Navy Cadets

The Army Cadets